$\mathscr{F}$INALLY HOME

LOIS GREIMAN

KENSINGTON BOOKS
www.kensingtonbooks.com

KENSINGTON BOOKS are published by

Kensington Publishing Corp.
119 West 40th Street
New York, NY 10018

All Kensington titles, imprints, and distributed lines are available at special quantity discounts for bulk purchases for sales promotion, premiums, fund-raising, and educational or institutional use.

Special book excerpts or customized printings can also be created to fit specific needs. For details, write or phone the office of the Kensington Special Sales Manager: Kensington Publishing Corp., 119 West 40th Street, New York, NY 10018. Attn. Special Sales Department. Phone: 1-800-221-2647.

Kensington and the K logo Reg. U.S. Pat. & TM Off.

ISBN-13: 978-0-7582-8124-1
ISBN-10: 0-7582-8124-2
First Kensington Trade Paperback Printing: December 2013

eISBN-13: 978-0-7582-8125-8
eISBN-10: 0-7582-8125-0
First Kensington Electronic Edition: December 2013

10 9 8 7 6 5 4 3 2 1

Printed in the United States of America

To Christian Greiman, a hero in the making

FINALLY
HOME

CHAPTER 1

Money can't buy happiness.

Casie Carmichael reminded herself of that comforting little maxim as she smoothed a hand over her newly purchased but slightly battered copy of *A Mano*. The author was a cowboy poet whose work had touched something deep inside Ty Roberts. And as Emily Kane said, she'd give a kidney to see the boy smile. Especially at Christmas.

So hopefully the scholars were correct, and happiness wasn't up for sale, because Casie couldn't even afford a down payment. The Lazy Windmill, the ranch she'd inherited less than a full year ago, was making a comeback, but the upswing was uncertain at best, and she knew enough to keep her expectations humble. Aiming too high brought nothing but trouble. In her mind, Casie called it the hungry horse syndrome: Eat too much and you were certain to come down with a bellyache.

She glanced out the window toward the sculpted white hills that rolled into forever. Her mother had not been a subscriber to any such belief. Kathy Carmichael had been a mover and a shaker. Perhaps others had seen her differently. But to Casie, she had been an undiminished dynamo until the day she died. At age forty-seven, when her only child was still trying to negotiate the slippery trail of her *own* future, Kathy had declared her intentions of returning to the rodeo circuit. Her husband had objected, but she'd merely laughed and paraphrased Calamity Jane: It wasn't too late to become a legend. That was three days before she'd been diagnosed with lymphoma. Perhaps it had also been the inauguration of Casie's hungry horse theory. But whatever the case, a host of events since that moment had done nothing to diminish her belief that asking for too much would destroy—

"No!" The single word rasped through the house, shattering Casie's introspection.

She jerked away from her bedroom window, catastrophe reflexes twitching. "What's wrong?" she called, but there was no answer. Racing through the doorway, she torpedoed downstairs.

"Don't!" Emily's voice was breathy with desperation.

"I'm coming!" Casie skittered down the stairs, stocking feet slipping on every worn tread, heart thundering in her chest. "What's wrong? What—" she began and shot into the family room, sure she would find the baby catatonic or Sophie dead on the floor.

But instead, Baby Bliss was slouched in her cushy swing like a tiny angel, and their intern Sophie was nowhere to be seen. Casie's mind absorbed those little factoids long before her body could adjust to this shocking lack of emergency. Her feet slowed gradually, carrying her farther into the room where Emily Kane, seemingly with all limbs attached and no arterial blood spattering onto the faded wallpaper, was valiantly trying to shoo an unrepentant cowboy back into the kitchen.

"What are you trying to hide?" he asked. Colt Dickenson had that dark, slow timbre to his voice and a steadier-than-earth stance passed down through his Native American roots. The girl tried yet again to shove him out of the room, but he simply leaned into her palms and shifted his diabolical gaze to the right. "Oh, hey, Case. What's going on?"

"What's going on?" Her heart was just now settling into a more sedate pace in her over-taxed chest. "I thought someone was getting murdered. That's what's going on."

"Nope," he said. Beneath the shadow of his ubiquitous Stetson, his jaw looked square and rough with a couple days' beard. "Em here's just excited about Christmas."

"Someone *is* going to get murdered," Emily said, "if you don't get out of here."

"Is that any way to talk to your baby's godfather? Hey," he said, leaning left to peer past Emily, who stood her ground like a small, mixed race soldier. "That looks real nice." The blue spruce they'd cut from the shelterbelt just a few hours before stood smack-dab in front of the window adjacent to the porch. "A little sparse on the left side and kind of tall for the room, but I could fix that if you'd just let me . . ." He took a step forward, at which time Emily smacked him in the chest with her fist. Her unruly dreadlocks swung with the force of her punch.

"Ouch," he said, though it seemed unlikely he felt the blow through the insulation of his canvas jacket. "Is that any way for a mother to act in front of her own baby?"

"Get out!" she insisted, then turned narrowed eyes toward Casie. "Tell him to mind his own business." But Casie's heart was still working on returning to its pre-emergency rhythm.

"Holy Hannah," she said, exhaling finally. "You scared about twenty years off my life expectancy."

"Oh." Emily's cheeks reddened a little. Eight months earlier, when she'd first arrived at the ranch, homeless and pregnant, Casie would have sworn the girl didn't know how to blush, but motherhood or some other form of ineffable magic had changed that and a host of other things. "Sorry," she said. "But he can't come in."

"I just want to see my goddaughter," Colt said. His eyes gleamed with mischief and something Casie didn't dare consider. She and Colt had known each other since grade school, when he had tormented her to distraction. During high school the torments had morphed into something closer to titillation. But only a fool would forget the wild-eyed boy's penchant for stuffing grasshoppers into chocolate milk cartons. "I'd better come in and make sure her momma's screaming didn't scare her."

"Your goddaughter is fine," Emily said. "You're the one who's going to need attention if you don't shape up."

"What's going on?" Casie asked and stepped cautiously into the breach. It was probably a mistake. Being close to Colt Dickenson was always fraught with a dozen dangers she could neither catalog nor fully understand. His tilted grin, for instance, made her intestines twist in an unacceptable manner. But a girl would have to be brain-dead to forget about sodden grasshoppers, or the adult equivalent, which she wasn't entirely sure she was capable of identifying at this juncture.

"I'm wrapping his gift," Emily said, nodding vaguely toward a box half enclosed in environmentally responsible newspaper. "And he's trying to peek."

"I'm not!" Colt said. He sounded genuinely offended, but despite the fact that he had spent a good deal of every day on the Lazy over the past several months, Casie wasn't positive he was genuinely *anything*. He *was* male, after all. And a rodeo cowboy. And inexplicably fond of insects. None of which suggested constancy.

"You just want to know what I got you," Emily insisted.

"Are you accusing me of lying?" he asked, and spread brown fingers over the place on his chest where a normal person's heart would reside. Colt Dickenson was not a normal person. Casie had decided that twenty years earlier, upon the discovery of a wood frog in the pocket of her denim jacket.

"Yes!" Emily said.

"How can you wound me like that?" Colt asked, eyes tragic. "I'm little Bliss's—"

"Seriously," Casie said, seeing no end to the drama in sight. "I thought the roof was coming down when you yelled."

"I know it. She's so loud," Colt chided, shaking his head at the little mother. "You've probably upset the baby. I'd better check on her."

"The baby's fine. It's you—" she began, but just then little Bliss woke with a bleat of despair. One tiny hand had escaped her swaddling and waved abruptly in the air. Emily glanced toward her with that wild expression reserved for new mothers and prey animals. "You stay out," she ordered, and went to console her infant.

Colt watched her go, then leaned one canvas-clad shoulder against the doorjamb as she lifted Bliss from her swing. His eyes, Casie noticed, were soft and warm now, and though his smile had ramped down from mischievous demon to happy sprite, it rarely disappeared completely. Maybe that was why it was so pathetically difficult to think like a rational person when he was near. But maybe there were other reasons. Reasons she was far too wise to explore, she thought, and turned away, but his next words stopped her.

"Hey, you're not expecting any new lambs, are you, Case?"

"What?" She pivoted back toward him, already on the alert for trouble. The ancient thermometer above the bunkhouse door hovered just above zero. She scowled. "No. No one should lamb for a couple of months yet." The thought of bringing new life into such inhospitable temperatures made her blood run cold. Literally. "Why do you ask?"

He shrugged, a slow movement of his left shoulder. A small hole punctuated his jacket's clay-colored sleeve, and the brown corduroy collar was beginning to fray. She had no idea why those foolish details drew her attention.

"It was pretty dark in the barn. I probably imagined it," he said and turned back toward the kitchen. "I'll do one more check before I head home."

"Home?" Emily asked and glanced over Bliss's silky head at him. "What are you talking about? Supper's almost ready."

"You don't have to check," Casie said and felt guilt twist in her stomach. Tending sheep wasn't Colt Dickenson's job. Then again, neither were any of the other tasks he undertook on a daily basis. "I'll take care of it."

"You don't know how she looks," Colt said.

"You didn't get a tag number?" Casie was already hurrying toward the front entry. Worry made her steps quick and her chest tight.

"I don't think she had one."

She winced. "I meant to get them all numbered last summer."

"Well . . . you can't rope no steer before you build your loop."

She glanced at him.

"Ty told me that," he admitted and grinned.

Tyler Roberts was barely sixteen years of age, but he was chockablock full of cowboy wisdom and proof positive that while hard knocks bowled some people over, they merely made others learn to stand on their feet.

But Casie put Ty out of her mind as she hurried toward the tiny foyer where outerwear was packed in a primitive wardrobe like kosher dills. "How'd she look?" she asked and snagged a pair of insulated overalls from a hook in the back. The floor creaked as she shoved her right foot into the appropriate leg. The foyer had seen some renovations in the past few months; the roof above the tiny alcove had been repaired and the front door replaced, but the floor needed work and a fresh coat of paint would not be amiss.

"Well . . ." Colt watched her as she shoved her second foot into the worn garment. "She was kind of a dirty white with a really short tail and a sassy look about her."

Casie rolled her eyes. The Lazy was home to two hundred and twelve sheep. Trying to distinguish one from another put finding a needle in the haystack in a far more favorable light.

"I meant . . ." She bent to guide her foot through the tattered fabric at the bottom of the overalls, then turned to see Colt drag his gaze up her body as she straightened. She felt her face flush and her breathing accelerate, but she ignored both. She didn't have time for untamed cowboys and feral hormones. "Why did you think she might be ready to lamb?"

His eyes were bright with nefarious thoughts to which she planned never to be privy. "I thought maybe she was bagging up."

"Oh no." Grabbing the end of the sleeve of her South Dakota State hoodie, she crammed her right fist into her overalls, then did the same with her left. "It's way too early for them to be lactating," she said, and after shimmying into the abused garment, struggled with her zipper. It was stuck again. No big surprise there. Apparently, overalls weren't necessarily meant to be passed from generation to generation like a family heirloom. And truth be told, she wasn't entirely sure to whom this particular article had belonged in the first place. It may well have been her father's. Growing up, his somber standoffishness had made him seem larger than life, but posthumously she realized he hadn't been much taller than her own five feet ten inches.

"Unless some were bred earlier than we intended," Colt suggested.

She gritted her teeth against such an unfavorable suggestion and pulled harder on the zipper.

"Here," he said, stepping forward. "Let me do that."

"I can dress myself," she said and yanked again, but just then the tab came away in her fingers. She glared at it in frustration and he laughed.

"You're such a bully," he said and pushed her hands away.

They were standing extremely close.

"I'm not a bully."

"You have to finesse things a little," he said, and gripping the garment near her crotch, seized the nub of the zipper in his right hand.

She stood absolutely still. Her face felt warm and her body fidgety. "I can get my own zipper." Her words were little more than an irritable mumble.

"I know you can." His voice was soft and deep as he tugged the tab effortlessly along her abdomen and over her chest. His index finger brushed her chin. His eyes were laughing as he lowered his voice. "Which makes me wonder if you secretly *want* my help."

"I don't—" she began, but he was already raising his voice to address the girl in the living room.

"Hey, Em, do you need me to lock the chickens up or anything?"

"I didn't let them out today." Her feet rapped quietly against the kitchen's old linoleum, coming closer. "Too cold."

"All right." He lowered his gleaming gaze to Casie's. She shifted hers away, feeling foolish. "We'll be back in a few."

"No hurry," Emily said and appeared in the doorway with Bliss hugged snug and content against her shoulder. She smiled, first at Colt, then at Casie, who refrained from rolling her eyes like a disgusted teenager. If the girl's matchmaking schemes were any more obvious, she'd lock them in the tack room together until their firstborn arrived. "The stew'll keep."

"Stew?" Colt questioned, voice level as if he didn't realize the girl's diabolical plans.

"Potato beef."

"With cheesy dumplings?"

"And honeyed carrots."

He sighed dreamily. "We'll be back," he repeated, then opened the door.

"Don't rush," Emily said, and kissing Bliss's forehead, hugged her even closer. "I'm going to feed the baby first anyway."

Colt cupped the infant's duckling-down head for a second, then stepped back, motioning Casie to precede him. She skittered her gaze away. Chivalry always made her twitchy. Maybe it would be different if she hadn't been dressed like a backwoods yeti, but maybe not.

Jack, border collie and resident security guard, smiled as he slunk toward them from the barn. He seemed impervious to the weather, but the brittle air snapped against Casie's cheeks and chilled the back of her neck, finding every chink in her well-insulated armor. She hunched her shoulders a little, trying to block out the South Dakota cold.

Reaching up, Colt tugged her hood out from under her overalls and snugged it over the experimental stocking cap Emily had knit last month. It was lumpy in the back and saggy in the front, but Casie didn't believe in looking gift horses in the mouth, especially when they were given by fragile teenagers intent on acting tough.

"Thanks," she said, and barely glancing at him, trudged through the snow toward the sheep barn. The wind was gusting from the northwest, making it a relief to reach the door, but Colt was already slipping past her to pull it open.

"After you," he said.

Casie flipped on the lights. Overhead bulbs illuminated scores of dozing sheep. Lying in clusters upon the straw, they looked soft and cushy in their reclining positions, but experience assured her they were not always as docile as they appeared.

"Where was she when you saw her last?" Casie asked.

"Near the corner over there," he said and motioned toward the east. He wasn't wearing gloves. His hands looked broad and sturdy. On the underside of his russet-colored wrists, the veins stood out in sharp relief.

Casie cleared her throat and pulled her gaze from his arm. She was fairly certain the sight of his wrists shouldn't made her feel faint. "I'll see if I can find her," she said. "You don't need to come along."

"But you don't know how she looks," he argued.

"Dirty white, I think you said," she reminded him and hopelessly scanned the endless animals that dotted the barn like so many moguls.

Colt chuckled quietly, careful not to frighten the ewes. "Come on," he said. "I might recognize her if I see her."

Perhaps she should have argued, but if there truly was a ewe about to lamb, it was imperative that they find her soon. The guilt involved in losing a newborn was something she tried to avoid at all costs, and the thought of looking for one pregnant sheep in this sea of gestating ovines was overwhelming at best. She was sure she wasn't allowing him to assist for any reasons other than practicality.

"Look for a red mark on her spine," he said as they moved cautiously through the woolly waves.

"What?"

"I intended to mark her with a big X so we could find her later, but all I managed was a little swipe of red before she got away from me."

"You could have told me that before," Casie said.

"And missed this chance at such a romantic interlude?" he asked, then grinned across the backs of a dozen ruminating sheep.

She caught his gaze. For months they had been dancing these same steps. It seemed as if he was always present, repairing equipment, doctoring livestock, cleaning cattle yards. There were times, entire minutes, in fact, when she was absolutely positive he was enamored of her. Why else would he stick around? But despite the entirely unpaid hours he put in at the Lazy, he had never once asked her on a date. Why was that . . . unless he was merely ever-present so that he could spend time with Emily? The two of them had formed a special bond early on. When the girl had first arrived, her relationship with older men had bordered on hero worship. Colt's presence seemed to be eroding that weird scenario. Although Em still periodically gazed at him as if he were an integral part of the Second Coming, she no longer acted as if the entire male populace held the key to the universe. Was that intentional on Colt's part? Did he arrive at the Lazy every single day in an attempt to foster a healthier attitude in the wayward teenager? Or did he have other reasons?

There were times when Casie was convinced that Colt was simply killing time. After all, he'd spent a good many years on the rodeo circuit. Maybe he was just enjoying some time off. But every once in a while, when she least expected it, he would look at her as he was now, making her heart leap into her throat and every flighty molecule she possessed scream for caution. Despite his irresistible wrists, she was nowhere near ready for a relationship. If her failed engagement had taught her nothing else, she had learned this much: She was a terrible judge of men. Always had been. And this one was looking at her as if his interest in the Lazy had nothing to do with boredom or needy teenagers or a dozen other reasons she had invented over the long winter months. It made her heart seize up and her palms sweat.

"Colt . . ." she began, desperate to clear the air, but he interrupted her.

"There she is."

"What?"

"The mother-to-be," he said, pointing toward the east door. "I think that's her."

She turned reluctantly away, knowing she should voice her concerns before her nerve abandoned her completely. "Where?" she asked instead.

"Just to the right of that trio there. See her?"

She scowled into the poorly lit distance. Colt had risked life and limb propping a twenty-foot ladder against the rafters to replace the burned-out bulbs only a few weeks earlier, but the barn seemed to absorb the sparse light like a black hole, casting most of the building into shadow. Half the ewes seemed to have a mark of something or other on their backs. "I think so. Maybe."

"It's a little hard to tell. But you head around that way. I'll cut to the right. We'll trap her between us and check it out. Easy as pie."

It was a decent plan, Casie thought, and did as suggested.

In the end, *easy* wasn't exactly the term she would have used, but the ewe with the red mark had been captured. The animal stood motionless, pink-tipped nose held high by Colt's right hand as his left kept her from backing away.

"Whatcha think?" he asked. He was breathing a little heavily. The ewe had not been partial to being captured and stood wide-eyed and resentful in his grasp. Her comrades had scattered to the edges of the barn like chaff in the wind, leaving a wasteland of scattered straw between them and the intruders.

Casie scowled down at the ewe in question. She was almost identical to the others, round as a barrel with spindly legs sticking out below her like a woolly hors d'oeuvre on toothpicks. But maybe her belly was a bit more distended than her peers'. Casie dropped to her knees, the better to examine the animal's udder, and sure enough, it did look engorged.

She pursed her lips as she rose to her feet.

Colt grinned. "You can cuss if you want to."

She *did* want to, but her cursing ability had been impugned in the past, and with three teenagers ensconced on the Lazy, this probably wasn't the perfect time to try to improve her prowess.

"How could this happen?" she asked instead.

Colt straightened a little, careful not to loosen his grip on the ewe. "Maybe you should talk to Em about that."

She scowled at him. "I meant, they weren't supposed to be cycling in . . ." She counted back on her fingers. Sheep were considered short-day breeders, which meant they shouldn't be ready to mate until fall. "July."

Colt shrugged. "Maybe she got her months confused."

She gave him a look.

He grinned. "Life'll make a liar out of you nine times out of ten."

"Let's get her in the pen," she said, but in the end Colt did most of the work. She merely followed behind and shut the gate once the ewe had entered a small wooden cell at the north end of the barn.

"When do you think she'll drop?" she asked.

Colt shook his head as he stepped through the makeshift gate. During the regular lambing season, dozens of these little crates would be set up along the walls, but right now only a few remained for this type of emergency. "Couple of days maybe. A week on the outside. Least that's my guess."

She blew out a breath. "Hope she waits till this cold snap ends," she said and hurried toward the hydrant in the corner, but Colt stepped past her.

"I'll get that," he said, and grabbing a nearby pail, filled it to a few inches from the top before carrying it to the crate.

Casie bent over a nearby fence to retrieve a slab of alfalfa, but as she did so, her exposed wrist scraped along the sharp end of a stray wire.

She jerked back with a rasp of pain, and Colt was beside her in a second, water bucket abandoned.

"What happened?" His brows were low, his tone concerned.

"Nothing." She shook her head and hugged her arm against her overalls. "It's no big deal."

"Then let me see it," he insisted, and tugging her hand toward his chest, made a hissing noise as the wound was revealed.

"It's fine," she said, though it stung like the devil. Three inches long, it was little more than a thin pink stripe except toward the distal end where a single drop of blood bubbled against her pale flesh.

"*Nothing!*" He tugged off her right glove. It was worn

through on the index finger. "Are you kidding me?" he asked, tone rife with drama.

"No, I'm not. It's—" she began, but he interrupted her.

"Buck Creger had an injury just like this in Laramie last fall. Lucky for him there was a medic on hand so they didn't have to amputate," he said and skimmed his thumb down her wrist.

Feelings shimmied away from his touch, making her nerve endings twitter like over-stimulated songbirds. She searched wildly for something to say.

"That's comforting," was all she could come up with.

"Is it?" he asked and raised his eyes to hers. It struck her hard, causing heat to rise in her cheeks and seem to begin a slow melt down the center of her being.

"I meant . . ." She swallowed. "I meant . . . it's comforting that he didn't . . ." For one wild second she couldn't remember what she was going to say. Hell, she could just barely recall they were standing in a sea of sheep instead of on a tropical beach somewhere, waves lapping at their ankles. "That he didn't lose his hand."

"Oh." He grinned a little, as if he knew exactly what she was thinking. "Yeah, but they had to take drastic measures."

She made a face at him. Colt Dickenson had been a wild-eyed risk taker long before he had become a nationally ranked bronc rider. Rarely had a year passed that he hadn't broken, lacerated, or bruised something near and dear to his heart. Three months ago, after his latest return from the rodeo circuit, there had been a new scar bisecting his right brow. She raised her gaze breathlessly to that area.

"I . . ." she began, but when she glanced up, the words froze on her lips. His eyes were dark, glowing with warmth and promise and a thousand emotions she dared not consider. "I can . . ."

"Can what?" he asked and raised his attention from her lips to her eyes.

She swallowed hard. "Listen, Colt . . . I just . . ." She tried to hold his gaze, but it was too steady, too bold, too appealing. And she couldn't afford to be appealed to. "You don't have to be so nice to me."

"I know." He grinned. His smile was little more than a slash of diabolical white beneath the rim of his dark Stetson. Rain, sleet, or arctic blast, he looked comfortable in a felt hat and canvas jacket while Casie needed what amounted to an insulated onesie and mukluks to keep the cold from seeping into her bones like permafrost. "It's not as if someone's holding a pistol to my head," he said and raised her wrist to his lips.

She tried to pull away. "I don't—" she began, but in that instant his lips touched her flesh.

Dynamite ignited someone near her solar plexus, causing shock waves to reverberate over the landscape of her body.

He smiled. "We'd better get you inside."

"But Red Stripe needs—"

"Less attention than you do," he said and swept his thumb across the palm of her hand.

She felt her eyes fall closed at his mesmerizing touch and yanked them wide open. Holy cats, what did it mean that she almost swooned when he touched her palm? "Listen!" she said. Her voice was marvelously brusque. "I'm perfectly fine. I don't have to go to the house. I can—"

"Not to the house," he said, and bending slightly, lifted her into his arms.

She made some kind of babbling sound that defied description. Marvelously brusque it was not. On the brink of unconsciousness? Perhaps.

"To the bunkhouse," he said. "I'm afraid you may not be able to make it all the way to the house."

"But . . ." Their faces were inches apart. His was full of such indescribable character that it made her tongue feel heavy and her head light. "The bunkhouse is farther than the—"

"Shhh," he chided. "You don't want to strain yourself."

"I'm not going to—"

"Hit the lights, will you?" he asked.

She did so, reaching to the side to throw the barn into darkness. "This is ridiculous," she said, but his breath felt soothing and warm against her check, his chest hard and capable against her shoulder. "I can walk to the house."

"The bunk—"

"The *bunkhouse*," she corrected, desperate to be practical. "I can walk to the bunkhouse."

"But why risk it?"

"Risk—"

"You have kids to think about."

"That's what I *am* thinking about."

"Really?" he asked, looking disappointed and mildly confused. "Then I think I'm doing something wrong."

She blinked at him, not sure what to make of that but determined to push through to the sensible her . . . the her that would make it to the house under her own steam and bandage her own minuscule scratch like a capable human being. "Listen. You have to put me down. What if the kids see—"

"You can't think about them all the time, Case."

"But you just said—"

"Sometimes you have to think about yourself."

"I do think about—"

"About what *you* want."

"I want—" she began, but they had reached the bunkhouse. "Get the door, will you?"

She didn't really know why she did as requested. It was a ridiculous situation, made even sillier by the fact that she turned the knob with her injured hand.

"What *you* need," he added, seeming entirely undistracted by their trip up the hill, completely unhindered by her considerable weight. At a hundred and thirty pounds, she didn't weigh *that* much less than he did. The best bronc riders, after all, were neither tall nor particularly beefy. But were they all made of this delectable stuff that he seemed to be comprised of? Did their muscles shift like magic beneath their clothes? Did their grins make a woman's respiratory system feel taxed and her heart bang like a blacksmith's hammer?

But it didn't matter, she reminded herself. She was an adult. An adult with responsibilities. "Listen . . ." she began, but in that moment she realized they were entirely alone in a room with a bed, and though she knew that should be of little consequence, said consequences loomed like towering giants. The bunkhouse was lit by nothing but the distant yard light and the waxing moon shining on endless miles of drifting snow.

"What do you need, Cassandra?" he asked.

"I . . ." His lips were inches from hers. His body felt warm and hard against her side, and his voice did weird, infuriating things to a system left too long to its own devices. But she found her voice. "I don't need anything," she said. "Put me down."

He delayed a full two seconds, but finally let her feet drop to the floor. "Okay," he said, "but a man can only wait so long, Case."

They stood facing each other, touching here and there: elbow, hip, thigh. His right arm was still curved around her back.

"I didn't . . ." She drew a deep breath, steadying herself. "I didn't ask you to wait, Colt."

He raised one brow. The world went absolutely silent. "Then come here," he breathed, and pulling her against his chest, kissed her.

CHAPTER 2

The breath left Casie's lungs like a tornado sweeping the heartland. She felt every nerve buzz and every muscle go limp. But by the time he pulled away, her mind was just beginning to blink back to life.

"I wasn't . . ." Her voice sounded ridiculously high-pitched, like Minnie Mouse on nitrous oxide. His right hand was cupping her neck while his left arm gripped her waist in a far-too-intimate manner. But truth to tell, it was entirely possible that if he removed that arm, she would have flopped to the floor like a fish out of water "I wasn't talking about *that*—"

"I call it the drought," he said and kissed her again.

Her knees sagged, but she braced them with cowgirl grit and pushed against his chest. Or at least that's what she *thought* she did, though, when her mind was a little less muzzy, she was sadly suspicious that her fingers might have been curled tight in the front of his jacket.

"The drought?" She didn't even know what she was saying. Why the hell didn't she know what she was *saying?*

"I think we could both use a little rain," he said and drew back a few scarce inches.

She glanced down. Her overalls had somehow become wide open. "How—"

"Zippers like me," he explained.

She scowled, first at her traitorous garment, then at him as she remembered a dozen high school cheerleaders who had talked about him with giggling giddiness. "I suppose hooks like you, too."

He grinned a little. "We could give it a try," he said, but she found her strength and pushed him away.

"Is this how you do it?"

"Do what?"

"Is this how you make all your conquests? Do you just . . ." She waved one wild hand at him. "Make googly eyes at them and they fall at your feet?"

He raised his brows at her. "Googly eyes?"

"I'm not that kind of girl, Dickenson. You must know that. You can't just flex your muscles . . ." She glanced toward his chest. There was little enough to see. He was, after all, dressed for winter, but his neck was bare, and somehow the sight of that dark little hollow between his collarbones made her feel a little giddy herself. She swallowed a giggle. "And think I'm going to . . . to . . ."

"Are you all right?" he asked and stepped toward her.

She jerked back. "Of course I'm all right! Why wouldn't I be all right?"

"I don't know. You're acting kind of funny. Are you feeling dizzy?"

The idea was overtly offensive. "No, I'm not feeling dizzy! Why would I feel—" she began, but just then a wave of something weird struck her. She steadied herself with a hand on the rough timber table beside her.

"Case?" he said, voice earnest now as he eased her toward a nearby chair. "What's wrong?"

"Nothing's—" she began, but her head felt as if it had become disconnected from her body. She slid onto the Navajo cushion that covered the nearest chair. ". . . wrong," she said, and exhaled forcefully.

"Here." He hurried to the cupboard. Having resided for decades in Hope Springs' granary, the little cabinet was weathered and scarred and bursting with character. When The Feed and Seed was renovated, Frank Pullman, its current owner, had donated the cabinet to the Lazy in exchange for partial board of his wife's geriatric gelding. Pulling a mug from the cupboard's depths, Colt filled it with water from the nearby tap and turned back to Casie. "Geez, woman, you have to eat."

"I eat," she said, and took a sip of water.

He nudged the cup back up to her lips. "As much as you drink?"

"What?" She scowled at him.

He tilted the mug toward her mouth again. "You drink like a dehydrated goldfinch. Finish that cup."

"Listen," she said. "I know how to eat *and* drink."

"Then prove it."

"I—"

"Prove it," he insisted, and pushed the cup toward her again.

Snatching the mug from him, she finished off the water, then snapped the empty vessel back toward him. Embarrassment sometimes made her cranky.

"There," she said. "You satisfied?"

He raised a brow at her, grin barely contained. "It takes a little more than that, Case," he said. "Even from you."

"What—" she began, then understanding his meaning, skipped her gaze away without dipping it toward his crotch. Her face felt warm.

He chuckled a little. "Sorry," he said, and crouching next to her chair, took her hand in his. "But you shouldn't give me such great opportunities if you don't want me to take advantage of them."

"I didn't give you any opportunities," she said, but she could muster absolutely no heat in her tone. Her face, on the other hand, felt as if it might incinerate before his very eyes.

"It's not too late to change that," he said.

She tried to ignore the feelings that shivered through her, but there was no point. She had to face the facts. "Listen, Colt—" she began, but he stroked her knuckles, causing tingles to dart off in every direction.

"I'm listening," he said, and kissed the faint veins that criss-crossed her right arm.

She blinked breathlessly.

"Case?" he said.

She shook herself back to reality. "I really appreciate everything you've done for us," she said and found his eyes with her own. "But you can't keep this up."

"There's some pretty hard evidence to the contrary," he said, and rising to his feet, turned away. Opening another cabinet, he reached inside.

"What do you—" she began, but he spoke before she made a fool of herself.

"You and the kids have your hands full. No reason I shouldn't help out some."

"Some!" She breathed a laugh. "You're here every day. I can't pay you for—" She paused and scowled as he pulled out a first aid kit that had been housed in the cabinet.

"How did you know that was there?"

He raised his brows at her. "I saw it when I was framing the new windows."

It wasn't until that moment that she remembered his wood-working skills. He had been instrumental in getting the old chicken coop converted into a bunkhouse for paying guests.

The poultry now lived in a cozy little room in the corner of the cattle barn.

He crouched down beside her chair again and reached for her hand, but she pulled out of his grasp.

"That's just what I'm talking about." She would have risen to her feet, but he was too close to allow her to do so without pressing up against him . . . an eventuality to be avoided at all costs.

"Windows?" he asked, and opening a tube of antibacterial gel, retrieved her hand again.

"You!" she said and waved frantically toward the ranch at large. "Doing all this work. I can't pay you for it."

"I didn't ask you to."

"I know! And that's the worst part."

Putting a dollop of ointment on his index finger, he smeared it over her cut. She was absolutely certain it shouldn't feel good. "What's the worst part?" he asked.

"You're so—" The word *gorgeous* popped into her head. She popped it back out with frenetic haste. "I just . . ." She glanced to the right. Outside, the half moon was framed in a sky as black as an Angus steer. "I don't want to disappoint Emily," she said.

He was watching her. She could feel his attention like sunshine on her face.

"What does Em have to do with this?" he asked and eased the ointment to the medial end of her scratch.

Casie refused to close her eyes at the luxurious feelings. "She's been through a lot." In actuality, Casie wasn't entirely sure what the girl had endured before her arrival at the Lazy. But drugs had been involved. And theft. Emily was naturally talented in a host of ways. There was no reason to believe she wouldn't be just as gifted a thief as she was a chef. "I don't want her to be hurt again."

"Me either," he said. His voice was low and steady.

She skipped her gaze to his, wondering if they were still talking about somebody else.

"I'm sorry," he said. The words were slow and earnest, his expression somber for once as he drew a deep breath. "I should have told you about the baby."

She glanced away, remembering the conversation they'd had just a couple of months before. Remembering the pain of learning that Colt's ex-girlfriend had been expecting his child. Remembering his agonized expression when he'd told her of the abortion, unsanctioned by him, but maybe not entirely unhoped for. "Yes. You should have."

"I'll make more mistakes," he said. His eyes were dark, his tone steady. "But they won't be with other women."

For a moment she considered pretending she didn't know what he was talking about, but there was no point. His hands were like magic against her skin, his gaze like moonlight on hers. She was drowning in it, falling under his spell, but she shook her head and pushed to her feet.

"That's what Bradley said."

He gritted his teeth and rose beside her, so close they shared the same breath. "You two were engaged when he cheated on you," he reminded her. "You'd agreed to marry him."

"I know it's different, but—"

"Different!" He laughed out loud. The sound was coarse and angry. "Do you really think I would have given another woman a glance if *we* were engaged?"

"Yes, I do. I mean . . ." She laughed, feeling crazy. "Come on, Dickenson . . ." She moved away, putting distance between them like a barbed wire fence. "You're not exactly marriage material."

"What am I, then?" he asked.

She shook her head. "You're . . ." She paused, fighting to find something that wouldn't make her sound like a lovesick imbecile. But he was so tempting, so rough and hard and hopelessly attractive. "You're the stuff dreams are made of, and I'm not the dreaming type." She turned away.

He said nothing to refute her statement. Nothing to assure her that she, too, was desirable. But what did she expect? She would never in a thousand years match his cosmic appeal. "No." She blinked back her tears and raised her chin as she shook her head. "You're not the marrying kind, Colt."

Still he said nothing.

She drew a deep breath, steeling herself as she turned back toward him.

But he was gone. Or at least, for a fraction of a second, that's what she believed, until her gaze dropped. He was kneeling in front of her.

Her breath jammed tight in her throat. Her heart ceased to beat.

"Casie," he began, but in that second the door burst open and banged against the wall.

She spun around just as Sophie Jaegar stepped into the doorway. The girl held a Winchester in both hands.

"Soph!" Casie gasped.

"What the hell!" Colt snarled, but just then Emily rushed up, breath wheezing as she careened to a halt.

"What's—" Emily began, then gasped as her attention dropped to Colt. He was just pushing up from one knee to curl his hand around the rifle barrel and shift it aside.

"Hey!" Sophie said, perfect face marred by a scowl of thunderous proportions.

"Hey what?" Colt asked, signature grin noticeably absent. "What the devil do you think you're doing?"

For a moment Sophie almost looked chagrined, but then she shifted her gaze from Colt to Casie and back again. "What are *you* doing?"

"Well, I'm not threatening your life," he said, still holding the rifle.

"I'm not—" Sophie began, then paused. Her scowl darkened even further, but she cleared her throat. "I thought you were someone else."

"Someone else!" Casie's voice sounded squeaky to her own ears. And her knees felt weak again, but maybe for different reasons. "Like who?" she asked, but Emily took that opportunity to jump into the conversation.

"Mr. Dickenson, were you going to—"

"Give me that!" Colt demanded and tugged the rifle from Sophie's hands.

She glowered but released it. "I thought you were burglars."

"Burglars?" Emily said, and tearing her gaze from Colt, glanced around the bunkhouse. "What would they burgle?"

"I don't know," Sophie said. She looked a little embarrassed and a lot angry. Far be it from Sophie Jaegar to come out of any situation looking less than in control. "There's been that rash of robberies in town. Kids stealing copper from old buildings and . . . I was worried about the horses."

"In the bunkhouse?" Emily asked.

"Maybe that bastard's still after Freedom," she said, referring to the mare they had rescued a few months before.

"He's in jail," Emily reminded her.

"Maybe he broke out."

"He didn't break—" Emily began, then drew a deep breath, forced a smile, and aimed it with deadly accuracy at Casie. "Hey," she said and grabbed Sophie's arm in a tight grip. "Listen, I'm sorry we interrupted . . ." She glanced at Colt. ". . . whatever you were doing. We're just going to . . ." She took a step backward, dragging the other girl with her. "Soph's going to finish up chores while I—"

"I already finished—Ouch!" Sophie said and tried to snatch her arm out of the other girl's grasp, but when Emily Kane set her mind to something, there wasn't much short of the apocalypse that could change her course.

"Then you can help me with supper," she said, ghoulish smile still pasted in place. "It's not quite ready, by the way. So just . . ." They goose-stepped backward in tandem. "Just take your time doing . . ." She waved. "Whatever." The door closed firmly behind them, all but reverberating on its hinges.

The bunkhouse dropped into silence.

"What was that about?" Casie asked.

"Paranoia?" Colt guessed and shelled out the Winchester's bullets.

"Yeah. Sophie's always worried about the horses."

He set the rifle aside, butt end on the floor, as he settled his shoulders against the wall. "I meant *you.*"

"What?"

He exhaled carefully, eyes narrowed, saying nothing for a moment, but finally he spoke, voice low, expression somber. "I'm not Bradley, Case."

"I know that, but . . ." She shook her head and shrugged.

"But what?"

"I can't . . ." She glanced away, feeling frantic, knowing she was being unfair. "You're not ready to settle down, Colt."

"*I'm* not or *you're* not?"

"What about your career?"

"What about it?"

"You're a bronc rider."

"I *was*."

"Was? What are you talking about? You're ranked thirteenth in the world." She shook her head, feeling frantic. "You can't just give that up."

"If Niagara can, I can."

She scowled. "What?"

"Niagara Falls, the horse that threw me in Dallas. Gave me this." He pointed to the crease in his brow, watching her steadily. "Maybe knocked a little sense into me. I heard they're retiring her. I might make them an offer."

"For . . ." Casie shook her head.

He shrugged. "Could be I owe her something. For the life lessons."

She opened her mouth, nerves jittery with hope, but she shushed them with a stern command. "You could never make the kind of money ranching that you made on the circuit."

"Probably true."

She scowled, entirely uncertain where to go from there, but she hurried on, sure there were a thousand reasons she should discourage him. "And what about . . . about . . ."

"What?" He narrowed his eyes at her.

She pursed her lips. Silence lingered between them.

"The women?" he asked.

She raised her chin. "You're a bronc rider," she said again, tone steadier now. "The term is practically synonymous with playboy."

"Are you serious?" he asked and took a step toward her.

She stood her ground. "Yes, I'm serious," she said. "Jess—"

"I told you I'm sorry about Jess."

"Sorry?" She laughed. "Holy cow, Colt, she was going to have your baby!"

"And you were going to marry Bradley. Now you're not."

"I . . ." She shook her head, trying to muster her thoughts. Glancing out the window, she sighed. "You don't want this," she said. "Not really."

"What don't I want?"

"The endless hours, the monotony, the—"

"The *monotony?* Are you kidding me?" he asked and waved a wild hand toward the door. "A teenage girl with daddy issues and a grudge just about shot us two minutes ago."

"And that's another thing you don't want . . . the kids. They're . . ." She shook her head, breathing hard. "They'll make you crazy. Just the other day—"

"You must be joking."

"No, I'm not joking. It's really hard. They need—"

"You think I don't know what they need?" he asked and took the few steps that remained between them. "Dammit, Case, what do you think I've been doing for the past two months?"

"Two *months?* As far as I know these kids are here for good, so this is a life sentence, Dickenson. This is up at dawn, to bed at midnight, with sporadic periods of insanity in between. This is dirty diapers and clogged drains and lawsuits and—"

"I know what I'm getting into."

"Listen, you've been great." She felt as if the air had suddenly evaporated from her lungs, but she dared not back down. Not for her own sake and not for his. "And I really appreciate it, Colt. I do, but—"

"Who do you think rushed Emily to the hospital when she was in false labor? Who do you think saved Curly and got Ty away from his dumb-ass parents and rocks Bliss to sleep when she's colicky?"

The image of him with tiny Bliss tucked against his flannel-clad shoulder was almost her undoing. She responded with anger. "So fine! You're Superman! Is that what you want to hear?"

"No! I'm not Superman. I'm just a man who—" he shouted, but he stopped abruptly, rocking back on his heels a little. "That's the problem, isn't it?"

"What are you talking about?"

"You don't trust men."

"That's not true. I—"

"Name one."

"What?"

"Name one man you trust."

She glanced out the window again, wishing she was gone. She detested controversy, would rather spend the night in a cold barn with a sick cow than argue about anything with anyone. Which meant she must be pretty close to her wits' end to be fostering this argument. "My dad . . ." she began, but Colt interrupted her.

"Let you down in a hundred ways," he said.

She pursed her lips, knowing it was true. In her entire life, Clayton Carmichael had never once opened up to her. Hell, if he hadn't died, she would have never known the ranch was in financial trouble, would have never guessed that without his wife, with whom he had feuded incessantly, he had no reason to go on living. "Fine," she said. "I don't trust men." She fisted her hands beside her thighs. "Would you?"

He opened his mouth, then gritted his teeth and shook his head. "No. Men are mostly bastards."

She nodded once, gaze steady on his. "I'll bet that's what Jess thinks."

Anger erupted on his face. "Are you going to throw that at me every time we argue?"

"You made a baby, Colt! Another human being! So yeah, the point's going to come up a couple thousand times," she snarled and waited for him to blast her, but instead, he studied her in silence for what seemed like forever.

"I've got a barrel full of faults, Case. I'm not denying that."

She laughed out loud, egging on his temper, but he drew a careful breath and continued.

"I'm stubborn as a cranky mustang, I need a hit of caffeine

first thing in the morning, and sometimes I'm an ass, but if I say I'll stick, I'll stick." He nodded at her, eyes hard. "You can take that to the bank."

"I've heard that before," she said.

For a moment she thought he'd whine or protest or scoff, but instead he just stepped forward, standing within inches of her.

"Not from me you haven't," he said, and grasping her set jaw in his right hand, kissed her square on the lips.

She felt her knees go weak and her brain go soft, but before she slipped to the floor in a puddle of soppy mush, he turned on his heel and left.

CHAPTER 3

"Where's Mr. Dickenson?" They were the first words out of Emily's mouth when Casie finally toed off her gone-through-hell Sorel boots and headed into the kitchen. Her feet felt wooden against the discolored linoleum.

"Man, that smells great," she said and studiously ignored the question as she sniffed the aromatic steam that drifted from the pot atop the Lazy's ancient stove.

"Mr. Dickenson . . ." Emily said, hurrying into the entry to search in vain before tromping irritably back toward the stove. "Where is he?"

"No one makes stew like you do, Em," Casie said.

There was a moment of tense silence, then, "You turned him down, didn't you?"

Emily held a wooden spoon in one determined fist near her hip, dreadlocks in wild disarray around her face. Casie opened her mouth, ready to attempt to allay the storm, but before she had a chance to try, Sophie stepped into the room from the stairwell.

"Is supper ready or what?" she asked. "I'm starving. Is that—" She stopped abruptly, perfect brow furrowing. "What's going on?"

"Nothing's going on," Casie said. To say her cheeriness was forced would have been a miscalculation of Clydesdale proportions. "Let's eat," she suggested, but Emily remained exactly as she was, arms akimbo and spoon held like an impromptu weapon.

"He asked you, didn't he?" she said.

Casie felt depleted and exhausted and as jittery as a spring colt, but she remembered that she was the adult here. When that did nothing to bolster her spirits, she told herself in no uncertain terms that she had nothing to be ashamed of. That proved to be fairly ineffective as well, so she punted. "Where's Ty?"

"Asked her what?" Sophie said, and lifting the cover from the pot on the stove, sighed before dipping a spoon into the broth that boiled up between the cracks in the dumplings.

The fact that Emily didn't take the girl down like a grizzly on a jack rabbit was proof enough that she was distracted by other catastrophes. "Mr. Dickenson asked Casie to marry him," Emily said and sharpened her glare. "Didn't he?"

"*What!*" Sophie asked, momentarily forgetting the broth that drizzled slowly back onto the dumplings.

"And you turned him down," Emily said.

"Who?" Sophie asked.

Emily shook her head, disapproval steaming from every pore. "What is wrong with you, Case?"

The girl's disappointment hurt far more than Casie would have ever thought possible, stinging on contact, burning with contempt.

"*Colt* Dickenson?" Sophie asked.

"Oh, for Pete's sake!" Emily snarled, turning toward the younger girl. "Who do you think we're talking about? *Monty?*"

Sophie ignored the reference to the elder Dickenson. "*Colt* asked you to marry him?" she said and dipped her spoon back into the broth. Steam wafted like fragrant magic into the air. "That doesn't even count as a proposal."

They both stared at her.

"I mean . . . come on . . ." She exhaled a laugh. "He's a *bronc* rider."

"Exactly!" Casie concurred, though, in truth, a dozen reasons to defend him came rushing to the fore. "See? Sophie understands, Em. Colt isn't ready to get serious. He's—"

"So I was right," Emily said and dropped dismally into the nearest chair. "He *did* propose. And you said no."

"No," Casie said and hurried over to crouch beside her chair. Somewhere inside, she knew it shouldn't matter so much what Emily thought. The girl was barely eighteen years old. She was bruised and unpredictable and fragile in ways that still weren't readily apparent. But somehow, somewhere along the battering life they shared, Emily Kane had become the soul of the Lazy Windmill. There was no explaining that. It was just a basic truth. "He *didn't* ask," Casie said.

Emily stared at her a second, then sighed. And somehow that sound was even more discouraging than her anger. "But he was going to." She smiled a little, a tiny tug of plump, cynical lips. "Colt Dickenson was going to ask you to marry him until Sophie barged in to shoot you."

"I wasn't going to—" Sophie began, then exhaled, breath cooling the stew. "Seriously, Colt Dickenson . . . married . . ."

Emily shook her head, never taking her gaze from Casie. "What were you thinking?"

"Listen . . ." Casie said, reminding herself yet again that *she* was the adult. This ranch was *her* responsibility. As were the teenagers and the livestock and the bills. "I know you're fond of him, but—"

"*Fond* of him? *Fond* of him! Casie, do you think men like that come along every day? Do you think they just pop up . . ." She raised both hands in wild unison as if a cowboy were magically conjured into the air between them. "Like sunflowers in June? Well, they don't. Things happen. People let you down. Or die. Or leave. Or—" She sputtered to a sighing halt, making Casie wonder again exactly what the girl had endured before arriving at the Lazy. What she had endured and how it would affect her in the long run.

"Colt Dickenson wants to get married?" Sophie mused. "To Casie?"

They both turned toward her. Emily's brows puckered. Casie felt heat strike her cheeks.

"I didn't mean it like that," Sophie said. "I just meant . . ." she began, but Casie rose to her feet.

"No, you're right. It would be like . . ." She shook her head. "Like hitching a mule and a Friesian together."

The kitchen went silent for a second.

Sophie scowled. "Which one's the mule and which one's the Friesian?"

"What's a Friesian, and what does that have to do with . . . No!" Emily said, slicing the air with her hand. "This is stupid. We're talking about Colt Dickenson."

"And *Casie?*" Sophie said, as if to clarify it further in her own mind.

"Yes, *Casie,*" Emily shot back. "Geez, Soph, try to keep up. Cassandra May Carmichael turned down—"

"He didn't actually—" Casie began, but her tone was weak.

"She was *about* to turn down Colt Dickenson, the sweetest, sexiest, most hardworking man in the state of South Dakota."

The house went silent. Casie felt pale. Colt *could* be sweet. No doubt about that. And he had been known to put in a full day of work before most people got out of bed. And yeah, those were fine qualities. Qualities she could maybe deal with on a day-to-day basis. But that sexy thing? She felt nervousness twitter along her spine again. She wasn't built for sexy. Had never been. She was meant to be serviceable, solid. Hell, *boring* made her all but euphoric.

"Well . . ." Sophie said and shrugged as she licked the spoon. "You're too good for him anyway, Case."

For a moment no one spoke. Casie creaked her head in the girl's direction, brows raised in absolute shock.

"What?"

"*What?*" Emily echoed.

Sophie scowled at their obvious surprise. "I mean, sure, the man's built like a . . ." She paused and shook her head, as if his physique somehow defied description, and hurried on. "And he's all right to look at if you like that rugged cowboy thing. But you're . . ." On the girl's usually aloof face was something indescribable, something that almost looked like admiration. "Hey," she said, jerking irritably toward Emily again. "Are we going to eat or what?" she asked, but in that instant the front door opened and Ty Roberts stepped into the kitchen. Sixteen, rangy, and reticent, he scanned them with soulful eyes.

Sophie fell immediately silent. For one wild second his gaze met hers, but he turned abruptly toward Casie. His angular face was shadowed by his ever-present baseball cap, his rough, capable hands were bare, and in his arms he cradled a still-wet lamb. "Sorry, Case," he said, newly lowered voice barely a rumble of disappointment. "Looks like we got us a little problem."

"Holy shorts," Emily said, pulling her gaze from Casie to lock it on Sophie, who stood immobilized near the stove. "You're *both* crazy."

"What?" Ty asked.

Emily sighed. "Nothing," she said and dropped her gaze to the lamb. "She okay?"

Ty shook his head and hugged the baby a little closer to his chest. "Awful cold," he said. "But the other two seem okay."

They all stared at the infant in silent unison. Emily spoke first.

"Put the lambing box in front of the oven. I'll dish up the stew."

The meal was amazing. Emily was a phenomenal cook. No one said different, but it was Sophie's proximity across the table from Ty that made it impossible for him to put two coherent thoughts together. Thus he sat in silence, grateful that three feet of aging wood separated them. On occasion, circumstances dictated that they sit side by side, but her nearness always made it difficult to eat . . . or breathe. Sophie Jaegar was not the kind of girl who made life easy.

"So you think her siblings are okay?" Casie asked and glanced at the box that sat on the floor in front of the oven.

The "lambing box" was nothing more than a corrugated container that had once housed some kitchen appliance long ago forgotten. It was frayed at the top and bent at one side, but newborn lambs were not known for their wild attempts to escape, and dozens had been warmed in that same crate just as this one was now, tiny head nestled into the terry cloth towel that cushioned the bottom, knobby legs folded under its angular form.

"They seemed to know which end was up," Ty said.

"So they were nursing?" Casie asked.

"Yeah." Their tiny tails had been twitching merrily while their smaller sibling had stumbled around blindly searching for a meal. But unlike cows, who had four plates at the dinner table, sheep only had two. It made no sense, since the former would almost invariably give birth to a single offspring, while ewes were known to produce three with disturbing frequency. Neither did it make sense that they would, more times than seemed logical, refuse to take one of those offspring while accepting the other two. That had been the case today. He glanced at the lamb, which, to his eyes, possessed all the charm of her siblings, and wondered why some mothers could love with selfless charity while others . . . He winced, mind jolting back to the present.

Casie was staring at him. "What's wrong?" she asked. Her voice was soft, as was her heart. There was no reason to bother her with the fact that the ewe had knocked this particular baby to the ground more than once. No reason to debate why she found this infant so patently detestable.

"Nothing," Ty said and glanced at the soup bowl in front of him.

"Is there something wrong with the stew?" Emily asked. She was different from Casie. Not so soft, but her heart was good as gold. She was loyal as a hound, tough as a screw. If someone asked, he might be able to admit he thought the world of her. After all, they'd been cut from the same tattered cloth.

"No. Course not. It's real good," he said and took a bite, though thoughts of mothers always put him off his feed.

"She'll probably eat when she warms up a little," Emily said.

"Sure. I ain't worried," Ty assured her, but it was an out-and-out lie. He worried about a whole lot of things and they all knew it. The crazy thing . . . the thing that still baffled him was that they cared. Oh sure, *Casie* would . . . she was the kind of person who'd take a kick in the head to save a June bug from a tornado, and Emily . . . Emily was his friend, had been ever since she'd refused to mind her own business in the foster home where they'd both been dumped years before. But Sophie . . . He chanced a look at her, but she was watching him out of the corner of her eye, so he yanked his attention away just as she did the same, heart beating a raucous cadence like it always did when she was near.

"Is everything okay with Angel?" Casie asked.

Ty zipped his gaze to her, already fretting even though the flea-bitten mare was doing as well as could be expected considering her advanced age. "She's doing real good," he said.

"Chesapeake didn't get in trouble again, did he?" In the past couple months Casie had become increasingly attached to the bay stallion Colt had delivered months ago with several other half-starved horses. It was a fact about which no one was particularly thrilled; Chester was as unpredictable as he was handsome.

"Nope," Ty said.

"Is something wrong with Free?" Sophie asked.

"She's fine, too." Freedom was no Angel. Goofy as hell and flighty as a songbird, she wasn't the kind of animal that appealed to Ty's need for calm, but since the day he and Sophie had found her tethered and neglected in a neighboring pregnant mare urine facility, the girl had been in love with the horse. And there wasn't no accounting for love. He glanced across the table once again. Sophie's long, smooth hair shone like a pampered sorrel's in the overhead light. The pink turtleneck she wore under her sleek zip-up sweatshirt matched its trim to perfection, and her earrings, though small and barely visible past the burnished sheen of her hair, probably cost more than he had earned in his life.

He curled his ragged fingernails into his palms and scowled at the unoffending stew.

"What about Blue? He didn't get that bandage off again, did he? Or Marley!" They'd spotted a trio of unclaimed horses in an

overgrown hayfield a few weeks ago. Sophie had named the un-
kempt buckskin after the Jamaican musician and worried about
the feral animals ever since, though they'd proven impossible to
track.

"I didn't see the wild band again. But everybody else looked
good out there 'cept this little one here." He nodded toward the
abandoned lamb.

"She'll be fine once she gets something warm in her belly,"
Emily said.

Ty shifted his gaze to the girl. To look at her you'd think she
was an urban brat, but she was an earth mother at heart, always
ready to nurture and console and feed. If life made any sense at
all he'd be in love with *her* instead of . . .

He stopped his thoughts abruptly.

"I'll mix up some milk," he said, and bumped gracelessly to
his feet, jostling the table as he did so. " 'Cuse me," he added,
but Emily was rising with him.

"What about dessert?" she asked.

"I don't need nothing. Thanks anyhow," he said.

"It's a new—" she began, but just then someone knocked at
the front door. They turned toward it as Colt Dickenson stepped
inside.

"I forgot to drop off the groceries," he said and set a reusable
Monsanto bag on the floor. The irony of the behemoth chemical
company stamping its name on an environmentally friendly
sack wasn't lost on anyone.

"Mr. Dickenson!" Emily's eyes lit up like firecrackers at the
sight of him. Ty glanced at Sophie, but if she was thrilled by the
cowboy's appearance, she didn't let on. Casie just looked tense,
her cheeks somewhat pink. "You're just in time for dessert."

"Thanks," he said. There was a stiffness to him this evening
that didn't usually exist. Colt Dickenson was generally as
smooth as river water. "But I promised Mom I'd fix the bathroom faucet tonight."

"It's a new recipe," Emily prodded. Emily was aces at prod-
ding.

"I'm sure it's top-notch," Colt said. "But I should get going."

"Plum cobblers. I'm thinking of adding them to my list of for-sale items, and I need feedback."

A few months earlier Emily had started selling jams and pies to their neighbors. Shortly after the denizens of Hope Springs had tasted her wares, she'd been invited to deliver breakfast pastries to the Pony Espresso in town. Increasing sales had made it necessary for her to find a vehicle in which to deliver her goods since Puke, Casie's old truck, wasn't exactly reliable. Colt had offered to give her a loan, but true to her frugal nature, Emily'd found an ancient pickup truck that appealed to her. Its dented fenders and broken headlights made Puke look like a thorough-bred by comparison. But it ran, if the wind wasn't too strong and God was feeling generous.

"They're still hot," Emily added and pulled a pan of steaming cobblers from the oven. Sugared cinnamon wafted from them like fragrant dreams, firing up Ty's salivary glands.

"Well . . ." Colt said, already weakening. "I don't want to mess up your experiment."

"Have a chair," Emily chirped and hurried to the cupboard for additional crockery.

Fetching mismatched bowls, she placed a cobbler in each and delivered them to the table.

"There you go. The topping's fresh from Bodacious," she said, referring to the goat she'd brought to the Lazy just a few months before. "I used honey from Colt's mom and plums from that little tree out back."

"Geez, Em," Colt said, settling into the chair next to Sophie, "if you grew your own cinnamon you'd never have to leave the farm."

She blinked. "Does cinnamon grow this far north? How would I plant it? Do you know anything about harvesting—"

Colt chuckled. "Don't go getting all riled up," he said and sliced into his cobbler. "I was just kidding."

She fell silent as the four of them tasted their dessert in unison. "What do you think?" she asked, brow already beetled.

"Man!" Sophie murmured and paused for a moment to stare at her cobbler.

"What?" Emily said, unclasping her hands.

"I just don't understand it," Casie said, ruminating slowly.

"Is it good?" Em asked, but just then Bliss made a noise from the other room and she scooted out to fetch her. By the time she returned, cuddling the baby against her shoulder, the topic had not changed. Sometimes Emily's experiments were gut-wrenching disasters, but when they worked, they worked.

"It's just . . ." Casie tasted another spoonful. "I mean . . ." She shook her head. "*I* can cook."

"Really?" Colt asked.

"No," Sophie murmured, not lifting her gaze from the cobbler as she took another bite.

The kitchen went quiet. Ty glanced from one woman to the next.

"I made that oatmeal once," Casie said.

"Oh yeah," Sophie agreed, savoring another small spoonful. "That wasn't bad."

Casie licked the back of her spoon, looking thoughtful. "And when Em was still laid up I made that pizza."

"It was frozen," Sophie reminded her.

"Well, yes," Casie agreed. "It was frozen before I started."

"And afterward it was burned."

"But I *did* make it and . . ." Casie took another bite and closed her eyes to the sensations. "Holy cats, Em, I just don't have any idea how you do this."

She sounded honestly upset, which, naturally, made Emily euphoric. "You really like it?" she asked and zipped her gaze from one to the other. Colt lifted his bowl. It was already empty.

Still cuddling Bliss, she snatched the dish from his hand and hurried to the stove for a refill. A shade of pink showed through her mocha complexion. "You sure it's not too tart?" she asked.

"I'll know more after my third or fourth helping," Colt said.

"You've gotta be careful," Emily said. "Or your cholesterol's going to be higher than your dad's."

He shrugged. "Mom's got him on starvation rations. So it's my duty to hold up the consumption standards of the Dickenson men. It's a tough job," Colt said.

Emily rolled her eyes but her smile spoke volumes.

Ty let the soft sounds of domesticity seep into his soul, spilling like mulled cider into his system, relaxing his gut and tilting his world toward perfect.

The remainder of dessert was consumed while a half dozen topics were discussed. In a matter of minutes, Sophie was mixing up milk replacer for the lamb, Emily was gathering up the dishes with one hand, and Ty was running hot water into the sink. Steam curled up like morning mist. The water felt heavenly as he dunked the first dishes inside.

"I can wash," Casie offered, but Colt shook his head.

"Let the boy do it," he said. "It's the only time he gets his fingernails clean."

"Can you dry, Soph?" Emily asked.

"Sure."

Ty didn't glance her way. Standing beside her at the sink would be almost as horrible as sitting next to her, almost as hideous as an early morning ride down a sunlit trail or earning an A on a poetry project.

"I'll feed little Lumpkin then," Colt said.

"Lumpkin?" Emily glanced at him.

The cowboy shrugged. "I'm running out of names."

"I'm sure glad I didn't ask for your input for Bliss."

"Well, I would have come up with something better than . . ." He glanced at the far wall, apparently thinking back to the traumatic months before the baby's birth. "Ixapos."

"I was never going to name her Ixapos."

"I'm pretty sure it was in the mix for a while," Colt said. "Sophie, wasn't Ixapos one of the ten thousand options?"

"I'm not sure," she said, pouring the freshly rehydrated milk into a funnel that sat atop a glass bottle. "But I do remember an Enheduanna."

"Enheduanna." Colt nodded. "That was it."

"Well, yeah! She was the first known author. It's a revered nomenclature," Emily said, using some of the ten-dollar words she'd practiced almost constantly during her pregnancy.

"Were you hoping to scar her for life or just—"

"Here you go," Sophie said and handed the bottle to Colt before hurrying out of the room. "I'll be right back."

"And wasn't there a Beelzebub?" Colt asked, raising his voice after the departing girl. But she was already out of hearing.

"Oh, for Pete's sake, there was no Beelzebub," Emily said.

"I'm pretty sure you're wrong."

"Why would I name her after the devil?" Emily asked and plunked the baby into Casie's arms. Bliss stared at her, dark eyes serious as storm clouds beneath gathered brows.

Casie's expression softened. Reaching up, she smoothed her hand over the baby's downy head, then sighed and closed her eyes as she cuddled Bliss against her heart.

The kitchen went silent. Colt stood absolutely motionless, watching, expression unguarded as he held the forgotten bottle in one large hand.

Ty glanced at Emily. Her eyes gleamed as if she'd just won the lotto, but in a second Colt jerked toward her with a scowl.

She struggled to squelch her grin.

"Bethany," she said.

"What?"

"I was going to name her Bethany."

"Who are you trying to kid?" he asked, seeming to come back to himself with some difficulty. "You never considered a single normal name in the whole twelve months you were pregnant."

"Gestation's only nine months," she reminded him.

"Well, it seemed like twelve."

"You should try carrying an elephant around in your belly."

"No matter how long it took, you did a first-rate job," Casie said and smoothed the baby's hair behind one seashell ear.

"Yeah," Colt agreed, staring at the duo on the nearby chair. "Not half bad."

"Do you want to hold her?" Casie asked.

Their gazes met for a second, calling a truce to whatever argument they had shared.

Time stood still. The expression on Colt's face was inexplicable, a nearly painful blend of hope and hopelessness. It made Ty almost hurt for him, though God knew there would never be anyone good enough for Casie Carmichael.

"What? No!" Colt said, finally shaking himself free from Casie's gaze. "I'm a manly man. Manly men don't hold babies."

"She's really soft," Casie said, and turning her face toward Bliss, drew in a deep breath. "And sweet-smelling."

"I like things hard," Colt said. "And stinky."

"She's growing like a buttonweed," Casie added. "Pretty soon she'll be asking for the keys to Puke and bringing home strange boys with tattoos and blue—"

"Oh for God's sake, give me that baby," Colt said, and setting the lamb's bottle on the table, reached for the infant.

After that there was crooning and teasing and laughter.

The kitchen felt as warm as summer sunshine. Steam and contentment swirled together in a moment of magic as old as time until . . .

"Emily!" Sophie yelled. "Why are there dirty diapers in the toilet again?"

CHAPTER 4

"Welcome to the Lazy," Emily said. The couple that disembarked from the rented SUV was handsome, svelte, and polished. Jack circled them, keeping this new human herd tightly packed. "I'd shake your hands, but . . ." She jostled Bliss a little. Baby was dressed in red cable-knit pants and a white sweater. The ensemble had been handcrafted by Cindy Dickenson and made the infant look a little like a Christmas balloon, arms and legs sticking out at incongruous angles. A red stocking cap with a tail as long as her body topped off the outfit. The white puff at the end was nestled near her little green booties. "I don't want to have to worry about shaken baby syndrome."

Max Barrenger and Sonata Detric laughed on cue.

"You must be Casie," the man said. He was five ten in his shiny new alligator boots. His hair was artfully tousled, and his coat was leather. Lambskin, if she wasn't mistaken. She'd have to keep him away from Lumpkin. Insecurity wasn't good for anyone.

" 'Fraid not," she said. "I'm Emily. Casie is . . ." She glanced around, but true to form, Case was nowhere to be seen. Generally speaking, the Lazy's owner would rather take a hoof pick in the eye than meet strangers. "On a tractor somewhere."

"Oh," Sonata said. Her hair was short, dark, and chic. "I thought Casie was a woman."

Emily refrained from laughing out loud. She might have been similarly prone to gender profiling in the past. "Turns out being female doesn't preclude one from feeding cattle," Emily said, and Max chuckled.

"What did you think, S.?" he asked. "That women were forbidden by law to operate heavy equipment?"

Sonata Detric raised carefully threaded brows at him. "Actually," she said, "I thought women would be smarter than to want to."

Emily felt a wave of protective resentment wash through her. An odd thing, perhaps, considering Casie was ten years her senior. "Well, I'm not sure if Case really *wants* to drive the tractor," she said. "But cows seem to get hungry every single day, and they're not very particular about who feeds them."

"So this really *is* a ranch," Sonata said.

That statement stopped Emily dead in her verbal tracks for a second. "Were you expecting something else?"

"Well, no." The woman tilted her chin up and laughed a little. The sound had a throaty musicality to it. "I mean, Max said it was, but—" She shrugged one trim shoulder. The coat she wore was winter white, probably cashmere, and belted snugly at a very narrow waist.

"Didn't you see our Web site?" Emily asked.

"Max made the reservations. I've been so busy with work that I just let him take care of things." She glanced around. Emily didn't bother to do the same. She knew what people saw: pastoral snow-covered hills dotted with white-faced cattle, woolly sheep, and shaggy horses. It was impossible to say if they also recognized the hope, fatigue, or gut-deep contentment that were part and parcel of the struggle to put the Lazy in the black. "I just thought—" She shook her head, looking befuddled.

"What?" Max asked and grinned. "Say it."

"Okay." She faced him with a mild blend of challenge and amusement. "I thought you were putting me on."

He laughed out loud. "I told you I'm a country boy deep down in my roots."

She shook her head. "We'll see how country you are when your BlackBerry doesn't work while you're out punching cattle," she said.

"Punching cattle?" He laughed. "Who have *you* been talking to?"

She grinned though she looked a little defensive. "I saw an episode of *Deadwood.*"

He chuckled again.

"Punching cattle is the correct term, isn't it?" she asked, turning toward Emily.

"Well, we don't do a lot of punching, per se," Emily said. "More shooing, a little nudging, a lot of feeding."

"Remind me never to trust HBO again," Sonata said and glanced around. It was a fair bet that Sonata Detric had never ventured more than fifty blocks from her favorite Macy's.

"You're going to love it!" Max vowed and hugged her with daunting enthusiasm. "Isn't she?" he asked, one arm remaining around his fiancée's tightly cinched waist.

"Guaranteed," Emily said, but one glance at the other's sleek boots made her a little dubious. Those things were not horse friendly. In fact, they might not even be *outdoor* friendly. The spiky heels were more likely to be seen in *Sex and the City* than in *Cheyenne,* which was Emily's current favorite. There was nothing like a little retro TV . . . and army boots, she thought, appreciating her own serviceable footwear. Paired with oversized cargo pants with enough pockets to house every conceivable baby necessity, they were killer. She turned away from her guests' rented Escalade. "Come on. I'll show you to the bunkhouse."

"Bunkhouse?" Sonata sounded uncertain at best, but Emily kept an upbeat tone.

"It sounds better than the chicken coop," she said, at which time uncertainty probably turned to terror in their new guest's mind, but when they had trudged up the hill and stepped through the rough timbers of the front door, the couple drew in their breath in unified surprise.

"My God!" Sonata said, eyes wide and lips parted. "This is . . . this is just adorable."

Emily glanced around. The building formerly occupied by the

Lazy's motley poultry wasn't a large space. Still, it had taken months to restore. While the foundation and the original log siding had remained intact, the roof and windows needed replacing. The process had seemed to take forever. But in retrospect, the exterior of the building had been completed fairly quickly. The threat of oncoming Dakota winters tended to hustle people along pretty efficiently. Casie's popularity coupled with Sophie's free riding lessons had inspired their neighbors to help speed the project along. Finishing the interior of the bunkhouse, however, had been almost entirely Emily's domain. Impeded by a nonexistent budget, a thousand chores, and little Bliss's impending arrival, decorating had been a challenge. But she was pleased with the results; the striped Navaho coverlet on the heavy timber bed contrasted pleasantly with the ragged-edged leather curtains, which had been salvaged from old coats bought at the local Salvation Army. The shutters, crafted by Colt from ancient barn wood, were weathered to a gunmetal gray and highlighted with olive lichen that had long ago dried but remained tenaciously intact. The basin used as a sink had been found in the Pollacks' abandoned attic. It was a copper hue that Emily had painstakingly matched to the hooks anchored beside the door. A few yards away, half hidden behind a privacy screen made from corrugated steel fencing, was a clawfoot bathtub. Sophie had discovered it half buried in a neighbor's shelterbelt. Neither removing it from the entwining roots nor scouring it clean had been a simple task, but, as Ty would say, "The best saddle horses can buck like mustangs when they first come out of the chute." In other words, each piece had been a pain to find, and a nightmare to restore, but she loved every inch of space, every bit of tilted floor, every grain of rust and floret of lichen.

"Wow," Max said, drawing Emily back to the present.

"*Who* is your decorator?" Sonata asked.

Pride bloomed stealthily in Emily's chest. Still, it wasn't difficult to be self-deprecating. Memories of her life before the Lazy, life with Flynn, had a way of keeping her humble. Had Casie not taken her in, little Bliss would have been born in a flophouse somewhere. *If* she'd been born at all. "We all just kind of pitched in," she said.

"Well, someone's got a good throwing arm then," Max said.

"I think you're being modest," Sonata added.

"It takes a village." Emily shifted Bliss a little higher against her shoulder. "Or in this case, about a dozen well-fed farmers and a lot of elbow grease."

"You're kidding me," Sonata said, and turning away finally, ran an analytical finger over a knothole in the nearest shutter.

"Believe me," Emily said, "I have the capped elbow to prove it."

"What's that?" Max asked.

"Capped elbow?" Bliss made a mewing sound. Emily bounced her a little more vigorously. "It's an inflammation on a horse's olecranon that . . ." She shook her head. Sophie was always spouting those ridiculous terms. Half the time Emily didn't even know she'd been listening. "I'm not the horse expert."

"Well, you've got a great eye for decorating," Sonata said. "If my people had this kind of talent, Pier One would be out of business."

"Who?" Emily asked, and Sonata laughed.

"Exactly," she said, then sobered rapidly and turned with an entrepreneurial light in her eye. "Say, you wouldn't be interested in—"

"Just quit," Max said and snagged her close to his side again. "We're on vacation."

"That doesn't mean I can't—"

"Yes, it does," he argued and shook his head as he turned toward Emily. "You'd better watch out, or she'll have you stashed away in the Village cranking out decorating sketches to pay for your caffeine addiction."

"Already there."

"What?"

"Not in the Village," she clarified. "Just with the caffeine addiction. Listen, I'll let you get settled in. Supper will be ready in about an hour."

"Great. I'm starving already," Max said.

Sonata rolled her eyes.

"What?" He rocked back on his well-shod heels and rubbed his hands together. "Us cowpokes gotta get plenty of grub," he said. "What are we having?"

"Chicken-fried steak, spiced yams, and pickled beets," Emily said.

"Chicken-fried . . ." Sonata stopped short. Her perfectly groomed brows had risen a quarter of an inch, but didn't dare settle a single wrinkle into her forehead. "You're kidding, right?"

Emily blinked. Bliss whimpered. "I didn't know steak was intrinsically amusing."

Sonata preened a smile. "Max told you I'm a vegan, didn't he?"

"Vegan?" Holy Pete. "No," she said, turning her gaze to Max and trying to refrain from looking either accusatory or terrified. "I didn't know."

"I haven't eaten animal products for . . ." She waved a slim hand. Her fingers were pale and delicate, her nails a perfect shade of pearl. "Years."

"I see," Emily said, but her mind was spinning. It wasn't as if she disapproved. After all, it was a wise choice for a crowded planet. Hell, if she had the discipline she'd go that route herself, but the Lazy went through about a gallon of heavy cream a day and butter . . . butter was like gold. And there were no substitutes no matter what the romance cover guy with the long hair said on TV.

"That's not a problem, is it?" Sonata asked.

"No. Of course not," Emily said, mind scrambling. "It's just that Bodacious needs . . . never mind," she said, smiling carefully as she turned toward the door. "It's not a problem at all."

"Bodacious?" Sonata asked.

"Our nanny goat." Emily glanced back at the woman. "Her previous owners were going to send her to slaughter, but Casie took her in. Well . . ." She shook her head and smiled. "I'm sure you're tired. I'll see you in a little bit."

"They were going to kill her?" Sonata said.

Emily sighed sadly. "She kept having babies, and they didn't want more kids, and now the little ones are weaned, so Bo has to be milked or she gets pretty miserable." It was a cock-and-bull sob story if she had ever made one up. And she *had*. But dammit, she didn't know how to cook vegan.

"Surely you can market the surplus," Sonata said. "Raw milk is worth a fortune in the city."

Emily shook her head. "I'm afraid it's illegal to sell unpasteurized milk in South Dakota stores. Otherwise the Lazy would be on the cutting edge. Our milk isn't just raw, it's produced by an all-organic, free-range, split-hoofed ruminant." That meant that the bothersome Bo could be found outside her spacious pasture more than in. She was, in short, the Houdini of herbivores, but Emily had learned to sling verbiage before she'd learned to walk. "Don't you guys worry about any of this, though. You're on vacation. Do you have any other dietary restrictions?" Maybe they only ate food that was harvested on a Tuesday or fruits that were picked on the Sabbath.

"Well, I do try to limit my oils, even those that are vegetable-based."

Emily refrained from rolling her eyes.

"Oh come on," Max said, leaning away from his fiancée a little. "Like she said, we're on vacation."

Sonata's scowl darkened. There was still not a wrinkle to be seen. "Fat molecules don't take a vacation."

"Bodacious needs to be milked," Max reminded her. "You don't want to make an innocent animal suffer because you're trying to keep innocent animals from suffering, do you?" he asked and winked at Emily.

Sonata scowled at him. "Okay," she said finally. "No veganism while we're here."

"Are you sure?" Emily asked. Inside, she was doing the happy dance even though Bodacious was about as innocent as Satan. "I don't want to compromise your morals."

"I'll live on the edge," Sonata said, then hastened to add, "but no meat."

"Of course not," Emily agreed, then hurried out the door before minds were changed. In a moment she was hustling into the sheep barn.

"Colt!" she called, storming through the scattering flock toward the isolated pen in the corner. "Colt?"

He stepped out of nowhere, scaring the life out of her.

"Holy . . ." She put one hand to her chest in an attempt to keep her heart confined. "Are you trying to kill me?"

"If I did, would I have little Bliss all to myself?" he asked and tugged the knit cap over the baby's tiny left earlobe.

"She's vegetarian," Emily said, ignoring his ridiculousness as best she could.

"Give her some time," he said, pulling down the other side of Bliss's cap. "She probably needs teeth before she can go full-bore carnivore."

Emily stared at him for a good four seconds before she realized what he was talking about. "Not Bliss. Sonata Detric. She's—" she began, but he was already grinning.

She drew air through her nostrils and glared at him. "Holy cow, you're a pain in the tail. No wonder Casie turned you down."

Sobering somewhat, he settled his lean hips back against the sheep pen. "What makes you think I proposed?"

She stared at him, nervous suddenly. She wasn't entirely unaware that she was meddling.

"Em?" he asked.

"Well . . ." She blew out a breath. "You're not a complete idiot."

He raised his brows.

"I mean, you're as sexy as Belgian chocolate," she said, and stole a peek at him.

His brows had jumped into his hairline.

"Oh, don't look so surprised. You know you're tasty. But Casie . . ." She shook her head and felt her gut tighten with emotion. "She's like . . ." She shrugged, searching for words. "Wild raspberries."

"I don't think I follow your—"

"Tasty *and* good for you. I'm just saying . . ." She exhaled heavily. "Don't give up."

"She's awfully skittish."

"Yeah, well, just give her . . ." she began, then shook her head and brought the conversation back to the crisis at hand. "What am I going to do?"

"About Baby's vegetarianism?"

"I'm going to slap you," she warned.

He laughed. "Geez, Em, simmer down. Why are you so wound up?"

"Why! Why? Fifty percent of our current guests don't eat meat. And we're on a cattle ranch. A cattle ranch!"

"So make her something else. It'll be fine."

"It's not that simple."

"Even for a virtuoso like you?" he asked.

She narrowed her eyes at him. "Maybe Casie turned you down because you're such a bull sh—"

"Hey, you watch your mouth in front of my godchild."

She glanced guiltily at Bliss, but the baby didn't seem to be taking notes. In fact, she had fallen asleep against her mother's shoulder, tiny mouth slightly open, downy lashes dark and lush against her Frappuccino cheeks. Emily absorbed the sight, drawing it into her soul. This was her family, her blood, her life. Everything else was irrelevant.

"You're right," she said, and sighed. "It'll be fine."

"Sure it will," he said and, leaning closer, placed a kiss on Bliss's flawless brow. "Do you need some help?"

"I would give my spleen for some help," she said and scowled. "What can you do?"

He made a face as he considered that. "I'm pretty good at riding broncs."

"Can you ride broncs while peeling potatoes?"

"Not sure, but I can probably manage without the broncs."

"Bingo," she said.

Two minutes later they were side by side in the kitchen. Emily had strapped Bliss to her back, and Colt was studiously beating eggs with a wire whisk. The chickens' productivity was considerably diminished during the winter months, but the available yolks were as bright as harvest moons.

Colt set the bowl aside. "Now what?" he asked.

"Now you . . ." She glanced at him and stopped short. He had found a half apron somewhere and subsequently tied the lacy garment around his taut waist. The frilly single pocket looked ridiculous against the frayed denim of his jeans. "What are you doing?"

He lifted his arms slightly and glanced down at himself. "I didn't want to soil my ensemble."

"If Casie sees you in that she'll probably never talk to you again, much less seriously consider marrying—"

"Hey." Casie's voice rang through the house as she stepped in through the front door. "It smells great in here al—" Her voice stopped as she appeared in the kitchen and caught sight of Colt in the apron.

"What do you think?" he asked, lifting his arms higher. He'd rolled the sleeves of his corduroy shirt away from his wrists, which were corded with muscle and ridiculously appealing. Emily squelched a sigh.

"I think you missed your calling."

"I should have been a chef?"

"You should have been a housewife."

He chuckled. The sound, low and fertile, rolled like distant thunder through the kitchen, stopping Emily's breath for a moment, but when she glanced at Casie, she realized she wasn't the only one affected. The other woman's eyes were wide, her lips slightly parted. Emily struggled with her grin and turned away, but Casie found her voice in a moment.

"I thought we were having steak," she said.

"I thought so, too, but apparently fifty percent of our guests are vegetarian," Colt said.

"Oh no."

"Oh yes," Emily countered.

"What now?"

"Colt says he knows his mom's recipe for egg strata."

"*Says* I know. Thanks for the vote of confidence, Em."

"Our reputation rides on these guests. You're only as good as your last satisfied—"

"Man, it's colder than the ice age out there," Sophie said and unceremoniously entered the kitchen. Why, Emily wondered, did she always look like she'd just stepped off the pages of *Vogue*? "Is the coffee on or should I—" She paused as she glanced around. "What's going on?"

"She's a vegetarian," Casie said.

"Who? Bliss?"

"Geez!" Emily said. "Everyone's a comedian. This isn't funny."

Sophie pulled the knit cap off her head and stared at Colt's frilly apron. "It kind of is."

"You don't like it?" he asked and pirouetted a little.

For a second not a female breath was drawn as their gazes shifted to lower regions.

"What?" he asked, scowling as he noticed their expressions.

"Nothing!" Casie said, and clearing her throat, turned away, already blushing.

Emily managed to refrain from pumping her fist in the air. "Beat up another egg, will you, Colt? Soph, I need some more Parmesan grated," she said and scowled. "Why didn't I learn to make my own cheese?"

"Because you only have two hands," Colt suggested. "Well, you know, besides our six."

For the next ten minutes they worked in concert.

"Tell me again why we're sweating bullets over one guest," Sophie said. Her hands were covered in flour. A little dusted her hair.

"So we don't starve to death over the winter," Emily said.

"Oh." Sophie made a "makes sense" expression. "Good reson."

Ty showed up a few minutes later and set the table as Colt mixed up Lumpkin's milk. She bleated hopefully from the living room. But true to his gregarious nature, Colt carried her back into the kitchen to feed her. Far be it from him to be out of the action . . . or maybe . . . Emily glanced wistfully toward Casie. Maybe there was something else that brought him back.

Whatever the case, everyone bumped knees and elbows as they passed the chair where he sat. But Lumpkin didn't take long to finish a bottle anymore. In a matter of minutes Colt was rising, stowing the lamb under one arm just as a knock sounded at the door.

Emily let in their guests.

"It smells terrific in here," Max said.

"Yes, it . . ." Sonata began, but then she caught sight of Lumpkin. "Is that a . . ."

They all waited.

"I believe it's a lamb," Max said.

"In the house?"

"Pretty cold outside for newborns," Colt said, and settling Lumpkin under his other arm, stuck out his right hand. "Hi. I'm Colt Dickenson."

"Maxwell Barrenger," said the other man and grinned as they shook. "I like your apron."

Colt grinned back and turned toward the woman who was just lifting her gaze from the apron's frilly hem.

"I'm Sonata." She thrust out a perfectly manicured hand and held his just a second longer than necessary. "Sonata Jameson Detric. It's very nice to meet you."

"Well," Emily said, sensing trouble brewing. "Let's eat."

CHAPTER 5

"I don't know what's wrong with it," Colt said, and cupping his hands in front of his face, breathed some heat onto them. It was colder than a witch's rear end standing beside the ancient pickup.

Emily scowled at the engine. Between it and the open hood, she could see Max approach from the bunkhouse. En route, he popped the collar up on his lambskin jacket and shoved his hands into the pockets. His blue jeans were creatively distressed, his cowboy boots shiny. "What's going on?"

Colt shook his head. "Can't seem to get Em's truck started this morning."

"That's a truck?" Max asked, staring askance at the vehicle.

"It was a *crazy cool* truck," Emily said and sadly put one mittened hand on the curved fender.

"Oh yeah?" Max said, tilting his head the other way, as if another angle might help him see things differently. "What century?"

Colt chuckled. "In the late forties, this little baby would have been top of the line."

"Yeah," Emily agreed, though she didn't have any idea what she was talking about. She just knew she loved the lines of it, and the substance. And of course, the price. The octogenarian who'd placed the ad in the *Hope Springs Gazette* had asked for three hundred dollars, but she had talked him down to two-fifty, five dozen eggs, and a quart of bread-and-butter pickles. The thought of owning her own ride for the first time in her life had conjured up images of independence and world domination. But in retrospect, perhaps she should have been a little suspicious when he had insisted that she take "the whole thing." Maybe that was a clue that some parts weren't necessarily attached with the kind of cohesiveness that one generally expects in automobiles. In fact, although the engine had started after some cajoling, she'd been forced to stop twice on her way to the Lazy to retrieve parts that had gone AWOL.

"It just needs a little tender, loving care," she said.

"And maybe a paint job," Max added, at which point Emily had to admit that the amalgamation of colors was more a lack of paint than an actual hue.

"A new carburetor," Colt said.

"And a seat," Emily admitted wistfully.

Max glanced into the truck's interior. "Huh," he said and not much else. There *was* a seat, but rodents, time, or some as-of-yet-undisclosed monster had eaten most of it away, leaving passengers and driver to perch as best they could upon the open springs.

"But the tires are good," Emily said.

Max raised his brows, obviously impressed. "You *are* an optimist."

"It's pretty much a necessity around here," she said, still staring dismally at her proudest purchase.

"Maybe it just needs a new alternator," Max said and reached into the bowels of the beast to touch an unidentified doohickey.

Emily glanced at him. "You know something about engines?"

"Nah," he said, drawing back. "I was just trying that optimist thing."

Colt chuckled. "Sorry I don't have more time to tinker with it right now, Em. I promised Dad I'd run an errand for him this morning."

"You'll have time to pick up our guest though, right?"

"I'll be there, but I guess you'll have to use Puke to make your deliveries."

"Deliveries?" Max questioned.

Emily hugged her arms to her chest, wrapping herself against the brittle cold. "I take pies and stuff to a couple neighbors," she said.

"Don't let her fool you," Colt warned. "Em here supplies half the county with baked goods. She's a regular Chef Boyardee."

"Nice reference," Emily said, pulling her gaze from her truck.

Colt shrugged. "Couldn't come up with anything better."

"Maybe your brain's frozen," Max said, hunching his shoulders against the cold.

Colt nodded. "Probably nothing a hot cup of coffee wouldn't fix." He glanced sideways at Emily. " 'Course, if I had a fresh-made sticky bun to go with it, I could maybe remember to talk to Les about Dee's troubles."

"Dee?" Emily said, and looking into his eyes wondered, not for the first time, what the hell Casie was thinking. If Colt Dickenson had the slightest interest in *her,* she'd have him hog-tied to her ankle before he'd finished that first cup of coffee.

"I thought I'd state my choice of names for the truck before you called it Ixapos or whatever."

"Enheduanna," Emily said and grinned. "Come on in, both of you. Coffee's on and the rolls will be ready in a few minutes."

"I'm pretty sure I'm still full from last night," Max said.

"You won't be," Colt assured him. "Not once you catch a whiff of those rolls."

"Well, maybe I'll have a little something now, then eat again later when Sonata's ready."

"You must not be the type to sleep in." Colt held the front door open for the other two to step inside.

"Pretty tough to do when your roommate is pacing your space like a Nazi on morning patrol," Max said.

"What?" Emily turned, toeing off her boots as she did so. "There's not a problem, I hope."

"No. No problem."

Emily scowled, worry troubling her stomach. "The temperature was okay, wasn't it? You weren't too cold? This is our first winter with guests and it's hard to—"

"The temperature's fine," Max said and laughed. "S. just isn't ..." He made a face as if trying to think of a term that didn't conjure up thoughts of concentration camps. "Let's just say she isn't the kind for cuddling when there are employees to be castigated."

"But this is supposed to be a vacation."

"Believe me," he said, "she wouldn't be happy if she couldn't be worrying about her business."

"Maybe I should go get her," Emily said. "Invite her for rolls and coffee."

"Not if you want to keep your head attached to your torso."

Emily glanced at him.

"She doesn't really like to be interrupted when she's chewing someone out. Why do you think I was out in the cold at—" He stopped and sniffed. "What *is* that smell?"

"It's magic." Colt winked at Emily as he stepped past Max. His stocking feet were silent on the old linoleum as he made his way toward the scrolled metal stand on the counter. It held six pottery mugs. Each of them was slightly different, except for the fact that they were misshapen. Emily had found them at a garage sale on her way home from a doctor's appointment. She could only guess that they were somebody's art project gone bad, but she loved every misbegotten one of them.

Taking two of the nubby cups in one hand, Colt set them on the counter, poured coffee into each, and handed one to the other man.

"Have a seat," Colt said and motioned to the chairs.

Emily sighed softly, beginning to relax. She didn't know why. It was going to be a crazy busy day and she still had deliveries to make. Dee (she rolled the truck's new name around in her brain for a moment, then gave it a mental thumbs-up) was on the blink, a new guest would be arriving in the afternoon, and Bliss wouldn't sleep much longer. But she loved it that Colt felt at home here. Loved it that others could sit in the kitchen and taste the warmth and smell the peace.

"How long has Sonata been . . ." Colt paused as he and Max moved toward the table. He was limping this morning, Emily realized, and wondered why his leg seemed to bother him more sometimes than others. Maybe she should try her hand at homeopathic recipes. "What does Sonata do exactly?"

Max laughed and wrapped his hands around the earthenware mug. It would take a minute for it to absorb heat from the coffee. But there was nothing more comforting than feeling warmth seep into the baked clay. "She's VP for Hearth and Home," he said and took his first sip. A moment later he raised his brows. "Whoa!"

"Is it too strong?" Emily asked.

"No." Max shook his head, looking dazed. "Not at all. I think I could wrestle it to the floor if I had to."

Colt laughed just as the front door opened. Casie entered the kitchen on stocking feet. Her nose was red and her fingers looked stiff as she wrapped her hands around her own cup of coffee.

"Good morning," she said, gaze touching on Colt for an instant before darting to Max. "How did you sleep?"

"Great for about six hours."

"Six—" Casie began, but just then there was a bump and a bleat from the family room. An instant later Lumpkin trotted into the kitchen, tiny hooves clattering like castanets, woolly ears bouncing as she rounded the corner and bumped her pointy nose smack-dab into Max's leg. "I'm sorry," Casie said, already sounding embarrassed as she hoisted the lamb into the air with one hand under her belly.

But then Bliss squealed from the other room.

"Guess everyone's hungry," Colt said.

Emily glanced at Casie before lifting her attention to the rolls.

"I'll get her," Colt said, taking one more sip of coffee before easing to his feet.

"Man," Max said, grinning at Lumpkin. "That is cute."

"Not so cute when she poops on the floor," Emily said.

"True for almost everyone," Colt added and sauntered from the room. In a moment he was crooning to the baby, and for a second Emily let herself absorb the low, soothing tempo of his voice. Not that she wanted him for herself. She didn't. Really. This once she would gladly adopt Casie's cautious approach to life and be content with what she had.

"Why in the house?" Max was asking. "I mean, I have to assume they don't *all* come inside. Do they?"

Casie laughed as she pulled a mixing bowl from the cupboard. "We try to keep a few of them in the barn."

Emily said a silent thank-you to whoever might be watching out for her.

"Could I take her while you get things ready?" their guest asked, and rising to his feet, took Lumpkin from Casie's hands. Holding the lamb out in front of him for a second, he studied her comical little face. "Is it because she's so cute?"

"What?" Casie asked, already retrieving the milk replacer.

"Lumpkin," he said, now cradling the woolly infant against his chest. "Is she inside just because she's so adorable?"

"Oh no. Well . . . she is cute," Casie said. "But she wasn't supposed to be born yet. In this weather, if they're not dried off right away, their extremities will freeze."

"Really?" He cradled two tiny black hooves in one hand.

"Probably not their feet, but their ears and tails for sure. Even in December, the mother could probably handle the job if she were so inclined."

"Could?" he asked.

"Sometimes mothers fu—" Emily stopped herself. There were times when gratitude turned to grudge without the slightest warning. And her own mother hadn't *completely* failed, she reminded herself. Jennifer Casper had kept her alive. Kept her fed. Emily remembered scraping the jelly jar empty on one cold November night. She'd been small for her age and knobby-kneed. When Mom was in a good mood she used to call her Big Bird because of those gnarly joints, but her mother hadn't awakened until evening that day. Still, there had been peanut butter in the cupboard. There had almost always been peanut butter.

She could feel Casie's sudden attention and lowered her eyes to carefully align slices of bacon in the pan, each one soldiered perfectly against the next. Emily cleared her throat. "Sometimes mothers reject their young," she corrected.

"You're kidding. She didn't want this one?" Max asked.

"Some of the very best ones are neglected," Casie said.

Emily didn't look up. Couldn't. Her throat felt too tight. The kitchen went quiet.

"I don't know if I should ask for clarification or just say thank you," Max said.

They turned toward him in unison, and he chuckled. "Mom took off when I was three."

An unidentifiable noise sounded in Emily's throat. She covered it with a cough.

"I'm sorry," Casie said.

Max shrugged. "Luckily, Dad had enough cash to buy me a new one."

Emily blinked at him, emotions boiling.

"Look what I found," Colt said, entering the kitchen with little Bliss tucked into his right arm.

"Wow!" Max said, gazing at the baby, then at the lamb. "I can't decide which one's cuter."

"If you've got a weakness for sticky buns, you're going to want to choose this one," Colt said, seating himself and propping Bliss on his lap. She slumped there like a tiny Yoda, blue eyes dark and wise.

"Good morning, Baby Bliss." Emily tried to say the words casually, like this was the norm. Like she had awakened every day of her life to share this familial magic. But Max's words had aroused something raw and needy inside her. "How are you today?"

"A little stinky," Colt said.

"Oh. Sorry." She raised her gaze to his, trying to bring herself back to the here and now. "I'll get her changed before—"

"Already done," Colt said.

Emily swallowed. She had no idea why that made her feel like crying. "Thanks."

"No problem," he said and set the baby on the edge of the table so he could see her face. It was a good face. An amazing face, with round eyes that swallowed you whole and soft black curls already wisping onto her milk-chocolate forehead. A face that generally made Emily cry or laugh or both . . . frequently at the same time. Maybe she needed help. "Better than having to clean up after that one," he said and motioned to the lamb just as Sophie stepped into the kitchen from out of doors. Ty followed a second later. "They're going to have to chase all over the house for that job, aren't they?" he said, wiggling Bliss until she grinned lopsidedly. "Unless they diaper her, too."

"That's cruel and inhuman," Sophie said.

Emily glanced at her. It wasn't as if she and Soph were bosom buddies or anything, but the girl looked cold enough to snap. Em handed her a cup of coffee. "The weather or diapering a lamb?"

"Both," she said, gratefully cradling the cup between chilled hands. "Besides, where would her tail go?"

"She's right," Colt said, still addressing Bliss. "Little Lumpkin will have to take her chances."

"What do you mean take her chances?" Emily asked and turned from the oven where she had just peeked at the rolls. They were starting to blush with that just-toasted look. Warm, sugar-laden contentment wafted into the air. She closed the door, poured another cup of coffee, and handed it to Ty. His gaze barely met hers for a moment as he mumbled his thanks and moved off for the closest empty chair. "Her siblings are doing okay, aren't they?"

"They have their mom to cuddle up to," Colt said. "But I'm sure Lumpkin will be fine."

Emily scowled. Worry was beginning to creep in. "But she'll be with the rest of the flock, right?"

"She *is* a sheep," Colt said.

Emily turned the bacon. It sizzled merrily, spitting forth flavor and heat.

"Why don't we put her in the basement like we did all the rest of the bums?" Sophie asked.

"She'd be all alone down there," Emily said and stole a glance at Bliss. She couldn't imagine being separated from her. It would be like death. Worse than death.

"Well, like Colt said . . ." Sophie shrugged, cradling her mug against her chest. "She is a sheep."

Anger spurred unexpectedly through Emily, and though Colt *had* said the same thing, her rage was directed at Sophie alone. "Like Freedom's just a horse?"

"I didn't say *just*. I said—"

"So, Max . . ." Casie's voice was raised from its usual quiet reflection, effectively reminding both girls that they did, in fact, have a paying guest in their midst. After one glance they emotionally backed off to neutral corners. "You grew up in Nebraska?" she asked and poured the reconstituted milk into an empty Coke bottle.

"Well, that's what I like to tell my urban friends. They think I rope buffalo on Sundays and Thursdays, but the truth is I spent . . . or *misspent* most of my youth on Park Avenue."

"In Midtown?" Sophie asked.

"Yeah." Max glanced up in surprise. "Are you familiar with the area?"

"A little," Sophie said. They all stared at her. Ty's face was expressionless, a leftover from the days when he'd been constantly careful to reveal nothing. "They make some pretty good pad Thai on the corner of Fiftieth and Sixth."

"The Tuk Tuk Boy," Max said, beaming. "I can't believe I found a Midtown girl out here in the Dakotas."

"I'm a little surprised myself." Casie said what they all were thinking. Sophie had never mentioned spending time in New York City. Apparently, they all had their secrets. And sometimes secrets hurt, Emily thought. She glanced at Ty. His hands looked rough against his misshapen mug. His hair was shaggy, and the color in his cheeks had not diminished as he held his gaze steady as a falcon on the contents of his cup. Not once did he shift his attention to Sophie. But Emily knew there was a spark there. In fact, maybe there was more than a spark. She turned her attention back to Sophie, perfectly groomed and carefully aloof despite early mornings and rank livestock. Ty, on the other hand, looked a little sick to his stomach.

Holy cats, love was like a carnival ride through hell. She was lucky to have made her way to Bliss without having to endure *that* agony, she thought, and tucked away ragged memories of professed love miserably melded with throbbing bruises.

"How about you, Tyler?" Max asked, shifting his gaze from Sophie to the boy. "Have you ever been to New York?"

Ty glanced at their guest. He kept his expression solemn, but his hands tightened on his mug. "No, sir."

"Well, you should try it. It's a fascinating place. My father used to say there's nowhere like New York City to put polish on a boy." He smiled at Sophie.

Ty lowered his gaze to his coffee again. Emily expected him to sink into his usual reticence, but in a moment he spoke. "A cow pony ain't a show horse just cuz you braid his mane."

The kitchen was quiet for a second, and then Colt chuckled. "Amen," he said.

Max laughed, Bliss gurgled, and the conversation turned to other things.

By the time breakfast had been devoured, Max had tried his hand at bottle-feeding Lumpkin, and Bliss had fallen asleep against the soft, waffled cotton of Colt's shoulder.

Her pink lips were parted, her tiny fingers curled softly against his chest.

"I'd take her with me," Colt said, stroking her back gently, "but it might get the townsfolk talking a little."

"Give her here," Emily said and took Bliss from his arms, letting the baby's solid weight ease into her soul.

"I didn't say I was adverse to the idea," Colt said and settled back in his chair. "Wanna ride into town with me, Ty? Or are you going to catch the bus to school?"

"You goin' right away?"

Colt glanced at the clock above the kitchen sink. It was almost seven thirty. "Should have already left," he said.

"Guess I better clean up a little first."

"There's something wrong when kids don't appreciate the smell of a little horse manure first thing in the morning," Colt said and rose to his feet. "Come on. I'll give you a ride back to the Red Horse, at least. Mom will probably want to feed you a second breakfast."

"How's she doing?" Casie asked. Cindy Dickenson had been experiencing chest pain and bouts of dizziness.

Colt shrugged noncommittally but there was worry in his eyes. "She's going in for more tests."

Ty rose beside him, glanced furtively at Sophie, and moved toward the front door.

"Does she need a ride to the clinic or anything?" Casie asked.

Colt watched her for a second, expression inscrutable, before he shook his head. "It's not likely Dad would let her go without him." His gaze was soft, but in a moment he turned his attention toward Max. "What's on your docket for today?"

"I'm considering snowshoeing. And I hear there's an art fair in Hope Springs. Thought we might take that in when Sonata's done chewing out her underlings." He grinned. "*If* she gets done with that. Until then . . ." He shrugged.

"If you're interested, I could hook you up with some of our local artisans while Sonata's busy," Emily asked.

Max cocked his head at her. "I thought you didn't have a vehicle."

"Hence the beauty of the plan," Emily admitted. "You could give me a ride in your fancy SUV while I make my deliveries."

He laughed. "Sounds great," he said. "Just let me check in with S. first. No point in making the woman you love mad, right?" he asked and paced toward the door.

Ty glanced at Sophie. Colt looked at Casie. No one turned toward Emily.

Love might be a carnival ride through hell, but sometimes a girl missed the Tilt-A-Whirl something awful.

CHAPTER 6

"How's she doing?" Casie watched Sophie clip a tie to Evie's halter.

The mare, pretty as a picture despite her winter fuzz, boasted a flaxen mane and three white socks. Heaving a sigh, she relaxed her left hind and dipped her muzzle into the bucket that hung below the quick release snap.

"Pretty well," Sophie said. "She seems to like the work and her body score is improving."

Casie ran her gaze over the mare's golden hide. When she had come to them, packed in Monty Dickenson's horse trailer with a half dozen other horses, she had been severely underweight, though she had hardly been the worst of the lot. But while her bonier peers had packed on the pounds fairly easily, the palomino mare had remained skinny as a rail. Now, however, thanks to a strict deworming schedule, dental care, and more feed than seemed necessary to sustain a pachyderm, she looked hale and hearty.

"What do you think? Can we trust her with guests?" Casie asked.

"Riding or driving?"

"What?"

Sophie glanced over her shoulder. A mischievous grin flashed. It was a rare expression on the girl's too-serious face. "You know I've been long-lining her." Her tone was devoid of that carefully nurtured disdain that had been all but constant during her early weeks at the Lazy.

"Yeah." Casie kept her own tone casual. This newly emerging Sophie Jaegar was a skittish creature and only made infrequent visits. But horses seemed to coax her out of hiding. So although Casie worried about the girl's safety, she tried not to complain about the long hours she spent in the barn. Even when Casie had seen her trailing behind the palomino, two long ropes strung from the rings of her bit, she had not interfered.

"A week or so ago I started having her pull some weight. Just a little at first. A log, then a hay bale."

Despite her vow to let the girl's shy happiness take flight, Casie felt herself pale. "Holy Hannah, Soph. I wish you'd tell me before you start things that are dangerous."

The girl laughed. "I'm working green horses, Case. Everything's dangerous."

"Well . . ." It was painfully true. "Just let me know when you're going to do something that's likely to get you killed."

"Will do," Sophie said, tone reminiscent of Emily's sassy demeanor. "But listen, she's been great. Hang on a minute. I'll show you."

It didn't take much longer than that for the girl to drop a surcingle around the palomino's girth. The mare finished up her oats while Sophie buckled the belly band in place and slipped the snaffle bit of a driving bridle between her teeth.

"Where'd you find the harness?" Casie asked.

"In an old trunk in the hayloft. I swear this place has everything." She fastened the throatlatch quickly in place, no small feat considering the cold. She'd set aside her bulky gloves some time ago, and fingers could only take a few minutes in these subfreezing temperatures before they began to seize up. "At first I thought I'd just use an open bridle, but I talked to my old riding instructor and she said I was likely to end up in Bennett County if I didn't put blinders on her. Apparently, it's best if they don't see the stuff they're dragging behind them." She slipped another leather strap over the mare's head, then flipped the traces over her golden back. In a second the girl had stepped behind the animal and tapped the long reins against her sides. They moved out in tandem, slow and steady. Once beyond the barn doors, Sophie tugged on the reins, urging the mare to a halt.

"Can you grab that for me?" she asked, nodding to the left.

Casie glanced around. An old-style sled was leaning up against the side of the barn, its twisted rope lying kitty-corner across the length of it. The runners were rusted, the red paint little more than flecks of uncertain color against the sandy wood grain, but the sight of it brought back memories of Casie and her mother racing down the hills in the pastures. She retrieved it with a mental sigh of nostalgia, but the current situation brought her own maternal instincts back to the fore. "Are you sure this is safe?" she asked, setting the ancient runners down in the snow a couple yards behind the mare.

"Not in the least," Sophie said and grinned again. Maybe it was that grin, that lovely carefree expression that was too often absent, that convinced Casie to allow this to go on.

"You're going to be the death of me," she said, moving the sled back a few inches. In a moment Sophie had hooked the rope to the traces that dragged behind the mare. Then, slipping on her gloves and making a here-we-go expression filled with equal measures of excitement and trepidation, she sank carefully onto the sled and gently slapped the lines against the mare's haunches. Evie turned her head back for an instant, as if to ask if they were sure this was a wise idea, then moved slowly into the clean snow of the pasture.

Once those first few terrifying seconds were past, the whole performance was a joy to watch. The figure eights were a little lopsided and the transition into the trot a bit bumpy, but it was all amazing.

"Soph!" Casie said when the mare was once again standing quietly beside the barn. "That's fantastic! Where did you learn to do that?"

"It's no big deal. I just . . ." She shrugged, and though her tone evidenced a trace of that cool boredom that used to be so commonplace, her enthusiasm was still entirely evident. "I just thought I'd give it a try. I guess some trainers start them in stone boats."

Casie searched her memory banks, but the term was notably absent despite the ridiculous amount of equine trivia she'd packed into her brain as a youth. "Stone boats?"

"It's just a really heavy thing on skids that you hook a young horse up to. The weight discourages them from doing anything too silly, I guess. Anyway, we don't have one of those, so I just decided to try this method. It'd be fun to drive her competitively. I bet she could be ready by next summer."

Casie stifled a wince. She didn't want to squelch the girl's enthusiasm, but although the Lazy's finances were better than they had been a year before, they were far from flush.

"If anyone could get her ready, I'm sure you could, Soph, but equestrian events are expensive . . . and that's not even considering the cost of a vehicle suitable for horse shows."

"You're right," Sophie said, then pursed her lips and stepped out of the sled. "There's no hurry now anyway."

"What do you mean?"

"Nothing," she said. Her tone had gone from excited to indifferent. Removing her gloves once again, she turned away to untie the sled. "It's not important."

"What's going on?" Casie asked, approaching slowly from behind. Having a heart-to-heart with Sophie Jaegar was a little like inviting a grizzly to a walleye dinner.

"I just . . ." The girl shook her head as she led Evie past Casie into the barn. Once there, she slid the leather reins through the metal rings at the top of the padded leather band that encircled the mare's girth. It was an odd, makeshift system, but necessity was often the mother of crazy inventiveness. "I guess Dad's going to Saint Thomas next week." Her voice was extremely cavalier. It was unnerving at best.

Casie winced and tread softly. This was tender territory. "So he won't be here for Christmas?"

"He said he'd be back before then. But he won't." Cavalier had made a sharp turn toward effervescent. God help them. "It's no big deal," she said and removed the surcingle from the mare's back. "I just wish he had told me before so I could have . . ." She paused.

"What?"

Sophie shrugged. The movement looked stiff. "Maybe I would have gone to Paris after all."

"Paris, *France?*"

"I guess Mother's going to be there for the holidays," she said and hung the truncated harness on a hook beside the end box stall.

Casie blinked in amazement. "You had the opportunity to spend Christmas in Paris?"

Sophie scowled as she slipped the bit from the mare's mouth and replaced the bridle with a blue nylon halter. "I've been there before."

"Really?"

"I was just a kid the last time."

"I hear it's gorgeous."

"It's all right."

"All right?" Casie asked and stroked the mare's butter-bright neck as Sophie hung the bridle next to the surcingle. Three new horse stalls had been added in the past few months, making a total of five.

Evie stood relaxed and content as Sophie tied her to the wall.

"All right?" Casie asked again.

"I flew back with Mother," she said. "Dad went home alone." The barn was absolutely quiet for a moment. A cow bellowed. The sound was low and strangely soothing. "They filed for divorce a few days later."

"Oh." Geez, love, or whatever it was, seemed more and more like a virus to be avoided at all cost. "I'm sorry."

"I guess it was supposed to be some kind of second honeymoon or something."

Casie did her best to hide her wince.

"Someone should have told them not to take their kid along, huh? Or maybe they should have told me not to be such a . . ." She stopped and pulled her gloves back on. Her hands looked stiff and red before disappearing inside the insulated nylon.

"Never mind," she said and fished a dandy brush out of a bucket near the wall. The short, stiff bristles looked hard and aggressive as she scraped them down Evie's neck, but the mare sighed happily and dropped her head.

Casie watched. "It's not your fault," she said.

Even from behind she could tell the girl was scowling. "I know."

Finding a currycomb in the same bucket, Casie moved to Evie's off side. The metal teeth dug into the mare's coat. She cocked a contented hip.

"Do you?" Casie asked.

Their gazes met over the top of the horse's golden withers. For a second Sophie said nothing, then, "This is going to be hard to believe. . . ." She pursed her lips. "But I haven't always been the jolly little elf I am now."

Maybe it wasn't appropriate to laugh, but Casie did so nevertheless. "No one's happy all the time, Soph."

"You are."

Her laughter turned to a kind of snort. "Are you kidding me?"

Sophie had returned her attention to the palomino. "Maybe not happy. Maybe just . . ." She gritted her teeth for a second as if the very idea made her angry. "*Nice.*"

"I'm not always nice."

Sophie exhaled her discontent. "Give me a for-instance."

"For instance whenever Dickie . . ." She paused, not really knowing why he put her back up. "Whenever *Dickenson* is around."

Sophie stared at her a second, then nodded solemnly. "I love that."

"What?" She paused in her currying for a second.

"When you snipe at him. It almost makes me feel normal."

Casie laughed again. "You *are* normal."

"Name one other kid whose parents have both run away from home." Sophie stared at her with solemn, haunted eyes.

Anger or something like it sprinted through Casie's system. Sophie's dad was handsome, congenial, and intelligent. Turned out he was also a pretty poor father. Unfortunately, he seemed to be the *good* parent. The girl's mother had never so much as shown her face on the Lazy.

"That's not your fault, either," Casie said.

"You know . . ." Sophie paused for a second, tilting the brush away from the mare's hip. Evie glanced back accusingly. "I really think it is."

"Honestly?"

"Yeah," she said and began brushing again, face a quiet mask of concentration.

"So your parents . . ." Casie shrugged, treading lightly, though the anger still sat like a lead weight on her chest. "They adored each other, did they?"

"Yes." The answer was flippant. Casie waited. Sophie could be dramatic and aggressive, but she was almost always honest. It was one of the scariest things about her. "They must have." A muscle jumped in the girl's jaw. "Why would they have gotten married otherwise?"

"So let me get this straight. . . ." Casie drew a deep breath, steadying her nerves. "You think that they were crazy in love. Ecstatic in each other's company. Then you come along, and bam . . . suddenly they can't stand the sight of each other."

Sophie's gaze never shifted from the mare.

Her downcast eyes somehow made Casie even angrier, and since she didn't have the parents upon which to cast her rage, she flung it wide. "They probably were lovey-dovey all the time. Cooing and laughing and tickling each other."

Sophie glared at her. "Don't be ridiculous."

"*Ridiculous?* Soph . . ." She paused. "Some couples are actually like that."

"That's disgusting."

"No, it's not disgusting. It's . . . Okay," she said, remembering the squirmy discomfort she felt around blatant acts of . . . anything. "The tickling would be kind of weird. But there are actually couples out there who enjoy each other's company . . . forever."

"What kind of fairy tales have *you* been reading?"

Casie laughed. "I'm telling you, Soph, some people's parents really like each other."

"Did yours?" The question was a challenge.

Both of them had stopped brushing now. Evie squared up on all fours and huffed her discontent.

"Mine were . . ." Casie rolled her eyes toward the ceiling. She'd spent a good deal of time trying to figure out what her parents were. Definitely not lovey-dovey. Her father had been stoic and hard. It was strange that while Casie had wanted quite desperately to be like her fun-loving mother, in hindsight, it seemed that she had put a good deal of effort into attaining the stubborn stoicism of her paternal side. "Sometimes they fought," she said.

"Sometimes?"

"Well, when I was a kid, I thought they fought constantly, but in retrospect I think . . ." She shrugged. "Relationships are tricky."

"She took his boat."

"What?"

Sophie exhaled and quietly resumed brushing. "She hated that boat. Hated it. But it was Dad's pride and joy." She cleared her throat. "She sold it a couple months after the divorce was final."

They brushed in silent unison for a moment.

"It doesn't really sound like they would have had an idyllic relationship with or without you, Soph."

She nodded, thinking. "In some ways that almost makes it harder."

"What? Why?"

Her brows beetled. "I mean . . . if it was just me . . . just the strain another human being put on their relationship . . . if that had been too hard for them . . . that would be one thing. But to think that that's just how they are. That mean. That . . . vengeful." Her lips twitched. "That's my heritage. My stock," she said and glanced up, eyes haunted.

Casie shook her head. "I don't know why love makes people crazy."

"If that's love I'd rather have the stomach flu."

Casie thought about that for a second, thought about the burbling insanity she sometimes felt in Colt Dickenson's presence. Thought about the euphoric angst he caused the rest of the time. "I'm not sure we always have a choice," she said.

"*I* do," Sophie said and led the mare out of the barn.

"Where are you going?" Casie asked.

"I'm going to work with Chester for a few minutes."

"What?" Casie asked and hurried after her. "What are you talking about?"

"The bay," Sophie said, not turning toward her.

"I know who Chester is." Casie caught up to her at the gate to the pasture. "But you can't work him."

"Why not?"

"Because he's not gelded yet."

"And he's not gelded because he's not trained."

"Soph!" Casie said and caught her arm. "I mean it, I can't take that risk."

"You're not risking anything."

"Are you kidding me? What do you think your dad will do if you get hurt"—she made a face—"again."

"Well, he won't find out, will he?" Sophie asked and turned Evie loose. "Because he's not around."

Casie shook her head. "I know you were looking forward to seeing him, but—"

"This isn't about him," she said and sighed. "Okay, maybe it is kind of. I mean . . . it just . . ." She gritted her teeth and turned away. "This is my world." She glanced around at the endless acres. "I thought maybe this once he could take an interest instead of running off to the Virgin Islands with some bimbo who hasn't been a virgin for . . ." She stopped herself.

"I'm sorry," Casie said, "but breaking your neck probably isn't going to help anything."

"You don't trust me, either!" she snapped.

Casie had to stop herself from taking a cautious step to the rear. So the mature Sophie Jaegar was gone again, replaced miserably by the twisted, angry Sophie. But Casie had seen her before. Was familiar with her moods.

"Fine!" the girl said. "That's just fine."

Casie steeled herself. "How about we both work him?"

Sophie narrowed her eyes but didn't immediately spew vitriol. "How do you mean?"

"We could pony him together."

"Don't you have chores to do?"

Casie forced a shrug, setting aside the thought of broken fences and yet-to-be-stacked hay bales. "They can wait," she said and watched the girl's shoulders drop a fraction of an inch as if they were no longer braced against the weight of the world.

CHAPTER 7

"Whoa," Emily said and wiggled her bottom into the Escalade's cushy seat. "This is even nicer than *my* ride."

Max glanced at her with wry appreciation. "High praise," he said.

"Yeah," she agreed and rolled her head sideways to glance into the backseat where Bliss was strapped into her carrier like a nuclear bomb. "What do you say, Buttercup?" she asked, but the baby's eyes were already drooping shut, downy lashes falling drowsily over plump mocha cheeks.

The sight did something funky to Emily's heart. She couldn't say what it was for sure, but the area near her solar plexus felt gooey.

"That's a nice sound," Max said.

"What?" She glanced at him. They had already turned onto the snow-packed gravel that led toward town. He'd slouched down in the seat a little and propped his left elbow on the armrest. With two fingers on the wheel, he navigated the eco-unfriendly vehicle like an aged farmer checking soybeans.

"That noise," he explained and sighed heavily to demonstrate. "The sound of love."

"I didn't do that," she scoffed, then sat up a little straighter. "Did I?"

"Yeah," he said and glanced at her. "You did."

"Oh, well . . ." She shrugged. "I just . . ." For a second she considered trying to downplay her feelings, to crack a joke or find a bit of sarcasm, but the truth was too easy, too obvious. "I didn't know."

"Didn't know what?"

"That she'd make my heart turn inside out."

The car fell silent. She glanced out the window. The whitewashed hills rolled silently into the distance, dotted here and there by a jagged line of rock or bent pine.

"It must be nice," he said finally.

"What's that?"

"To love like that."

She turned her attention back to him.

"I mean . . ." He laughed. "I'm crazy about Sonata. Don't get me wrong."

"Yeah." Emily blinked, wondering where this was going. She was a little embarrassed to realize that sometimes, with Bliss so overpowering in her mind, it was difficult to remember that other people had problems, other people had issues and hopes and aspirations. For just a second she wondered if her own mother had ever felt the same way. Wondered if Jennifer Casper had ever made *her* baby the center of her universe . . . before she'd stepped out of her life and never looked back. "She seems great."

"She is!" He nodded emphatically, but the edges of his eyes seemed a little pinched.

"Classy," Emily added.

"She's a hard worker, too. And smart."

If she wasn't mistaken, there was a "but" coming. Emily didn't want to hear any buts. Mostly she just wanted to stare at Bliss. But that didn't seem right, either. Casie would inquire, show an interest, and probably solve any impending problems. That's what made Casie special, what made her different from . . . say . . . Emily's mother. And when she looked at it in that light, the choices were pretty clear. Exhaling softly, she focused all her attention on the driver. Max Barrenger was medium height with a stocky build and a face that had seen some years. "So how did you meet?"

"Skiing," he said. "In Vale. I was racing down a black diamond when someone came tearing past me like she'd been shot out of a cannon. I nearly broke my neck trying to beat her to the bottom."

The "cute meet," Hollywood would call it. "Did you manage it?"

He chuckled. "It takes a stronger man than me to beat S. at anything."

Emily smiled, then pointed to the left. "That's a really nice area. When you're ready to snowshoe that would be a good place to park your car."

He glanced at the narrow, snow-covered approach. "I don't have to worry about getting towed?"

"Seriously?" she said, and he laughed as he turned toward her.

"I guess there's not a shortage of parking out here."

"Not so much."

He nodded as he looked back toward the road. "It *is* beautiful."

"Yeah," she agreed. Maybe there had been a time when the vast spaces had intimidated her, but now they felt like home and freedom and security all rolled into one. She didn't know how much of that was because of the place and how much was because of the people, but she would make herself worthy of both of them. She *would,* she vowed, and hushed the doubts that gnawed nastily at her psyche. "I think so, too."

"You did it again."

"Did what?"

He sighed dramatically.

"I did not."

He grinned. Crow's-feet bracketed his eyes and a little silver edged the hair around his ears. "You look at the land kind of like you look at your baby."

She shrugged. "Well, it's a good place to be."

"Are you from here?"

"No." She glanced out her window again. Stray memories

started nudging in, needy, angry memories that eroded her peace. She shoved them back into the dark recesses of her past where she kept the sleepless nights and grinding insecurities.

"Let me guess." He narrowed his eyes, looking worldly wise. "I bet you grew up in . . ." He studied her. She knew what he would see: wild dreadlocks, milk-chocolate skin, crafty eyes. But maybe she'd learned to hide that craftiness. Or maybe, when she wasn't looking, it had receded a little, settled back into the shadows, waiting. "Seattle," he said.

She opened her mouth to refute his statement, but he held up a hand, shushing her.

"Just wait. There's more. Your mother was an artist. Thus the cool . . ." He motioned toward his own mostly dark hair. " 'Do."

"Cool 'do. Yup." Her hair was crazy. There wasn't really a good euphemism for it. Years ago, she had wished it was straight and smooth like her mother's, but that was before she'd realized her childish dreams had no bearing whatsoever on the future. It had taken her longer to realize that Jennifer Casper's *own* dreams had little more influence than her child's. Such was the sharp blade of addictions.

Max grinned, drawing her back to the present. "And your dad . . ." He narrowed his eyes as if divining the past. "Your dad was an oceanographer."

"Oh boy," Emily said, forcefully dispelling old demons.

He laughed at her tone. "Who worked late hours trying to . . ." He wiggled his fingers at her. "Save the blue gill whale."

"I don't think there's any such thing as the blue gill whale."

He shook his head as if to dismiss such nonsensical logic. "But the long hours took a toll on his marriage."

"Didn't they just?"

"Hence the divorce." He made a face. "It was sad but amicable. Maybe their struggles are what gave you such depths."

Depths? she thought, but before she could question his wild assumptions, he spoke again.

"Maybe that's even why you're such a great mom."

There were a thousand elements to dispute about his story. Or maybe she should just laugh, but his last statement touched a sensitive chord in her, pinging it gently. "You think . . ." She paused, stilling the telltale tremor in her voice. "What makes you think I'm a good mother?"

He stared at her, mouth quirked in a smile, but eyes solemn. "I've been around."

"Yeah?"

He glanced out the window again. "Hither and yon."

There was pain in his voice now. Casie would probably delve into that. Not that Emily Kane could ever be the woman Casie Carmichael was, but . . . "You have kids?" she asked.

"Look at that!" he said and touched the brakes sharply.

Emily jerked her gaze to the right. A quartet of wild turkeys was searching for goodies along the roadside. "Aren't they great?" she asked.

"They're huge."

"Yeah," she agreed just as three of them took to the air, sweeping low over the reeds that poked at bent angles through the snowdrifts. "It doesn't really look like they should fly, does it?"

"Man, that would make a great shot."

"Are you a hunter?"

"Me?" He laughed. "No. I meant it would make a nice picture."

"Oh. You're a photographer."

He shifted his shoulders a little. "That's kind of a grandiose term for what I do, but yeah. I like to fiddle."

"What kind of camera do you have?"

"My favorite for action shots is the four hundred–millimeter Nikon."

"You have a telephoto lens?"

"Yeah, but it's heavy as a mother. Not that mothers are, umm . . ." He made a face. ". . . Fat or anything."

"Nice save," she said and turned the conversation back to cameras. There was something about photographs that had always appealed to her . . . the way they could capture a moment and hold it forever. Memories slipped away. People left. Things changed. But photos held true to the moment, clinging with timeless tenacity. "I just have a little ELPH PowerShot. It only has a twelve times zoom, but it's red so . . ." She shrugged.

"Totally makes up for its lack of capabilities."

"But that doesn't mean I wouldn't give my spleen for one of those old-school Kodaks," she said.

"Those Six-Twenty folding cameras?" he asked, gazing raptly across the console at her.

"They are *sweet*."

"Can you tell Sonata that? She thinks I'm obsessed with those old cameras. But life's not all about work."

"Sometimes it kind of has to be," she said.

"But sometimes it's about . . ." He shrugged. "Finding yourself. Sometimes it's about family and friends and . . . old-timey pictures."

"Like those sepia pics."

He sighed dreamily. "Anything that requires a developer is orgasmic."

"We could share a darkroom," she said.

He stared at her, brows slightly raised.

Blood rushed to her face in a flush of heat. "I didn't . . ." Panic filled her. She jerked her attention to the passenger window. "Turn here!"

He did so without comment.

"It's just . . . just a little farther. Right behind those trees."

"On the right?"

"Yeah." Holy shorts, she was an idiot! Maybe there was a time when she had thought sex was just another biological urge, but things were different now. She glanced into the backseat. *Everything* was different now, she thought, and zipped her gaze back to Max.

"Listen . . ." he began, but she cut him off at the pass.

"The Frenches have lived here for about a hundred years, I

guess. It's just the two of them now. All their kids moved east. But Fred and Birdie can finish off a rhubapple pie in about an hour and a half, so I try to bring one by every other day or so. She's teaching me to crochet, but she's got some arthritis so it's kind of slow going. Cindy Dickenson, though, Colt's mom, she's fantastic and she has alpaca. Did you know their fiber is twenty times warmer than wool?

"Turn in here."

"Here?"

"Yeah. That's great," she said and wrenched her door open before the vehicle came to a complete halt. In a second she had speed-walked to the tailgate and was yanking at the handle.

Max approached slowly from the left.

"You okay?" he asked.

"Yeah, of course. I just . . ." She gave the mechanism another ineffective tug. Her face still felt hot. "I just want to get this done before Bliss wakes up."

"Okay," he said, and pushing her hand aside, smoothly opened the door.

She pulled out the nearest pie, checked the label on the aluminum foil, and hurried up the slanted steps. Fred French was glaring at her from the stoop, khaki pants cinched just below his armpits.

"Where's your truck?" he asked and jerked his knobby chin toward the Escalade.

"It just needed a little rest."

"A little rest! It needs a tombstone. And I told you, we don't want no more pies."

"I know you did, but I had an extra and the dog's getting fat."

He glowered at her, then shook his head. "Well, here you go then," he grumbled and held out a much-folded bill.

"Mr. French," she said, backing up a step. "You know I can't take your money."

"Why not?" His wrinkled lids shifted over rheumy eyes. "We ain't no charity, you know."

"I know that. But *Mrs.* French is teaching me to crochet and—"

"Well, I ain't my missus and I don't do no crochet," he said. Shoving the bill into the thigh pocket of her cargo pants, he snatched the pie out of her hands and slammed the door in her face.

"I know that," she said to no one.

Silence stretched out on all sides for a moment. Somewhere in the shelterbelt behind them, a pheasant called. The sound was sharp and staccato in the morning air.

"Your Web site was right," Max said. "Dakotans *are* friendly."

"And New Yorkers are hilarious," she said, tromping back to the Escalade.

Bliss was still sleeping. Emily pulled Fred's money from her pants pocket and stared at it as they traversed the bumpy yard.

"Must be a pretty good pie," Max said and nodded toward the hundred-dollar bill.

She scowled at it as a dozen weird emotions fired up inside her. Her eyes stung, and that was weird, too, because she wasn't the sniffley sort. "I'm not a skank," she said.

"I beg your pardon?"

"I don't know why he gave me this." She tightened her grip on the bill.

There was a long moment of silence, then, "I didn't think you slept with the old codger, if that's what you mean," he said, lips twitching.

She didn't laugh. On the other hand, she didn't cry, either, so all was well. "I didn't mean anything by that darkroom comment."

"I assumed as much."

She took a deep breath. "Just because I'm a single mother doesn't mean I'm easy."

"Okay."

"I'm not trying to steal you from your girlfriend or anything. She seems really great. Not that you don't. You do, too. But I wouldn't ever . . ."

He was staring at her as if she was one bushel short of a full load. She cleared her throat. "I, ahhhh . . ." She nodded at her own insanity. "I might still be a little hopped up on estrogen or something."

"You think?"

She stared at him, nodded once, and took a shot at being normal. "Take the next left."

CHAPTER 8

The sun was as bright as an egg yolk in the endless azure sky. Casie lifted her face to its welcome rays as she rode along. Beneath her, old Maddy, the pinto mare Colt kept at the ranch for guests to ride, lifted her knees in a mincing prance. The unexpected afternoon warmth made everyone a little giddy. Or maybe it was the dark stallion she led from Maddy's back that put the bounce in the old girl's step.

Hormones. Just when you thought they had taken a long sabbatical, they'd pop up again. It wasn't as if Casie herself had time for such things, not when she had a ranch to run, but thoughts of Colt Dickenson kept creeping under her skin, disturbing her calm, amping up her adrenaline.

"He *is* handsome," Sophie said.

"What?" Casie swung her attention to the left. Jack smiled up at her as he slunk along beside the mare, tongue lolling with joy.

Sophie rode with almost unconscious ease. She raised her brows. "I was talking about Chesapeake," she said, shifting her gaze from the stallion that pranced beside Casie's mount. "Who were *you* thinking about?"

"Oh . . ." How old would she have to be before she quit blushing? "That's who I was thinking of, too."

For a moment Sophie just stared, brows a little raised. Beneath her, the red dun seemed staid and dependable. But maybe that was just part of the girl's magic. *Casie* had had her share of problems with Tangles. "Sure," she said.

"It was," Casie lied, but never well.

"Listen, Case, I know Colt can seem a little . . ." Sophie paused, gazing off toward the Lazy in the distance. "Well, he's maybe too hot for his own good, but I think you need to give him a chance."

"I *am* giving the colt a chance," she said. "I'm exercising him, aren't I?" she asked, and raised the stallion's lead line as proof.

Sophie scowled, then heaved a sigh. "Oh, for Pete's sake, Case. I'm talking about—"

"Let's lope."

"What?"

"Ponying him isn't going to do him much good if we don't wear him out a little."

"Casie . . ."

"I need you to make sure he doesn't fall behind," she said and jerked her chin toward Chesapeake. He was wearing a bright green halter with a chain tucked under his jaw for control, but that didn't mean he couldn't drag her off her horse if he so desired. "Okay?"

Sophie nodded reluctantly.

"All right." Casie glanced toward the house. It was less than a full mile to the west. "Let's keep it slow."

"Don't tell me. Tell the wild child there," Sophie said, gazing accusingly at the bay.

He tossed his head twice and curled his upper lip as if smelling something fascinating.

"Maddy's not in heat, is she?" Sophie asked and ran her gaze over the mare, checking for any signs of estrus.

"She shouldn't be," Casie said. "She's about a hundred years old and it's the dead of winter."

"Yeah, well, we seem to have a lamb frolicking around the Christmas tree . . . just in case we forgot that hormones sometimes fail to shut down just exactly like they're supposed to."

"Life'll make a fool of you," Casie said and drew an invigorating breath. "You ready?"

"If you are."

Casie gave a single nod and squeezed her legs. Maddy lifted seamlessly into a lope. The three-year-old, however, simply lengthened his trot, trying to keep up without breaking stride.

"Can you give him a little encouragement?" Casie asked, glancing over her shoulder and raising her voice.

Sophie dropped behind the bay, pushing him a little. He raised his head and sped along, extending his trot.

"Hup," Sophie urged, and riding alongside, slapped his haunches with the loose ends of her reins.

Young and full of himself, Chesapeake bucked once and leaped into a flowing lope. He was poetry in motion. Casie grinned as she watched him move fluidly beside them, but Maddy shook her head, demanding attention as she powered into a gallop. After that it was a wild ride home. Snow sprayed up from their pounding hooves. Condensed air steamed from their nostrils like flame from a fiery dragon. Wild exhilaration stormed through Casie. A hundred nagging worries flew away beneath their mounts' flying feet. A dozen tensions eased from across her back.

The final hill lay ahead. Something like freedom filled Casie's soul. She breathed it in and turned toward her companion.

"I'll race you!" she yelled.

"Are you kidding?" Sophie asked, but her cheeks with flushed with the thrill of the ride.

"Scared?" Casie asked.

"You're on!" Sophie shouted, and letting Tangles have some rein, she leaned over the gelding's crest.

"Let's see what you've got," Casie said, and the mare, game as a bobwhite, leaped into the race, challenging the stallion beside her. The earth sped like a locomotive beneath them. Air whistled past. Casie grinned into the wind.

And then it happened. A pickup truck appeared over the top of the hill.

Chesapeake, full to the brim with testosterone, reared, jerking Casie backward.

She tried to release his lead, but in the heat of the moment, she hadn't realized the rope had become wrapped around her hand. One second she was galloping full tilt up the hill and the next she was on the road, being dragged across the gravel as Chesapeake backed frantically away.

The pickup slammed to a halt and the stallion spun. Terror flared through Casie like a wildfire, but suddenly her glove was yanked from her hand. The bay, finally free, leaped madly away, leaving his handler belly down on the road.

"Casie!" Sophie was beside her in a second. "Are you all right?"

"I'm fine," she said, and clambering to her feet, turned to check on her mount. "Is Maddy . . ." she began, but even before she realized the old mare was quietly nosing along the side of the road, she saw Colt sprinting toward her.

He slowed as he drew nearer, but she could see his face was red and his hands fisted at his sides.

"Hey," she said, though she really wasn't sure what she was planning as a follow-up to that clever gambit.

"Are you trying to kill me?" His voice was very low. A muscle jumped in his stubbled jaw.

She cleared her throat and glanced toward his vehicle a few dozen feet away. A young man was just stepping out of the cab. "You picked up our guest, huh?" she asked, and as surreptitiously as possible, curled her fingers into her palm. Insulated gloves or not, Chesapeake's nylon lead had peeled off some skin.

Colt ignored her words completely and gritted his teeth. "Or are you just trying to drive me crazy?"

"It's my fault," Sophie said.

They turned toward her in slow unison. Since when did Sophie Jaegar take the blame for anything?

She scowled, first at one, then at the other. "I was supposed to keep him up beside Maddy."

Colt narrowed his eyes, then returned his dark gaze to Casie.

"Look what you've done," he said, lips twitching just a little as he nodded toward the girl. "You broke Sophie."

"You okay?" asked the young man who strode toward them.

"Sure." Casie gave him a smile. He was tall and narrow,

dressed in low jeans and a hooded sweatshirt. "I'm fine." She thrust out her injured hand. "You must be Lincoln."

He blinked at her, long lashes slow over metal-gray eyes. "Yeah. Hi. Are you . . ." He skimmed his gaze to Sophie, stared at her for a heartbeat, then shifted his attention back to Casie. "You own the Lazy Windmill?"

"Yup, that's me. Casie Carmichael," she said, but he was already staring at Sophie again. It was a little disconcerting. Not that Casie thought she was model material or anything, especially not when she was swaddled like a winter infant. But Lincoln Alexander wasn't *too* much her junior, and besides, barely ten square inches of Sophie was visible between her scarf and her stocking cap. "This is Sophie Jaegar."

He scowled at her, not quite the enthusiastic response Casie had anticipated after such careful inspection. "Hi," he said.

Sophie barely nodded before turning to watch Chesapeake come charging back toward them. "Should we try to catch him or do you think he'll go straight home?"

"He'll follow the mare," Colt said.

"I think we should probably—" Casie began, but he interrupted her.

"Lincoln had a long flight."

"Oh. I—"

"Maybe you could show him the bunkhouse."

Casie raised her brows, irritated.

"I should probably catch—" she began, but he spoke again.

"You must be cold."

"What?"

"Take my truck. I'll look after the horses."

"I can—"

"Please!" he said, but the single word was forced between clenched teeth.

She squelched her scowl and acquiesced with a certain lack of grace. "Okay," she said and stepped toward his pickup. Her hip twinged, but she ignored it. "So you're from Detroit, Lincoln?"

"Yeah." He glanced back as he turned with her. "Thereabouts."

"So what brings you all the way out here?" Her hip complained again as she pulled herself into Colt's big four-wheel drive.

"Are you sure you're okay?" he asked and slid easily into the passenger seat. Apparently, it was no big deal when you were ten feet tall and hadn't been dragged down the road by a rank stud horse.

"Sure. Yes." She eased sideways a little and watched as Colt caught the bay by his flapping lead. "I always dismount that way." She smiled, but her guest didn't smile back. She cleared her throat. "Are you here on business or . . . ?"

His brows were low as he stared out the passenger window. Colt was just swinging into the saddle, movements cowboy smooth. "I just needed some time away."

"Are you a student?" she asked and managed to put the truck in reverse despite her chafed palm.

"Yeah. Well . . . no, not anymore."

She nodded, waiting for him to continue. When he didn't, she backed past the Lazy's driveway, then put the truck in gear and turned slowly toward the house. In the past, she'd thought *she* was a poor conversationalist, but this young man had her beat. She glanced toward the top of the hill. Colt was just turning his head to speak to Sophie. The sun beamed down on him like a spotlight. The collar of his canvas jacket was pulled up and brushed the dark, curling tendrils of his hair. His hands were steady, his body perfectly positioned on the old pinto's back.

She felt a little sick to her stomach. The flu or infatuation? It was impossible to differentiate.

"Do you?" Lincoln asked.

"What?" She jerked her gaze to her half-forgotten guest.

His frown deepened a little. "You don't live here alone, do you?"

"Well, no. Why do you ask?"

"No reason. It just seems . . ." He glanced around the yard as she pulled up to the bunkhouse. "Like a lot of work for one person."

"I have good help. So . . . where are your bags?" she asked, and turned in her seat a little.

"Who helps you?" he asked.

She shifted her attention back to him, nerves jangling a little as she remembered the recent spate of trouble in town.

"Colt Dickenson, for one," she said and nodded toward the road. For a moment she was despicably grateful for his presence.

"The cowboy?"

"Yeah," Casie said. "He's ranked thirteenth in the PRCAA." Good grief! Why did she feel the need to mention that? She was beginning to sound like Emily.

"Anybody else?"

"A lot of neighboring men help out."

He stared at her.

She fidgeted a little. "You never know when they're going to be hanging around."

Lincoln was gazing into the long side mirror that projected out from the truck. Glancing into the rearview, Casie saw that Colt and Sophie were just turning into the driveway. Jack loped on ahead as Chesapeake jigged beside Maddy's placid form.

"Is he new here?"

She pulled her attention from the images framed in the mirror. "I beg your pardon?"

"He seemed worried about you." His brows were pulled low over storm-cloud eyes.

"We've . . ." She blinked. "Been friends a long time."

"Oh. Well . . ." He exhaled softly as if relieved. "I guess I'll lie down for a while."

"You did bring luggage, didn't you?"

"Sure," he said, and stepping outside, reached behind his seat to pull out a duffel bag. It was the approximate size of one of Em's honey loaves.

Casie raised her brows. "*How* long are you planning to stay?"

"Through Christmas."

She glanced at his bag again.

He looked down, hiding his eyes. "I like to travel light."

"Oh. Sure," she said, and tried to sound as if guests arrived every day of the week with little more than the clothes on their backs. But she didn't quite sell it. Sonata Detric traveled with two suitcases the size of pack mules, a carry-on bag, and a Coach purse.

In a second, Casie was handing a key to Lincoln Alexander. "Your room is on the far end."

He nodded, not seeming to care in the least.

"If there's anything you need you can just call the number that's printed by the phone."

"Okay," he said and turned away.

"Otherwise, dinner will be ready in a couple of hours."

"Dinner?" He twisted back. He had a lean, hungry look about him.

"Yes," she said, nerves cranking a little tighter. "We'll let you know when it's—"

"Are you the cook?"

"No. I . . ." She shook her head and forced a laugh. "We'd never get another guest if I was."

He watched her for a second, then nodded once and strode off toward the bunkhouse, strides long and quick.

She scowled after him.

"What's wrong?"

Casie jumped at the sound of Colt's voice. He was still astride Maddy, but the young stallion was notably absent. She glanced behind to see that Sophie was leading him and Tangles toward the barn.

"Case . . ." Colt said. His voice was a low rumble. "What's wrong?"

"Nothing." She brought her attention to his face. It looked entirely different without its usual cocky smile. But no less appealing. Just older, more mature. "He's just a little . . ." She paused as she shifted her gaze to the bunkhouse where her guest had disappeared. "Did he seem kind of strange to you?"

"Strange? What do you mean?"

She glanced at him. His eyes were narrowed beneath the brim of his Stetson, his dark brows lowered.

"Nothing," she said, but he didn't drop it.

"Strange how?"

She shook her head. "Never mind. The trouble in town has just made me a little skittish, I guess."

"You think he's a thief?"

"No! I didn't say that. He's just . . ." She forced a laugh. "He asked a lot of questions."

"About what?"

She shouldn't be slandering a paying guest. Okay, technically, maybe she shouldn't be slandering *anybody*, but. . . . "About who else was on the ranch."

He glanced toward the bunkhouse again, then nodded as if to an unheard voice. "I'm staying the night."

"What?"

"Tonight." His gaze was as steady as an osprey's on hers.

"You can't stay. We don't have an extra—"

"This isn't up for debate," he said and pivoted Maddy away in a flashy maneuver that would have made John Wayne drool.

CHAPTER 9

By the time evening chores were done, Emily was busy with supper preparations. Colt could hear her humming tunelessly to Willie Nelson's best as he toed off his boots in the entryway. Hanging his jacket on a hook inside the old wardrobe, he stepped into the kitchen in time to see the girl stare out over open fields, halfheartedly stirring the contents of a pot. From the scratchy radio above the refrigerator, Willie crooned on about heroes and cowboys.

"What—" Colt began, but she squawked and spun toward him, dreadlocks bobbing.

He jolted back in surprise. "Will you quit doing that!"

"Holy shorts! Will you—" She glared at him. "Wear a bell or something!"

He grinned, heart rate diminishing. "What were you thinking about?"

"Nothing."

"Really?" he asked and, approaching, stared into the pot. "Because you seem to be stirring water."

She blinked as if returning from a dream. "It's not water."

"It looks like water."

"It's broth."

"Is that water with salt in it?"

"No. It's . . ." She waved a hand at him. "Why aren't you scrubbing potatoes yet?"

He chuckled. "Because I don't know how many you need."

She hurried to the refrigerator, pulling out items seemingly at random. "Just start in. I'll tell you when to stop."

He studied her in silence. In this house of perplexing women *she* was usually the one he understood the best. "You okay?"

"Of course I'm okay. What happened with our new guest?"

"What do you mean?"

"Our guest. Lincoln Alexander. Didn't he show up at the airport or what?" she asked just as Lumpkin trotted in from the living room. A diaper had been pinned around her hindquarters. Her tail, already bobbing merrily, had been thrust through a hole in the cotton.

"Seriously?" Colt asked, staring at the ridiculous sight.

Emily shrugged. "It was *your* idea. What about Alexander?"

"I delivered him to the bunkhouse a couple hours ago." He found a stiff-bristle brush in the top drawer and pulled a bowl of dark-skinned potatoes from the pantry. "Did you think I'd forget?"

"You *are* kind of old," she said and nodded toward the taters. "Can you dice them, too?"

"Not if you're going to insult me."

"It wasn't an insult," she said and scowled at nothing in particular. "I like old. Always have."

"Why doesn't that make me feel better?"

"I don't know," she said, and pulling a few leaves from one of the vines that grew on the windowsill, dropped them into the so-called broth. "What's he like?"

"Who?"

"Geez, Dickenson, are you getting senile or what?"

"Listen, missy . . ." he said, tone insulted.

She turned toward him, already looking guilty, and he squirted her in the face with the sprayer.

Jumping back, she squawked like a scared chicken and he chuckled. "Don't get sassy with me, youngun."

"You got me wet."

"Shocking," he said. "How many potatoes?"

"I don't know until you tell me about the new guy. Is he nervous, stodgy, funny, dopey?"

"You make him sound like one of the nine dwarves."

"There were seven dwarves . . . and will you hurry up with those?" she asked, pushing his arm toward the potatoes.

He picked up the first one.

"Think about it," she said, stirring with her right hand as she added cream with her left. Fragrant steam was beginning to waft into the air. Emily Kane was the only person he knew who could make water smell good. "Sonata, for instance . . ."

"Only eats food that food eats?"

She grinned a little, then corrected herself sternly. "There's nothing wrong with vegans."

"Except they're abnormal."

"And impossible to cook for."

He chuckled. "What about Sonata?"

"You can pretty much just glance at her and think . . ." She nodded as she stared out the window again. "Vegan or not, she's still a half-a-potato kind of girl."

"She *is* pretty skinny."

"It's not that she's . . . Okay, yeah," she said, scowling at the inoffensive sauce that smelled a little like heaven. "She *is* skinny. But so is Casie, and Casie can eat."

"Are you kidding?"

"Well, she doesn't eat as much as *you* do. But then . . ." She made a face. "Neither does any other creature not used for draft purposes."

"So now I'm old and *fat?*"

"Not fat," she said and raised her wooden spoon at him. "Yet."

"Sometimes I wonder why I help you out."

"I think it's because of my cinnamon rolls."

"I'm so easy," he sighed, and she laughed. It was a nice noise, relaxed, rolling softly through the warmth of the kitchen. The sound made him smile. It wasn't as if Emily had ever been difficult. Oh, she had convictions that bordered on pushy, but she was kind. She might be surprised to hear it, but she had *always* been kind. Early on, however, there had been a brittle caginess to her, a crafty defensiveness that had all but disappeared over time.

"So the guest . . ." she said, pushing him back on track.

"He's young. At least by my curmudgeonly standards. Eighteen, maybe. Tall. Scrawny."

"Is he hot?"

"If you make me stand here and scrub potatoes while discussing teenage boys I'm going to have to put that apron back on."

She grinned, face barely visible past her falling dreadlocks. "Does he look hungry?"

"Yeah," he said and scowled at the potato he was working on. "He does, kind of."

"What does that mean?"

He chuckled, coming back to himself. "You're the one who asked."

"Yeah, but I didn't think you'd make it sound like we were discussing the meaning of life." She peered askance at the growing pile of nubby tubers. "One more should do it."

He finished off the last one and moved to the wooden cutting board. It was two inches thick, crisscrossed with a thousand scars, and looked as if it had been sawed straight from a scrub oak in the back pasture.

"So tell me more about Hungry Guy," she said.

He shrugged, feeling a smidgeon of angst return as he remembered Casie's words. "I'm not sure what to think yet," he said, not wanting to color her perception unnecessarily, but he should have known better than to bother hiding his feelings; Emily was one eye of newt short of being a witch. "He's quiet."

"Sophie's quiet," Emily said. "Doesn't mean she's a mass murderer or anything. Of course. . . ." She squinted and peered into the middle distance as if debating the possibility.

Colt grinned. "I doubt Soph has killed more than a couple people."

"You're right. She's still young."

"Takes a while to annihilate whole masses and—"

The door opened. They glanced guiltily at each other, and in a second Sophie had stepped into the kitchen.

"When's dinner?"

"Gotta ask Em," Colt said, trying not to grin.

Emily glanced behind her. "You look nice," she said.

Her tone was innocent, making Sophie immediately suspicious. "What's going on?"

"Nothing," Emily said. "Where's Casie?"

"She should be here in a minute." The girl's tone was still cautious, but she had moved toward the stove, easily distracted by the scent of Utopia.

"It might hurry supper along if you set the table," Emily said.

Sophie moved toward the hutch that occupied the east wall of the expansive kitchen. Well . . . hutch was a kindly euphemism for an ancient cupboard that had been pulled out of some long-forgotten barn and left to languish in disrepair for years on end. Despite its tilted stance and cracking paint, Emily loved it like a child. Or maybe those were the features that made it endearing for her. Colt wondered what she saw in *him*.

"How many?" Sophie asked.

The front door opened and closed.

"Case?" Emily called, raising her voice.

"Yeah?"

"As long as you got your boots on, will you make sure Max and Sonata will be here for dinner?"

"Sure."

"And tell them it'll be ready in half an hour or so."

"Okay," she said and headed back out.

"So everyone's eating?" Sophie said.

"Far as I know."

"Which makes eight."

"Unless you count Colt as two."

"I *do* have a big personality," he said.

Emily snorted. Sophie ignored him as she set bright, mismatched plates around the table.

"You did want the skins left on, right?" Colt said, gazing at the nubby tubers.

"Yeah. That's where most of the nutrients are."

"Which means approximately none," Sophie said.

"That may be true of store-bought potatoes, but these are Lazy Taters. Planted with love and nurtured with care."

The front door opened and closed.

"I don't think potatoes actually know how you feel about them," Sophie said, fetching glasses from the top shelf of the hutch.

"Then maybe it's the cow manure fertilizer that makes them so tasty."

"Let's not use that as a selling point," Casie suggested and stepped into the kitchen. Her cheeks and the tip of her nose were pink from the cold. She rubbed her hands together. Did they hurt? Colt watched her, silently assessing. "Smells good in here. What can I do?" she asked, and in that second he saw that she was favoring her right leg.

"Sit down," he ordered. The command was a little gruffer than he had intended.

The kitchen went quiet. Three pairs of female eyes turned to him in question.

"The baby's up," he explained lamely, hearing Bliss awaken in the living room. "Someone has to hold her." With that he hurried away.

"What's happening?" Emily asked.

He ignored the question although it was a fairly good one. After all, Casie had made it perfectly clear that she didn't need him in her life. So why the hell was he here?

Bliss blinked up at him and cocked a toothless smile. Something hurt for a second near the center of his chest.

Maybe this was why he showed up every morning at the crack of dawn, he thought, and reaching down, lifted the baby to his shoulder. If he weren't such a manly man he would be perfectly content to sit in the nearby rocking chair and discuss world problems with this tiny bundle that warmed his soul, but the potatoes called. The irony of the situation was not lost on him as he toted Bliss back to the kitchen . . . where Casie had taken his place at the cutting board.

He spread a steadying hand across the baby's shoulders and glowered at Casie's back. "That's my job." His tone, he discovered, was no more convivial than before.

"Since when are you so hepped up about potatoes?" Emily asked.

"Since about an hour ago," Colt said.

Casie tightened her jaw and said nothing.

"What happened an hour ago?"

"You going to tell her?" Colt asked.

"I'm an adult, you know," Casie said. Her pouty tone might have belied her words a little.

"Then sit down and act like one."

Both girls were staring at them now.

"What's going on?" Emily asked.

"Dickenson's being stubborn. That's what's going on," Casie said.

"Me?" he countered, and felt an angry burble of protectiveness shoot through him. "Talk about the kettle and the pot."

"Is someone going to tell me—"

"Nothing hap—" Casie began, but Sophie cut her off.

"Oh, for crying out loud! Why don't you two just get a . . ." She stopped herself, heaved a sigh, and started off in another direction. "Casie came off a horse."

"What? No!" Emily said, drying her hands on a nearby towel. "How? Are you okay? Sit down."

"It's no big deal," Casie said. "I wasn't even—"

"Sit down!" Emily repeated and yanked out a kitchen chair.

Colt stifled a grin.

"You know this is actually *my* house, don't you?" Casie asked.

Colt had to turn away to hide his glee.

"Exactly," Emily said, nodding bossily at the chair. "What do you think would happen if you were seriously injured?"

"The point is that I *wasn't*—"

"What if you lost the ranch?" Emily's eyes were so wide with earnest worry that she could have made a boulder weep. Casie wasn't a boulder. "What would happen to Bliss?"

All activity stopped. Casie sank guiltily into the chair.

"Talk to me!" Emily demanded, and with one glance at Colt, tugged Bliss from his arms before settling the baby onto her mentor's lap. Casie hugged the infant to her chest. There was something about the sight of the two of them together that made it difficult to breathe . . . the somber mocha face juxtaposed against the other's peachy complexion.

Cassandra May Carmichael *wasn't* the most beautiful woman in the world. Somewhere in the left-thinking part of his brain Colt probably knew that, but she had sucked him in from the moment he'd seen her standing knobby-kneed and pink-cheeked in front of Mrs. Littleman's chalkboard. Her short, caramel-colored pigtails had stuck out at odd angles beside her ears, and her eyes had been so round and guilelessly blue that he'd felt an immediate and inexplicable urge to put grasshoppers in her lunch bag.

Love was a hard thing to figure, he thought, and longed preposterously for a lively crop of arthropods.

"Did you know Sophie trained Evie to pull a sled?" Casie asked in a hopeless attempt to change the subject.

"Soph's a magician with horses," Emily said, tone matter-of-fact. "But so are you. How did you fall off?"

"I *didn't* fall off." Casie's tone was defensive as she cast a sideways glance at Colt and fiddled with the baby's homespun bootie. She shifted under his gaze. He still made her nervous. They'd known each other for twenty-odd years. Had attended the same school for twelve. Had kissed once in Grady's pasture under a crescent moon. That memory made *him* a little fidgety. Not because he regretted it. Hell no! It was because he regretted every day he'd spent *not* kissing her since that moment. He regretted every stupid deed he'd ever done to push her out of his mind. Sure, she was too good for him. But it was entirely possible that she was too good for *any* man. So why shouldn't *he* be the lucky bastard who spent the rest of his life trying to make up for those damned grasshoppers?

Emily shook her head as she put biscuits in the oven. "So Sophie's lying?" she asked and drew Colt back to the conversation with some difficulty. "You didn't fall off a horse?"

It was an absurd thought. Sophie rarely fabricated anything . . . unless it somehow involved abused horses. Then it was no holds barred.

"I was riding Maddy, so you know it can't be *too* serious," Casie said, which was just idiotic, because it had been proven time and again that falling off *any* horse wasn't exactly good for your longevity.

"While leading Chesapeake," Colt added. He didn't really know why he acted like a tattling twelve-year-old when she was around.

"You were leading that crazy stallion?" Emily asked.

"He's not crazy. He's really got a pretty good mind for a three-year-old. It's just that he's—"

"A *stallion!* He could have killed you!" Emily jerked her gaze to Colt. "How could you let her do that?"

He blinked, but in a moment he realized he should have known this would somehow turn around and bite him in the rear. "It's not my fault if she thinks she's Jim Shoulders."

They stared at him in unified silence.

"The Babe Ruth of rodeo," he added in exasperation. Apparently, unlike Willie Nelson, *their* heroes had *not* always been cowboys.

Emily glowered.

"So . . ." he said, grinning sheepishly as he glanced at Sophie. "You're teaching Evie to drive, huh?"

Silence again, then Casie buried her face against Bliss's chubby arm and chuckled at his evasive maneuvers. Emily shook her head.

By the time Max and Sonata stepped into the fragrant warmth of the kitchen, Sophie was reenacting the scene on the road and Emily was laughing out loud. For the life of him, Colt couldn't have said why Casie was the one hand-whipping Bodacious cream while he dandled the baby against his chest.

"Are we too early?" Max asked.

"No, you're right on time." Emily was just carrying a pot from the stove to the table.

"That's good, because S. is starving," Max said. Sonata rolled her eyes and he laughed. "What have you got there?"

"Burgundy cream sauce." Emily lifted the pan and offered a spoon to Max. "Want to try it?"

"If I must," he said and tasted the velvety mixture. "Yowsa" was his only comment.

Emily smiled and handed a clean spoon to Sonata, who took a tiny sip.

The front door opened and closed again, signaling the arrival of their third guest.

"Is it too salty?" Em asked, shifting her gaze from one to the other.

"It's not too *anything*," Max said.

"Except fattening," Sonata suggested.

"There's no such thing here on the Lazy," Emily assured them.

"Really?"

"Believe me," she added. "If there *was,* Mr. Dickenson would be as big as a barn."

Colt raised a brow and gave her his best don't-mess-with-me expression.

She grinned. "Instead of being the hottest bronc rider on the—"

But in that second Lincoln Alexander stepped into the kitchen. Emily raised her smiling face to welcome him, but her eyes went wide and the pot slipped from her fingers to crash onto the linoleum.

CHAPTER 10

"So what brings *you* to the Lazy Windmill, Lincoln?" Max asked.

The lazy lasagna, as Emily called it, had been consumed by everyone but Sonata and wildly applauded. Dessert was now being served. Apple-plum bread pudding steamed into the air like culinary magic. Lumpy and variegated, it was a homely dessert, but each serving was baked in its own muffin tin and capped with Bo's uber rich cream. Chances were excellent it was going to taste far better than it looked.

The young man glanced across the crowded expanse of the Lazy's battered kitchen table, wintery eyes solemn and unblinking. He had been almost entirely silent during the meal. But then Emily had been almost as reticent. What was that about? The question nagged at Casie. Emily was usually as chatty as a mynah bird. In the past, half of what she said had been lies, but that had rarely stopped her from participating in their mealtime conversations.

Lincoln Alexander shrugged. "I just needed some time to think," he said finally, voice low, left fist tense beside his empty plate.

"Yeah?" Max glanced up before dipping a spoon into his pudding. "About what?"

The boy's brows lowered the slightest degree, and for a second it almost seemed he wouldn't answer, but finally social expectations or some other equally powerful force prompted him. "I'm working on something."

No one spoke. All eyes were on him, waiting for clarification.

His gaze slipped to the left for a second, but never actually met anyone's eyes. "I'm an artist. Sort of," he said.

"Sort of?" Max's tone was curious.

"What kind of artist?" Sonata asked.

"Metal."

The room went entirely silent again but for Max's spoon clicking against his bowl. "You're a sculptor?"

"Guess you could say that."

Casie felt Colt glance at her, but she didn't glance back. She'd been a fool to let him see that the boy had spooked her. Now she'd be forced to spend time convincing him to go home for the night since she sure as hell couldn't have him sleeping on her couch. Holy cow, what if he didn't sleep fully clothed? Her stomach twisted. Maybe she should have gotten a flu shot.

"Do you cast your work or do you prefer fabricated art?" Sonata asked.

Lincoln shrugged again. The movement was stiff. "A little of everything."

The room fell into silence, each thinking his or her own thoughts as they stared at him. Only Emily had turned away.

"Well . . ." Max said, leaning back in his chair, dessert already finished. "What time is breakfast?"

"Max!" Sonata scolded.

"What?" He turned toward her, both chagrined and amused. "I was just wondering."

"We haven't even left the table yet."

"Eight o'clock," Emily said, and reaching down, curved a hand reverently against Bliss's head where it rested on Colt's shoulder.

Casie watched her. Not only had the girl been almost entirely silent during supper, but her usual sense of humor seemed to be completely depleted.

"It's a date then," Max said and winked at Emily. She didn't even seem to notice. "I'll await it with bated breath."

"You're going to await it while you burn off that bread pudding," Sonata said and stood up, her own dessert all but untouched. "Does anyone happen to know where the nearest gym is located?"

"Gym?" Colt asked, rising too, right hand large and steady against the baby's sleepily curved back.

"It doesn't have to be anything fancy," Sonata said. "A Stair-Master and some dead weights would do for a day or two."

Casie shifted uncomfortably. It wasn't as though she expected the Lazy to be a five-star inn, but she always felt oddly guilty when a guest desired something she couldn't or wouldn't supply.

Colt, however, seemed to be of an entirely different mind. He shrugged, then stroked the baby's back in absent adoration. Bliss sighed in her sleep, plump lips parted and lax against the soft flannel of his shirt. "There are some pretty good hills behind the bunkhouse," he said.

Sonata smiled. "I'm afraid I need something *tonight* before those calories congeal."

Colt canted his head a little, lips twitching into a mischievous grin. "According to my seventh-grade science teacher, those hills have been there for a few million years. I gotta think they're out there right now."

Sonata raised perfectly groomed brows at him. "It's dark."

His grin amped up a notch. "Not with the moon on the breast of the new-fallen snow," he said.

"You're kidding, right?"

"There's not a gym within fifty miles of here," he assured her.

She raised a brow, silently assessing him for a moment. "Then how do *you* stay in such great shape?"

The room went silent. Casie felt a muscle tic in her jaw, but, perhaps realizing the inappropriateness of her question, Sonata tore her gaze from Dickenson and turned toward her.

"Surely, *you* must work out," she said.

"Case works like a pack mule," Colt said. "Doesn't matter if she's recently broken a couple legs coming off a horse."

"What?" Sonata asked, but Casie desperately steered them back on track.

"Unfortunately, we don't have a lot of time for a regular exercise regiment," she said.

"But we do have three hundred hay bales that need stacking," Sophie added.

They all turned toward her.

"I'm just saying . . ."

"Hay bales?" Sonata repeated.

Max shifted his gaze to Emily, but she was catching no one's attention tonight. "Where are these bales going to and from?"

"This isn't something you have to worry about," Casie said. "I'm just sorry we don't have a gym for you to use."

"It's not a problem," Max said. "Sounds like we can burn some calories right here on the farm. What do the bales weigh?"

Colt shrugged. "Fifty pounds. Maybe sixty."

"You could think of it as a sixty-pound lat machine, S." Max grinned at her.

She lifted her chin at the challenge. Her white blouse was tailored and pressed, her cuffed trousers pleated. "Sounds good," she said.

Max's brows shot toward his hairline, and Sonata smiled. "We came here for a ranch experience, right?"

"Oh no," Casie said and rose nervously to her feet. The last thing she needed was guests suing her for medical compensation when their backs seized up in the middle of the night. "That's not necessary."

Sonata turned toward her, spine straight as a T-post. "Max assured me this vacation was all inclusive," she said.

"I'm not going to make you lift bales," her fiancé assured her. "You'll ruin your Christian Diors."

She cocked her head at him. "I thought I'd wear my Nikes."

He chuckled. "I'll check the GPS. Maybe there's a gym in Rapid City that's open all night."

"Not necessary," Sonata said. "I think this sounds like a great idea."

The two of them stared at each other for a prolonged second . . . the modern version of pistols at dawn.

"Okay," Max said, standing abruptly. "I'm in."

Sonata smiled. "What do we wear?"

"Really," Casie said, trying again. "We don't need to take care of those bales until morning."

"Why wait?" Sonata asked.

"Listen," Max said, looking smug. "I'd pay good money to see little Miss New York City throwing bales."

"Honestly . . ." Casie began, but Colt stood up.

"If they're game to help, it'd be nice to get the job done tonight. Then Ty can sleep in tomorrow morning."

Casie scowled. Ty had left immediately after evening chores to finish up an English paper; if he was willing to forego Em's lasagna, it must be important.

"There you go." Max shifted his gaze to Emily for an instant. "Thanks for supper. It was awe-inspiring."

"I *do* feel inspired," Sonata said, but for an instant her gaze shifted to Colt.

Lincoln rose to his feet.

"Is there anything you need before breakfast?" Casie asked as the young man moved toward the door.

"No." The word was barely audible as he shuffled past the others. Snagging his hooded sweatshirt from a peg in the entry, he stepped alone into the darkness and closed the door behind him.

"Not a big talker," Max said, then rubbed his hands together. "Well, should we meet you back here after we get changed?"

"This is a really dirty job," Casie said. "And hard. You don't want to—"

"Oh, but he does," Sonata said. There was a confrontational light in her eyes. "And I do, too."

Casie searched for another argument, but Colt spoke first.

"You have gloves?"

"Sure."

"If you use them for bales, you're never going to want to wear them again," Sophie warned, putting another set of dishes on the counter.

They stared at her in question.

"The hay gets stuck in the lining," she explained.

"We'll supply the gloves," Colt offered.

"Okay then," Max said, and raising a hand, ushered Sonata out the door.

The kitchen went quiet.

"Well," Colt said. "That's nice of—"

"What are you thinking?" Casie asked. She rounded on him, temper flaring.

He scowled as Emily took Bliss from his arms. "I'm thinking we have eight tons of hay to move, and you need to get off that leg."

"My leg is fine," she said, though she *had* kind of been dreaming about a long, hot bath.

"Your leg is not fine. You're limping."

"I'm not . . ." she began, then glanced toward Emily; she'd been trying to convince the girl to quit lying since the day they'd first met. "Well . . . you *always* limp."

"This isn't . . ." he began, then gritted his teeth. "You talk to her, Em," he said, but the girl was already turning away.

"I'm going to feed Bliss."

They stared at her in unison. "You okay?" Colt asked.

"I'm just tired," she said, but her grip seemed tight on Bliss's well-padded bottom and her eyes looked wary. "I'll do the dishes later."

"If you're not feeling well, Case and I can do them."

Casie tried not to stiffen at his words, but who was he to volunteer her time?

"No, I'll take care of them," Emily said and took a step toward the stairs, but in a moment she twisted back around. "Do you know how to install locks?"

"What?" Casie said.

The girl's brows were low, but she shrugged as if to lighten her words. "It's just that . . . there's been that rash of burglaries in town."

"Is there something bothering you, Em?" Colt asked.

"No, I just . . ." The tendons in her throat tightened almost imperceptibly. "Nothing. It's fine," she said and hurried away, Bliss hugged against her shoulder.

"What was that about?" Colt asked.

Casie shook her head, but Sophie was already slipping past them toward the entry. "Are we going to get this done or what?"

"Don't you have homework to do?" Casie asked.

She ignored the question as only a well-versed teenager can. "The horses are my responsibility," she said.

"Since when?"

"Since Freedom joined us. I think stealing horses might still be a hanging offense in the state of South Dakota."

"You did the right thing taking her," Casie said. "I know I wasn't too thrilled at the time . . . seeing how you could have been killed and all. But I'm really proud of you for saving her. Not to mention getting that whole pregnant mare cesspool shut down."

For a moment quiet gratitude flooded the girl's eyes, but she shrugged away the moment. "We were lucky to find homes for the others. But it looks like Free and her baby are mine for the foreseeable future at least so I'll be helping with the hay."

"The girl makes a fine point," Colt said.

"Good point or not, her father will still skin me alive if she fails a single one of her classes," Casie reminded them.

"Also a good point. How 'bout you both stay inside?"

"What?" Sophie asked.

"No," Casie said. She wasn't entirely sure why the idea made her angry. After all, the thought of a hot bath made her sigh with longing and maybe he was just trying to help out. But how many other women had he helped out in the past? The memory of Sonata's obvious interest in him made her stomach knot up.

Irritation danced in his eyes, but he kept his voice even. "Em needs you," he said.

She faltered for a moment, remembering the girl's atypical silence. But the realization that he was manipulating her won the day. "Sophie can take care of Em."

Colt shifted his dubious gaze to the girl who lifted a haughty brow.

"Can't you," Casie said. It was more a statement than a question.

"I suppose I can make sure the house doesn't burn down around her, if that's what you mean."

"There you go." Casie moved past Colt toward the door. "You can't ask more than that."

"You . . ." he said, clenching his jaw, "are the most stubborn person on the planet."

"Really?" She felt anger burn through her. She hated being angry. Hated being jealous and petty and wound up like a kid's Christmas toy. All emotions Colt Dickenson brought out in bushel baskets. "These aren't even your bales."

"Yeah, but they're my horses," he said.

She gritted her teeth as she stepped into her overalls and remembered the day he had brought those rangy broncs to the Lazy . . . just swinging by on his way to the killer sales in Canada, he'd said. He'd manipulated her then just like he was manipulating her now. She knew that. But looking back, she wasn't sure what she would have done differently. Those dark, wild eyes staring at her from the confines of the trailer had drawn her under. And maybe, just maybe, the challenge in *his* eyes had had a little something to do with her decision. "Fine. Suit yourself," she said and attempted to yank her zipper sassily closed. Unfortunately, she'd forgotten about the broken tab. Her empty fingers snapped into the air, making him grin as he straightened from pulling on his boots.

"Need some help?"

"No, I don't need any help!" she said and tugged desperately at the nub.

He shook his head. "Twenty-nine years old," he mused. They were standing less than three feet apart. Close enough for her to smell the leather of the gloves he held in one hand. "And you're still running scared."

She snapped her head up. "Am not."

"Really?" he asked and stepped up close.

She could feel testosterone roll off him in waves. Could all but taste the flavor of him on her lips. He took the one remaining step between them and tugged up her zipper. His knuckles brushed her neck, sending off a tiny tendril of something skittering across her skin.

She knew she should step back, knew she should escape. Maybe he wanted her now, but how long would that last? He wasn't her type. She needed someone solid and steady, someone *boring*. He was about as boring as a heart attack, as humdrum as a wildfire. And when he was near, she was no better than kindling waiting to be consumed by the flame. But he was leaning in, chiseled jaw coming closer, sexy eyes half closed. Their lips were inches apart.

"Stay inside." He breathed the order against her lips.

It took her a moment to make sense of his words, to realize he was manipulating her yet again. "No."

A tic twitched in his jaw. "You have to soak that leg."

"This is *my* ranch!" she said and stepped back a pace, putting a little much-needed space between them.

"That doesn't mean you have to do every damn job yourself."

"It means that I can if I want to."

His lips were tight as he turned toward the door before swinging back. "Stay in and I won't mention today's fiasco ever again."

She shrugged, oh so unconcerned.

"If you insist on coming out, I'm putting you in the tub myself the moment we're back inside."

The thought fired up an unacceptable spark of glee somewhere in the middle of Casie's being, but she doused it with manic speed.

"Try it!" she challenged.

His brows quirked up in unison with his lips.

"Okay then," he said and motioned toward the door. "After you."

CHAPTER 11

"All right!" Max clapped his gloved hands together. Frost flowed from his lips into the chill night air. "Let's get this done."

"How about Max and I throw the bales onto the loft and you ladies stack them," Colt said.

Casie considered calling him a poopyhead and telling him that *she* would throw and *he* could stack, but even in her current state of inexplicable anger, she wasn't deluded enough to think that was possible. She could no more throw a sixty-pound bale through the air than she could fly to the moon.

"That work for you?" he asked. She couldn't help but think it sounded like a challenge.

"Sure," she said. "That's fine. The ladder's over here," she added and motioned Sonata toward a dark corner where rickety rungs climbed ten feet into the loft. It only took her a few seconds to reach the top. Just a little longer to realize her guest wasn't immediately behind her. She glanced down.

Sonata was standing at the bottom, looking up, face a perfect pale oval beneath her jaunty red beret.

"Sonata?"

"Yes. I'm coming," she said and put a tentative foot on the first dowel.

"You okay, honey?" Max asked, glancing down from the top of the hay wagon.

"Of course," she said again and took a step up.

Max grinned. The hay upon which he stood was stacked twelve feet high. Colt was beside him, already tossing off the ropes that had held the bales in place during transit.

"We can still go find that elusive gym," Max said and winked at Casie, but Sonata kept climbing, eyes straight ahead, movements slow and stiff.

It took half a minute for her to reach the top. Beads of perspiration dotted her smooth brow and her lips looked taut.

"Everything all right?" Casie asked.

Max was still grinning from the hay wagon.

"I'm fine," she said and took a shaky breath. "Just tell me why the bales have to be up here."

"They don't," Casie said. "Not tonight anyway. Please, let us take care of this."

"S. and I have a little bet," Max said. "The person who cries uncle first has to pay for our next vacation. I'm thinking African safari." His grin amped up a little. He rubbed his hands together. "Let's get this party started."

"I'm in a bit of a hurry to get back into the house myself," Colt said and glanced at Casie. His eyes seemed demonically bright in the dim light, reminding her of his bathtub threat. "You ready?"

She gave him a challenging glare though her stomach felt queasy. "Whenever you are."

He nodded and dragged the first bale up by its strings.

It was then that Lincoln Alexander appeared below them.

"Where do you want *me?*" he asked. His hands were shoved into the pockets of his sweatshirt and his head was bare.

From above, the boy looked more slender than ever, barely as heavy as one of the bales.

"Not much room up here," Colt said. "But we'd appreciate your help in the loft."

He nodded once, then clambered up the ladder.

Sonata shuffled carefully away as if just the sight of such careless disregard for vertigo shook her foundation.

Once on top, Lincoln shifted his weight and waited.

Colt tossed the first bale. It hit the plywood beneath Casie's feet with a reverberating thud.

Sonata swore almost inaudibly and widened her stance as if steadying her sea legs.

"You'll get used to it," Casie said, and not knowing what else to do to reassure her, grabbed the twin twines and carried the tightly bundled hay to the back wall.

Lincoln retrieved the next one and placed it carefully beside Casie's. Sonata had moved toward the middle of the loft, and Max was positioned to make the next pitch.

His face was a mask of concentration as he heaved the bale sideways. It soared through the air, struck the edge of the platform, and toppled dismally to the ground.

"I'll get this," he promised.

Ten minutes later his breath was coming hard and he'd only managed to get three onto the loft. Four others, however, had joined their fallen comrades belowdecks.

"It takes some practice," Colt said and tossed another bale onto the floor near Casie's feet. Despite the frigid temperatures, he'd already removed his coat and rolled up his sleeves. The muscles flexed in his corded forearms. Sonata raised her brows as she watched. Casie felt heat flush her cheeks. Exercise, she thought, was very effective in raising one's body temperature.

"I got it," Lincoln said, and lifting the newly arrived bale from in front of her, stacked it among its mates.

"There must be an easier way," Max said. His face was a little red.

"Yeah," Colt agreed, and shifting another bale, tossed it sideways. It landed on the plywood and slid to within five inches of Sonata's feet. She shuffled back but finally gritted her teeth and bent to haul it away. "The Lazy could benefit from a few modern conveniences." He made another toss. "Or *any* conveniences."

"What would take *our* place up here?" Max asked, breath rasping a little as he bent to grasp two more twines.

"A hay elevator," Colt said.

"They make such a thing?"

"They do." Colt tossed another bale and added a grin as Casie hauled it away. "But then Case would have to invest in a bench press."

"You two married?" Lincoln asked.

The question seemed to come zipping out of left field.

Casie shifted her gaze to him. The boy looked pale but un-taxed as he stood near the edge, legs spread and brows low over gunmetal eyes.

"Nah," Colt said and turned his amused glance on Casie. She felt the heat of his attention like the spark of a Roman candle. "I'm just the hired help."

Lincoln tightened his fists, making Casie notice for the first time that his hands were bare. She winced. There were few things more egregious to skin than baling twine and coarse-stemmed alfalfa. Small abrasions already bedeviled his knuckles. Surely that would upset an artist. Wouldn't it?

"You need gloves," she said, but he didn't seem to notice.

"You and . . ." Lincoln paused and clenched his jaw as he jerked it toward Colt. "You married to the girl?"

"What?"

"The girl . . . in the house." He pursed his lips, expression sober. "Is she your wife?"

Colt scowled, dark brows low over suddenly cautious eyes. "Which girl are you talking about?"

"The baby . . . she doesn't look like you."

No one spoke. They seemed to be holding their collective breath.

"Emily's a friend," Colt said. Something in his stance suggested that he wanted to add "and none of your damned business." His protectiveness simultaneously moved and irritated Casie. Life was just so damned confusing.

"She do all the cooking?" Lincoln asked.

Colt shifted his gaze to Casie and back. "Most of it. Why?"

He shrugged. The movement was stiff, his expression dark. "I was thinking maybe you could use some more help around here."

Casie blinked. Holy cats. What was this all about? "Your art must keep you pretty busy."

"I can do other things," he said and turned to her, expression earnest.

Casie longed to glance back at Colt, but she didn't need his support. "I'm afraid I can't afford another employee right now," she said and resisted adding "or *any* employees."

"Okay," he said and fell silent.

After several seconds of uncomfortable quiet, Colt threw another bale. Things speeded up a little after that. Max tossed one for every four of Colt's, but his attempts were getting better.

Unfortunately, the work was becoming increasingly difficult. As the stack on the wagon got lower, the throwing distance became longer and the pile in the loft higher.

Everyone's respiration rate had escalated a little. Sonata had ceased carrying the bales to the growing stack and was now dragging them as far as possible. Lincoln worked in silence. Max grunted as he heaved another bale. And then there was a gasp. Casie spun toward the wagon just in time to see him topple to his knees. He teetered on the edge. Colt leaped forward and grabbed his jacket.

For one frantic second, she was sure they would both crash to the floor, but suddenly Colt fell backward, dragging Max with him.

The three in the loft stared wide-eyed as Max lay on his back, gasping for breath.

"You okay?" Colt asked, crouching over him.

Max swore with breathy vigor.

"Max?" Colt said, but the other man was rolling slowly onto his belly.

"Come on, Sonata," he said and crawled carefully toward the edge of the rack.

Sonata's stance had widened even farther, as if the flooring beneath her was not to be trusted. Still, she wasn't giving up. "Are you crying uncle?"

"And every other imaginable relative." He groaned.

"I'm so sorry," Casie said and hurried down the ladder to watch him creep toward the floor.

"Not your fault," he assured her and put a hand to the small of his back as he reached the ground.

Worry crashed over her. It wasn't as if she needed more lawsuits against her. The pending problems with Ty's parents were enough. "I'd better call a doctor. Or do you want me to take you to the emergency room?"

"No. I'm fine. It's probably just a ruptured spleen or something."

Casie felt herself blanch as Sonata crept down the ladder.

"I'm kidding," Max said and placed his right arm across his fiancée's shoulders. "I just need to rest a little. You can't keep us cowpokes down for long," he said and limped out of the barn with a grimace.

Casie watched them disappear into the darkness.

"You should go with them," Colt said.

She glanced up at him.

"Make sure he's okay," he added, but she shook her head.

In a moment she was back in the hayloft. The remainder of the job was uneventful but difficult. By the time the wagon was empty, her arms ached and her right hip throbbed with the beat of her heart. She glanced at Lincoln.

"Thank you," she said. "That was really nice of you."

He nodded, brows low above overcast eyes.

"I can . . ." She shuffled her feet against the hay-strewn plywood, trying to relieve the pain in her hip. "I can take some money off your tab if you like."

He stared at her.

"In exchange for your help," she added.

"Not necessary," he said and strode toward the ladder. In a moment he was down. In another he had slipped from view.

"What's with him?" Colt asked, voice low.

She shook her head, a half dozen worries gnawing her. "Maybe I should check him out."

He raised his brows, expression amused. "You a sleuth now?"

She pursed her lips, remembering she was angry. "Could be."

He chuckled. "Well, your investigation's going to have to wait until after your bath."

She jerked her eyes to his. Panic spewed through her, but she tried for a sassy comeback.

"I don't think I need one as much as you do," she said and sniffed at him with noisy disdain, but honest to God, he still smelled good. What kind of sense did that make?

"Well, maybe we can wash each *other's* backs then," he said.

Panic twisted into something a little more confusing, but she held on desperately to her cheeky demeanor. "Very funny," she said and turned away to hide her face.

"Since I'm staying the night," he added.

She pivoted back toward him. Anger and excitement mixed dangerously inside her, but she calmed herself with a deep breath. "I appreciate the offer," she said, making certain her tone implied the opposite. "But—"

"It's not an offer. It's a fact."

Anger won. "This is *my* place," she said. "This is—"

"And those girls are *your* responsibility."

She didn't like cursing. She reminded herself of that now. "You think I don't know that?"

"You act like you don't."

"I do not act—"

"Em's scared."

"What?" she asked, surprised despite herself.

"Why else would she ask about locks?" He gazed toward the bunkhouse, where their latest guest had disappeared a few moments before. "What does it take to scare a girl like Emily Kane?"

She hated to admit it, but he had a valid point. "Okay," she said. "You can stay. But just tonight."

"Of course," he said, and grinned as he returned his gaze to hers. "You sound like you think I'm trying to make a move on you or something."

She stared up at him, a thousand questions quivering on the tip of her tongue.

"No," she said and looked away. "Of course not."

"Good. Cuz no means no, right?"

His eyes were so damned enchanting, drawing her back.

"Right?" he asked.

"Right! Yes."

"*Yes?*"

"I mean *no!*"

He raised his brows at her.

She gritted her teeth and backed away. "You'll have to stay downstairs," she said and nodded at her own wisdom.

"Of course," he agreed. "Just as soon as you're done with your bath."

CHAPTER 12

Colt watched Casie's eyes widen. With desire? With fear? Hell, he couldn't even guess. They'd known each other for a couple decades and she was still an enigma. But he knew this much . . . he wasn't leaving tonight.

"We had an agreement," he reminded her.

She shook her head, but he continued as if he hadn't noticed. "If you insisted on stacking hay despite your injury . . ."

"I—"

He raised a hand to forestall any arguments. "Which you did," he added. "Then I was to make certain you got safely into the bathtub."

"I didn't agree to that."

He exhaled as if wearied by the whole debate and forced his gaze away from her. It took some effort because, regardless of every irritating little detail about her, she was still hopelessly alluring, like the sun after a long winter or hope in the midst of despair. "I believe you said . . ." He narrowed his eyes, mimicking deep thought, but he wouldn't have had to waste a second on remembering their earlier discussion. She'd been fiery and firm, standing up for herself and her ranch. The way she should be, the way she used to be before her dumber-than-snot fiancé had drained her of confidence. " 'Try it.' " He grinned despite himself. "Those were your exact words."

For a moment he thought she would retaliate and waited, but

she merely preened a smile at him. "I'll take a bath," she said. "Without your help."

"But how do I know you'll make it to the tub?" he asked. "I mean, it's been a long day. Maybe you'll just fall into bed without properly soaking your joints."

Her smile was becoming a bit more brittle. "I promise to bathe."

For a second his mind stepped back and felt the need to inform him that this might be the silliest conversation he'd ever had. But he was not adverse to silly. If anyone needed a little more silly in her life, it was Casie May Carmichael.

So he shook his head. "You came off Maddy pretty hard. Could be you injured yourself more seriously than you think."

"You don't have to worry about that."

"But I do," he said, and though he didn't mind in the least if she thought he was being glib, it was the truth. He worried about her all the damned time. And what the hell was that about? Half the women he had dated, and there had been a considerable number of them, had been rodeo queens or Miss something-or-others, which meant they'd risked their lives running horses on a daily basis. Which also meant the majority of them had taken some nasty spills. By comparison, Casie had just kind of slipped gently off Maddy, like a duckling gliding from the nest. Yet seeing her fall had been like taking a hammer to his thumbnail. "I worry." It was the horrible truth. "What if you collapse while getting into the tub?"

"Oh, for Pete's sake! I'm not going to collapse," she said and turned away.

"You might have hit your head," he argued, following her with dogged, and he was certain irritating, tenacity.

"I didn't."

"Brain injuries are nothing to fool around with."

"I don't have a brain injury."

She didn't mention that she didn't fool around, he realized, and thought that was a hopeful point to ponder.

"I had a buddy in Cheyenne once," he said, gearing up for a

much fabricated tale. "Name was Mick. But we called him Mayberry. No idea why. Anyway . . . he was a bulldogger who—"

"Colt!" She jerked abruptly toward him. "I just stacked three hundred bales of hay with no ill effects."

He shrugged, doing his not-so-fantastic best to control his grin. Man, he loved it when she got fired up. Which might be pretty perverse on his part, because there were few things that made her more wigged out than those messy emotions. "Two ninety-eight maybe," he said.

She scowled.

"Sonata stacked at least two."

She rolled her eyes and turned away.

He went with her. "And the kid, Lincoln . . ." He was a little embarrassed that he had forgotten about the boy for a minute. After all, he was the supposed reason for this little sleepover. "He must have stacked five at least." Actually, Lincoln Alexander had done pretty well despite scraped knuckles and lacerated forearms. He was stronger than he appeared, Colt thought, and wondered if that realization should make him feel better or worse.

He glanced at the bunkhouse as they reached the porch, but she stopped and turned toward him, one booted foot on the bottom step.

"Really," she said, voice low, brows bunched over oh-so-earnest eyes, "you can't come upstairs."

"Why not?" he asked and tried his utmost to match her solemn sincerity.

"Because I'm trying to set an example for the girls!"

He raised his brows and waited to the beat of three before speaking again. "It's not like we're going to sleep together."

"I—"

"Is it?" He tilted his head a little.

"No!"

"Then what difference does it make if I help you with your bath?"

"They'll know!"

He allowed himself a tiny chuckle. "Well, of course they'll know, Case. It's not like I'm invisible."

"And they'll think . . ." She shook her head.

He did the same, though he wasn't sure why . . . maybe to help her reach some sort of less-than-asinine conclusion.

"They'll think there's something going on."

He continued to stare at her with blank fascination.

"Between us!" she explained, as if he was so remarkably obtuse that he hadn't quite followed her thought process.

"Oh!" He stepped back a startled pace. "Well, that's just wrong. I mean, you said you weren't interested. Right?"

"Right."

He scowled as if troubled by an unacceptable thought. "You don't think I'd take advantage of a woman who's not interested in me, do you?"

"No." Her answer sounded truthful, which was something of a relief, but the dilemma didn't seem to be settled in her own mind.

"Then you have nothing to worry about."

"But they won't know that."

"Won't know what?"

She pursed her lips. It was entirely possible that he was being intentionally difficult. "That there's nothing between us."

He swore in silence and upped the wattage of his innocent expression. "So the girls' opinion is your only concern?"

"Yes," she said, and though her answer sounded suspiciously like a question, he doggedly took it at face value.

"Not a problem," he said and marched past her up the porch steps with steely resolve.

He heard more than saw her spin around to follow him. "Colt!" Her voice was breathy, but he ignored her.

"Colt!"

"Just a minute." He was in the house now and toed off his boots in deference to the recently scrubbed floor. "Girls!" He raised his voice once he saw that the kitchen was empty.

"Colton!" Casie hissed.

He waved a hand behind him. "I'll clear this up," he told her. "Emily? Soph!"

"Don't—" Casie began, but the teenagers were already clattering down the steps. In a second they had burst into the kitchen.

"What's wrong?" Emily's face looked strained. Sophie's was stamped with her signature irritation.

"Hey," he said and kept his own expression carefully serious. "Sorry to bother you."

"What's going on?" Emily asked, gaze sprinting from one to the other.

"We need to talk to you," he said.

"I was doing homework," Sophie informed them.

"This will just take a minute. I wanted to make sure you didn't have any objections to my sleeping on the couch tonight."

"What?" Emily asked.

Sophie had a pencil stuck above her left ear. "Why would I care where you sleep?" she asked.

"This is ridiculous," Casie said through gritted teeth, then raised her voice a little to include the girls. "You can go back to—"

"I just wanted to make sure you weren't uncomfortable with the idea," Colt interrupted.

"Why?" Emily asked, looking from one to the other again.

"Why would I stay, or why would you be uncomfortable?" Colt asked.

Emily narrowed her wily eyes. "Both."

"Well . . ." he began, and now he watched her carefully. "I'm a little nervous about those burglaries in town. I'd just feel better if I was close by for a while."

She nodded slowly as if accepting the idea. And he wasn't sure what to make of that. The day Emily Kane didn't question every single event that crossed her path was the day that something was wrong.

"How are you feeling about that?" he asked.

Emily shrugged.

"I think we should do target practice," Sophie said.

Colt shifted his gaze to hers. "What?"

"Casie can shoot," Sophie said. "I want to learn, too."

That gave him pause. The idea of Sophie Jaegar carrying a loaded anything was cause for alarm.

"Okay," he said. "That's . . ." Terrifying. "A good idea. But for right now, I'm going to hang around some. Okay?"

Sophie shrugged. "Seems like you're here all the time anyway," she said. "Hey, is there any of that lasgna left?"

"A little." Emily's tone was vague, as if her mind was elsewhere, but that's all Sophie needed to hear. She brushed past the others, making a beeline for the fridge.

"We just wanted you to know that there's nothing going on between us," Colt said, and turned sideways so as to address both girls.

Beside him, Casie fisted her hands against her thighs and looked as if she would like to silently disappear into the worn linoleum.

Sophie gave them one more scowl before she pulled the refrigerator door open.

"What?" Emily asked and shook her head a little, as if the whole conversation made no sense whatsoever.

"We know you're impressionable young women," Colt explained. "And we don't want you to think that there's any hanky-panky going on."

Emily lifted her brows, but Colt soldiered on, managing a straight face with what he considered admirable aplomb. "Casie's made it clear she's not the least bit interested in me."

The woman beside him moaned quietly, but other than that the house was as silent as death for the count of five.

"Are you serious?" Emily asked.

"It's not that . . ." Casie began, but her voice dwindled to a halt.

They all turned toward her. Sophie was eating leftovers straight from a glass container. Classiness, it seemed, did not extend to lazy lasagna.

Casie cleared her throat. "It's not that I'm not *interested* in . . . Mr. Dickenson."

Oh good, she was now referring to him by his last name, he thought, and blinked with innocent bonhomie.

"I mean . . . we're *friends*. It's just that . . ." She halted again and looked at Colt, as if she thought he might help her out of this hole. But why on earth would he have dug the hole in the first place if he didn't want her in it? "We don't . . ." She took a deep breath. "I'm just not really . . ."

"She's not attracted to me," Colt said.

"Holy shorts!" Emily sounded earnestly peeved.

"I'm going to bed," Sophie said and headed toward the stairs.

"Okay." Colt nodded and did his utmost not to crack a grin. "I just wanted to let you know that if you see us in the bathroom together or anything, ours is a perfectly platonic relationship."

Sophie just raised a dismissive hand as she headed upstairs with her late-night snack.

But Emily remained where she was for another few seconds. She stared at them both in dismay, then shook her head and followed in her comrade's footsteps. The ancient stairs creaked one at a time until the doors closed and the house went silent.

"Well . . ." Colt turned toward Casie, rubbing his hands briskly together. "Good. I think that went pretty—"

"Are you out of your mind?" The words were hissed.

"No," he said and shook his head, perfecting his baffled expression as he did so. "I don't think so."

"You don't just . . ." She paused as if to catch her breath. "What's wrong with you?"

"I'll make you a list sometime," he said brusquely. "But right now we should get you into the tub before that leg stiffens up."

"Listen . . ."

"Come on, Casie. We had a deal."

"We did not have . . ."

"Just relax. We already determined that you're not interested in me and that I'm too . . ." He shook his head. "We'll call it vanity. I'm too *vain* to push myself on a woman who isn't attracted to me. Ergo—"

"*Ergo?*"

"Ergo." He grinned a little. Far be it from him to actually *be* vain, but he was fairly certain that women didn't find him entirely repulsive. "No harm can come of this," he said, and bending slightly, shifted his arms behind her back and thighs. In a second he was cradling her against his chest.

"What are you doing?" The words were little more than a hiss against his cheek.

"Carrying you," he said and took a step toward the stairs.

"You can't—"

"I can."

"You shouldn't—"

"Shhh," he said. "We don't want to wake the baby."

"I'm not going to wake—"

"Good. Maybe you should put your arm around my neck."

"That's not—"

"Oops," he said, and tripping, tipped her toward the floor.

She gasped and swung her arm across his shoulders.

"Sorry about that," he said and traipsed quickly upward.

"Colt . . ." She seemed to be whispering now. The sound did something devious to his insides, but he kept his tone conversationally smooth.

"Yeah?"

"I'm serious."

"Isn't that the truth!"

"We can't do this."

"Do what?" he asked and tilted his lips toward hers the smallest degree.

He actually felt the breath stop in her chest. Felt his own bottle up tight in his lungs, but he rallied. Dammit, he'd been fighting this battle too long to quit now.

"Do what?"

"*This!* Us."

"Why not?"

Her lips parted. Her fingers tightened on his neck. The change was almost imperceptible, and yet, beneath the warmth of her hand, he felt his skin tingle with desire. A desire that was reflected in her eyes. He leaned in.

"Because of the hungry horse syndrome."

"The hungry horses." He nodded. "Sure."

She shifted away slightly, expression surprised. "You know what I mean?"

"Not even vaguely."

"When horses get too hungry, they tend to eat too much."

"Okay."

"Then they colic because they were greedy."

He narrowed his eyes as they reached the landing. "So you think wanting to love and be loved is greedy?"

"Well, I just . . . Not for everyone."

"Just for you."

"Yeah, I mean, look at everything I have."

He didn't bother to glance at the threadbare carpet and faded walls. Instead, he let her feet slip to the floor when they reached the bathroom. She didn't step back. But her voice was breathy when she spoke.

"This ranch. The kids. The horses. It's enough for me. It's more than I deserve. I can't—"

"I can honestly tell you that that's the dumbest thing I've ever heard," he said and kissed her. For a moment, he thought she would pull away, but she didn't. She kissed him back. Need roared between them. She pressed up against him, soft and warm and firm.

"Casie," he said, but her name was little more than a breath. Her eyes were round and vulnerable, as deep as forever. He kissed her again and she didn't resist. She *wouldn't* resist. Not this time. Not tonight. He knew it.

But that would be a mistake. She wasn't ready.

The truth struck him like an ax. He tried to back away, but his legs, his damned legs wouldn't work. He was stuck, lost in her eyes, in the possibility that she might care. That maybe this wasn't just a moment of weakness, that maybe deep down she wanted him as desperately as he needed her.

But how would he know? If he took advantage of this miracle, how would he ever be sure that he hadn't been selfish? He tried to shift away from her again, and lo and behold, his right foot shuffled back a couple scant inches. The left followed with resentful slowness.

Her fingers slipped farther around his neck. Her lips were bright and moist. They parted. He watched them move, leaned in, then stopped himself with an amount of discipline he would have sworn he didn't possess.

"Gotta go," he said.

"What?" She breathed the word. It almost sounded like desperation in her voice, almost looked like sadness in her eyes. He couldn't make her sad. That would be cruel. He wasn't a cruel man. But—

"Gotta get that!" he said, and realizing with tragic relief that the phone had been ringing for some time, stumbled out of the room and down the stairs.

CHAPTER 13

"Hello?" Colt's voice sounded a little hollow to his own ears. Sex deprivation could do that to a man.

"Hello? Is this the Lazy Windmill Stables?"

He rubbed the back of his neck, relived the feel of Casie's fingers against his skin, and glanced toward the stairs. What kind of idiot was he? He had probably just blown his last opportunity with her. Because for a moment, just an isolated second in time, she had wanted him. He was sure of it.

Or was he just seeing something he wanted to see instead of something that was really . . .

"Hello?"

"Oh. Yeah," he said, jolting back to the present. "This is the Lazy."

"To whom am I speaking?" The woman's voice was as sleek as polished jasper and already a little peeved.

"This is Colt Dickenson." He glanced toward the stairs again. What would happen if he dropped the receiver and bolted back to the bathroom to pick up where they had left off?

"Oh, Mr. Dickenson." The voice on the other end of the line changed dramatically. "It's nice to finally speak to you."

He dragged his attention from his imaginings and scowled at the phone. "What's that?"

"Are you alone?"

"What?"

She chuckled, the sound sexy and low. "I'll explain myself in a moment, Mr. Dickenson, but first you must disclose whether you're alone."

"Yeah," he said. Very, very alone. And whose damn fault was that? "I'm alone. Why?"

"Sophie Jaegar's not in the room?"

Something flared in his gut, some weird, feral instinct that might have been protectiveness, which was pretty damned odd, because really, Sophie needed protection about as much as a porcupine needed a shotgun.

"Who is this?" he asked.

"She's not there, is she?"

"No. Not at the moment."

"Good." There was a breath of a pause, almost as if she was waiting for a drumroll. "This is her mother."

He glanced at the stairs again. Was Casie in the bathtub yet? Was she the type to linger there? He earnestly hoped so.

"Monica Day-Bellaire," she added.

He brought himself painfully back to the matter at hand. "Oh. Did you want to talk to—"

"No!" she said, then laughed again. "No. You must not tell her I called."

"Okay."

"I want to make it a surprise."

The beginnings of caution were creeping into his psyche. "Make *what* a surprise?"

"I will be visiting soon."

"Visiting . . . *here?*" he asked. It wasn't as if he and Sophie Jaegar were best buddies, but even *he* knew that the girl didn't have a real top-shelf relationship with her mother.

"Yes. It is, after all, the holidays." Her voice was almost a little preachy now, and wasn't *that* messed up. "Time for family."

For a moment he wondered if he should suggest that maybe she could have thought of that sometime between New Year's and Thanksgiving, but he didn't make mention. "When are you coming?" he asked instead.

"As soon as I can. I realize it's quite spontaneous. In fact, I considered simply showing up, but then I thought I had best apprise you and Ms. Carmichael of the situation."

Well, consider him apprised. He rubbed his hand over his eyes. "All right."

"Sophie will be there, won't she?"

"As far as I know. But—" But what? But don't come because the Lazy has enough whack jobs already? Don't come because I have a sneaking suspicion your daughter despises you? Don't come because I need as much of Casie's scattered attention as I can possibly get? "But I don't think there's room here for another guest, Mrs. . . ." What the hell was her name?

"Ms.," she corrected. "Ms. Day-Bellaire. And you don't need to concern yourself. I'm sure I'll be able to get a hotel room in the city."

For one forgetful second he was actually relieved. Until he realized how ridiculous that statement was. "What city?"

She paused a second, then laughed. "I guess I've been gone longer than I realized. I forgot how charmingly rustic it is out there. Well, not to worry. I'm certain I can share a room with my daughter."

He didn't bother to ask if she had ever *met* her daughter, because even though he didn't consider himself to be a social genius, he had a sneaking suspicion that might be considered rude. "With Sophie?" he asked instead.

"I'm sure she won't mind."

Was she serious?

"It'll be like . . ." She paused. "Like going to camp."

"Do you *like* to camp, Ms.—"

"Oh. What?" she asked, obviously addressing someone else. "Yes. Just one minute. I'm sorry," she said, returning to him. "I'm afraid I've got to run. It was very nice talking to you, Mr. Dickenson. I'm so looking forward to meeting you in person."

"Maybe you should talk to—" he began, but the phone went dead. He stared at the receiver, exhaled heavily, and glanced toward the steps. True, he had been intent on escaping the house while he still had the ability to control his legs, but he had the feeling all hell was about to break loose, and if he didn't inform Casie, it was likely to break loose on *him.*

Replacing the receiver, he mounted the steps very slowly, exhaled again, and rapped softly on the bathroom door.

But the water was running. There was no answer. He tried again, but no louder. Despite whatever impression he might have been trying to give, he cared about the teenage girls down the hall quite a lot and had no wish to adversely affect them, but it did seem fairly important that he speak to Casie soon. So when there was still no answer, he put his left hand over his eyes, turned the knob, and stepped inside.

There was a gasp, a splash, and the sound of a shower curtain being zipped across a rod.

"Sorry," he said and hoped that the hand that shielded his eyes also did something to hide the grin that was trying to creep onto his face. "I need to talk to you."

"Now?"

"Yeah. Sorry."

"About what?"

"About . . ." He stepped forward, stubbed his toe, and hopped a little bit. "Can I uncover my eyes?"

"No!" she hissed and shut off the water. "Is something wrong?"

He shuffled forward a couple extra inches. His earlier visit to this room had seemed strange enough, but this was stranger still. If he ever stopped to consider how many women he'd seen naked, this scenario might very well seem ludicrous. But none of those women had been Casie May Carmichael, had they? "I'm not sure," he said.

"You're not sure if something's wrong?"

"Right."

"Can't it wait?"

"I don't think so."

"Okay, well, I'll get out in a minute. But you have to—"

"You need to soak," he said. "I know you think you're not seriously injured, but sometimes people are wrong, Case." He heard her splash, and somehow that whisper of sound sent a wave of wild images cascading through his mind. She was naked in every last one of them. The idea made him feel strangely squirmy. "Listen . . ." he said, wondering uncomfortably if she could tell how her nakedness was affecting him. "I guess this *can* wait till morning."

"No. I'll get out."

"How about if I blindfold myself?"

"What?"

"You must have something I can use for a cloth."

"Are you kidding me?"

He smiled a little at her tone, but corrected himself in a moment. "A washcloth or a sock," he said and felt around blindly with his right hand as he bumbled forward again. Feeling something against the wall, he patted downward. Surmising it was the toilet, he lowered the lid and eased himself down atop it. "A towel? A sweater? A pair of under—"

"Oh for heaven's sake, you can open your eyes."

Huh. "You sure?"

"Yes." Her voice was as quiet as his.

He removed his hand slowly. She was, after all, like the sun. But unfortunately, the day was overcast with a high probability of storms; the curtain remained closed. Still, just the knowledge that she was naked only inches away did upsetting things to his equilibrium. And how sad was that?

"Colt?" she asked from behind the curtain.

"Yeah?"

"What's wrong?"

For a second he had actually forgotten why he was there. He shook his head at such a pathetic situation. It wasn't as if he was a pubescent hayseed. "I just . . ." He grinned, finding a fair amount of humor in the situation. "I gotta tell you, I'm having a little trouble concentrating when you're naked in there."

No response.

"You *are* naked, aren't you?" he asked.

"Of course I'm . . ." she began, then stopped herself. "I meant why are you here? Is something wrong at the bunkhouse?"

"As far as I know, your guests are fine."

He was the one having heart palpitations.

"Is it the horses?" Was she beginning to talk to him like he was mentally handicapped?

"They seemed okay, too, last I checked."

"The cattle—"

"All the livestock's fine," he said. "But I . . ." he began and sniffed. It smelled like apricots, he realized, and spied the peach-colored bottle perched on the edge of the tub. "Do you always take baths?"

"What?"

"I was just curious if you prefer them to showers."

"Why are you here, Dickenson?"

Judging from her prissy tone, he had to assume she had gotten over her breathlessness of a few minutes before. For reasons entirely unknown even to him, he found that mildly amusing.

"Sophie's mom's coming tomorrow."

"*What?*" she rasped and snapped the shower curtain open a couple scant inches.

He stared, breath held, which was just ridiculous, because seriously, all he could see was her head, part of her shoulders and about two inches of back, but all those inches were naked. And he couldn't help zeroing in on that fact.

"You *are* naked," he said.

"She's coming here?"

"Shh," he said, and shrugged. Holy crap, she had pretty skin, all creamy smooth and rosy from the heat of the water.

"She's coming *here?*" she repeated, voice low now.

"That's what she said."

"Why?"

"Because it's Christmas. Time for family."

"Are you serious?"

"I wasn't the one who said it."

"She actually *said* that?"

"Yeah."

"No," she breathed and dropped her head against the shower wall. This new and improved position offered him an extra couple inches of viewing pleasure. "Sophie's going to have a cow."

She'd put her hair on top of her head, but a few wispy ten-drils had come loose and curled now with gentle adoration against the soft scroll of her ear. Her skin looked dewy soft and could really use a kiss. Right there where—

"Colt?"

"Yeah?" he asked and zipped his attention to her face.

"Do you think we should wait till morning to tell her?"

"Tell who?"

"Sophie," she hissed. "When should we tell her?"

"Oh. We *can't* tell her."

"*What?*" Her eyes had gone wide. She grasped the shower cur-tain in one soapy hand. The sight of those fingers, slim and wet and strong, did something terrible to his already uncertain in-nards. Maybe it was the fact that she was naked. Or maybe . . .

"Colt!" she said.

He tried not to jump. "I agreed to keep it a secret."

"What? Why would you do that?"

Good question. "Because Sophie needs a mother."

"Well, I just . . ." She huffed a laugh and shrugged. For rea-sons not readily apparent, that motion seemed to interfere with the rhythm of his heart. "Maybe the woman should have real-ized that before the middle of December."

"True, but better late than never, right?"

"I don't know," she said earnestly, and rolling her head side-ways, stared at the far wall. Her left foot rose in unison. He could just see it and one delectable ankle past the opposite end of the curtain. Water dripped from her heel as tiny, exuberant bubbles glistened against her skin. "I'm worried she might do more damage than good."

Her toes were small and very pink. The nails were painted red, a deep scarlet hue that surprised him. The thought of the oh-so-sensible Casie Carmichael polishing her toenails cranked up his considerable attention.

"Aren't you?"

He dragged his gaze from her toes. It was not a simple task, which was somewhat disturbing. They were, after all, just toes.

And yet . . . He felt his attention being pulled in that direction again.

"Colt?"

He snapped his gaze back to her face. "What?"

"Aren't you scared?"

Yes, he was. If the sight of her bare toes created this kind of havoc, what would the rest of her body do to him? She had a rocking—

"Colt!"

"Yeah," he said. "Pretty scared."

"I mean . . ." She shook her head. The cords in her neck stood out in sharp relief against her pretty throat. The hollow between her collarbones was a deep, soft dell just waiting to be explored. "I know Sophie wants a mother. I know she feels neglected and abandoned. I'm just afraid . . ." She winced. "What if she has some kind of bomb to drop?"

"Soph's mother?" he asked and tried to concentrate on their conversation.

"Yeah. What if she's planning to remarry or something?"

"You think she'd show up at Christmas time to tell her daughter that?"

She sighed. The high tops of her breasts rose and fell. Colt kept himself from swooning like a half-starved debutante. "Her parents separated while they were on a family vacation together."

"Well, that's just screwy."

"Sophie said it was no big deal."

He swore softly.

"Yeah," she said.

"So what do we do?"

"Leave home?"

He chuckled. "Or we could send Soph to my folks' house. Tell Ms. Day-Bellaire that we don't know where she is."

She rolled her eyes at the absurdity of his suggestion.

"There's more," he said.

"What?"

"She wants to stay here."

She canted her head a little and raised her brows. "She what?"

"She wants to stay—"

"Well, she can't!" Casie rasped. Her expression was nothing short of horrified. "There's no room at the inn."

He kind of wanted to laugh, but he was a little bit afraid. "She said she can stay with Sophie."

"*Where?*"

"In her room. She said it would be fun. Like camping."

"Was she kidding?"

"I don't think she's that kind of woman, Case."

"Then she's on drugs."

"Maybe it won't be so bad."

"Are *you* on drugs? Colt—"

"Shhh."

"Colt," she said, softer now as she leaned toward him, revealing more creamy skin. "It's the holidays."

Merry Christmas to me, he thought, and forced himself to look her in the eye. "I know that."

"If she comes here and . . ." She shook her head. "Sophie could be devastated."

"Or she could be happy."

"Have you . . ." She squinted a little as if deep in thought. "Are we talking about the same girl?"

"Well, I'm not saying she'll be ecstatic," he admitted. "But she might be . . . mildly content." He stared at her, so beautiful and vulnerable and painfully empathetic that he felt an overwhelming need to shield her from life. "You can't be everything to everybody, Case."

"What are you talking about? I don't want to be anything to anyone."

That wasn't true, but maybe she didn't know it. He wasn't entirely sure she was capable of lying. "Sophie deserves to have a mother."

She stared at him, then blinked. "You think I'm trying to take her mom's place?"

"It's not that I think you're *trying* to." He drew a careful breath. "I think you *have*. Or maybe you've taken the place her mother *should* have had. But at what cost, Case?"

She shook her head. "First of all, I haven't taken anybody's place." She leaned forward for emphasis, nearly baring her breasts completely.

"And in the second place?" he asked, gaze eighteen inches lower than he knew it should be.

"In the second—" she began, then realized where his attention lay and snatched a towel from the floor. By the time she was covered and he had forced his eyes upward, her cheeks were pink.

"I like the second place even more than the first place," he admitted.

She gritted her teeth and almost shifted her gaze away, but she held steady. "I get more from those girls than I give them," she said.

He stared into her eyes, almost able to forget all those places that mesmerized him. "And therein lies the magic of Casie Carmichael," he said.

She narrowed her eyes a little and tilted her head as if awaiting a trap, but there was none. No trap. Unless it had been laid for *him*.

He shrugged. "It's why kids are drawn to you, Case. Why they seem to show up from . . . who knows where."

She still stared. Maybe she herself was a little baffled about how the Lazy had ended up with so many teenagers.

"Because you make them feel as if you need them more than they need you."

"Maybe I do," she said, and suddenly her eyes were very earnest, her mouth achingly soft. "And maybe that's what scares me."

For a moment he almost leaned down, almost drew her into his arms, but the time wasn't right, and if he had learned anything from riding broncs, it was that timing was everything. One wrong move, and a cowboy could find himself flat on his back with a broken heart and a shattered clavicle.

"Maybe it shouldn't scare you," he said. "Maybe it should make you realize how amazing you actually are."

Her lips parted, those beautiful, irresistible lips. "You think I'm . . ." she began, then scowled. "That's not funny," she said.

"And I'm not laughing."

Her expression went serious. He could feel her weakening. And that was bad. Really bad, because *he* had weakened years ago. Had damn near fallen apart the very first day she'd stood in front of Mrs. Littleman's classroom with those stupid lopsided ponytails and gigantic eyes. If she stood up right now, there would be nothing in the world to stop him from lifting her into his arms. Nothing to keep him from ruining any small chance he had with her. But she was rising. Dear God, she was—

"Hey, Case," Sophie said, voice loud on the far side of the door. "I've got to brush my teeth. Are you decent or what?"

CHAPTER 14

"Good morning," Casie said and smiled as she turned from the stove.

Ty nodded. He knew he should be more effusive, more extroverted and loquacious. Emily had once told him he had the social skills of a potato. Luckily, she said, potatoes were the Lazy's most versatile tuber. "Morning," he managed and tried not to worry about the hole in his left sock. If Colt's mom saw it, she'd buy him new ones. There would be no questions asked or blame handed out. He would simply find them atop his dresser, and it was that silent thoughtfulness even more than the money expended that would exponentially increase his debt.

"How's Angel today?" Casie asked, and pouring a second cup of coffee, handed it to him. He took it in fingers numb with cold and wondered if she looked a little stiff.

"Seems okay," he said. "Maybe a tad sore on her left fore again."

She nodded, leaned her hips against the countertop, and took a sip of coffee. "The ground's as hard as granite. It probably makes her more tender."

He exhaled and curled his palms around the mug. The heat was comforting, relaxing muscles he hadn't known were tense. It was kind of like love, curling into places you were sure had shut down for good. "Thought I might keep her inside more, where I can keep her comfortable."

"Do you think that's a good idea?"

He searched her eyes, already worried that he'd upset her. Even potatoes worried. "I'll pay for the straw."

Her brows dipped a little. She went entirely silent.

The nagging worry amped up a notch. His stomach clenched. Was she angry with him? Were finances so bad that—

"How many hours do you think you put in here a day, Ty?" Her gaze was extremely steady on his.

He shrugged, agitated by her attention. "Couple, maybe."

She smiled. The expression did something weird to his gut. "A couple in the *morning*," she corrected.

He gripped his mug tighter. "A man ain't no better than the work he does before breakfast." It was something his grandfather used to say. Grand would have liked Colt's dad. And probably Colt, too, come to that.

"Then you're a very good man," she said.

For one terrible second he thought he might cry. What kind of man would *that* make him? He blinked and glanced away.

"I'm sorry I'm so late," Emily said, rushing into the kitchen, baby at her shoulder. "Bliss—oh, Ty. Thank God you're here. Take her, will you?" she asked, and with that pressed the solid little bundle into his arms. Bliss was dressed in a green oversized sweater that swallowed her tiny fists. One sleeve seemed to be a couple inches longer than the other. At this rate, Bliss would be lucky to be out of her mother's experimental cable-knits by August. "She's been so crabby. And she just adores you. Caffeine! Thank you, Jesus," she said and poured herself a cup. "I swear she didn't sleep more than thirteen seconds all night. She didn't keep you awake, did she, Case?"

"No," Casie said.

Ty caught a glimpse of her face. She was lying. He knew it. But Casie would do that. For others, she could lie.

"That's good," Emily said, then turned toward Ty, mug cupped in her hands. Her sweater was green, too, also with sleeves of varying lengths. She must have found a really dynamite sale on yarn. "How's Angel?"

He shrugged as he settled the baby into the crook of his arm. She still seemed shockingly tiny. Had he ever been so small, so vulnerable? Had his mother ever looked at him and felt that almost painful tug in her gut?

"She's a little sore again, I guess," Casie said.

"Oh no." Emily sighed as she set her coffee aside and pulled a carton of eggs from the refrigerator. "Can't Sam do anything for her?"

Ty glanced toward the stairway, hoping Sophie wasn't within hearing. She didn't seem to care for the female farrier who worked on Angel. He didn't know why. It would be understandable if Casie held a grudge against her, because there had obviously been something between Sam and Colt at one time, but Case didn't appear to care much. Maybe she realized there wasn't a woman alive good enough to polish her boots, but he kind of doubted it.

"Ty?" Emily asked as she glanced over her shoulder.

Bliss complained quietly. He bounced her on his arm and returned to the conversation with an effort. "I think Sam's done 'bout all she can do. Pads to reduce concussion. Bars to prevent contracted heels."

"What's that?" Emily turned on the oven while simultaneously pulling ingredients from the cupboard.

"It's when their feet don't expand proper."

She made a face as she cracked the first egg. "Why do you want big feet anyway?"

"Not big," he said, and lifting Bliss in both hands, raised her above his head in a slow sweeping motion. She brought her tiny fists together and gave him a toothless grin that made his heart hurt. "But their hooves take the weight of a thousand pounds of horse, so they gotta be able to spread a little on impact. Iron don't allow for much of that, so we took some precautions."

She nodded. "What are you going to do?"

"What's for breakfast?" Sophie asked as she clattered down the stairs. "I'm—

"Oh." She stopped short before entering the kitchen. For a second she was framed by the doorway. As if she were the center of the universe, the center of his world. Her hair swung free, as shiny as an agate against her trim shoulders. Her eyes were the wide, deep green of a summer pond, able to showcase a dozen emotions at once. "Ty." She blinked. "Good morning."

He nodded and tucked the baby back against his chest, fingers splayed across her tiny shoulders. Sophie stared. Her lips parted a little. From the corner of his eye he thought he saw Casie and Emily exchange a glance, but he wasn't sure. Sometimes it was hard to focus on everyday stuff when she was near. And sometimes it was hard to breathe.

"We were just discussing Angel," Emily said. "I was saying maybe he should have Sam come back out. What do you think, Soph?"

The girl snapped her gaze from his, arched brows already descending. "What?"

Em's grin was a little impish. It was impossible to guess why. "I said, that Sam is a marvel, don't you think?"

"Em . . ." Casie's voice was soft and sounded sort of like a warning.

They all glanced toward her, but she lowered her eyes and sipped her coffee.

Sophie shrugged, but the movement was stiff as she moved toward the coffeepot. "I think we should hire someone else."

"Why?" Emily asked. Her tone had gone from mischievous to innocent in a heartbeat. There was no use pretending; he didn't understand women.

"Angel's not cured. So we should get someone else in here." She shifted her gaze to Ty. "If you don't mind."

Bliss squawked a little. He cradled her tiny head with one chafed hand and bounced her more vigorously. "You got someone in mind?" he asked.

Sophie stared at the baby's back or maybe she was looking at his hand there. Maybe his fingernails were dirty again, but she didn't look disgusted. Her eyes were wide and liquid, like a lost puppy's or a broken doll's.

"Soph?" Emily said. "You okay?"

"What?" she asked, jolting back into the conversation. "Of course I'm . . . I'm going to go . . . feed Jack," she said and all but galloped toward the entry.

Emily chuckled softly.

Casie said something under her breath. Ty couldn't quite hear what it was.

"I didn't do anything," Emily said and chuckled again, but in a matter of seconds the front door opened and Max Barrenger stepped into the kitchen.

Casie turned toward him, expression concerned and hopeful and guilty all at once. "How are you feeling?" she asked.

"Me?" He put a hand to his back and arched a little. "I think I'll survive, if Emily's breakfast is as good as her supper."

"What will you survive?" Emily asked.

"I just about fell headfirst off the wagon last night."

"Are you speaking metaphorically or . . ." Em paused, allowing him to fill in the blanks.

"I *wish*," Max said. "I was throwing . . . correction . . . *attempting* to throw a bale onto the loft." He shook his head. "If Colt hadn't grabbed me I would have splattered like a water balloon. Is there coffee?"

"Here," Casie said and hurried to pour him a cup. Ty had been right: She was limping, but she was doing a fair job of hiding the pain. He scowled. "Are you sure you're okay?" she asked.

"Absolutely." Max stepped forward to take the mug from her hand. "Is this going to stop my heart?" Apparently, he had already tasted Em's coffee.

Sophie arrived. Ty ignored her as best he could. But heart palpations are not easily disregarded.

"You might want a good cardiologist on speed dial just in—" Emily began, but then another man stepped into view. She stopped midsentence.

"Morning," he said. The newcomer was tall and lean. His hair stuck up in odd tufts as if he'd been wrestling with it during the night.

"Hi," Emily said and turned abruptly back toward the stove.

The young man shifted his attention to Ty. Their eyes met. The other didn't turn away.

"Ty, this is Lincoln Alexander," Casie said.

Max was pouring fresh cream into his coffee. He glanced up. "So, what's your job here at the Lazy, Ty?"

There was a second of silence, which Casie filled. "He keeps the place from falling apart."

Ty felt his cheeks redden, but the younger man was already speaking. His eyes were serious, his lips unsmiling. "How long have you worked here?"

Ty studied him, wrestling with a half dozen questions. Who was this guy and why did he want to know? "Six months or so maybe." He looked over at Casie. Did she seem tense? "But I'm here a lot," he added and tightened his grip on the baby. "And I just live down the road if trouble stirs up."

Max glanced toward him, brows raised. The attention made Ty fidgety, but there was too much at risk to sissy out now. "And Colt . . ." The door opened again. It was a pretty good bet that it was Dickenson himself. So far as he knew the man hadn't come home last night. There was the sound of him toeing off his boots in the entry. In a moment he was stepping into the kitchen. "He's here near *all* the time."

"Morning," Colt said, and nodded at the guests before looking at Ty. Their gazes met. Had he spent the night here or elsewhere? Ty wasn't sure which might be worse. He glanced at Casie. She looked edgy but not miserable. His own tension eased up a little. "You get Dad's steers fed?"

"Yeah," he said. Bliss mewled softly and wriggled a little in his arms.

"Any problems?"

Ty shook his head and bounced the baby. Lincoln's brows lowered the slightest degree as he watched.

"That gimpy one was eating?"

"Yeah, he seemed better."

"I owe you one," Colt said, and crossing the kitchen, poured himself a cup of coffee. "You want some?" he asked Lincoln and lifted his mug a little.

"No thanks."

Colt raised dark brows. "You're really *not* from around here," he deduced and took a slug from his own cup.

The kitchen went quiet for a second, then, "You can all sit down," Emily said. "Breakfast will be ready in a minute."

They shuffled toward the table as a unit, but Max spoke as he pulled out a chair. "Let me guess," he said. "You're from . . ." He shook his dark head. "Bangor, Maine."

"Detroit," Lincoln corrected and settled his lank body into the nearest chair. He wore a long-sleeved collarless thermal under his Hard Rock Cafe T-shirt. His hands looked pale, his knuckles scuffed against the dark fabric.

"Yeah? How's the Motor City faring these days?"

"All right, I guess," he said and shrugged as he put one nervous hand atop the table.

Max laughed. "You must not be in the auto industry."

"Not directly."

"Indirectly?"

"Dad worked for Chrysler."

"Got laid off?"

"Died."

Emily dropped a metal lid. It clattered like a castanet onto the counter. She muttered an apology under her breath.

"I'm sorry to hear that," Max said. "Pass the sugar will you, Colt?"

"Were you able to be with him?" Colt handed him the sugar bowl, then set his cup near his plate before stepping away to retrieve the cream pitcher from the counter.

Lincoln curled his fingers up a little. "No."

"That's tough," Colt said. "I always worried something would happen to my folks while I was on the circuit."

Lincoln remained silent.

"You have a job you couldn't get away from?" Max asked.

Lincoln shook his head, face expressionless.

"Hey," Max said. "If your old man worked for one of the Big Three, you must know something about cars."

They all stared at Lincoln. His brows dipped toward never-tell eyes. His body language was taut. "A little, maybe."

"You ever work on Dodge trucks?"

" 'Fraid not."

"Well, you don't have to be afraid," Max said. "Unless you look inside Emily's old vehicle." He laughed. "That's a pretty scary sight."

Casie poured the contents of a teakettle into a ceramic mug. Steam rose from its curved top. "You want some spiced cider, Lincoln?"

"Okay."

"It turns over but it doesn't start," Max said.

"My *dad* was the mechanic," Lincoln said and accepted the cider with a nod.

"You must miss him," Casie said.

"Sorry, Emily," Max said as she set a large cast-iron pan in the center of the table. "I guess there's no one here who can help you."

Lincoln tightened a white-knuckled hand near his plate and glanced at Max, brow furrowed.

"Don't worry about it," Emily said, and lifted the lid from the pan. She had mixed bacon and bits of apple into the bright yolks. Eggstacy, she called it. "Help yourselves."

"It's your truck?" Lincoln asked, addressing Emily.

"Yeah," she said but didn't glance toward him.

"What year is it?"

She merely shrugged.

"I'm not sure," Max said and reached for the ladle that protruded from the pan.

Lincoln watched him, unmoving, as the other man filled his plate.

"This smells terrific, Em," Max said.

"Thank you," she said, but her tone seemed tight. "Isn't Sonata coming?"

"She's not a breakfast person. Guess I'll have to eat her share."

"You don't know the year it was made?" Lincoln asked, body absolutely unmoving.

Max shook his head and turned toward Colt, who had just returned with a clean cloth diaper.

"Forty-eight maybe," he said and draped the unbleached cotton over Ty's arm. Easing into a chair, he reached for his coffee again. "Could be a little older," he added and narrowed his eyes against the steam as he took a sip.

"You the one that bought it?" Lincoln asked.

"What?" Colt asked, and setting his mug aside, took the basket of biscuits Em handed him.

"The Dodge," Lincoln said. "Did you buy it?"

"No. Emily came home with that herself."

Lincoln nodded, lips pursed. "You mind if I take a look at it?"

"You'll have to ask her."

He raised his attention to Emily. Their eyes met. She smiled, but maybe the expression was a little too bright, a little too brittle. "Of course not. But don't go getting any ideas."

He stared at her, unspeaking, and she laughed.

"It may look like a piece of modern art, but it's not," she said and turned blithely away.

"Do you need more coffee, Mr. Barrenger?"

"Will you call me Max? I feel like I'm a hundred years old already after last night."

"That's right," Colt said. "I'd almost forgotten. How are you feeling?"

"Like an idiot."

Colt chuckled. "It might not be a bad idea to take it a little easy today. Maybe soak in a hot bath for a while."

Sophie shifted her gaze to Casie, who didn't look up from her plate. What was that about? Ty wondered and tried to dish up some eggs while holding Bliss steady. Emily came up behind him.

"I can take her."

"Naw, that's all right," Ty said and hoped like hell they didn't realize the baby was a shield of sorts. Something to hide him from the world.

"Don't you have to . . . oh shoot," Emily said as the lamb burst into the kitchen, tail switching rhythmically through the hole in its ridiculous diaper.

"I'll get her," Sophie said, and pushing back her chair, stood up.

The lamb trotted over, bleating hopefully. Sophie scooped her up, one hand under her belly, just as the doorbell rang.

"Are you expecting more guests?" Max asked.

Casie made a face. "I'm afraid three's all we can handle. We're not exactly a convention center," she said and scooted her chair back, but Sophie turned automatically toward the door.

"Just sit."

Her footfalls were light and quick across the floor. The door just creaked a little as it opened, then, "Mom?"

"Darling!" The voice from the entry was polished and enthusiastic. "It's so good to see you."

CHAPTER 15

"A lamb! In the house! How adorable. But don't just stand there, sweetheart. Invite me in." The words were singsong, bursting with buoyancy and confidence. Emily stood frozen in place beside Ty's chair, one hand just resting on Bliss's head until the twosome appeared side by side in the kitchen.

Sophie's mother entered the scene like a celebrated starlet, head thrown back and eyes alight. "Well, Sophia," she said, smiling at each of them in turn, her neatly tailored jacket moving with her like a second skin. "Aren't you going to introduce me to your friends?"

Sophie looked as if she had swallowed turpentine. Even Lumpkin seemed to be in shock, but Soph did as told, marching out the names like a death roll before turning slightly toward the older woman.

"This is my mother."

Absolute silence filled the kitchen until Emily was able to shake her brain loose. "Mrs. Jaegar . . ." She was trying to sound unfazed, but she could barely manage lucid and ran out of words right at that point.

"Day-Bellaire," Sophie's mother corrected, and dropping her arm from around her daughter's waist, strode farther into the kitchen, heels clacking assertively against the aged linoleum. "But you must call me Monica." She pronounced her name with a long e sound and lifted her chin just a tad when she said it.

Her hair was a color so bold and light it dared you to call it platinum. Combed smoothly back on the right side, it lay in a cool sweep across her brow on the left. She had high cheekbones, full red lips, and not a line on her patrician face. "You must be Emily."

"Yes, I . . ." It wasn't often that she was at a loss for words, but just now every syllable was at a premium. "Yes."

"I've heard so much about you."

From who? Emily wondered, but even in her current state she knew better than to voice such a question out loud.

Casie stood up, eyes wide, face pale. "Welcome to the Lazy."

Monica Day-Bellaire turned with crisp precision and thrust her hand toward Casie. "It's so nice to meet you, Cassandra."

"Yes, I—"

"How can I ever repay you for making my daughter so happy?"

Happy? They turned toward Sophie in unison. She looked shocked. But maybe if one looked closer, it would be clear that she was also angry. And confused. And scared out of her wits. Happy wasn't even on the charts.

"She simply loves it here, don't you, darling?" she asked and turned slightly to extend perfectly manicured fingertips toward her daughter.

Sophie shifted her attention to Ty for a second, but he dropped his gaze almost instantly to the tabletop. Emily could feel agony rolling off him in waves and almost winced. For those whose mothers were monsters, even someone like Monica Day-Bellaire was miraculous.

"Mother," Sophie said, face pale. "What are you doing here?"

"Well . . ." She turned and swept her hand reverently down Sophie's loose hair, as if she couldn't be close enough. "You didn't think I'd be able to stay away forever, did you? I just had to see the ranch that has brought the color out in your cheeks. And don't you look fabulous!" Sliding her fingers down Sophie's arms, she stepped back a pace. "You've filled out, I—"

"Mother!" Sophie said, then drew a steadying breath. "I thought you were in Paris."

"Well, I was of course. And it was just lovely. The cathedrals, the Louvre! But you remember how it was when we were there together. And I remembered, too. Remembered how you loved *les jardin* and suddenly I simply couldn't bear to be there without you another minute."

"But your symposium—"

"Is already done," she said and lifted an elegant hand as if to wipe away any lingering worry. "I was the keynote speaker. They wanted me to stay and expound on Munchausen syndrome, of course." She rolled her eyes toward the ceiling. There was still a water stain above the sink. "But I said no. It's Christmas, and I wanted to be with my beautiful daughter for a little while at least before her father insisted on whisking her away."

Emily hadn't thought Sophie could look more miserable, but she was wrong. "You needn't have hurried," she said. "Dad's in Saint Thomas."

"What?" her mother asked and reared back a little.

"He has a business meeting there."

"Oh, bunny . . ." Monica said and looked enormously mournful. "I'm so sorry he let you down again."

Sophie pursed her lips, trapping whatever she was thinking inside her head. But her brows were lowered, a sure sign that such a miracle wasn't going to last for long. "You . . ." she began, but Emily leaped into the breach.

"Mrs. Day-Bellaire—"

"*Monica*, please," she repeated, elongating the e sound again.

"Monica," Emily corrected, careful to do the same. "Won't you have some breakfast with us?"

The woman scanned the table, then lifted one narrow hand to her chest. There was no diamond on her ring finger, but a good-sized rock adorned her pinkie. "My goodness! What a sumptuous spread, but I really mustn't."

"There's plenty," Casie said and stepped away from the table. "Please. You must be hungry after your flight."

"Well . . ." She tilted her head as if fighting a losing battle. "Okay. The airlines are so tight-fisted these days. Maybe I will have a bite."

Casie took her plate with her, though she'd barely touched her meal. Emily hurried to bring clean crockery.

"Coffee?" she asked as Monica slipped into the abandoned chair.

"Coffee would be heavenly. You're a godsend."

Hurrying to the counter, Emily filled a mug and handed it off. Monica sipped it in silence as they all stared. She raised her brows with dramatic surprise. "*Mon dieu!* That's strong. But that's how we Francophiles like it, isn't it, Sophia? Remember the demitasses we had in Alençon?"

Sophie's eyes seemed to be shooting daggers. Colt spoke, sacrificing himself to the blades. "I can't believe you were able to get here so fast," he said.

"Well . . ." She put down her cup. "I was already in New York when we spoke. And I must admit, Colton, I wasn't sure how long you would be able to keep our little secret. So when my friend, Captain Whittington, said he could pull a few strings to get me here early, I jumped at the—"

"Wait a minute," Sophie said, turning slowly toward Colt. "You knew she was coming?"

Colt opened his mouth, maybe to lie, or plead the Fifth, or beg for mercy, but Monica spoke first.

"It's entirely my fault, honey," she said and dished up a little eggstacy. "I made him swear to keep my visit a secret. I so wanted to surprise you. And I have, haven't I?"

Judging by the expression on her daughter's face, she was not only surprised but pretty damned mortified, too.

Sophie opened her mouth, closed it, then turning robotically, set the lamb on the floor. "Blue needs his bandage changed."

"Now?" Monica asked and looked woefully crestfallen as she glanced around the room. "Surely someone else can see to it."

"I—" Casie began, but Ty spoke over her in that deep-water way of his.

"She oughtta take care of him herself."

Monica raised a brow at him. "Why is that?"

He gazed at her, cheeks a little pink, eyes so serious they could make you cry. "If you got a string girth that don't gall, you don't go switching to fleece."

Monica Day-Bellaire blinked at him. "I don't think I—" she began, but just then the front door opened and closed. She scowled. Colt cleared his throat.

"Your daughter's been treating that wound herself for weeks. She knows what she's doing."

"Oh." Monica forced a smile. "Well . . . my Sophia always did have a way with horses. Did she tell you about the time we rode in Central Park?"

"I don't think she did," Colt said and rose to his feet. "Can I get you some spiced cider, Monica?" He, too, used the long e sound. Maybe it seemed a little silly in the warm comfort of the Lazy's battered kitchen, but maybe it was just classy. Emily wasn't the kind of girl who could necessarily tell the difference.

"I'm stuffed already," Monica said and glanced down at her plate. Two and a half tablespoons of eggstacy languished there.

"It's high in antiphiliaries and low in calories," Colt said.

They all stared at him, and he grinned.

"I don't have any idea what it's high in, but Em here made it herself and it's damn good," he said and lifted the kettle from the stove. "Want to try it?"

"Well sure." She laughed. "If it's high in antiphiliaries."

Colt poured her a half cup. It steamed aromatically. She lifted it tentatively to her lips.

"That's excellent. Where did you get the recipe?"

Emily flushed with pride, then reminded herself that this wasn't *her* mother; she had no reason to try to impress her.

Ty stood up. "Guess I better be going," he said.

Emily hurried around the table to take Bliss from his arms. The baby had dropped off to sleep long ago. "Already?"

"Got some things to do."

"What things?" she asked and eased Bliss onto her shoulder.

"Just things."

"What—"

"I asked him to check the yearlings' water tank," Casie said. "The float keeps sticking."

Hogwash. He just wanted to escape the suddenly uneasy confines of the kitchen, Emily thought, but when she glanced at Ty, she saw the flash of gratitude in his eyes. She shifted her gaze briefly around the faces near the table and wondered who was going to save *her.*

Ty stepped into the cattle barn. It was quiet, dusty, cold. But it was still his favorite place on earth. The barn was where peace lived. But not right now. Right now Sophie Jaegar was in it. Making it seem alive and essential and scary as hell.

She was crouched beside the steel-gray colt, unwrapping the bandage from the foreleg he'd injured on a twisted wire fence. Blue fidgeted, but the girl didn't move. Six hundred pounds of horsepower, but she didn't retreat. She never retreated. Not until today. Leave it to a mother to make that happen.

The colt shuffled sideways again as she pulled the wrap free. She turned a little as she tossed it aside. In profile, she was almost too pretty to bear. She'd pulled a black stocking cap low above her brows. But she'd left the house without a coat so Ty had brought it with him.

"Just relax. We'll be done in a minute. It'll be okay," she said. Her voice was raspy. She swiped the back of her hand across her cheek.

That was when something in Ty's gut clenched up tight. Sophie Jaegar didn't cry. And she certainly didn't allow others to *see* her cry. He should leave. Should back away now, but she looked so small and lost hunched beside the colt's wounded leg.

He cleared his throat and knew the moment she realized he was there by the stiffness of her body.

He shuffled his feet a little. "You're gonna catch your death."

She reached to the side for the new bandage material, but her hair was an amber screen of silk, hiding her face from him. "I'm fine."

He took a few steps forward, hoping he'd given her enough time to compose herself. "Casie wanted me to bring your coat." It wasn't a complete lie. She *would* have wanted him to if she'd realized the girl had left without it.

She glanced up. Her mouth was pursed, her brows low. A storm brewed in those bottle-green eyes. "I'm not cold." That *was* a lie, but he didn't call her out. Mothers could make people do a mess of crazy things. Lying was the tamest of the lot.

"Sure, I know," he said. "But it'd make her feel better if you wore it anyhow."

"She's not the boss of me!" She stood abruptly, scaring the colt. He reared a little, but she just stepped away.

"I know," he said and held his ground in the face of her anger. "She just don't want you getting sick, is all."

"You *would* take her side."

He didn't comment. He wasn't sure where they were going, but he'd cinched up long ago for this particular ride. "If you'll put it on, I'll help you with the colt," he said.

She glared at him for a second, then stepped forward. Snatching the coat from his hand, she slipped her arms into it. Her movements, usually as smooth as ice, were jerky and quick. She yanked her hair out from under the collar. "She knew!" she said and glared at him.

"I don't know what you—"

"Casie!" she said. "Your idol. She knew Mother was coming and she didn't tell me. She just let me be . . ." Her words stopped short. A muscle jumped in her cheek. She turned away.

He shook his head. "Maybe Dickenson knew, but that don't mean Case did."

"Don't be naïve," she said, but her voice was very soft. "They're all alike."

"All who?" he asked and took a few steps toward her.

"Adults," she said. "You can't trust any of them."

Ragged memories whispered through him. "That ain't true."

"Yes, it is. They don't care what—" she began and swung toward him, but when her gaze touched his face, her words trembled to a halt. The muscle in her cheek bounced again. He hoped like hell she couldn't read the painful thoughts that stormed through his mind, but her eyes clouded. Those little-lost-girl eyes that made him want to cry like a baby every time he saw them. She swallowed. Her throat contracted. "She's not perfect, you know," she said. Her tone was rough but quiet, her eyes haunted.

"I know."

"She should have told me."

He didn't try to argue, though it was hard to hold back. "Yeah."

"She just . . ." She turned away. "Why did she come here?"

He didn't ask who she was talking about. Sometimes he wasn't the sharpest tool in the shed, but he knew that much. "Could be she just missed you, Soph."

"No, it couldn't," she said, but her voice was barely audible now.

"She's not . . ." He chose his words carefully. Sophie didn't spook him like she used to, but even a coyote knows to be cautious sometimes. "She can't be all bad."

She snorted. "You don't know her."

"No," he said. "But I know some things."

"Yeah?" Her tone was derisive as she pivoted toward him, the old Sophie come back to haunt them all. "*What* do you know, Tyler?"

"I know moms," he said. His stomach felt hollow.

She winced, and he cursed himself for sounding like a baby.

"I didn't mean it like that," he said. "I just meant . . ."

"I'm sorry."

The apology caught him off guard. He tightened his hands into fists. "You don't have nothing to be sorry for."

She exhaled a soft laugh. "Are you kidding me? Your mother . . ." She motioned toward his face where the bruises used to be most obvious. He felt his gut knot up. She winced again. "And I complain because *mine* doesn't..." She breathed out, trying to relax. "Well..." Bending, she lifted the new cotton bandage material from the ground. "Let's just say she's never going to win Mother of the Year."

He shrugged and retrieved the Vetrap. "I suppose that depends on her competition."

She laughed. Actually laughed. Not that hard-edged noise she made when she felt threatened but a gentle sound somewhere between tears and relief. "Well, I'll sure let her know if Emily and you want to enter *your* mothers," she said, and crouching beside the colt's left foreleg, began wrapping the bandage around his cannon.

He bent down beside her, easing out a wrinkle in the cotton. "Maybe we could have a least worst contest," he suggested.

She chuckled, and it was that sound, that low note of gratitude and hope, that made him want to cry. What the hell was wrong with him? "How long you think she'll stay?" he asked.

"Hold that, will you?"

He reached for the bandage. Their fingers brushed. Fire ignited. She inhaled sharply and turned toward him. Their eyes met. Fear or something like it flamed through him. He watched her swallow and turn abruptly away.

"I don't know," she said. Her tone was breezy now, as if she didn't have a care in the world. "If she says she'll stay a month she'll be gone tomorrow. Off to some"—she shook her head as she tore open the plastic containing the self-adhesive wrap— "workshop on narcissism or androphobia. Ready to cure the world's emotional ills. It's such a joke," she said and wound the stretchy material aggressively around the leg.

"Make sure you don't get it too tight," he said. "We don't need no bowed tendon to worry about."

She wiped her hand beneath her nose. "I used plenty of padding," she said, but she eased up on the tension a little and exhaled heavily. The barn went quiet. She finished wrapping the leg, but her hands remained on the bandage.

"How do you do it?" she asked and turned toward him finally.

He felt her attention like a sock to the gut. "Do what?"

"Stay so normal."

For a second he just stared at her, then he laughed and jerked to his feet. But she rose with him and grabbed his arm before he could pivot away.

"I mean it," she said. "Why aren't you . . ." Maybe he would have been able to turn away if it weren't for her eyes. "Why aren't you bitter or mad or mean or . . ." She shook her head. "Why aren't you crazy?"

"You kidding me?" he asked.

The world was quiet again. Off to the right a calf bellowed.

"No," she said and stared up at him, eyes so earnest they sucked him in, rolled him under. "I'm not."

She stared at him. Every ragged instinct in him wanted to run, to hide, to escape. Every instinct except that one niggling impulse that wanted to take her in his arms, to pull her against his chest, and let her cry on his shoulder, or maybe he'd cry against *hers*. In which case he'd never be able to show his face again. He drew a deep breath. He wanted to lie something awful, but her eyes wouldn't let him. "It's cuz of you," he admitted. "You and Case."

"Me and Casie? We're nothing alike," she said and looked at him as if she trusted him. As if she believed in him. It was damned near terrifying.

"Maybe angels don't know they're angels, neither," he said.

"I don't . . ." Her lips parted slightly and stayed that way. She blinked. "I'm not like Casie."

He didn't argue. Didn't dare, maybe.

"I'm like my mother."

"Yeah?" he asked and jerked his chin toward the grullo. "How many worthless colts has *she* saved lately?"

"That's different." They were standing very close. Close enough to feel the warmth of her breath. "She doesn't like horses."

"What does she like?"

She shrugged. "She spends a lot of money on her hair."

"Well, that probably don't need no saving," he said.

She almost smiled a little. Almost broke his heart, but then her eyes went wide and she jerked her attention to the left. Lincoln Alexander stood only a few feet away, silent as a ghost as he watched them.

CHAPTER 16

"What are you doing here?" Ty's voice was deep and quiet as he turned toward the older boy.

"You got any scrap metal lying around?" he asked and turned to Sophie, making her wonder how much he had heard.

Ty shifted a little closer to her, body stiff. "You'd have to ask Casie 'bout that. She owns the place."

He nodded once as if thinking, then asked, "So you live around here?"

"That's right."

Lincoln lowered his brows and shoved bare hands into the pockets of his sweatshirt. "With your parents?"

Dark emotions shadowed Ty's eyes, highlighting a blatant lack of trust, but the man was Casie's guest and Ty wouldn't compromise that. "No."

Lincoln shifted his gaze back to Sophie. She raised her brows at him, half daring him to ask. It must be pretty clear to everyone what *her* lineage was. Like mother, like daughter. Everyone knew that. Except Ty, maybe.

Lincoln Alexander cleared his throat and shuffled his feet. "How about the girl?"

They stared at him.

"Emily?" Ty asked. Sophie felt her muscles knot up at his defensive tone.

"Is that her name?" he asked.

"What about her?" Ty asked.

"How long has *she* been here?"

"Why you wanna know?"

Lincoln shrugged, eyes narrowed a little. "Just curious."

"Then you should ask *her,*" Ty said.

Angel thrust her head over the nearby stall door and bobbed for attention.

Ty lifted one hand to the mare's neck but kept his gaze on Lincoln.

The older boy shifted his attention to the gray. "How come he's inside?"

"Angel's a mare," Ty said.

The boy shrugged. Not caring. "How come *she's* inside then?"

"She's got some trouble with her feet."

Lincoln hunched his shoulders against the cold as if he could bundle his body heat inside his chest cavity. "What kind of trouble?"

For a moment Sophie thought Ty would refuse to answer, but he spoke finally.

"Horses' hooves ain't very big, considering the size of the animal. Sometimes stress or whatnot will cause the insides to swell."

Lincoln nodded, thinking. "What do you do for that?"

"Medicine, rest, special shoes."

"Special how?"

A muscle bunched in Ty's jaw, but he went into the stall. Angel nudged his pockets, frisking him for treats.

Sophie watched as he ran a hand down the mare's left foreleg. His fingers were chafed, his nails ragged, but his touch was as gentle as a love song. It was his damned hands that got her every time. "See here?" he asked and lifted Angel's hoof so that the sole was exposed. "Most shoes don't have this bar across the back like this."

Lincoln nodded.

"It keeps pressure on the frog to keep the foot healthy," Ty said and set Angel's foot back into the deep straw. "You got an interest in horses?" he asked.

"I've got an interest in metal."

Ty scowled. He wasn't the only person on the Lazy who failed to understand how people could be uninspired by the equine species.

"I do some sculpting," Lincoln said, "but I don't know much about iron."

Ty shrugged and stepped back out of the stall. Lincoln followed suit. "They been shoeing with iron since time out of mind," he said and kept walking, ushering the guest from the barn, out of their sanctuary, or was it just Sophie who thought of it that way?

Lincoln glanced around the interior of the barn. They'd made considerable headway in cleaning up the mess left by Casie's dad, but they still had a ways to go. Old farm equipment and castoff appliances cluttered the area. Emily's ancient truck had been hauled inside and stood as desolate and silent as an abandoned house.

"Looks like most things around here haven't changed in a while," Lincoln said.

Sophie wasn't sure if it was an insult, but judging by Ty's expression he wasn't considering it a compliment.

"Change ain't always good," he said. "It's just different."

"That must be the truck they were talking about."

Ty nodded, looking as if he'd just about reached his social interaction limits. "That's Em's."

"It doesn't run?"

"It's spotty at best."

They stepped outside and glanced across the yard. Max Barrenger was just firing up his shiny Escalade when Emily descended the porch steps, Baby Bliss cuddled against her shoulder.

"He must be helping her with her deliveries this morning," Sophie said and wondered dismally where that left her mother.

"Looks like it," Ty agreed.

"How long will they be gone?" Lincoln's brows lowered over gunmetal eyes as he watched the trio by the Escalade.

Ty shifted his attention back to their strangely curious guest. "There's always *someone* 'round the Lazy."

Their gazes met, gray on amber. "Good to know," he said and strode stiff and silent across the yard toward the bunkhouse.

"What have we learned about that Lincoln guy?" Sophie asked. Her mother was asleep upstairs, allowing her jittery stomach a temporary reprieve. She tentatively tasted a chunk of rutabaga she'd been chopping. It wasn't awful.

At eleven fifteen Casie was busy slicing beef into tiny morsels. Emily had returned from making her deliveries two hours before and was dicing onions just a few inches away. She shrugged.

Lumpkin pranced through the room, dark hooves shiny, tiny diaper askew.

"You didn't check him out?"

"Maybe you haven't noticed, but I've been kind of busy." Emily's voice was waspish. Sophie glanced at Casie, who raised her brows a tad. Everyone knew which of them had been designated Wicked Witch of the West. Give Sophie a pair of striped tights and pointy shoes and she'd have to keep a weather eye out for falling houses.

"I didn't mean you *should* have," Casie said. "It's just that you usually do. It's like having our very own bloodhound."

"Sorry," Emily said, but she didn't expound.

"You don't have to be sorry." Casie's voice was quiet and typically upbeat. "I'm sure he's a perfectly nice guy."

"I think he's weird," Sophie said, remembering the conversation in the barn.

"Weird how?" Casie asked and watched as Lumpkin made a dramatic twist in the air and tore off toward the living room.

"Snooping around," Sophie said. "Asking a lot of questions."

Casie shrugged. "He's from the city. He's probably just curious about how we live. That's part of the appeal of the Lazy, I guess. To see a different way of life and—"

"Sophie's right. We should get rid of him," Emily interrupted. They turned toward her in tandem surprise.

"What happened to 'Trust your neighbor but brand your calves'?" Casie asked. It was something Ty had said on more than one occasion.

"I thought we needed the money," Sophie added.

"We don't need it *that* bad," Emily said, and setting the onions aside, quickly wiped her hands on a washcloth. "Let's just give him his deposit back."

"Are you kidding me?" Casie asked. "We can't do that."

"Of course we can."

"We don't have any *reason* to do that. Do we?" Casie asked and peered carefully into Emily's face.

There was a long moment of silence, then, "No," she admitted. "But that's just it. When I Googled Lincoln Alexander, all I came up with was a ninety-year-old politician and a toddler who can play 'Chopsticks' with his toes."

"I would have guessed he was somewhere in between those two ages," Casie said.

Sophie didn't even bother to give her a look. "Did you try Facebook?"

"Of course I tried Facebook. You think I'd eschew the most irritating of all social media?"

"Excuse *me*," Sophie said, but Emily's shoulders drooped.

"I just . . . I don't trust him, that's all."

"Why?" Casie's voice was concerned, her expression solemn.

"Because . . ." Emily shook her head as if at a loss. "*Lincoln Alexander?* That doesn't even sound like a real name. And why is he asking so many questions?"

"He's asking you questions, too?"

She winced. "No, but . . ." Pursing her lips, she hammered away at a chicken breast. "You know who doesn't show up in a search?"

"People who think their lives are nobody else's business?" Casie guessed.

"Criminals!" Emily corrected. "Murderers, rapists, arsonists, embezzlers—"

"Emily . . ." Casie said, interrupting quietly. "If you know something about—"

"Thieves," she added. Her voice had gone soft.

Casie glanced sideways as the lamb trotted through with a sock in her mouth. Sophie shrugged. Casie tried again. "If you knew anything about this guy, you'd tell us, wouldn't you?"

"I'm not a thief!" Emily said. Her face looked unusually pale, her eyes tortured. "Not anymore," she added, and tossing the washcloth onto the counter, rushed from the room.

The kitchen went quiet. Casie exhaled slowly. "Do you have any idea what that was about?"

"Insanity?" Sophie guessed.

"I'm serious."

"So am I," Sophie said and returned to chopping vegetables. "Speaking of which . . ." She drew a careful breath, wondering if she was even close to sounding casual. "How long have you known my mother was planning to come?"

The air around her seemed to tighten. She felt rather than saw Casie turn toward her.

"I'm sorry about that, Soph." The words were very quiet. "She asked Colt not to tell you."

"How long?"

"She called last night."

"Figures," she said and callously decapitated a carrot. "Something must have fallen through."

"What do you mean?"

She shrugged. The movement almost hurt. "Her current *amour* must have had other plans."

"I'm sure she just missed you and—"

"Of course she missed me. She always misses me. Who wouldn't?" she asked, and because she needed something to do with her hands, scooped up the chopped vegetables and dumped them into the nearby pot. It steamed and splashed.

"People make mistakes, Soph. Your mother's probably no exception. But she's here now."

Sophie glanced toward the stairs above which Monica Day-Bellaire was sleeping. "I know she's here," she said. "In *my* bed."

"I'm sorry," Casie said again, and lowering her voice even more, glanced guiltily toward the doorway. "I didn't know what to do with her."

Sophie deepened her glare, but it was almost impossible to be angry with Casie Carmichael. That was probably the most irritating thing about her. Letting her shoulders drop a little, she forced out a hard exhalation. "Welcome to my world," she said.

Casie scowled a question.

Reticence seemed like a wise course, but maybe it was too late for that. "She's always been . . ." She shook her head, searching for words. "Bigger than life. Jetting off to Istanbul, dissertating in Luxembourg, skiing in Zermatt. But she was never able to just be . . ." She winced at her own words. Was her tone as whiny as it seemed? "I know I shouldn't complain. I mean, Ty's mom . . ." She picked up the cleaver again, gripping it hard, but still she couldn't force out any more words.

"We're all disappointed in our parents to some degree," Casie said.

"Colt's not," she argued, somehow managing to sound even more childish.

"Well, Colt was such a little—" Casie began, then stopped herself.

Sophie raised her brows, intrigued. "Such a little what?" she asked, but the other woman had returned to vigorously slicing beef.

"He was lucky his parents didn't turn him loose with the coyotes."

Sophie felt a smile tug her lips a little. "Ty thinks Monty Dickenson's a saint," she said, but Casie didn't seem to notice.

"How could he have fit inside?" Casie's voice was very small.

"What?" Sophie asked.

"My locker," she said, seeming to come out of her trance a little. "Did you know a sophomore boy can fit inside a regular-sized school locker?"

Sophie had seen such antics in movies, but *she* didn't seem to be the type of girl who prompted that kind of behavior even if she *had* been sent to public school.

"I was in a hurry between classes," Casie said. "Had to get to chemistry. God forbid I made the teachers the least bit unhappy. Had to earn A's. Had to . . ." She paused. "I actually felt my heart stop when he jumped out."

"Then what happened?"

"He laughed."

"Did you hit him?"

"No," she said, sounding disappointed. "He was too low."

"Mentally or—"

"Physically," she said. "He had fallen on the floor laughing. Literally fallen on the floor." She narrowed her eyes. "So I kicked him."

"You what?" She was trying to imagine the scenario. But honestly, Casie Carmichael was the least aggressive person she had ever known. Usually, anyway.

"It was the first and last time I ever saw the inside of the principal's office."

"What happened to Colt?"

"He had to go to detention. But he didn't care. He was such a . . ." She ground her teeth and stopped herself. "What I'm saying is . . ." She shook her head as if trying to remember where their conversation had taken a wrong turn. "Parents make mistakes. But your mom's here now."

"I wish she wasn't." It was more honest than she had meant to be, but the words slipped out unbidden.

"She's trying, Soph," Casie said. "Maybe you should, too."

The kitchen went quiet. Sophie released a long breath. "I don't know if I can."

Casie glanced at her, brows half lifted in a knowing expression. "If you can train a thousand pounds of recalcitrant equine to pull a sled, you can do this."

"Horses don't jet off to Zurich and miss the piano recital you've practiced for since June."

"Not generally," Casie agreed. "But they don't usually catch the red-eye back to Nowhere, South Dakota, to spend the holidays with their daughters, either. Keep that in mind, huh?"

Lumpkin pranced up, tinsel gleaming shiny as a tiara between her woolly ears.

Sophie sighed and reached for the lambkin, who bleated cheerfully. "If she can forgive *her* mom, maybe I should be able to, too," she admitted.

And on the stairs nearby, Monica Day-Bellaire hoped it was true.

CHAPTER 17

"That was literally the best meal I've ever eaten," Max Barrenger said. Beside him, his carefully groomed fiancée smiled, but her expression seemed a little tight.

"I've never believed that old axiom that the best way to a man's heart is through his stomach," she said. "But I'm starting to see the error of my ways." She patted Max's slightly protruding belly. "I may have to get some of your recipes, Emily."

"And do what with them?" Max asked and laughed. "Use them as coasters?"

Casie watched as Sonata raised her brows.

Emily pushed nervously to her feet. "It's just because the ingredients are so fresh," she said.

"Believe me, that's not all it is," Max argued. "But S. has an interesting idea. Have you ever considered writing a cookbook? I think it could be a big hit."

"It would never work," Colt said.

Max scowled at him, giving off the slightest whiff of antagonism. "Why's that?"

"Em doesn't use recipes. Her meals never taste the same twice."

There were four men around the table; Ty and Colt watched Emily with protective zeal, Lincoln and Max with unconcealed interest. What did the girl have that drew men like fruit flies? True, she could make ambrosia from a pint of manure dust and a dollop of vinegar. But she wasn't exactly beautiful in the traditional sense. Not like Sophie. Casie let her gaze drift to the younger girl for a second, then glanced back at Emily. Perhaps it was because Em truly didn't know she possessed that indefinable spark that drew people to her. Whatever it was, Casie was jealous. It was as simple and as demented as that.

She bit off her bad karma and reminded herself that she truly loved Emily. It was Colt who made her crazy. Him and his grin and his grasshoppers and his oddly flexible body. She would have been better off if she'd never opened her locker door, she thought, and almost smiled at the idea of him hunkered down in the dark after the last cheerleader went home.

"Recipe or not," said Monica Day-Bellaire breezily, "it was a wonderful meal."

"Thank you," Emily said. Her cheeks were a little rosy, either from the heat of the kitchen or from the flattery. She looked flustered, making Casie wonder if perhaps she had read the girl wrong from the very beginning. Maybe it wasn't simply that she longed to impress *men*. Maybe she needed to impress adults regardless of their gender. Abandonment, she thought . . . not a fantastic idea. "But you haven't tasted dessert yet. There's rhubarb crisp and suet pudding. Which would you prefer?"

"Oh, dear," Monica said, "I'm participating in a symposium with a group of my fellows in two weeks and I must—" she began, then glanced toward Sophie and stopped herself. Her mouth softened, and her shoulders dropped a quarter of an inch. "Never mind," she said and, laughing, shrugged disarmingly. "I'll have a piece of each."

The rest of the meal passed quickly. Lincoln Alexander left the table first. The door opened and closed almost silently behind him. Ty and Colt returned to the Red Horse soon after. Casie ran warm water into the kitchen sink and tried to pretend she didn't even notice their leaving.

"Well, I'm going to hit the proverbial hay early," Sonata said and rose lithely to her feet before glancing down at her fiancé. "Are you coming?"

He pulled his attentive gaze from Emily. "I think I'll stay and nurse my coffee for a little bit longer."

Her brows dipped a little toward her carefully made up eyes. "You're just hoping for another piece of rhubarb crisp."

"Actually, I prefer the pudding," he said, and lifting his empty plate, gave Emily a hopeful glance.

Sonata made a little snort of disgust. "I thought we were going snowshoeing in the morning."

"That's just it," Max said. "If we're going to be trekking through the wilderness, I want to make sure I have enough energy to save you when we're accosted by grizzlies."

"You think another six hundred calories is going to help you fend off wild animals?"

He shrugged. "We don't want to take any risks."

She rolled her eyes and headed for the door. "You have your key with you, don't you?"

"I think we're safe out here, S.," he assured her.

She gave him a tilted glance. "Just don't wake me when you come in," she said and took some of the tension with her when she left.

Monica Day-Bellaire rose to her feet. "How about if Sophia and I do the dishes?"

"Oh no," Casie argued and slipped another plate into the warm water. "You're on vacation."

"It's a vacation just to be here," she said.

"Honestly, I like this job. It helps me warm up."

"Well . . ." Monica turned toward her daughter. "Maybe you could show me the stables then."

"They're not stables. They're just—" Sophie began, but Casie shifted her gaze surreptitiously toward the girl, who stopped in her verbal tracks and pursed her lips.

"You don't have the proper clothes," she said.

"What clothes do I need?"

"Something that wasn't purchased in Milan." Sophie's tone was punctuated by disdain and maybe a dash of almost indistinguishable pride.

"She can wear my overalls if she wants," Casie said, and Sophie laughed.

"I doubt—" she began, but Monica stopped her.

"That would be wonderful."

Even Sophie Jaegar, blasé soul that she was, couldn't quite hide her shock, but she bumped her expression quickly back to one of nonchalance.

In a matter of minutes they were out the door.

Casie exchanged a sideways glance with Emily, who shook her head once.

"I take it those two aren't exactly BFFs," Max said, watching them from his kitchen chair.

Casie sighed. "They're trying."

"There you go." Emily set a bowl of suet pudding in front of him. "The stuff grizzly fighters are made of."

"You're a lifesaver," he said.

"I might be the opposite."

He closed his eyes and made a dreamy noise as he tasted his first bite. "How do you mean? This stuff is heavenly."

"Far be it from me to discourage anyone from appreciating my desserts," she said, "but there are about five thousand fat grams per serving. One more bowl and your heart is likely to drop from your chest cavity into your shoes."

He laughed. "I think we might want to try a little different angle when we market it."

"Don't be ridiculous," she said, but her eyes looked happy.

"I don't think you realize your own worth, Emily."

"Oh, I'm aware," she said. "It's about a hundred and twelve dollars after my last stellar purchase."

"Which was . . ."

"The truck."

"Shrewd move," he said and took another bite.

"I'm full of them," she assured him, and taking a large covered bowl from the refrigerator, dumped the contents onto the flour-sprinkled counter. In a moment she was kneading the dough with rhythmic cadence, dark knuckles caressing and punishing.

Taking his dessert with him, Max rose to lean his hips against the counter and watch her work. He took another bite. "I'm telling you, Em, you could make a fortune. I know a little something about big business."

She narrowed her eyes as if considering. "I think I'm probably more of a small business–type of girl."

"But you have a baby to think about now. It'd be shortsighted to turn down a possible fortune."

She shrugged. Her cadenced kneading was strangely soothing.

"Tell her, Casie," he said, but just then Bliss gave a small mew of despair.

Elbow deep in dough, Emily glanced up.

"I got her," Casie said and hurried into the living room.

The voices behind her murmured on as she bent over the ancient bassinet.

Inside, Bliss blinked up at her, dark eyes wide with infantile wisdom.

"Hey," Casie said and lifted the baby from her blankets. "What's going on?"

The tiny mouth lifted into a cheeky grin.

"Your momma's in there stealing hearts . . . or stomachs," she said and wiggled the infant, prompting a wider smile. The feelings perpetrated by that silly expression were indescribable, making Casie wonder where she had gone wrong. Or had she gone right? Maybe this was what she was meant to do . . . live independently, give others a chance to get their lives on track, to gain perspective and mend fences. It could seem like a lonely life to some, but her track record with men suggested she might be better off alone.

She ruminated on that while she changed Bliss's diaper and snapped her onesie back in place. After rinsing the cloth in the toilet, she dropped it in the stainless-steel bucket and propped Bliss back against her shoulder. The baby felt soft and substantial against her chest, life in bloom. She closed her eyes to the poignant feelings for a moment, then bumped herself out of her reverie and marched back into the kitchen, where Emily was folding the dough into a long, fat roll. The smell of warm butter and cinnamon drifted cozily into the air.

"You wouldn't be *just* an overseer," Max was saying. "You could cook as much as you like. That's the beauty of it. You'd have all the time you wanted to experiment instead of—

"Ohhhh," he sighed as he caught sight of Bliss. "Look at *her.*" He shook his head as he put his bowl on the counter. "She gets cuter every time I see her. Just like her mama."

"Can you hold her for another minute?" Emily asked, glancing at Casie. "I'm almost done."

"Here, let me have her," Max said, and wiping his hands on his designer jeans, reached for the baby. Bliss eyed him critically as he held her out in front of him. "Wouldn't she be the perfect face for a baby food jar?"

"Baby food!" Emily said and laughed.

Max joined in. "Okay, maybe I'm getting ahead of myself. It will be a strictly adult menu for now . . . with a picture of you *and* Bliss on the label."

"You *are* a dreamer," Emily chuckled, but Casie couldn't ignore the fact that her tone wasn't altogether dismissive.

"Never underestimate the power of dreams," Max said.

The front door opened. Monica Day-Bellaire's voice was soft from the entryway. "So you're breaking the palomino all by yourself?"

"I think she had quite a bit of training before she came here," Sophie said. Her voice was still cool, but it had lost that caustic edge it so often used to contain, and was buffered by the sheen of excitement she always exhibited when talking about horses. "I'm just continuing her education. She's super-intelligent."

"And so beautiful. Palominos have always been my favorite."

"Since when did you have a favorite horse?" Sophie asked.

"I was a girl once, too," Monica said. "You know that, right?"

Sophie didn't respond for a moment.

Monica laughed. "I wasn't always a stodgy old psychiatrist," she said. "Hey, you know what would be great?" Her tone was bright with excitement. "If we bought a farm somewhere."

Casie shot her gaze toward Emily, who glanced back, eyes wide and brows winging toward her hairline.

"What?" Sophie's voice was very soft.

Casie returned her attention to Bliss. The baby looked perfectly content cuddled against Max's shoulder, and in that second, it dawned on her that her whole house of cards could crumble to nothing in less than a heartbeat.

"I don't mean an establishment this big," Monica said. "Just something small. How many acres would you need for, say . . ." She paused. "A herd of fifteen?"

"Fifteen?" There was an awed breathiness to Sophie's voice.

"Well sure. I mean, you'd want enough space to take in animals that have been neglected or abused. But you'd have to promise never to steal another horse."

"I didn't *steal* Freedom . . . exactly."

"Oh, Sophia, I just can't tell you how wonderful it is to spend time with you again."

"Yeah." The girl's tone was iffy but stronger. "It's great."

"Come on," said the older woman, "let's go see if there's any dessert left."

A moment later they stepped back into the kitchen. Sophie's cheeks were flushed from the chill outside air. But maybe there was something else that made her face pink and her eyes bright. And maybe that something sparked an ache in the middle of Casie's chest. What would she give to have one more day with her own mother?

"Cassandra . . ." Monica said, voice exuberant. "Join us for a second dessert?"

Casie's stomach twisted with something oddly akin to jealousy, and for one fragile moment she was poised on the brink of telling her that some people didn't deserve second chances, didn't deserve families and fortunes and prestigious careers. But just then the phone rang.

"Sorry," she apologized and lifted the receiver from the jack on the wall before stepping into the hall so as not to disturb the others.

"Hello?"

"Is this the Lazy Windmill?"

"Yes. Sorry." She'd not only forgotten her professional salutation but the appropriate upbeat tone. What would this place be like without Emily to keep them all on track? "This is the Lazy Windmill. Can I help you?"

"I hope so." The voice on the other end of the line paused for a second, as if the speaker was gathering her strength. "I can't think of a thing to get my sister for Christmas."

Casie scowled, moved a little farther into the hall, and plugged her free ear with the pad of her index finger to drown out the laughter that bubbled from the kitchen.

"I'm sorry, I'm not sure what—"

"She's been a little . . . blue. I thought it might be a good idea to get her out of the city. I'm thinking maybe she'd enjoy some time on a ranch somewhere. She's good with . . ." She paused. "She's always liked horses."

"That's very nice of you. When were you thinking?"

"Do you have any openings for the middle of January?"

Laughter rang in the kitchen. Casie glanced inside. The people gathered there could have been on a movie poster, beautiful, happy, and bursting with possibilities. Emily was chuckling. Even Sophie was smiling. Casie felt her heart lurch. The way things were going, the Lazy could be entirely empty by New Year's.

CHAPTER 18

"Hey."

Ty jerked toward the noise issuing from the dim depths behind him. Though the building was referred to as the cattle barn, the south end housed enough rusty equipment to make a redneck hoarder jealous. Lincoln Alexander stepped out from behind Emily's ancient Dodge.

"Sorry." His brows were low over winter-sky eyes. He thrust his hands deep into the pockets of his sweatshirt. "Didn't mean to startle you."

Ty lowered his head. Fear made him angry; he was angry a fair amount. "What are you doing out here?"

The older boy lifted one boxy shoulder. "Just looking over that old truck."

Ty's first instinct was to remind him that the Dodge was none of his business, but that's not how Casie would handle the situation. Come to that, neither would Colt. *Monty* Dickenson, however, had once told him to speak his mind and ride a fast horse. But Ty had learned early on that sometimes there wasn't no horse fast enough. "How come?" he asked.

Lincoln shrugged. "It's a classic."

Ty didn't respond. Even under normal circumstances, he rarely had a clue what was expected of him. Since Monica Day-Bellaire's arrival at the Lazy, he'd felt as if his tongue were looped in a hangman's knot. Worry rolled from Sophie like stink off a pig, and he had no idea what to do about it.

Lincoln shifted his slight weight. "I was wondering if you'd mind if I tinker with it some."

Ty stared at him. "It ain't my truck."

The other boy glanced toward the house and shuffled his feet a little. He wore black high-tops with white laces, shoes reminiscent of the fifties' shows Em favored. His jeans rode low on his hips. And his sweatshirt wasn't thick enough to do much of anything in these inhospitable temperatures. Maybe in L.A. he would have looked cool and felt warm. In South Dakota he looked like a frozen nut-job. "Maybe I could get it running."

Ty scowled. "Why would you wanna do that? It ain't your truck." His words sounded too aggressive. Not what Casie would want. He backed off a little. "You're a guest. You don't owe us nothing."

A tendon jumped in the other's throat, testament to tension or anger. Ty wasn't sure which. "What do *you* owe them?"

"What?"

"This isn't your place, either."

Ty lifted his chin a little, fighting unacceptable emotions. "What are you getting at?"

"I'm wondering what keeps you here, working like a slave."

"I don't work no harder than anybody else."

"You must be getting *something* out of it." He narrowed his eyes a little more. His thin lips turned down at the corners. "Or maybe you're just *hoping* to."

Ty squared his shoulders. "I don't know what you're talking about."

"Maybe you think this stuff *should* be yours."

"What stuff?"

The other boy glanced toward the house, teeth gritted. "The sun hasn't even thought about getting up yet, but you're out here . . ." He waved toward the two horses that occupied the stalls. "Slopping muck. Either you're trying awful hard to impress someone or you've got something planned. I'm just wondering which it is."

Ty felt his face flush. He didn't roll out of bed at five thirty every morning to impress anybody, he told himself, but Sophie's lost-girl eyes flashed into his mind. He pushed away the mental images. "That ain't none of your business."

"You're not her type. She—" Lincoln began, then drew a deep breath, shook his head, and glanced toward the stalls again. "How's that old horse doing, anyway?"

Ty scowled, trying to keep up. No one had to tell him that Sophie Jaegar was light-years out of his league, but who was this city dude to weigh in on the situation? "What you talking about now?"

"The horse with the bad feet."

"Angel?"

"Yeah, I guess. How's she doing?"

" 'Bout the same as usual," Ty said and turned away, but Lincoln stopped him with a raised hand, then hurried off in the opposite direction. In a moment he had returned. "I was thinking this might help," he said and held up an odd mesh structure shaped into a rough oval.

"What's that?"

Lincoln deepened his scowl and handed it over. "It's a horseshoe."

"No, it ain't."

The high-tops shuffled.

"It's big as a barrel," Ty added.

"Well, her feet hurt, right?"

"Yeah."

"So maybe if her weight was distributed over a larger area, it would get rid of some of the pain."

Ty scowled and hoisted the odd metal in his hand. It felt as light as thistledown. "What's it made of?"

"Nickel phosphorus tubes."

Ty lifted it closer to his face. "Don't look like tubes."

"They're small, mostly air. It's what makes them so light."

"Where'd you get it?"

"I brought it with me."

"Why?"

Lincoln shrugged and shoved his right hand into his pocket

again. His left looked chapped and cold. "I like experimenting with stuff."

"Don't you have nothing better to do?"

He hunched his shoulders. "Listen, if you don't want my help, you can just say so."

Ty shifted his weight and glanced toward Angel. She bobbed her head over her stall door, impatient for breakfast. "I can't pay you nothing."

The wintry eyes were steady. "Let me work on the truck."

Why the hell was he so fired up about that damned truck? It wasn't worth a hill of beans. "Like I said, that ain't my decision."

"You're her friend, right?"

"She's . . ." His stomach tightened as he thought about how Emily looked with Bliss in her arms. How she made Casie laugh. How she made the Lazy feel like home. "Yeah," he said. "I guess."

"Then she probably won't make a fuss if you ask her."

"Why do you want to—"

"Just ask her," he said, and snatching the metal oval from Ty's hand, hurried stiffly from the barn.

"Hey, Ty," Emily said. She looked sweet and young as she glanced over her shoulder at him, the exact picture that had made his stomach queasy only a half hour before. Bliss's fuzzy head lay against her chest. "Want some coffee?"

He nodded and moved toward the counter, but she had already poured him a cup. It felt warm and friendly as he wrapped his chilled fingers around it. He nodded toward the tiny bundle slumped in her arms. "She keep you up again?"

Emily smiled, eyes tired. "Sleep's overrated."

He didn't necessarily think that was true. His room at the Red Horse was as pink as an antacid tablet, and there was still a My Little Pony poster on the wall beside the window, but the bed was soft and the space his own. He'd never admit to anyone how much he loved that room. "Maybe I could make your deliveries today."

Her grin amped up a notch. Mischief lit her eyes. There wasn't no one like Em to upend the ugly side of life and see the funny underneath. "It's a long ways on horseback," she quipped.

He shook his head at her. "I have my farm permit."

"But nothing to drive."

Disappointment coiled in his stomach. He glanced out the kitchen window. Being a burden was getting pretty damned old.

"But hey, walking's eco-friendly, right?" she said, and after dipping a piece of bread into a bowl, dropped it into a hot skillet where it sizzled happily.

"Maybe Casie wouldn't mind if I borrowed Puke," Ty said, stomach queasy at the thought of asking for favors.

"You're kidding me, right?" she asked and faced him square on.

"I've drove it before."

She stared at him, then laughed and shook her head. "Ty, Casie would lend you her *liver*."

"What are you talking about?"

She raised one brow. "You gotta know she thinks you walk on water."

He felt his face heat up, felt his chest swell and his psyche crumble. Yeah, he was pretty sure Casie thought well of him, but he was absolutely *certain* he didn't deserve it. "I don't know what you mean."

She stared at him, then shook her head. "Tyler James Roberts," she said. "When are you going to realize you're the best thing that ever happened to this place?"

The bile in his stomach turned to turpentine. In the past, he had combated taunts with aggression or silence. Neither had improved his life much. Still, words could hurt more than bare knuckles to the face. "It ain't nice to tease, Em."

She chuckled, eyes steady with a softness that confused him. "Someday you'll know your worth." She hefted the baby a little. "Can you hold her for a minute?"

He set his coffee mug aside, trying to battle the uncertainty in his soul as he reached for little Bliss. She sighed, soft as a bunny as she snuggled against his shoulder. Dandelion-down feelings settled over his being, tightened his throat, stung his eyes.

"What have you been doing out there?" she asked. The sun had not yet risen, but he wasn't the only one who was awake, he thought, and remembered his conversation with Lincoln Alexander.

He shrugged. "I like to get Chester's pen cleaned up first thing."

"Colt could do it," she said and added three more slices of French toast to the pan.

"It ain't his job," Tyler said.

"No," she agreed, "it's Casie's." She tilted her head a little. "Or Soph's."

He felt his cheeks heat up. "That colt can get a little rank sometimes. I feel better knowing the job's done before I head out."

She stared at him again. Such direct attention always made him feel itchy. "I'll try to stand by with a boat," she said.

"What're you talking about?" he asked and stroked Bliss's back when she mewled.

"In case the water gets too rough for walking on."

He scowled and reached for his coffee to hide the heat in his cheeks.

She smiled. "I'd be jealous as heck if . . ." She paused, shrugged one shoulder. "Ah, fudge, who am I kidding?" She flipped a piece of bread. "I *am* jealous as heck."

He felt his heart lurch. What were the chances that in six months' time he would meet so many people who made life worth living?

"Oh, don't look so hangdog," she said and laughed. "Hey, did you know that Mr. Barrenger wants to market my recipes?"

"What?" He paused with his mug halfway to his lips.

"Sit down," she said and motioned to a chair. He did as told. "He thinks he can make me a brand name. Put my products on grocery shelves from sea to shining sea."

"Is that what you want?"

She flipped another piece of toast. The scents of nutmeg and tranquility filled the kitchen. "Who doesn't want to be rich?"

It was a question he had never contemplated. "Would you have to leave the Lazy?"

"I'd need more room than we have here to experiment with new recipes and stuff. He says he could build me a state-of-the-art kitchen."

"I thought him and that lady were pretty serious."

"Sonata? Of course." She looked surprised and a little insulted. "They're engaged." She flipped three pieces of toast in rapid succession. "What does that have to do with anything?"

He watched her closely. Her movements seemed jittery, her body tense as she sprinkled the bread with cinnamon and sugar. "Seems to me a man don't go hunting deer when he's got venison cooking at home."

She stared at him a silent moment, then laughed. "You've got this all wrong. There's nothing going on here."

"Then why's he driving you all over the county?"

"He's a nice guy," she said and placed his breakfast ceremoniously in front of him before taking Bliss from his arms.

He kept his gaze centered on hers. "Even a snake can say please."

"I don't even know what that means," she said and sat down across from him.

He frowned. "I don't want you getting hurt no more, is all. You gotta think of the baby."

"I *am* thinking about the baby. I don't do anything *but* think of the baby. That's why I have to make some money."

"You *are* making money."

She made a dismissive sound.

"More's not always better, Em," he said.

She shook her head. "Like you and I would know that." Her words drilled painfully through him, reminding him of his past, of his family. Shame and regret and guilt all in one ugly muddle.

He cut into his breakfast. Dakota toast, she called it. "I'd just feel better if you had your own truck."

"I do," she said. "But as it turns out it's too old to be modern art and too big for a paperweight."

"Maybe we can get it running."

"You and I?" she asked.

He shrugged, not exactly sure where he was going with this. Maybe he was being selfish. Maybe he just wanted to convince her so that Lincoln Alexander would continue with Angel's shoes. In retrospect, oversized lightweight plates might be just what the doctor failed to order. He glanced up at her. "That guy, Lincoln Alexander, he said he'd like to fiddle with it some."

"When did you talk to him?"

He raised his head at her strange tone. "You don't like him?"

"No! I mean . . . I don't know if I like him or not. I don't know him."

"Then what's the problem?"

"I don't take favors."

He stopped chewing, swallowed. "You messing with me?"

"No, I'm not. . . . Okay, so I've accepted a few favors from Casie."

He stared at her.

"And Colt. And his folks and Mrs. French and Mr. Sommers and . . . The point is," she said, interrupting herself with a scowl. "I don't trust him."

"Why not?"

"What's he doing here?" she asked and leaned forward with sudden zeal. "Does he look like a country boy to you?"

"No. But lots of our guests look as city as traffic lights. Mr. Barrenger don't exactly make me think of longhorns and wide-open spaces."

"At least he's got the boots."

Thinking of those shiny alligator boots made Ty cock his head in question.

She had the courtesy to look chagrined. "Okay, that's not a good example. But he *enjoys* country life. Alexander doesn't even pretend to be interested in . . ." She waved her free hand. "Anything."

"He says he just needs some time away."

"Away from what? We don't know anything about him. Maybe he's planning to rob us blind."

"Seems like we're pretty near-sighted already, Em."

She stared at him a second, then snorted but didn't give up. "I think he's after something."

"Like what?"

"Something valuable. Maybe something we don't know about."

"If we don't know about it, how would he?"

"Casie lived in Saint Paul for years. It could be her old man hid something on the ranch while she was gone. And . . ." She shook her head, thinking. "You know how small towns are. Maybe rumors got around. Maybe . . ." She stopped. "Maybe there's nothing. Maybe he just *thinks* there's something and he's trying to find it."

"Well, how 'bout we let him fix your truck while he searches?"

She scowled. He watched her.

"What's going on, Em?" he asked.

"Nothing."

"You're sure you don't know him . . . from before or something?"

Her expression was somber now, her eyes earnest. "I'm very sure."

"Then why not let him fiddle with your truck? He's only gonna be here a little while. Why not—"

"That's another thing! What nineteen-year-old can afford our rates?"

"He's nineteen?"

She blinked at him. "I don't know how old he is. How would *I* know? And why are you drilling me, anyway?"

He raised his brows at her tone. "He don't look old enough to tie his own shoes. That's all."

"Oh, well . . . I asked him his age . . . just to make conversation. He said he'll be twenty on the third of February. Do you believe that?"

He shrugged. "Why not?"

"That's my mom's birthday. I don't trust anyone with those stats."

He was quiet for a moment, thinking back. Maybe he hadn't exactly gotten the pick of the litter when it came to parents, but at least they had kept a roof over his head. Yeah, his mom had been as unpredictable as a rattler, but she hadn't abandoned him completely. "I'm sorry, Em," he said.

"She refused to tell me who my dad was. Said she didn't know." Her tone was reflective. "But I think she was lying. Barry, boyfriend number eighteen, had droopy earlobes. Especially the left one. His was pierced."

He stared at her.

"My earlobes droop, too," she said, coming to the point suddenly. "I mean . . . not that it matters. I don't need a father, but sometimes it'd be nice to have some clue about the other half of your DNA."

Melancholy washed through him. She didn't deserve to be alone. If anyone should have good in her life it was Emily. She was tough and creative and . . . His thoughts stopped. She *was* tough. And she *was* creative. Creative about everything. Especially lying. And when she lied, she thought it most effective if she elaborated. She had told him that herself.

He settled his fork against the edge of his plate. "You can tell me the truth, Em," he said. "And you don't have to change the subject. If you don't want that Lincoln fellow messing with your truck, I'll just tell him no."

"You think I'm lying?" Her tone was breathy.

He said nothing.

"I thought we were friends," she said. There was pain and disappointment in her tone. He was pretty sure it was real.

"I thought we were, too, Em." He said the words with gut-wrenching slowness. She stared at him, eyes bright.

"Fine. That's fine then. You want him to play around with

the truck, go ahead and let him," she said and hugging the baby to her shoulder, disappeared up the stairs.

Sophie appeared a couple seconds later. "What was that about?" she asked.

He glanced up at her. Her hair was as sleek and smooth as a thoroughbred's, her lavender pullover and dark jeans freshly washed and perfectly fitted. But it was her eyes that always stopped him dead. Her better-than-thou eyes that begged for acceptance. That begged to be worthy. It was a dichotomy he could neither understand nor ignore.

"I ain't sure."

She poured herself a mug of coffee and curled her hand around the heat of it. Her nails were trim and clean, her fingers slim.

"What do you think about that Lincoln guy?" he asked. Her eyes were as green as summer above the edge of her ceramic mug.

"You know me," she said. Her lips twisted a little. She didn't smile often, but when she did, he felt it like an anvil on his chest. "I don't like anyone."

"That ain't true."

Their gazes met. His heart stuttered.

"You like Casie," he added.

She nodded, all humor gone from her wide, save-me eyes. "Casie and—" she began, but just then Monica Day-Bellaire breezed into the kitchen.

"Good lord, it's freezing in here." She rubbed her hands together. "Look at you," she said, smiling at her daughter. "You're the spitting image of your grandmother at her first cotillion. Sometimes I think I did you a terrible disservice by taking you out of that world. But . . ." She brightened. "You could slip back into it any day if—"

"Mother!" Sophie said. Her tone was raspy. "Ty was just asking me what I thought of Lincoln Alexander."

"Oh!" Monica Day-Bellaire said and turned with guilty surprise to stare across the table at him. "I'm so sorry. I didn't even know you were here. But you can hardly blame me. I haven't seen my daughter in ages. And she's so beautiful, isn't she?"

"Mother!" Sophie said. Her cheeks were flushed, but Ty knew he should be the one who blushed. He had no right to think about her like he did. She was beauty and brilliance and old money.

He was nothing more than a dirt farmer's son.

"Excuse me," he said and bumbled, hapless, to his feet. "I got work to do."

CHAPTER 19

Emily glanced up from rolling out piecrusts when Casie entered the kitchen. Lumpkin jumped up from her blanket near the stove, floppy ears bouncing as she trotted toward the door. Bliss slept soundly in her backpack. "Where've you been all day?"

"The water tank in the cattle pasture froze," Casie explained. The weather had taken a turn for the worse. "Took me half the morning to get it chopped out." Bending, she lifted the lamb from the floor. "Is it feeding time?"

"Isn't it always?"

The woolly infant bobbled excitedly as Casie dumped powdered milk into a bowl.

"Did you get that tank taken care of?"

Casie shook her head as she set the baby back on the floor where it nosed her pant leg and wildly waggled its tail. "I went to town to buy a new heater, got the wrong kind, went back to town, ordered the right one." She sighed as she whisked the milk. "I was hoping to get the tack room finished before the next guest arrives."

"We *have* a next guest?"

"Didn't I tell you?"

"I barely know we have *any* guests."

"How do you mean?"

"No one showed up for dinner. I kept it warm until two."

"You're kidding."

She shook her head. "Sophie and her mom went shopping in Rapid City. I guess they won't be back until tomorrow."

"Oh." Casie's voice was quiet, her tone solemn.

"Don't," Emily said, not looking up as she placed a piecrust in the waiting tin.

"Don't what?"

"Don't feel sorry for me."

"I'm not. I just—"

"I don't need a mother," she said and bounced, gently jostling Bliss, though she hadn't made so much as a peep in over an hour. "I *am* a mother. And maybe the luckiest person in the world."

"I wasn't feeling sorry for you," Casie repeated, but she was going to need a lot more lying practice. "If you had any more men in love with you, they'd have to take numbers and stand in line."

Emily snorted. "Ain't that the truth? Everybody's jonesing for a mixed-race hippie girl and her bastard baby."

"I've noticed that myself."

"Yeah?" Emily didn't like to admit it, but she was feeling a little alone, a little self-pitying, a little pathetic. "Name one."

"Colt," Casie said and poured the reconstituted milk into its waiting bottle. "He thinks you're the Virgin Mary and Julia Childs all rolled into one."

She laughed. "If you weren't so demented, you and Mr. Dickenson would have your two-point-five children and a minivan by now."

"Don't be ridiculous."

Emily turned on her, half angry, half appalled. "Seriously?"

"What?"

"Are you honestly trying to tell me that you don't know how he feels about you?"

Casie chuckled as she lifted the lamb back into her arms, but her expression was strained. "*Colt* doesn't even know how he feels about me. He just . . ." She shook her head. "Wants what he can't have."

"And he can't have you?"

"He . . . I . . ." She paused. Lumpkin sucked noisily at the bottle, tail wiggling madly. "He's not ready for this, Em."

"*This?*"

"This!" She nodded toward the ranch at large. "The dull, the drama, the boring, the baby." She laughed a little, but the truth lodged like an icicle in Emily's veins.

"So it would be different without me and Bliss?"

"What? No. No!" Casie's face looked pale suddenly. "I didn't mean it like that, Em. He's crazy about Bliss. And you! You know that."

"Yeah." She nodded and turned back to flute the edges of the piecrust. "He loves us."

"He does!"

"Lots of people love us like . . ." She shook her head. "Like people love artichoke dip or fondue. They just wouldn't want to make a steady diet of it."

"Emily . . ." Casie's voice sounded tortured. "You're not the reason Colt and I aren't together. You know that, don't you?"

"Well, it doesn't look like I'm helping the situation."

"You're wrong. Absolutely wrong. This has nothing to do with you. Colt and I . . . we're totally different. He's like a thunderstorm and I'm . . ." She shrugged. "Bathwater."

Emily stared at her. How could so many people be so entirely unaware? Sometimes it almost made her wonder if she was as deluded as the others. "Rainwater, maybe," she corrected.

"What's the difference?"

"Not much. Except rain's essential for life."

Casie gripped the nipple more tightly against the lamb's persistent tugs. "The point is, what happens or doesn't happen between Colt and me has nothing to do with you. You believe that, right?"

"I almost have to," Emily said, though worry still gnawed at her. "Since you're the worst liar ever."

"Well . . ." Casie shrugged, but the motion seemed tight. "We can't all be virtuosos."

"It's a sad truth." The kitchen went silent except for Lumpkin's enthusiastic sucking.

"I know you want us to get together, Em," Casie said finally, attention tight on the lamb. "And I appreciate that fact. But Colt is used to dating Miss Rodeos and Miss . . ." She shrugged. "Wyomings."

"And Miss-takes."

"What?"

"I'm just saying . . . maybe he's ready to be happy instead."

Casie turned toward her, silent for a second before speaking. "Look at you, calling the kettle black."

"What are you talking about?"

"Max Barrenger."

Emily felt her heart rate quicken, felt guilt and hope mix up to a dumbfounding infusion inside her. "What about him?"

"Do you think he goes around the country offering to finance *everyone's* business?"

"He's just being a man. Men say things they don't mean."

"That's not true."

"Really?"

Casie frowned. Memories of her ex-fiancé were probably marching through her head like army ants. "Well . . . not *all* men," she corrected.

"And this from the woman who habitually turns down *Colt Dickenson's* advances."

"He's not . . . advancing."

Emily stared at her, then hissed in frustration and rolled her eyes. "If I had a guy like Mr. Dickenson mooning over me, I'd have him hobbled and blindfolded before dessert was served."

"Hobbled and—"

"What I'm saying is . . ." Emily began, then shook her head and tried a new tack. "He's one of the good guys, Case. Hell, he might be the *only* good guy left."

"What are you talking about?"

"I'm talking about men. . . . They don't . . ." She shook her head. "Relationships . . . they're not meant for girls like me."

"I don't think Max Barrenger believes that."

She made a psffting sound again. "He just likes my sticky buns."

"He likes them, all right, sticky or otherwise."

"Don't be lewd!" Emily scolded, fully aware of their suddenly inverted roles.

Casie chuckled but sobered in a minute. "Are you considering his proposition?"

She shook her head. "I'm not going to ask him to spend money on a plan that will probably never work out. Besides, I can't leave the Lazy. Who'd take care of Bodacious and the orchard and the chickens and—"

"I wasn't talking about his business plan. I was talking about his personal plan."

"You're crazy. He's going to marry Sonata."

"Then he's a fool."

Emily glanced at her. Their gazes met.

"If he spends any more time staring at you, his eyeballs are going to dry out."

"He's just being nice."

"Nice is when you say please and thank you. Infatuated is when you leave your girlfriend during your vacation and spend the day driving a new mother around the country."

Emily's gut clenched, but she fought down the queasiness. "Spinsterhood has made you delusional. Max and Sonata left for town right after breakfast. A man's gotta be in love to drive sixty miles in weather like this."

"Believe me—" Casie began, but Emily stopped her.

"I'm not a home wrecker." Worry gnawed at her because, to tell the truth, she wasn't sure what she was.

"There's not a home to wreck yet, Em."

"Families . . ." she began, then took a deep breath and continued carefully. "I don't know much about them, but I won't be breaking any up."

"You can't break up something that doesn't exist," Casie said, but Emily shook her head.

"Let's change the subject."

There was a pause. Casie sighed. "Okay," she said. "How about Lincoln Alexander? What do you think of *him?*"

"I think he's a douche bag."

"What? Why?"

Emily swallowed, tamping down a thousand wild emotions. "He didn't show up for dinner, either."

"What's *he* doing?"

"I don't know."

"Did you knock on his door? Make sure he's all right?"

"I'm not his mother."

"I'm not his mother, either. But if he drops dead on the Lazy, I'll still be liable."

"He's not going to drop dead," Emily said. "Unless he's doing drugs or something?" She glanced up. "Is that what you think?"

"No!" Casie gave her an odd glance. "I never even considered that . . . until you mentioned it. Do *you* think he's doing drugs?"

"I don't know. How would *I* know?"

"Holy Hannah." Casie set the empty bottle on the counter, placed the lamb on its tiny hooves, and rose to her feet. "I'm going to go check on him."

"Are you sure that's a good idea?" she asked, but Casie was already pulling on her jacket.

"Why wouldn't it be?"

"He—" she began, but just then the front door opened. They turned toward it in unison.

Max Barrenger stepped inside. "What's cookin', good-lookin'?"

Suddenly nervous, Emily shifted her gaze back to Casie. But her mentor just raised her brows and retreated without another word. The door closed behind her in a matter of seconds.

Emily cleared her throat. Lifting the second crust from the counter, she eased it into the waiting pie plate, which boasted two chips and a crack. "Supper won't be ready for an hour at least," she said.

"Well . . ." Walking up behind her, he peered over her shoulder. "Sonata's on the phone. Will be forever. Do you mind if I stay here? Soak up the scents?"

"It's a free country," she said.

"Is something wrong?" His voice was quizzical, a little wounded.

"No. Of course not," she said and, feeling fidgety, slipped Bliss's sling from her back. The baby drooped contentedly, downy lashes dark against her mocha cheeks.

"Here, let me help you," he offered and hurried forward to lift the baby, backpack and all, against his chest. "Should we have called earlier to tell you we weren't going to be here for lunch?"

"No. That's fine. You're on vacation. Sonata wanted to go into town. You did the right thing."

"Sonata wanted to have a conference call with her underlings to make sure they fulfilled their thirty-million-dollar-a-year quota," Max corrected.

"Thirty million . . ." The number made her queasy, but Max shrugged it off.

"Money's just money, Emily. There are more important things in life."

"Are you sure?"

He laughed. "Positive."

"Can you give me a for-instance?"

He grinned as he stepped into the living room to lay Bliss in her bassinet. "Fun," he said as he returned. "When was the last time you had any fun, Emily?"

"I have fun every day."

"So you like making pennies an hour cooking for strangers?"

"It's practically orgasmic."

He raised his brows at her. "If it's orgasms you want . . ."

She backed away, verbally and physically, immediately chagrined. "I didn't . . ." She shook her head. "That's not what I meant. I wouldn't . . ." She swallowed. "Sonata seems like a really nice woman."

"Does she?"

"Yes. She . . ."

"She's not as nice as you."

"Mr. Barrenger . . ."

"*Mr. Barrenger?*" He grinned charmingly and bent at the

knees to search her eyes. "You make me sound like I'm the headmaster of Miss Spinster's Finishing School for Snobs or something."

She made a face, despite herself. "Do finishing schools still exist?"

He chuckled, and stepping closer, cupped her cheek. "You're so beautiful."

"No, I'm not!" Panic skittered through her. "Sonata—"

"Doesn't need me." He stared at her, longing clear as daylight in his eyes. "I never thought I'd be the kind of man who needs to be needed. But maybe everybody does," he said, and leaning forward, kissed her.

She knew she should draw back, but he thought she was nice. He thought she was beautiful. And he should know. He was older, wiser. And it felt so good to be touched, to be—

"I wish I could say I'm surprised."

Emily jerked away, gaze stabbing to the left. Sonata stood five feet away, eyes steady, voice calm.

"But I suspected as much."

"S. . . ." Max began, but she was already turning away.

"Don't bother," she said and disappeared into the entryway.

"S.!" Max said again and hurried after her. The door slammed a moment later. Then slammed again as he rushed outside.

"I'm sorry," Emily whispered. But she was entirely alone. Seconds ticked away.

"Did you know Lincoln is—" Casie began, then stopped short as she stepped into the kitchen.

Emily blinked, coming back to the present, back to reality.

"What's wrong?" Casie asked.

"I'm sorry," she said again.

"For what?"

"I didn't . . ." She shook her head. "I don't know how—"

"What happened?"

She looked Casie in the eye for the first time since her arrival. "Do you think it's possible to beat genetics?"

"What?"

"My mother . . ." She swallowed and forced herself to go on. "She didn't know who my father was."

"Emily . . ."

"That's what she said, anyway. And maybe it was true. Maybe I should hope it's true, because otherwise she was just too cruel to tell me."

"What happened?"

"Max . . ." She shook her head.

"Max what?" Casie stepped up closer and took Emily's arms in a firm grip. "Did he do something to you?" Her voice had risen, but it was hard to focus. A thousand mistakes were roaring through Emily's mind.

"I'm a terrible judge of character."

Casie swore under her breath and pivoted toward the door.

It took a moment for Emily to realize what was happening. A moment more to grab Casie's sleeve and swing her back around.

"It's my fault."

Casie took a deep breath, visibly trying to calm herself. "What's your fault?"

"He . . . I kissed him."

Casie blinked, exhaled, narrowed her eyes. "That's all?"

"All? *All?*" Emily asked and laughed. Agony vibrated through her. "He's practically married."

"He didn't hurt you?"

"What's wrong with me?"

For a moment Emily thought Casie wouldn't respond. But she was wrong again.

"You're lonely." She said the words slowly, succinctly, as if they explained everything, but it wasn't enough.

"That doesn't give me the right to . . ." She shook her head. "I'm no better than my mother."

Casie stared at her for several seconds, then drew a deep breath and spoke. "You don't know that."

Emily blinked at her, broken, pained. Even Casie saw the truth. Even Casie, with the golden heart, couldn't deny reality.

"You don't know that because she abandoned you," Casie said. "Got high. Got wasted. And left her nine-year-old daughter to fend for herself."

Emily shot her gaze toward the living room where Bliss slept. Fear rolled like a damp fog through her soul. "You don't know I won't do the same."

"I do," Casie argued. Her voice was very soft but ultimately certain, absolutely calm. "That's exactly what I know."

"How—"

"Because you're good. Because you're kind and caring and smart and loyal."

She shook her head, but Casie squeezed her arms and caught her gaze again. "And maybe Max knows that, too. Maybe he sees it in you. Maybe he can't resist it."

They stared at each other. The world went silent. Colt Dickenson stepped into the quiet a moment later.

"Did you know that Lincoln kid is—" He stopped, eyes darting from one to the next. "What's going on?"

Emily winced.

"Case?" he asked.

"Max Barrenger made a move on Emily." She spewed the words out in a rush.

For a moment the world went absolutely still, then he nodded and turned toward the door.

"Where are you going?" Casie asked.

"To rip his head off," he said and slammed the door behind him.

CHAPTER 20

"Colt!"

"Mr. Dickenson!"

"Colt!" Casie said, and running after him, grabbed his sleeve just as he reached the first step.

He swung toward her with a snarl. "What!" His chest felt tight. His muscles vibrated with the need to be called to action.

"You can't kill him."

He snapped his gaze to Emily. She looked small and terrified in the backlit doorway. "Why the hell not?"

"Because it was my fault. I was—" Emily began, but at that moment, the Escalade's lights flipped on. It roared to life and fishtailed down the driveway, leaving a lone figure in its wake.

All three of them stared at Max Barrenger, standing alone in the frosty yard.

"Excuse me," Colt said and tugged at his arm, but Casie held on like a pit bull. He scowled at her hand.

"Come back in the house," she ordered, but he shook his head. Rage didn't visit him often.

"Later," he promised and tugged again.

"I'm sorry," Emily said. "Don't blame him. Please—" she began, but he pointed a gloved finger at her.

"You . . ." He shook his head, a thousand wild thoughts romping through it. "Go to your room."

The porch went silent. Emily raised her brows and took a surprised step to the rear.

"You can't make me," she said, then turned to Casie. "Can he?"

"I . . ." she began.

Max took a step toward the house. Colt squared off, seques-tering the women behind him. A noise issued from his throat. It sounded a little like the growl of a mad dog. He felt Casie's grip tighten on his arm.

"Maybe you'd better go, Em," she said.

There was a moment of indecision before the girl turned and sprinted into the house.

Max was getting closer. Colt stepped onto the porch stairs, all but dragging Casie with him. He heard her swear quietly but barely noticed.

"What the hell's going on?" he asked.

Max Barrenger stopped short. "Sonata, ahhhh . . . forgot something in town."

"Yeah?" Colt said. "Did she forget you were a two-timing bastard?"

"Emily told us what happened," Casie rasped.

"Oh." Max exhaled heavily. His breath was frosty white in the darkness. "I see. I'm sorry if that distressed you, but she's a grown—"

"*Distressed* me?" Colt said. Honest to God, he could feel the hair rise on the back of his neck. "You think it distressed me?"

Casie slid her hands lower, clasping his right fist with both hands. "Emily's been through a lot," she said. "We . . ."

"You're damn right it distresses me!" Colt growled. "You've got no right to come here with a woman on your arm, then make a move on a girl half your age."

"I know it was a mistake," Max said. "I just . . . Things haven't been right with Sonata and me for months. When I met Emily . . ." He shook his head. "She's like a breath of fresh air. Everything just fell together like—"

"Fell together?" Colt rasped. "You think things just fall to-gether for her, you f—"

"She's very special to us," Casie said and dragged down the fist Colt wasn't aware he had raised.

"I know she's special," Max said. "That's why I . . ." He stopped himself, maybe because of the growl that was rising from Colt's throat again. "Listen," he soothed, lifting both hands in front of him as if to ward off any forthcoming violence. "It's colder than a witch's . . ." He shifted his gaze hopefully from one to the other. "Can we finish discussing this inside?"

"Of course," Casie said.

Max gave her a grateful nod and headed toward the kitchen, but Colt crowded him back. "Not that way. The bunkhouse," he ordered.

He turned reluctantly. Colt dogged his heels.

The interior of the guests' room seemed uncomfortably bright after the dimness outdoors. Max turned. "Listen . . ." he began, but Colt didn't.

"No, *you* listen!" he snapped, jabbing a finger at him. "Emily Kane is our *daughter*—"

"What?" Casie said.

"What?" Max echoed. "I didn't even think—"

"Well, don't bother starting now," Colt said, crowding in a little more. "All you need to know is that she's ours."

"You and—" He turned his attention from one to the other.

"That's right," Colt said.

"Okay."

"You mess with our daughter, I'm gonna mess with your face."

Max puffed out his chest. "Just hold on a minute. You can't—" he began, but Colt pressed forward.

"I can," he countered.

"I didn't even—"

"And you're not going to," Colt said. He leaned forward, teeth grinding.

"Okay. All right." Max backed away, but tension still hung in the air like a toxin.

Max cleared his throat. "I just want you to know that I really care about her."

Colt narrowed his eyes. "Not like Sonata then," he said, and turning, walked out the door before he did something Max would regret.

Casie delayed a moment, then hurried after him, catching up after a few strides.

"Well . . . that was . . . weird."

"What did you expect me to do?"

"Not claim her as your daughter."

He shrugged. The movement pulled the muscles tight across his shoulders. He rolled his head a little, trying to ease the tension. It was patently ineffective. "Well, I thought you'd get mad if I killed him."

"It was just a kiss."

"Just a . . ." He turned toward her. The porch light shone on her face. Her eyes were bright, her lips canted up the slightest degree. He raised his brows at her. "You think this is funny?"

"No," she said, but there might have been a whisper of humor in her voice. "No, obviously it's not—"

"That bastard made a move on Emily!"

"I'm aware of—"

"She's just a kid."

"She's eighteen."

"That's my point!"

"I was *sixteen* when you kissed me."

For a moment he felt like he'd been gut punched, but he carried on. "I wasn't engaged to be married."

"You were dating Mandy Fenno."

He swore in silence, then exhaled, removed his hat, and ran his fingers through his hair. His brain hurt. "Your father should have horsewhipped me."

She laughed. The sound was like Christmas, lighting his life, settling his stomach. And suddenly he could think of nothing but her. "Marry me," he rasped.

"I . . ." She sputtered. "Colt . . . I . . ."

"Just do it," he said. He hadn't meant to ask her, not now. Not until he'd won her over, but life was unpredictable. Things happened. Men came along. People *died*. "Just say yes."

"Colt . . ." She was holding his arms again. "You're upset."

"Upset?" He was curious where she was going with this.

"You're feeling . . . paternal . . . or something. And I appreciate that more than I can . . ." She raised her right hand, then lowered it, carefully tucking her fingers against her palm. "I've got to go," she said, and jerking away, rushed up the stairs and into the house.

Colt watched her leave. There was a clink of noise in the darkness. He turned to see Lincoln Alexander watching him.

A host of undistinguishable emotions swirled through him. Damned if he didn't really want to hit someone. But he supposed Casie would be angry if he did. "You need something?" he asked instead.

The boy shuffled his oversized feet. "You know where I can find a twelve-volt, hundred-amp alternator?"

CHAPTER 21

"So you think these will make her more comfortable?" Ty asked and stared at the two metal oddities Lincoln Alexander had crafted. Calling them horseshoes seemed overly optimistic.

The older boy shrugged. "Worth a try, maybe."

Ty nodded dubiously. They were crazy-looking things, no doubt about that, but Sam was a farrier who seemed game to try new methods . . . and strangely willing to venture out to the Lazy day or night. But maybe that was because of Colt Dickenson. Ty mentally winced. It wasn't as if he *wanted* Colt and Casie to get together. God knew there wasn't a rodeo cowboy in the universe who was going to be good enough for her, but just maybe she wanted him anyway.

"Try them if you like," Lincoln said and turned away, but Ty couldn't let it go at that. Debt weighed like grinding millstones on his back.

"What do I owe you?"

Lincoln shook his head. "I was just trying stuff. No guarantees."

An odd meld of anger and appreciation boiled up inside him. Emotions were sneaky little bastards, especially after so many years of making sure he had none. "So what do you want for them?"

"It's payback," he said. "For letting me tinker with the truck." He nodded toward the vehicle behind him. A million unidentifiable parts were spread atop a canvas dropcloth. One corner of the plastic sheeting he'd hung from the rafters was folded back into a makeshift doorway. A portable heater blazed inside.

Ty scanned the area. "Why are you doing this?" he asked.

"You work on horses that aren't yours. I work on that."

Ty stepped inside the enclosure. The gossamer plastic whispered in an unseen breeze. "How do you know what to do?"

"My old man was always trying to teach me about engines." There was something unsaid in his tone, but before Ty could figure out what that was, Colt strode in. Months ago Ty had thought of his walk as a swagger, but now he wondered if it was a memento of some ride gone wrong.

"I see you found that alternator," he said and eyed the draped area with interest.

Lincoln nodded. Truth to tell, he didn't seem a whole lot more socially adept than Ty himself. And that was saying something.

"Seems like a lot of work for somebody else's truck."

The boy shrugged. "I'm thinking of getting my own someday. Just practicing on this one."

Colt studied him in silence, then shook his head and turned toward the misshapen metal in Ty's hand. "What you got there?"

It was a struggle to remember that he didn't care what Dickenson thought. "Horseshoes."

Colt's brows raised under the low brim of his hat. "You sure?"

Ty tightened his grip on the feather-light metal. "Lincoln thought they might help Angel."

"Yeah?" Colt asked and reached for one shoe before shooting his attention back toward their guest. "You know something about blacksmith work?"

The boy shook his head and shoved his hands in the pockets of his ever-present hoodie. "I just know something about metal."

"And trucks," Colt said.

"A little."

"That reminds me, Case said there was a delivery for you."

Lincoln remained very still, but there was increased tenseness in him now. "I ordered a couple things."

"They're on the porch."

He looked eager to be gone. "I'll get them off of there," he said and turned away.

"You need some help carrying them?"

"Nope," he said and walked with long, measured strides out of the barn.

"Not a big talker," Colt said.

For a moment Ty wondered if the cowboy's words were a direct reflection on Ty's own laconic nature, but Emily had once told him that not everything was about him. He had refrained with some difficulty from telling her he was pretty sure *nothing* was.

"Well . . ." Ty shuffled his feet, stirring a little dust in the cold winter air. "It don't take no words to mend a fence."

"You think he's got fences that need fixing?"

Ty shrugged, jittery under the older man's gaze. "It's just something Grand used to say."

Colt studied him, thinking his own thoughts. "Could be your grandpa was nobody's fool," he said and glanced out the wide door toward the house. "Looks like Sophie's back."

Ty resisted the instant and insidious need to peer around the corner just as he defied the urge to hide like a skittish toddler. The desire to see her fought almost constantly with the ache to run away. Painful curiosity won out. He stepped forward just as Ms. Day-Bellaire's rented car pulled up to the house. "You think her mom will buy that farm they talked about?" He tried to keep the gnawing angst out of his voice, but he wasn't likely to make it on the big screen.

Colt shrugged, then pinned him with a look that was somewhere between understanding and amusement. "Might be good for Sophie if she did."

Ty was pretty sure it was his turn to say something, but a half dozen confusing emotions choked back his words. Colt spoke again.

"Could be it's time her folks came through for her."

A few of those unwanted emotions spewed up, causing him to speak. "Her mother ain't never going to take Casie's place."

"Wouldn't make much sense for her to try. But maybe she can just be herself." Colt exhaled, dropping his head back a little with the breath. "Monica Day-Bellaire," he added, giving her first name that long e sound she'd insisted on and shaking his head a little as he gazed out the door.

It was at that second that Sophie Jaegar stepped from the passenger side. She was like music come to life. Like poetry in motion. Her hair swung in rhythm to her movements. She was carrying three shopping bags and stood very erect, her shoulders drawn back, her chin high, like a mustang testing the wind. Like the wind itself. Like magic in—

He yanked his embarrassing thoughts to a halt as he sensed more than heard Colt speak.

"What?" Self-consciousness spilled warmth over his cheeks and down his neck.

"I asked if you were okay."

"Oh, yeah." He shuffled his feet and wished to hell he was more like the cowboy who would never be good enough for Casie Carmichael. "Sure."

Colt's eyes crinkled a little at the corners, but his expression almost looked more like understanding than humor. Could be his own gut crunched up a little from time to time. Living this close to a woman who was too good for you was hell on a man's digestive system.

Laughter sounded from outside. Both men glanced in that direction as Monica exited from the driver's side of the vehicle. Sophie spoke and the older woman laughed again.

Ty felt his muscles knot up. "Looks like she's working on coming through for Soph right now," he said. He didn't mean to make it sound negative, but where had she been for the last six months when her daughter needed a friend?

"Dad says sometimes all we can do is cinch up tight and hope to God," Colt mused. Ty nodded, but in that moment he realized the cowboy's gaze had slipped toward the hip shed where Casie had disappeared some time before. Sympathy felt bitter and out of place in Ty's soul; he didn't even like Colt Dickenson. But losing the woman you loved would be like extinguishing the sun. He shivered and hunched his shoulders against the cold. "Casie ain't nobody's fool."

Dickenson shifted his gaze back to Ty. "Maybe that's what I'm worried about," he said.

From the yard, Monica Day-Bellaire laughed again, but Ty kept his eyes on the cowboy. "You thinking you ain't good enough for her?"

Colt drew a deep breath and narrowed his eyes as he glanced back toward the house. "That possibility *has* crossed my mind," he said, lips twitching up the slightest degree. "What do you think?"

Ty drew a deep breath through his nostrils. "This is the first time I thought you was," he admitted, and Colt laughed.

The kitchen was full for the first time in days. But the diners were atypically quiet . . . except for Monica Day-Bellaire.

If Sophie's mother felt the tension in the room, she was even better at fakery than Emily herself. And not many people could say that.

"So your lovely fiancée left already?" Monica asked, addressing Max.

Emily kept her eyes on her entrée, though she could feel Max's attention light on her face for an instant.

"I'm afraid she had to get back to work."

Colt sat between Ty and Lincoln Alexander. The three of them hadn't spoken five words altogether. Emily sensed the stress like repeated hammer strokes between her shoulders and felt entirely incapable of doing anything about it.

"I should return to work, too," Monica said, "but I just can't bring myself to leave this little piece of Utopia." She smiled. "Not to mention my daughter." Reaching out, she brushed a hand down Sophie's hair.

It was a silly act, singularly showy, Emily thought, and yet she felt jealousy curl like a smug cat through her system. She dragged her gaze away.

"So you had fun shopping?" Casie asked. She sat directly across from Ty and didn't seem a hell of a lot more relaxed than the men.

"It was wonderful. Just wonderful. I thought I'd miss the city, but you know . . ." Monica glanced at Sophie again, eyes soft. "That old maxim is absolutely right; it's not about the goods. It's about the company you keep."

"Here, here," Max said and raised his cup.

No one but Monica joined him. They clicked their cider-filled mugs. The sound was sharp in the stillness. Then Max cleared his throat, and Monica looked around, perhaps cognizant of the tension for the first time.

Her eyes settled on Lincoln Alexander. "Sophia tells me you've crafted a new type of horseshoe for Tyler's mare. Is that correct?"

Lincoln raised his gaze from his plate. His eyes looked silver in the overhead lights, his shoulders squared. He shrugged. "I'm just trying some stuff."

"What?" Emily asked. The word escaped against her better judgment, too strident. Too coarse. All eyes turned toward her. She swallowed and dished coleslaw into an oversized bowl. Softening her tone, she tried again. "I didn't know you were an expert on horses."

He speared her with his hoarfrost eyes. "There's a lot you don't know about me."

The kitchen went silent. Emily forced a laugh into the abyss. "Well, I'm sure that's true. It takes more than a couple of meals together to know *everything* about someone."

They all stared at her. She smiled. "More slaw?" she asked and handed the bowl to Casie.

"I don't think he plans on nailing the shoes on himself," Colt said, shifting his attention away finally. "But I have to admit, he's got an interesting idea there."

"How so?" Monica asked, high brows arched over carefully groomed lashes.

Colt settled back in his chair a little, stretching out his wounded leg and hooking an elbow over the back of his chair. He looked hopelessly alluring that way, as earthy as the miles of rolling acres outside their door. Either Casie Carmichael had the self-control of a saint or she was dumber than a post.

"I'm sure he can explain it better than I can," Colt said.

Lincoln shifted uncomfortably in his chair. He was twenty pounds underweight and had barely touched his meal. Maybe Emily resented that more than anything.

"The shoes are made of a bunch of tiny tubules filled with air."

They all stared at him.

"It makes them extremely strong."

"But they're metal, right?"

"Nickel phosphorous."

"That sounds expensive," Monica said.

Emily could feel Ty's tension crank up a notch at the mention of money. Sophie scowled.

"Exciting, though," her mother added. "Cutting-edge technology right here at the kitchen table. It's probably where most great innovations begin."

"I'm just fiddling."

"Well, you never know," Monica said. "Necessity is the mother of invention, and Sophia tells me Ty takes extraordinary care of his aging mare."

For a moment Emily thought Sophie might dispute having said anything even remotely positive about Tyler Roberts, but the girl pursed her lips and turned her gaze back to the table. Her flushed cheeks matched the color of Ty's nearly to perfection.

"I didn't mean to embarrass you," Monica said, watching Ty. "I think it's wonderful you have the desire and the wherewithal to care for her as you do."

Ty shifted almost imperceptibly in his chair before he spoke. "Lincoln ain't charging me nothing."

"Oh." Monica raised her brows and smiled a little at the older boy. "An inventor *and* a philanthropist."

"It's not like that. I'm just—" Lincoln began, but a knock

sounded at the front door, freezing the conversation for a moment.

"You expecting someone?" Colt asked, looking at Casie. In the past six months he'd gotten a little jumpy about the number of men who wandered through the Lazy. Only a few of them seemed overtly interested in the ranch's owner, but apparently Colt Dickenson wasn't a complete idiot. He appeared to have a *modicum* of sense, even if he did think he could send grown women to their rooms like they were pouty adolescents. Emily felt tears well up as emotions mixed like fermenting alcohol. She hated being told what to do. And he wasn't her father. So why did her chest feel so funky every time she remembered his disappointment?

"Not tonight," Casie said, snapping Emily back to the present as she placed her milk glass on the table. But Colt beat her to the punch, rising before she had a chance to push back her chair.

"I'll get it," he said. In a moment he had disappeared into the entryway.

"I bet you have a lot of unexpected guests around mealtime," Monica said. "This stuffed squash is exemplary, Emily."

"I thought it was a little dry."

"Not at all," Monica countered. "It's wonderful. Did I detect a hint of . . ." She narrowed her eyes a little. Her makeup was expertly applied, her brows brushed upward like feathery wings. Small gold hoops adorned her earlobes. ". . . Tarragon in the sauce?"

"Just a little," Emily said and tried her damnedest to sound normal. "I'm surprised you could taste it."

"Mother's a gourmet," Sophie said.

Emily wasn't certain what to make of the girl's tone. Pride? Resentment? It was entirely possible there was a trace of both in that one simple statement. Welcome to the world of unfettered emotions. A world Emily had hoped she'd left behind in the maternity ward.

"Thank you, darling," Monica said. "But I'm afraid I'd have to find time to cook to be considered a gourmet. I used to enjoy dabbling a bit, though, when life wasn't so hectic. Recently, things have been—"

Her words stopped cold. Her carefully groomed brows sprang upward as Colt stepped back into the kitchen. Beside him was Philip Jaegar, Sophie's father and Monica Day-Bellaire's erstwhile husband.

CHAPTER 22

"Daddy!" Sophie's voice was taut, her knuckles bone white against the handle of her fork.

Ty tightened his fist beneath the table and remained very still, though every odd instinct quarreling inside him insisted that he leap from his chair and step between the girl and her father. How damned strange was that?

"Hey, Soph," Jaegar said. He carried a red paper bag in one hand. A long, narrow box and two chunky square ones peeked over the top. All were wrapped in bright green foil and multicolored ribbon.

"What are you doing here?" Sophie had smoothed her tone a little. But her cheeks were brushed pink, her eyes as bright as the packages he carried.

He shrugged and grinned sheepishly. Philip Jaegar was charming. "I couldn't stay away from my best girl at Christmas." He shifted his gaze slightly to the left. A tendon in his neck jumped a little. "You didn't tell me your mother was here. How are you, Monica?" Ty couldn't help but notice that he did *not* use the long e sound when he said her name.

"I'm well." Her tone was crisp, her chin lifted another half inch, as if facing a contingency of her peers . . . or possibly a firing squad. "I didn't realize how lovely the Lazy Windmill was."

"Well . . ." Jaegar smiled again. The expression looked a little predatory. "Nobody kept you from coming here for the past six months. But I suppose Paris *is* more appealing in—"

"Daddy!" Sophie said and jerked to her feet. "I thought you were in the Caribbean."

Some emotion passed over Jaegar's eyes. Shame maybe.

"I left early," he said. "There was an estate closing in town that I had to take care of, but enough about me. How's everyone else?" He scanned the faces around him. Casie looked worried, Max curious, Monica mad enough to spit. "Emily, it smells heavenly in here. As always."

Casie was the first to recover. "You must be starving. Here . . ." She hurried forward to pull a folding chair from the living room closet. "Have a seat."

"Oh no," he demurred immediately. "I won't bother you. I just wanted to—"

"It's no bother," Emily said. Ty was pretty darn sure she was wrong about that, but as Colt had once said, she had a need to feed. "There's plenty left. You know I always cook for an army."

"Really," he said. "I'll just drop off these gifts and be on my way."

"You don't want to hurt Em's feelings," Colt said. "You know how sensitive these culinary artists are." He grinned a little as he took the chair from Casie and nestled it next to Lincoln's. "Sit down."

"I really shouldn't," Jaegar said, but he was already moving toward the table. There weren't a whole bunch of people who appreciated home cooking more than Philip Jaegar.

Emily set a plate in front of him just as Bliss began to cry from the other room.

"I got her," Ty said, and pushing back his chair, left the crowded kitchen behind him.

The baby grinned crookedly as he lifted her to his chest, a small, tight bundle of life against his heart. By the time he drifted back toward the table, Jaegar had taken his first bite and was extolling its virtues.

Lincoln lifted his gaze to Ty as he entered the room. Their eyes met for an instant and then the older boy rose to his feet. His movements were jerky, his body tense.

"Don't you want dessert?" Casie asked.

"Naw," he said and left the kitchen. In a moment the door closed behind him.

His exodus was greeted with a moment of silence.

"He must not have tasted your apple dumplings yet, huh, Em?" Jaegar asked. "Otherwise you'd have to pry him from the table with a crowbar."

"I prefer her suet pudding," Monica said. "It's Sophia's favorite, too, isn't it, darling?"

Sophie blinked. She looked a little like she was going to be sick. "I like them both."

"You should taste her raspberry turnovers," Casie said as she glanced from one parent to the other. "They're better than . . ." She paused. The woman was an excellent equestrienne and the kindest person Ty knew, bar none, but she wasn't exactly a maestro in social circles herself.

They all stared at her.

She swallowed.

"A poke in the eye?" Colt guessed.

Monica laughed.

Emily huffed. "A poke in the eye? Really?"

Colt grinned, though there had seemed to be a bit of unusual tension between him and Casie today. "So . . ." he said. "Philip, tell us about your vacation."

Sophie's father wiped his mouth with a cloth napkin as Ty returned to his seat, Bliss at his shoulder.

"Well, the weather's better than it is here. I'll say that."

"It was unseasonably warm in Paris," Monica said.

He ignored her. "And the water's as blue as . . ." He shook his head. "A robin's egg."

"I do have a weakness for Palm Passage, but the shopping can't compare to . . ." Monica began. And the verbal swordplay began.

The remainder of the meal was spent with Casie and Colt volleying carefully between the two as Sophie's expression got tighter and tighter.

By the time Philip Jaegar rose to his feet, there was enough tension in the room to wind a clock. "Well, I'd better be getting back to town."

"I packed up some leftovers and divinity for you." Emily lifted a brown paper bag by the handles.

"That's very sweet of you," he said, but he didn't even bother to employ his killer smile. Instead, he glanced back at his ex-wife. "It's supposed to snow tonight. You should probably be going, too. If you run into the ditch, you're not going to want to walk far in those boots you spend so much money on."

She gave him a smile. It could have been award-winning, except for the twitch of disdain at the corners. "How nice of you to worry about me, Philip, but I'm staying here tonight."

"At the Lazy?" He shifted his gaze between Max and the front door, where Lincoln had disappeared some minutes earlier. "I thought there were only two guest rooms available."

Monica canted her head, smile warming a little at the sight of his obvious irritation. "Casie was gracious enough to allow me to bunk down here," she said.

"In the house?" Philip looked as if the idea was beyond ludicrous.

She arched a brow at him. "You're surprised?"

He chuckled. The sound was a little gritty. "Emily's cooking must be even more enticing than I realized if you're staying here. I seem to remember a night at the Waldorf when you complained because the towels weren't lined up to your satisfaction."

Monica's smile amped up a little. "And I remember you're a—"

"Look at the time!" Casie said.

They all glanced at *her* instead.

She laughed. It sounded a little maniacal. "I didn't realize it was so late. I mean, I suppose things would just be gearing up in . . . wherever the Waldorf is . . . but I have to . . ." She ran out of words.

". . . Get to bed," Colt finished for her. Their gazes met for a second. "And I should get Ty home." He rose to his feet. "Mom doesn't roost well until her brood's in the coop."

Ty tried to control his blush. It was embarrassing to be

treated like a baby. Embarrassing and so damned wonderful he felt his throat close up. But he wouldn't let himself be overrun by emotions. Not tonight. He glanced at Sophie. Her lost-girl eyes looked tortured. He steeled himself. No, he wasn't nobody's hero, but he'd do this thing that needed doing.

"I'll take Bliss," Casie said, seeming relieved to have something to do with her hands.

"Well . . ." Jaegar sounded a little embarrassed himself. But not near as much as he should. "I guess I'll get going, too."

"I'm so glad I don't have to traverse those roads," Monica said and gave a delicate shiver. "Rooming with Sophia has been absolutely wonderful. I can't thank you enough for allowing me to stay, Casie. We've been giggling like schoolgirls at summer camp. Or maybe *winter* camp."

God help them all, Ty thought, and spoke into the void. "I'll carry your leftovers, Mr. Jaegar."

"Oh, okay." They turned toward the door.

It only took Jaeger a moment to settle into his coat. Ty wasn't exactly current on men's fashion, but he was pretty sure that single garment cost more than Angel's annual feed bill.

Outside, it was still and quiet, cold with the kind of sharp ache that settled into your bones like a cancer.

Jaegar turned at the steps. "I can get that, Tyler," he said and reached for the leftovers, but Ty pulled the bag back a little.

"I got it," he said and pushed himself down the stairs toward the man's car.

His Cadillac was as red as a candy apple. The interior light blinked on as he pulled open the driver's door.

"She thinks real good of you," Ty said, bolting into the silence.

Jaegar stopped, half in, half out of his vehicle.

Ty gritted his teeth. "Sophie," he explained and braced himself. "She missed you."

Jaegar tilted his head a little, softening. "That's nice of you to say, Tyler. I know she thinks highly of you, too."

He wanted to nod, wanted to believe it was true, but that wasn't the point. "Don't you mess that up."

Jaegar straightened but remained in the open doorway. "What do you mean by that?"

Every cowardly molecule in Ty wanted to back away. He didn't know nothing about family. It would have been better if he'd been raised by a pack of wolves, but he'd started down this path and he'd finish the course.

"It's just . . ." He tried to swallow his fear. But it was deep in his bloodstream, making his limbs stiff, his throat tight. "It ain't fair for you and Mrs. . . . Day-Bellaire . . . to put her in the middle like that."

Jaegar slammed his car door. He was a good three inches taller than Ty. Three inches taller, fifty pounds heavier, and infinitely wiser. Ty swallowed his bile. "Like what?" the man asked.

"Like she was a horse to be traded or something," Ty said and tightened his fist around the paper handles of the bag. "She's got feelings. And she's got heart." He felt his eyes burn with tears. Good God, if he started bawling he'd never be able to show his face at the Lazy again. He shook his head. "She's got more heart than any one of them mustangs she worries about."

"I think I know my daughter better than you do."

"Then quit treating her like crap!" Ty snapped.

"Who do you think—" Jaegar began, but just then Colt stepped into the cold. His frosty breath bubbled into the night air. In a matter of seconds he was standing beside them, a jagged triangle of men so different they barely shared a species.

The silence was all but painful. Colt raised his brows.

"Young Tyler here was taking me to task," Jaegar said. His tone was stiff.

Ty clenched his free hand into a fist. He knew he had no right to speak to Sophie's dad like that, especially not after he'd loaned him money for Angel's vet bills. But he wasn't going to apologize. Not this time. No matter what Dickenson—

"Well, Sophie needs *someone* to stand up for her," Colt said.

Somewhere in the distant pastures a coyote sang. A quartet answered. Ty released the breath he hadn't realized he'd been holding.

Jaegar pulled his back a little straighter. "You think *I* don't stand up for her?" he asked. "Who took care of her when that . . ." He stabbed a finger toward the house, then paused, not loosing the vitriol that trembled on his lips. "Her mother abandoned her."

A hundred arguments rushed through Ty's mind, but he kept himself from speaking and shifted his gaze back to Colt. Sometimes the man was dumber than dirt, but he knew how to keep folks from punching a fellow in the face, and that might be a skill worth learning. They exchanged a glance.

"She's here now," Colt said.

Jaegar raised his brows in question.

"Your ex-wife. She's here now, trying to make things right."

Jaegar laughed. The sound was harsh in the brittle cold. "She's just soothing her conscience before she jets off to Venice or somewhere."

"Sophie's just a girl, Philip," Colt said. His voice was soft. "She shouldn't have to choose between the two of you."

"I'm not making her—" Jaegar paused, drew a deep breath, and turned his eyes toward the sweeping hills that framed the Lazy. His face looked hard and angular in the diffused light. Snow began to fall softly. "Okay." He nodded once. "I suppose you're right. It *is* Christmas."

"That's all we're saying," Colt said and shifted his gaze back to Ty. "Well, we'd best get home before Mom worries herself sick."

Ty nodded and handed over the leftovers.

In a minute the two of them were alone in Colt's pickup truck.

He turned the key, then glanced across the chilly distance between them, brows raised in question. "Could be there's not a faster way to get yourself a beating than to tell a man how to raise his own kids."

Apologies and explanations crowded to the fore, but Ty had never been any good at either. "Sometimes a donkey don't know he's an ass till somebody tells him his ears is too long," he said.

Colt stared at him a second, then threw back his head and laughed.

CHAPTER 23

"Monica?" Casie forced a smile and tried not to pass out. She detested confrontations as only a pacifist raised by natural combatants can. "Do you have a second?"

The older woman raised her arched brows. Even after the pitched battle with her ex-husband only a few minutes before, there was not a hair out of place. She was sophisticated, intelligent, and sleekly sexy. The impregnable feminine trifecta. Casie tugged self-consciously at her sweatshirt. It had seen better days. Hell, it had seen better days ten years ago.

"Of course, Cassandra," Monica said and glanced at the closed bathroom door. She was carrying a leather toiletry bag that looked like it might have been custom-made in warmer climes. Her nails had been brushed with a clear lacquer. Her skin looked smooth and soft. Not at all as if she had spent endless hours delivering calves and shoveling horse manure. "I suppose Sophia will be a minute anyway."

Casie nodded. Of the three women who usually shared that single bathroom, Sophie was the one who tended to monopolize the space. But compared to her carefully polished mother, the girl was a speed demon. Casie cleared her throat and kept her voice low. "Downstairs?"

"Oh!" Monica gave a slight lift of her shoulders. "Certainly," she said and stepped onto the stairs. She walked very upright with a minimum of body movement. Her arms were almost perfectly still, as if she only did one thing at a time so as to perform it with precision.

Monica preceded Casie into the living room. The Christmas tree lights glowed softly. A dozen handmade ornaments were sprinkled among the store-bought ones. Only a topper was missing. From the nearby kitchen, Emily was adding a rapper beat to a George Strait classic. At any other moment it might have been amusing. But Casie was entirely focused on the up-coming conversation.

"What can I do for you, Cassandra?" Monica asked. Some-how, without apparent effort, she made it sound a little like a formal interview . . . or a gargantuan favor.

Casie refrained from clearing her throat again. Neither did she hide under the couch as she dearly longed to do. "Sophie is . . ." She'd rehearsed this conversation a half dozen times in the fifteen minutes since the ulcer-inducing meal they had shared with Philip Jaegar, but there was no way this was going to be anything short of painful. "We think a great deal of your daughter."

"Oh . . ." Monica Day-Bellaire smiled. She wasn't classically beautiful perhaps, but it was ultimately clear that she looked ex-actly as she wished to. "That's very kind of you to say, Cassan-dra. I cannot tell you how much I appreciate your opening your home to her."

"It's been my pleasure," Casie said, though, truth to tell, it had also, at times, been monumentally terrifying and a colossal pain in the rear. She did clear her throat now, then hated herself for the weakness. "That's why I wanted to talk to you."

"Oh?" The winged brows rose again, though barely a single wrinkle showed in the woman's alabaster skin.

"She . . ." Casie tapped her index finger against her blue-jeaned thigh. Right about now it would be fantastic to have Emily's lying skills. And yet she hoped to God neither of the Lazy's resident teenagers would get wind of this conversation. ". . . Admires you a great deal."

"Well . . ." Her smile was beatific. "She thinks highly of you, too, Cassandra."

That wasn't exactly the message she had been trying to convey, but she moved on. "She cares for her father, too."

The woman's smile stiffened, but just the smallest amount, a tribute, perhaps, to her exceptional self-control. "Well, a girl *should* respect her elders, regardless of their shortcomings."

Okay. Casie forced herself to continue. "I don't want to see her hurt."

Monica scowled, then nodded slowly as if deep in thought. "I could try to get a court order to keep him from visiting her, I suppose."

Casie blinked. "What?"

"She's growing up. If she signed a legal document stating she wants no further contact with him, perhaps the court would agree to—"

"I didn't mean he shouldn't be allowed to see her."

"Oh . . ." Those classy brows rose again as if she couldn't possibly have been more surprised. "Well, what did you mean?"

"I meant . . ." She was floundering badly. "Perhaps while you're here you could try to remember that she's not as . . ." Casie thought of the little lost girl that sometimes showed through Sophie's jaded eyes. "Don't get me wrong, your daughter's tough."

"Did you know her great-grandmother was the first woman in the state of Kentucky to get her pilot's license?"

"No, she didn't tell me that."

She canted her head a little. "Neither Lillian Meier nor her daughter, my grandmother, was exactly warm and cuddly, I'm told." She smiled. "Mother never appreciated their need to achieve, but I always understood that drive. I believe Sophie does, too."

Casie wasn't sure where this was going exactly, but she tried to stay on track. "Yes, she's a hard worker."

Monica stared at her a second. "Oh, you mean here on the farm," she said and laughed a little. "Yes, I'm sure she is, and that's very nice, but once she realizes her true potential, she'll be far more driven, I'm certain."

Casie watched her, but in her mind, she saw Sophie astride Freedom, her eyes on fire, every muscle in synch with her mount. "You don't think she'll continue with horses?"

"I'm sure what you do here is very important," Monica said, though something about her expression belied her words. "But I believe my daughter is destined for other things."

"Maybe," Casie said and couldn't forget the way the girl seemed to unwind when in equine company. "But maybe this is the kind of life she wants for herself."

Monica laughed. "Perhaps you're right, Cassandra. Is that all you wished to speak to me about?"

Casie wanted nothing more than to say yes, that was it, nothing important to discuss here, but she trapped the words between her teeth. "Please be careful," she said instead.

Somehow Monica could smile with her mouth while questioning with her eyes. "Be careful of what?"

Casie glanced toward the stairs, hoping like hell that the object of their discussion couldn't hear them. "She's more sensitive than she seems."

"Well . . ." Monica said, and now there was a hint of pity in her eyes, as if she believed Casie was casting her own shortcomings onto Sophie's hardened psyche. "I'll certainly keep that in mind. Now if you'll excuse me—"

"What you do now will affect her forever." Casie said the words a little more quickly than she had intended, imbuing them with too much force, too much emotion.

Monica twisted back toward her, eyes narrowing a little. "I'm afraid I'm uncertain what you're—"

"You gotta quit sniping at your ex," Emily said.

They turned in unison. The little mother stood in the doorway with the baby at her shoulder. Casie had no idea when she had entered the room. The kitchen radio was playing a Keith Urban song.

"I'm sorry," Monica said, but her tone rather suggested the opposite. "What did you say?" Her expression was haughty, bordering on outraged, but Emily was cool under fire.

"Sophie seems like a hard nut, but like Ty would say . . ." The girl shook her head once, dreadlocks brushing her shoulders as she rocked Bliss in her arms. ". . . Even bucking bulls ain't bulletproof."

The older woman scowled as if uncertain whether to be offended or just confused.

"Your squabbles with Mr. Jaegar are making her feel bad," Emily explained.

Monica pulled her shoulders back an additional half inch. The movement reminded Casie a little of a cobra preparing to strike. "Philip has always been jealous of my relationship with Sophia. He's . . ." She shook her head, the movement short and sharp. "My grandmother warned me that his people weren't . . ." She paused as if to find the perfect phraseology. "As . . . ambitious as we are."

Casie and Emily stared at her in mute immobility. The younger woman was the first to rally.

"I'm sure he's intimidated by your success," she said.

Casie blinked at her, but Emily was unruffled.

"You're an extremely strong individual," she added.

"It's a curse," Monica said. "And a gift, I suppose."

"Of course," Emily agreed. "That's why you're going to have to be the bigger person."

Monica watched her, unblinking. Casie was just as mesmerized, though she had seen the girl work her magic a hundred times. Manipulation was an art form where Emily Kane was concerned.

"How do you mean?"

The girl shrugged as if just working her way through the miasma. "Maybe you've heard the expression 'Kill him with kindness'?"

Monica's lips, lightly glossed and carefully outlined, tilted up a fraction of an inch. "I believe I *have* heard that phrase."

Emily shrugged, casual as Fridays, but if one knew her well, one might discern the diabolical gleam in her eye. "Not that we want to make Mr. Jaegar look like a villain."

"Of course not." Monica's lips curved slightly downward, just hinting at less-than-charitable thoughts. "It *is* Christmas," she said.

"It is," Emily agreed.

"Very well. After all, there is nothing that makes a man more uncomfortable than perfection."

Perfection?

Emily refrained from rolling her eyes. Casie could not have been more impressed if the girl had sprouted wings.

"Great," she said. "Well, I'm going to check the chicken's heat lamp, then I'll hit the hay." She jostled Bliss gently as the baby dozed against her shoulder. "For a couple hours at least."

"Sleep well."

Emily yawned. "You too."

"Oh, I will." Monica's voice was almost a purr. In a second, she had disappeared up the stairs.

Casie glanced at Emily. She still didn't roll her eyes. Holy Hannah, the girl was a master.

"I'm going to put Baby down," she said. "Would you mind keeping half an eye on her while I run outside?"

Casie shook her head. "Anything for our evil genius."

Emily tugged her coat tightly against her chest, glanced back toward the house, and knocked softly on the bunkhouse door. Not a sound could be heard. Snow settled softly on her shoulders. She hunched them against the cold and knocked again.

After a silent lifetime, footsteps could be heard on the floor inside. She held her breath. The door opened a crack. Lincoln Alexander scowled at her.

Gathering every ounce of strength she possessed, Emily pushed her way inside. The room was dim, lit only by the lamp perched beside the bed. It cast an amber glow around the room, illuminating the oil paintings on the wall, the cowhide rugs spread across the hardwood floor. She reminded herself that she had done this, had cleaned and decorated and organized. But it was cold comfort.

She pulled her attention back to Lincoln. His eyes were as steady and focused as she remembered.

"How'd you find me?" she asked and held his gaze. He was skinnier than he used to be, but his hands were the same, long-fingered and nimble.

He didn't answer but watched her with quicksilver eyes, eyes that could make people believe in him, could make people care. But she wouldn't be a fool again. Not now. Not when Bliss slept just a few yards away.

"You've done well for yourself, Ellie," he said.

She tightened her fists and remained exactly where she was. "I'm legitimate, if that's what you mean."

He made no response.

She drew a deep breath. "I want you to leave."

"I paid for a full week."

"I'll give you your money back."

His eyes sparked. "They trust you with the finances?"

She felt her gut twitch. "I'm not the person I used to be."

He watched her again, eyes unblinking, lips a hard line. "How old's the baby?"

Terror crept over her like a cold tide, but she wouldn't show it, wouldn't give in. "She's not yours, if that's what you're wondering."

His fingers twitched. The fingers of an artist . . . or a pickpocket. "How old?" he asked again.

"She's not yours!" she repeated, then lowered her voice, hoping to hell Max couldn't hear her through the ancient log walls.

Something flickered in his eyes, but she couldn't read his thoughts. Had never been able to, not even when she'd been infatuated by him. Not even when she'd thought him a genius and herself lucky to be at his side.

She'd been a fool. But she couldn't afford to be one again.

"I'll expect you to be gone before dinner tomorrow," she said.

"Where'd you learn to cook?"

For just a second, just a fractured moment in time, she almost asked if he'd enjoyed her meals. God help her! How needy was she? Even now. Even after all she'd been through.

"If I'd known you were so talented, I wouldn't have had to steal all those potpies."

She remembered sharing those pies. Remembered laughing when she'd realized he'd snuck an entire cheesecake in under his shirt.

"I want you gone," she repeated and turned away, but he caught her arm.

Feelings flared through her like fireworks, sprinting off in every direction.

"I didn't come here to cause trouble for you, El."

She tamped down the sparks, quashed the feelings. She wasn't her mother, needing a man to make her whole. Needing someone despite the consequences. "Good," she said. "Then I'll say good-bye now."

"I paid for a full week," he repeated, and there was a light in his eyes that reminded her of his intensity.

"Do as you please," she said and yanked her arm from his grasp. "I'll probably be gone before then anyhow."

His brows lowered.

"Max Barrenger offered to finance my products," she said and shrugged. "I'll be leaving with him as soon as I wrap things up here."

CHAPTER 24

"No, please, you deserve the honors," said Monica Day-Bellaire and handed Philip Jaegar the angel to place atop the Christmas tree.

"You should do it," he countered. "It's just such a pleasant surprise to have you here for the holidays."

"There's no place I'd rather be." She wore a cashmere sweater in a dusky periwinkle shade that made her seem almost soft, almost accessible. Still, Sophie watched the exchange with taut mistrust. Her father had arrived shortly after breakfast with a new batch of gifts, two of which were for his ex-wife. Tension sat like a block of salt in Sophie's gut.

"Hot chocolate?" Emily asked and entered the room carrying a tray of mismatched mugs. Tiny Christmas bulbs hung from her ears, accenting the red sweater and plaid skirt that topped her striped tights. Army boots and cargo pants were notably absent.

Sophie narrowed her eyes, wondering if there was some connection between her parents' weird behavior and the girl's even weirder ensemble. But Emily just smiled. "How's Freedom?"

"Fine."

"And Angel?"

Sophie deepened her scowl. "She's well."

Emily smiled. "How about Marley?"

"What are you up—" Sophie began, but her father chimed in, interrupting them.

"Who's Marley?"

Emily's lips twitched a little, but her eyes remained suspiciously innocent. "He's one of the wild horses your daughter worries about."

"Wild horses?" her mother asked.

Sophie lowered her brows. Her parents were acting flaky enough already without letting them slither deeper into her life here at the Lazy.

But Em seemed to have no such concerns. "There's a little band of mustangs that appeared a couple months ago. We don't know where they came from."

"What do you mean . . . appeared?"

"Sometimes people just turn horses loose or drop them off out here in the boonies when nobody's looking."

"You mean, like stray kittens?"

"Kind of," Emily agreed and distributed the hot chocolate. Sophie took a mug and glared over the rim at her. "But bigger."

"What do these horses eat?"

Emily shook her head. "Anything they can. That's where the problems start. Especially in the winter. They'll venture onto people's property. Sometimes they're shot so they don't compete for the cattle's feed."

"That's terrible," Monica said.

Emily shrugged. "With the changing weather patterns, hay is at a premium."

"How much is it going for now?" Philip asked.

Emily shook her head. Her lips twitched again. "Soph would know the answer to that better than I."

Sophie shifted narrowed eyes to her father. "Seven dollars a square, eighty per round."

They stared at her, expressions blank.

"A lot," she explained.

"How many horses are there?"

"Three that we've seen."

"Why don't you just go catch them?" Monica asked. "Surely someone would take them in."

Sophie blinked. Emily slipped unnoticed back to her refuge in the kitchen. "They're wild horses, Mother. You can't just hold out a carrot and expect them to hop in a trailer."

"Well, how about a tranquilizer gun?"

Was she kidding? Sophie wondered but managed to keep the sarcasm out of her voice. "Do you happen to have one?"

"No. But I'm sure I could find someone who does."

She nodded. When would this hell be over? "What do we do with them after they're sedated?"

Her mother's brows rose. "Well, we can't just let them starve."

"I wish that was true," Sophie said. "But—"

"Your mother's right," her father agreed, and walking to the couch, picked up his coat. "Come on, ladies."

"Where are you going?" Sophie asked.

"To save some horses."

Emily added the chopped black walnuts to the bowl and refused to think of the purloined potpies she had feasted on less than a full year before.

How had Linc found her? And why?

"It's like . . ." Max Barrenger shook his head and closed his eyes. "Like a fresh-baked orgasm."

But it didn't matter. Not in the long run. He had no power over her. Not anymore.

"Maxwell Barrenger the Second calling Emily Kane."

"What?" she said and glanced up at him.

"I was extolling the virtues of these cookies," he said. "Where were *you?*"

"I'm sorry. I've got a lot on my mind."

"That's why you should say yes."

"What?"

He smiled. The expression was self-deprecating and warm. "Wouldn't you like to have more time for Bliss?"

She scowled.

"I know it sounds cliché, but they grow up really fast, Em."

He had a faraway look in his eye. "And you don't get second chances."

She glanced toward the bassinet. Bliss was getting so big already, and she *did* worry about losing precious time. But despite what she'd told Linc on the previous night, she knew she'd be an idiot to leave the Lazy with Max, a fool to trust a guy she had barely just met, to think some miracle man was going to come along and mend all her financial woes. She didn't believe in fairy tales. Hadn't for a long while.

"You need some time off," he said. "Have you ever skied the Alps?"

She glanced up at him and laughed at his hopeful expression. "Do I look like someone who has time to ski the Alps?"

He grinned. "You don't look like you have time to blow your nose. But if your preserves were on supermarket shelves across the United States, you could do a little shooshing." He made a swaying movement with his hips as if he were gliding down some distant mountain.

"I don't think I'm the shooshing type."

"But maybe Baby Bliss will be. And how will you ever know if you're trapped here on the Lazy forever? Don't get me wrong," he hurried to add. "This is a great place. A fantastic place. But you could have an amazing future ahead of you, Emily. Why not embrace it? Why not let me show you—" he began, but just then the front door burst open.

"Did you notice his color?" Sophie's voice was atypically ebullient from the entryway. "So unique! I think he's a true Spanish mustang."

"He was spectacular!" Monica's voice evidenced a matching enthusiasm. "They all were."

"Following their tracks was a fantastic idea, Neeca," Philip Jaegar said. "Not strictly legal across private property maybe."

His ex-wife laughed. "You've *never* cared about a little thing like legalities when you want something. Remember our honeymoon?"

Jaegar chuckled as he ushered the women into the kitchen.

Sophie's eyes were bright, her mother's hair tousled. They looked like a family you'd find on the cover of a Christmas catalog.

Something clenched in Emily's gut, but she perked up her smile. "I'm guessing you had a successful day."

"Mom bought a hundred bales of hay from Elmer Langley," Sophie said.

"Highway robbery," Monica complained and smoothed back her platinum hair. "For that kind of money you'd think he would have been willing to feed it to those wild horses by hand."

"These old farmers are notoriously independent." Jaegar chuckled. "I'll never forget the look on his face when we drove up in the pickup truck."

Monica shook her head. "There's no one more stubborn than Philip Timothy Jaegar when he sets his mind to something."

He grinned down at her, hand still resting on the small of her back. "I've been meaning to buy a new car for months."

"Those wily old goats will probably relate to you better now that you're driving a truck, anyway," Monica said.

"Wait a minute." Emily raised her brows, addressing Philip. "You didn't buy a new pickup just to deliver hay, did you?"

He shrugged, mischievous grin stamped on his handsome features. "It's not as if it was brand new. It has a couple thousand miles on it."

"Oh, well then . . ." Emily said. She felt strange, as if she were having an out-of-body experience. What would it be like to have that kind of money, to have the opportunity to be your kid's hero at the drop of a hat?

"That's the way to do it," Max said. "It's nice to get your ride right off the showroom floor, but you pay through the nose for that privilege. Might as well let someone else drive the bugs out of it."

"Exactly," Philip said and checked his wristwatch. "Well, I'd better run. I still have some phone calls to make tonight. See you tomorrow, Soph?" Leaning down, he kissed her forehead.

"Sure," she said.

He nodded, smiled, and turned toward his ex-wife. "There's still no one I'd rather have ride shotgun when I'm breaking the law," he said, and she laughed as their eyes met.

For a moment Emily thought they would break into a kiss. She and Sophie seemed to be holding their collective breaths, but in a moment he turned and breezed out the door.

"Well . . ." Monica's cheeks were brushed with pink, her eyes bright. "I must look a fright. I guess I'll run up and dress for dinner. You should, too, Sophia, honey. We're going to want to get an early start tomorrow."

"An early start at what?" Emily asked.

Monica swept the hair behind her left ear. A square-cut diamond winked in the lobe. "We're going to look at farms for sale."

"Oh." Something panged near Emily's heart. "That's great," she said.

"Well . . ." Monica's gaze seemed to caress her daughter's face. "Sophia deserves to have somewhere to keep her strays."

There was adoration in the woman's eyes, tenderness in her touch.

"Don't you think?" she asked, glancing up.

Emily shook herself from her trance. "Absolutely," she said, but she didn't sell the line.

"Come on, honey. Let's go get changed," Monica said, and the two hurried up the stairs together.

The kitchen went quiet.

"Well . . ." Max broke the silence as though it were lake ice. "It looks like they had quite a—"

"I'll do it," Emily said.

He canted his head at her. "What?"

A knot grew in her throat but she spoke around it. "I'll go with you."

"Honest to God?" he asked, and taking the three steps that remained between them, rested his hands on her arms.

"Why not?" she asked. "I've never stayed in one place this long in my entire life. And you're right, Bliss deserves more. Deserves . . ." The knot tightened, but it was time to leave. Time to soar from the nest. And in so doing, maybe Casie would feel free to soar, too.

"This is going to be great," Max said, and leaned in. She turned her head, letting him brush her cheek with his lips. "I'm so happy," he murmured.

"Yeah," she said. "Me too."

CHAPTER 25

"You got her coming along real good," Ty said.

Sophie cued the palomino for a halt and glanced at him. He was handsome. There was no doubt about that. His cheekbones were high, his lips full, his jaw square and lean. But those features were almost forgettable, because it was his tender workingman's hands that drew her gaze. She had to fight to keep her attention on his face. And how damned freaky was that? "She's a fast learner."

He lifted one shoulder and slipped his fingers into the front pockets of his jeans, hiding his ragged nails and callused palms.

Silence stretched between them, making Sophie's movements feel jerky as she eased the bit between the mare's teeth, replaced the bridle with a nylon halter, and tied her to the wall beside the bag of hay.

"I heard you was buying some land," he said finally.

She chuckled. The noise sounded ridiculous, like a poor laugh track from a cheesy sitcom. "Not me. My mother . . ." Butterflies flittered in her stomach. Everything was happening so fast. Good things. All good, and yet . . . "And she's just looking."

She glanced at him out of the corner of her eye. His hands were still mostly hidden. Thank God.

"So you'll be leaving the Lazy." It was half a question, half a statement.

The butterflies turned to bats, scratching Sophie's intestines. She shifted her gaze back to the mare and unbuckled the surcingle that encircled her heart girth. "It won't be for a while yet," she said, and wondered how she would bear it. This grand, oft-dreamed-of event . . . how would she stand it?

"I suppose your dad can find a good deal pretty fast," Ty said.

"Maybe. I guess he had a few places for Mom to look at, but she should be back today." Sophie had had homes before, of course, private rooms in lavish houses, but none of them had looked out over an ancient windmill to the horse-speckled hills beyond. She barely remembered the brick Tudor where she'd lived until the divorce. The modern condominiums and European flats she'd shared with her solo parents since then had always had a two-dimensional feel to them regardless of the checks paid to sundry decorators.

Silence again, painful in its intensity.

"You got a minute?" Ty asked finally.

She turned toward him, surprised by the tone of his voice. He was always serious, always solemn and quiet, but there was an extra nervousness to the question. "Sure," she said, stomach jumping. "I'll just put Evie away and—"

"She don't seem in no hurry to leave," he said and watched the mare pull hay from the hole in the cotton bag hung up for that purpose.

"Oh. Okay," Sophie said and walked toward him. Their gazes met. Silence sifted between them, but he turned away in a moment and walked outside.

She followed him into the waning daylight, but hadn't taken three steps beyond the barn's newly restored doors before stopping short. The Lazy's old sleigh stood in the snow before her. But the shafts had been replaced. They shone black and glossy, running straight and parallel toward the curved dash that preceded the new red-velvet seat.

"Oh . . ." She exhaled heavily and glanced toward him. "Ty . . ." He stood absolutely still, devastating hands tucked deep in his pockets. "How . . ." She shook her head and stepped forward to run her fingers over the tufted seat. "You did this?"

He shrugged, then shook his head. "It's Monty; he's got a knack for fixing stuff."

"Colt's dad," she said, but without half trying she remembered Ty hurrying away before dessert on a dozen occasions, remembered the streak of black paint that marred his jeans, that edged the crescents of his jagged nails.

"Yeah . . ." He shifted his weight, uncomfortable under her gaze. "He thought . . ." He shrugged. "Thought it would be good for you to have a nice cutter."

She stared at him. She wasn't built for reading between the lines, for dissecting dialogue and deciphering moods. She was made for stating the facts and bearing the consequences. But he was different, kinder, better. And she could be cautious. "Why would he think that?"

He scowled. "Guess he musta heard you was training a driving horse."

"From whom?"

"What?" He shifted again, eyes wary, shoulders pushing hands deeper into hiding.

"Who told him?" she asked.

"I don't know." He looked belligerent now and a little desperate. "It ain't no secret you got a way with horses."

She skimmed her fingers over the delicately scrolled metal rail that ran along the top of the shiny wood side. "Did you have to replace the original brass?"

He shook his head. "Once I got it off there, it wasn't real hard getting the dents out of it. It was getting it screwed back in that took—" He paused.

She shot her gaze to his. He deepened his scowl. "That's what Monty said, anyhow."

She'd caught him in a lie. Maybe under different circumstances she would feel as if she'd won a round, but her soul hurt.

For a moment he looked like he would bolt, but he managed to stay put. "Well . . . I'd best be getting back to—"

"Casie will really appreciate this," she said and cleared her throat. "And Emily." She nodded. "They'll be able to drive it in parades and stuff to advertise the ranch."

His brows lowered beneath the frayed brim of his stupid cap. "It ain't *Casie's*."

She blinked at him.

"I mean . . . it used to be. But she didn't want it no more. Wasn't doing her no good like it was." He glanced away again. "Said you should take it with you."

Her eyes stung and her throat felt dangerously tight. "I won't have a horse to pull it," she said, but her voice was just a whisper.

He shifted his weight as if to step toward her, but then he settled back on his heels. A muscle jumped in his hungry jaw. "You will soon enough," he said. "Your dad'll buy you some."

She swallowed. "They won't be like the Lazy's horses."

He chuckled. But his eyes looked bright. "These old nags?" He waved a soulful hand vaguely toward the herds scattered across the hills. "Not hardly." The muscle jumped again. "They'll be thoroughbreds. Pedigreed back to some Bedouin tent somewhere."

She took a step toward him, drawn in by that one haunting hand. "What if I . . ." She stopped herself, physically and verbally.

He winced as their eyes met, then drew a deep breath and nodded. "You gotta go, Soph," he said. "They're your family."

"You left *your* family." Her words were barely audible in the chill stillness.

He shuffled his feet and glanced off toward where he'd grown up not three miles to the west. "I think you know why that is as good as anybody does."

It was because his parents were ogres. She knew that, but . . . "It's not as if Monica and Philip are going to win any parental awards."

"They're trying, though." He drew a deep breath as if searching for calm. "So you gotta try, too."

She didn't respond. Couldn't.

"Well . . ." he began again, but she stopped him.

"We could hitch it up."

"What's that?"

"The cutter," she said, and wondered if she sounded as pitiful as she felt. "We could give it a test-drive."

He glanced away. "I don't know. I should probably get to doing chores."

"Yeah," she agreed, but suddenly she seemed to be channeling Emily's manipulative ways. "Don't worry about it. I'm sure Evie will handle it just fine."

His brows lowered. "What do you mean? You think it'll spook her?"

"Horses don't generally love the idea of dragging terrifying stuff around behind them."

"I suppose you're right."

"You don't have to worry about it, though. Like I said, she's a fast learner."

He shuffled his battered boots for a moment and glanced over the hills before turning resolutely back. "Then we might as well hitch her up."

"What?"

"Well . . ." He cleared his throat. "It won't take much time, right?"

In the end it took nearly a half hour just to figure out the harness; Evie wasn't the only one new to the process. Neither handler was exactly certain what to do with all the straps and buckles, but finally they had the sleigh hooked up.

Sophie glanced at Ty, stationed beside the mare's neck. Evie pulled another hank of alfalfa from the bag they'd brought with them to the arena.

"What do you think?" she asked. Her nerves were cranked up tight. Cart horses could get in some spectacular wrecks.

"She seems pretty calm."

"Maybe that's because she's waiting to surprise us." Sophie had learned early on that horses were unpredictable at best.

"She was good when we dragged it around her." That had been Ty's idea. And a pretty good one, she thought.

"I guess there's only one way to find out."

He nodded. The motion was tense. "How 'bout I take the lines and you stand back there a ways and tell me how to do things?"

She scowled at him. "Why would I stand back there?"

He shrugged. He wasn't much better at lying than she was. "You'll be able to see her reactions, guess what she's gonna do."

"Why don't *you* stand back there?"

"I don't know her like you do. It only makes sense—"

"Ty . . ."

He paused, expression somber.

Jack crouched in the snow a few yards away, ears pricked at the tips as if he absorbed every word.

Sophie exhaled carefully, broaching a subject that had lain neglected since her accident months before. "It wasn't your fault."

"What's that?"

"My concussion."

"I know that. I just . . ." He stopped himself again, but finally pushed on. "I just don't want a repeat performance, is all."

She knew she should be insulted. Who did he think she was? Some weak-kneed city girl who couldn't take her blows? She should tell him that she could look out for herself. She raised her chin, prepared to say just that, but he had one hand curled around Evie's bridle while the other caressed the mare's neck with feather-soft strokes.

She winced at the sight of his fingertips against the golden hide.

"I don't really want you to get hurt, either." She said the words very softly, as if she was about to cry, as if she *were* that weak-kneed city girl. She turned away and closed her eyes for a second. In her mind, his hand still stroked the mare's neck. She tried to shake the image from her brain. "How about you get in the sleigh. I'll stay close to Evie. Calm her if she gets upset."

"No."

She turned toward him.

He shook his head, eyes intense. "I'll take her bridle. You takes the lines."

"Why?" A hint of her usual recalcitrance slipped through now. It was about damned time.

"Because you know what you're doing and I'm . . ."

"What?" she challenged.

"I'm heavier. Can hold her down better if she rears or something."

It was the funniest thing she had ever heard. She almost laughed out loud. "You could just say you're stronger, Ty. I wouldn't hold it against you if that's what you're thinking."

He winced, expression pained. "Truth is, I was thinking that you was prettier."

She felt her breath hitch in her throat, but tried to swallow such foolishness. It wasn't as if this was a secret. She'd been told she was beautiful from the day she was born. But somehow it had never mattered until this moment. "I don't . . ." She tried to glance away, failed, and tried again. "I don't know what that has to do with anything."

"If you was scarred, I'd blame myself till the day they put me under," he said.

She blinked, caught in the moment.

"And . . ." He shrugged. A hint of rare humor touched his eyes. His lips twitched up the slightest degree. "Your dad'd kill me."

Sophie's heart ached. How had she lived so long without seeing him smile? And how would she go on after this? she wondered, but reached hopelessly for normalcy. "It's really my mother you should worry about."

"Oh I do. She scares the living daylights out of me," he said, and she laughed despite herself.

"I'll let you take the bridle if you promise to let her go if she rears."

"If I let her go, what good would I be doing?"

Sophie glanced toward the house. "Have you ever thought about what would happen if I allowed *you* to be injured?"

He scowled at her.

"Casie would have my hide."

He reared back a little in surprise. "She wouldn't never blame you."

"Are you kidding me?" she asked.

For a moment she thought he would argue, but maybe even *he* couldn't completely ignore Casie's adoration. "She cares a whole lot about you, too, Soph."

"She'd trade five of me in for one of your *boots.*"

He squared his jaw a little. "There ain't but one Sophie Jaegar," he said.

For all she knew that might be the smoothest insult she had ever heard, but it didn't feel like it. She swallowed, trying to ease the pain in her throat. "Just . . ." She glanced at Evie, calm as toast in her traces. "Just be careful, okay?"

"You too."

With that she nodded and paced back to the sleigh. Once there, she stepped tentatively onto the floor and pulled her weight upward. Evie flicked back her ears. Ty tightened his hold on her bridle and spoke quietly, soothing her.

Sophie settled cautiously onto the seat and took a leather rein in each hand. "Okay," she said and slapped the lines gently against the mare's haunches. "Walk."

Evie pushed forward, felt the resistance, and stopped in her tracks, turning her head in question.

"Walk," Sophie repeated and slapped the reins a little more assertively.

"Come on, girl," Ty said and tugged at the bridle.

Evie stepped forward. The sleigh lurched . . . and she bolted.

"Whoa!" Sophie commanded, but it was Ty's weight on the bridle that pulled her to a halt after a few frenetic strides.

"You okay?" he asked, one hand on the mare's neck again.

"Yeah. I'm fine," Sophie said and tried to swallow her fear.

"You wanna try it again?"

"Do you think I'm crazy?"

"This *was* your idea, so I kinda gotta assume . . ."

She laughed. The sound was jittery but still did something to calm her nerves. "Okay," she said and braced her feet against the dash again. "Nice and slow."

He nodded. "Come on, girl," he said and stepped forward, urging the mare along after. She took a step. The sleigh dragged behind. She tucked her hindquarters under her, but Ty was already pulling her to a halt. "Good job. That's right. No trouble here. Nothing to be scared of."

It was a complete falsehood, Sophie thought, but twenty minutes later, Evie was pulling them both around the arena. Now and then she would jiggle a little, but for the most part she was the epitome of sensible.

Sophie blew out her breath and smiled at Ty, who sat only inches away. "Do you want to try her on the road?"

"What was that question about crazy?"

"Even if she freaks out, we should be able to stop her if we're both on the lines."

"You think so?"

"Well . . . like you said, you're stronger."

"I didn't say that," he countered. "Although . . ." He grinned a little, the slightest twitch of his lips. "I *am*."

She laughed out loud. Euphoria felt strange. "What's the worst that could happen?"

He narrowed his eyes in thought. "We could both die."

"Besides that."

"The horse could get injured. We could wreck Em's raspberry bushes. Jack could bust a leg when we run over him. That new rental car Max got might—"

"Open the gate," she said and he did.

After that there was no stopping them. The sun smiled down like a kindly cherub, casting diamonds on the snow that slid beneath their runners. Jack barked as he raced alongside.

By the time they returned to the ranch, Evie's steps were slow and flatfooted.

Ty stowed the harness as Sophie led the mare back to her pasture companions.

Evening eased into darkness. The moon, a small sliver of gold, drifted over the hills, gilding the world.

The two of them were silent as they headed toward the

house. Sophie cleared her throat. "Thank you." Her voice was little more than a murmur.

"My pleasure," he said.

"Really?" She glanced toward him.

"Do I look crazy?" he asked.

She chuckled, and as their gazes met in a soft meld of feelings, he slipped his hand carefully around hers.

CHAPTER 26

"I've got an . . ." Philip Jaegar began, but Monica jumped in.

"*We,*" she corrected, eyes alight.

Philip smiled. "*We,*" he agreed. They had returned to the Lazy less than an hour before. "*We* have an announcement."

Ty held his breath. He could feel Sophie's angst from across the table. Her gaze slipped to his, wide and earnest.

"We found a place."

Emily and Casie exchanged glances. Em's eyes looked tired.

"A place?"

"A farm," Philip said, and reaching up, clasped his ex-wife's perfectly manicured fingers. "A home."

Absolute silence met that declaration.

Philip inhaled heavily and grinned. "Sophie, honey . . ." He paused, but whether it was for dramatic effect or out of honest excitement, it was impossible to tell. "Your mother and I are getting back together."

Sophie's mouth formed an O as round as her eyes, but Ty had no idea what the expression meant. Hope? Fear? Sometimes the two were so tightly enmeshed, it was impossible to tell the difference, even in one's self. How many times had *his* mother checked into treatment? How many times had he hoped?

"That's great." Colt's words fell into the void like a block of ice. "So you'll all be living together."

"Yes."

Colt nodded. "Where's this land at?"

"That's the best part," Philip gushed. "It's not just land. It's got an existing house."

"Which we'll raze," Monica said.

Her husband grinned. "Which we'll raze," he agreed. "But we'll be able to live in it while the new one is being built."

"Where's it at?" Sophie asked, repeating Colt's question.

Jaegar exhaled. "The prettiest place in the world."

Sophie paled a little more.

"California," he said.

Ty felt something crack in his chest.

"That's where we've been the past few days," he continued, tone rife with exuberance. "Your mother thought I was crazy when I suggested it, but once she saw the place—"

"Oh, Sophia, you'll just love it," Monica said. "The hill upon which we'll build our home overlooks the vineyards."

"There are vineyards?" Sophie's voice was as pale as her cheeks.

"She doesn't care about the vineyards," Philip said and laughed. "Tell her about the barn."

"Oh, the barn!" Monica said, and squeezing her husband's fingers, rolled her eyes as if in ecstasy. "It's got stained glass windows, an air-conditioned lounge, and a separate stall for bathing horses."

You could have heard a cricket chirp. Casie spoke into the abyss.

"That sounds . . ." She shook her head. "Wonderful."

"Hot water!" Philip added suddenly. "It's got hot water in the barn."

"Not that you'll need it," Monica said. "Because the climate is so much better than . . ." She paused and shivered dramatically as she glanced around the table. "Well . . . let's face it, this isn't exactly Nirvana."

"But I thought . . ." Sophie began, then stopped herself.

"What, honey?" her father asked.

"I thought we were going to have a place around here so we could take in Marley and his band."

"I'm sure there are horses in California that need help, too," Monica said.

"Sure," Philip agreed, then frowned a little as if noticing his daughter's expression for the first time. "Or . . ." He brightened. "We can take Marley down there with us."

Sophie tilted her head a little. "I don't think—"

"Well . . ." He waved his hand. "We'll worry about that later. For now I'd like to make a toast." He raised his water glass. "To new beginnings."

They all chimed in.

Ty hoped to hell he wasn't going to be sick.

"Did you get those hinges welded?" Monty asked. Colt's dad didn't wear a hat, but his hair, just turning silvery gray, was as thick as thatch.

Ty stopped shoveling feed to the heifers and rested the edge of his scoop on the ground. Seventy-three angus yearlings were spread out in an arc around him. Steam rose from their nostrils as they masticated their meal. Ty tightened his grip on the handle. "I guess that sleigh took longer than I planned."

Monty nodded. "You did a good job on that, but the welding's got to be done, too."

"I'll get at it tonight," he said and returned to his current task, but Monty wasn't finished.

"What'd your girl think of it?"

"*My*—" Ty actually jumped. "Sophie ain't my girl."

"Whose is she then?" he asked.

"I . . ." Ty's nerves were hopping. His face felt warm. "She's her own girl, I suppose."

"Just cuz a horse ain't branded, don't mean it's not yours."

"She ain't . . ." Ty began, but then he recognized the spark in the older man's eyes. It was the same look Colt often got. Generally speaking, someone punched him in the shoulder shortly after. Ty drew a deep breath and glanced toward the west where the sun was just sinking beneath the snow-covered slopes. There wasn't no way in hell he was going to take a swing at Monty Dickenson. "She's moving to California."

Dickenson lowered his bushy brows.

"Her folks are buying some land there."

"I thought her parents were divorced."

"They're getting back together."

"Oh." Monty nodded. "What are you going to do about that?"

Ty caught his gaze. "What . . ." He shook his head. "Ain't nothing I *can* do."

Dickenson stared at him, letting the silence grow before he spoke again. "I been around some time now," he said and shook his head. "Can't come up with one time out of a thousand that's been true."

Off by the barn a cow bellowed. Night settled in a little snugger.

"You saying I should do something?" Ty asked.

Monty shrugged. "What do you *want* to do?"

"I wanna—" Ty tightened his fist on the shovel handle. A dozen wild scenarios raced through his head like skittish broncs. "I don't want her to get hurt," he said finally.

The smallest hint of a smile toyed with the old cattleman's lips. "Then I suggest you open the chute gate and choose your best pickup horse."

Ty stood in silence for a second, but the reference escaped him. "I don't know what that means."

"Every cowgirl gets throwed eventually, son," he said and turned away. "Smartest thing you can do is make sure her landing ain't too hard."

CHAPTER 27

Casie tied a bow of baling twine around the spindle of the antique spinning wheel hidden in her bedroom. She'd traded three full fleeces of unprocessed wool for it. Fleeces in the grease, was the colloquial term. Four days ago she'd been excited about handing out Christmas gifts. But now everything was turned upside down. Emily seemed atypically distant, Sophie would be leaving within the week, and Colt was barely speaking to her after his surprise attack proposal and her subsequent refusal.

She ran her fingers over the picture frame that housed the photo of Freedom. Autumn colors blazed in the background as the mare galloped across the pasture. Her nostrils were flared. Her mane, thick as brambles, blew in the wind. It was a pretty picture, but it was the unfettered joy in the chestnut's eyes that had convinced Casie to give it to Sophie. Emily had taken the shot. Colt had crafted the frame from weathered barn wood. Casie herself had had almost nothing to do with it. Nevertheless she had looked forward to seeing the girl's reaction.

Now, she was less certain. After seeing the Coach bag and matching luggage Monica had purchased for her daughter, the picture seemed cheesy beyond compare. Besides, Sophie would be gone by Christmas. Still, what else was she going to do with it? Sighing, she picked up the homey gift and traipsed down the hall toward the smallest of the house's three bedrooms. The door was shut. She knocked once. "Hey, Soph, can I come in?"

There was a moment of silence, then soft footsteps before the handle turned. The girl's expression was sober, her eyes bright. Beyond her, a trio of boxes sat filled and sealed. Her newly purchased suitcases sat beside them.

"So you're ready to go, huh?" Casie said and fought to keep her voice level despite the pang of disappointment that unexpectedly jolted her heart. She and Soph had had their share of skirmishes, but maybe those very battles were part and parcel of the reason it hurt to see her bolt away like a mustang from captivity. Maybe, despite the energy Casie expended to avoid confrontations, heated disputes could actually bring people closer together. It was a disturbing possibility. The girl shrugged. "Thought I'd just get it done now."

Casie nodded, then jerked herself back to her reason for coming. "Well, it's not much for all your hard work, but I wanted to give you this," she said and handed over the photograph.

Sophie took it in silence and blinked at it.

Casie cleared her throat and shuffled her feet a little. She had no idea why she couldn't grow up. Why she couldn't interact with others with a modicum of maturity. She didn't need to have the sleek panache of Monica Day-Bellaire. But maybe she could be as socially adept as, say . . . your average kitchen chair. "The frame's made from old barn wood."

Sophie nodded, lips pursed.

"Emily took the picture."

Still the girl said nothing.

"She has a way with . . ." Casie shook her head. "Things. Anyway . . . I just wanted you to have it."

"Thanks," Sophie said and momentarily lifted hooded eyes to Casie. "Well . . . I'd better get back to my packing."

"Sure," Casie said and took a cautious step back, though she wanted nothing more than to shoot down the stairs and outside like a loosed missile. "Hey, I'm really happy for you, Soph."

Sophie nodded, then glanced to the right as Lumpkin came charging up the stairs, ears bouncing. "Did you know it has an indoor arena?"

Casie shook her head, losing track of the conversation as she lifted the lamb into her arms.

"Our new farm. It's got an indoor."

"Oh." Casie forced a smile. "That's great."

"Just a small one. But I won't have to freeze my fingers anymore while bridling up."

"It sounds fantastic."

"Yeah." Sophie tilted her chin up a little in a mannerism reminiscent of former days. "Nothing but the best for Philip and Monica Jaegar Day-Bellaire."

Casie canceled launch mode and drew a careful breath. "They love you very much," she said.

Sophie shrugged casually as if to say it didn't matter either way, and Casie, unable to be an extrovert a moment longer, turned briskly away.

"You didn't have anything to do with this, did you?" The girl's words were quick and terse, drawing Casie back around to face her.

"With what?"

"This . . ." She gave a sparse wave. "My parents acting so . . ." She searched for the right word, lips twisting a little. "Nice," she said.

Casie laughed. "They just want to be a family again, Soph. Enjoy it."

There was a long, breathless pause, then, "Sure," she said and shut the door.

Not much later, supper was served. Casie had stolen a handful of minutes to groom Chesapeake and ease a saddle onto his back. With Sophie leaving, training horses would be entirely up to her again.

Lincoln Alexander was typically silent throughout the meal. Ty was the same. Even Max Barrenger seemed a little subdued as he complimented Emily's latest feast.

"Here here," Philip said and raised his glass. It was three-quarters filled with a dark merlot he had ordered from their soon-to-be ranch in California. "To Emily Kane, the best pastry chef this side of the Mississippi."

"The best chef anywhere," Max corrected, attention sharp

on the object of their conversation. Casie couldn't help but notice that Colt's brows lowered as he watched Max watch the girl.

"They *are* lovely biscuits," Monica said. "But there's a little place just a few blocks from my flat in Manhattan that makes the best beignets I've ever tasted."

"Beignets?" Casie questioned. She wanted nothing more than to fall facedown onto her mattress and stay there for a week, but Em was no longer leading the extroverts' ball and someone had to dance the dance.

"It's a French word," Monica explained as she swirled her merlot. "It means 'fluffy.' They are *très bon*. But filled with about a thousand fat grams per donut. I have to watch how many I eat."

"Well, you won't have to worry about that anymore," Philip said, and staring into her eyes, took her hand in his.

She smiled up at him. "Why's that?"

"Well . . ." He turned slightly to wink at his daughter. "You'll be so busy mucking stalls and stacking hay that those evil little fat grams won't have a chance to settle in. Isn't that right, Soph?"

His daughter didn't respond. Her knuckles looked white against the red plaid tablecloth.

Monica laughed. "As you may have guessed, Philip Thomas Jaegar, I'm not really the stall-mucking type."

"You never know," her husband quipped and grinned as he leaned toward her slightly. "I didn't think you'd be the type to sell that flat in Manhattan, either."

Monica's threaded brows rose as she reared back a scant inch. "What makes you think I am?"

"Well . . ." He laughed again, jolly as an elf. This wasn't his first glass of merlot. "We're buying a farm in Napa County, California."

"Which will make a nice little getaway from the city."

The smile dropped slowly from Jaegar's chiseled face. "I thought you wanted me to sell my condo."

Monica laughed and glanced conspiratorially at the others

around the table. "*Everyone* wants you to sell that condo, Philip. It's so . . ."

His back stiffened a little. "What?" he asked.

There were four seconds of dead silence before Casie managed to jolt to her feet. "Anyone ready for dessert?"

"Pedantic," Monica said and ignored her completely.

"Not for me, thank you," Philip said but never turned from his ex-wife. "You know we'll need to sell both properties in order to make that down payment."

She raised her chin a notch. "What happened to your savings?"

"There's raspberry crisp," Casie said. "It smells terrific."

"My savings!" Philip said and choked a short laugh. "You must be kidding. I've been paying you enough alimony to—"

"Folks!" Colt said, shifting his gaze from Jaegar to Day-Bellaire. "Maybe this isn't the time or place for this discussion."

"That alimony—" Monica began, but Colt pushed himself noisily to his feet.

"You might want to take this outside," he suggested.

Philip glanced around as if surprised to find they weren't entirely alone. "You're right. Of course," he said. "Darling . . ." The word sounded a little strained. "Let's let these people eat, shall we? It's a beautiful night for a walk."

She stared at him a second, then stood and turned toward the entryway. In a moment the door had closed behind them.

"Marriage," Max said, grinning. "It's not for the faint of heart."

Colt glanced at Casie, eyes troubled. "How 'bout that dessert, Em?" he said.

She jerked herself from her trance and handed him a plate.

"No!" The single word sounded perfectly clear from the porch.

Colt shifted his gaze to Sophie. She looked taut as a bowstring, but he forced himself to sit back down. Ty's expression was no less strained. "You did a real nice job on that sleigh," Colt said, but Tyler's attention was riveted on the girl who sat across the table from him. Colt cleared his throat. "How long did that take you?"

The boy jerked his attention to his left. His expression was pained, his face pale, but he forced himself to speak. "Your dad done most of the work."

"That's not exactly the story I heard. He said you hardly slept for—"

"I knew it!" Monica's voice was little more than a growl. "You've always wanted to bring me down to your level."

"My level? My *level?*" Philip laughed. "You still believe you're on some impregnable pedestal that—"

"This is exactly why I'm keeping my flat," Monica said.

"In which case, there will be no farm!"

"That's fine with me. I was just trying to make my daughter happy, but you're the same controlling bastard you've always been."

"And you're the same snotty—"

Colt and Sophie jolted to their feet simultaneously. He stormed toward the door just as she swiveled toward the stairs.

"Soph," Ty said and followed her from the room.

"Hey." Colt's voice was quiet but clear from the porch. "Maybe you two want to go for a drive or something."

"I'm not getting into a car with—" Monica began, but her words were drowned by Sophie's as Colt shut the door behind him.

"You're no better than me!" The girl's tone was low and strident.

Ty's voice was soft. "I know that."

"You're so smug. You think just because you're Casie's darling, you can change, but you can't. You'll always be white trash!" she said and sped noisily up the stairs.

In the absolute silence that followed, Casie was certain she could hear Ty's heart crack, but in a moment an engine roared to life. It was followed by another. Colt stepped back into the house just as Ty strode past him, eyes cast toward the floor as he hurried outside.

"What happened?" Colt asked.

Casie shook her head.

Max grinned. "Merry Christmas," he said.

Later that night, when the kitchen was all but empty, Max was still grinning. "Daytime TV's got nothing on this place, huh?"

Emily scowled as she cut out Christmas cookies on the liberally floured counter. "Do relationships ever work?"

"Relationships?" He leaned to the side to see her face better. "Sure. Lots of them."

She glanced up. "Are your parents together?"

"Mine? Yeah. Just not with each other." He laughed. "Come on, Em, why don't you take a break with that?" he said, and took her hands. They were dusted with flour. "Hey, tell you what . . . how 'bout you take tomorrow off?"

She shook her head. "It's Christmas Eve tomorrow. I'm going to have to glaze the ham and make fresh rolls and—"

"Wouldn't it be a lot easier if I just treated everyone to a meal in town?"

"What town?"

He laughed. "I don't know. There must be one around here somewhere."

"Not one with a restaurant that's open on Christmas Eve."

"No kidding?" He reared back a little, looking shocked.

"None whatsoever. Everyone wants to be with their family this time of year. Well . . . you know . . ." She felt odd tonight. So jittery and out of sorts that she considered waking Bliss just to feel her heart beat. "Everyone who *has* a family."

He smiled and caressed her knuckles.

"We're going to have such fun together, Em. We'll zip line in Costa Rica and golf at Pebble Beach. We'll go parasailing off Antigua and . . ."

"Perfect my recipes."

"What are you talking about? Your recipes are already perfect."

"No, they're not. If I'm going to get my products into supermarkets, I'm going to have to keep experimenting and develop a marketing plan and have an industrial kitchen that—"

He laughed. "You are such a cute little thing."

"I'm not—"

"I'll get you a state-of-the-art kitchen, we'll hire a team to put together a marketing plan, and as for experimenting . . ." He squeezed her hands and moved closer, expression suggestive. "I'm all for that. I don't even mind if we do some of it in the kitchen."

She stepped back a pace. "What about Bliss?"

"What about her?"

"Where is she while we're zip lining and parasailing and . . . whatever."

He shrugged. "Back at the resort slugging mai tais, I suppose," he said and laughed at her stricken expression. "I'm just kidding. We'll get her a nanny."

Emily lowered her brows, gut clenching.

"Oh, don't look so disgusted. We'll find someone wonderful for her. Someone to handle the dirty diapers and upset tummies so we can enjoy life a little."

"I *am* enjoying life."

He smiled. Lifting her hands, he ran a thumb across her palm. "Your calluses suggest—"

"Would you have slept with me?"

"What?" he said and scowled at her.

"That night we . . ." She winced. It was just a kiss. She had told herself that a thousand times, but smaller things had caused castles to crumble, families to fail. "Would you have slept with me?"

"Well, no," he said and grinned. "I mean, this place is like Grand Central Station. Where would we have gone?"

She exhaled. "So the fact that you were with Sonata wouldn't have mattered?"

"Sonata's a great girl," he said and sobered. "She really is, but the chemistry just wasn't right. I knew that for—"

She pulled her hands out of his. "I want you to leave," she said.

"What?"

She stepped back a pace, putting distance between them. "I'm sorry."

"What are you talking about?"

"This is my home," she said and waved a little frantically at the space around her. "This is my family."

He stared at her, then chuckled as he lifted a twisted dreadlock from her shoulder. "Believe me, Em. This is *not* your family." He smiled. "I know you're nervous about leaving. Anyone with your background would be, but they're just using you here. You must be able to see that."

"Using me for what?"

He chuffed a laugh. "Look at you. It's eight o'clock at night and you're still working like a dog."

"I like to work."

"You're being ridiculous."

"I want to stay here."

"Listen, Em, we have a deal. Let's not—"

"The deal's off!" Panic roared through her. What the hell had she been thinking? The Lazy Windmill was where peace lived, where Bliss blossomed, and hope had a chance.

"It's not—"

"Leave!" Her voice had risen a little. The tone was harsh.

"Don't get hysterical," he said and took a step toward her.

"Mr. Barrenger . . ."

Emily jerked her gaze to the left. Casie stood in the doorway. Her expression was tense. Their eyes met for an instant before the older woman shifted her attention back to Max.

"It's been a long day," she said.

He lowered his brows and faced her. "I'm sorry if we disturbed you. But Em and I have a few things to hash out." Reaching out, he took her hand again, curling his fingers forcefully around hers. He was stronger than he looked. "How about we go for a drive and discuss—"

"There's nothing to discuss," Emily said and pulled back, but he tightened his grip.

"You don't belong here."

"You're wrong."

His expression hardened. "Emily—"

"Get out," Casie said.

He turned on her, smile taut. "Emily and I had a verbal agreement. Perhaps it won't hold up in court. But I can cause you a good deal of legal trouble."

"Legal trouble?" Casie said, and laughing, raised her right hand. The pistol there gleamed in the overhead lights.

He stumbled back a pace, dropping Emily's hand as he did so. "Just a minute!"

"She asked you nicely." Casie stepped forward.

"You're crazy."

"That's entirely possible," Casie said and cocked back the hammer.

The front door opened and closed. Colt's voice could be heard from the entry. "Longest damn day in the history of—" He stepped into the kitchen and stopped. "Hey, Case."

"Hi." Her voice was as steady as a rock, her hand the same.

"Why are you pointing a forty-five at Maxwell Barrenger's head?"

"He seems reluctant to leave Emily alone."

"Ahh." He stepped forward a few tentative paces. "That's unfortunate, but you probably shouldn't shoot him just the same."

"Why not?"

"Well, it's frowned on in certain circles."

"South Dakota operates under the castle doctrine."

The house went silent.

Max darted his gaze from Emily to Colt. "What the hell does that mean?"

"It means we can protect our homes," Colt said, and shrugged. "I think she plans to shoot you."

"You're *all* crazy!" Max said.

"Not *me*," Colt argued. "But Casie does have a wild side. The quiet ones . . ." He shook his head. "You've got to watch out for them. You should see what she did to Ty's mother. It wasn't pretty."

Max backed toward the door. Colt turned to watch him go.

"It's been a pleasure having you at—" he began, but Barrenger took that opportunity to bolt.

"The Lazy," Colt finished and turned back toward the women. Emily swallowed. Casie lowered the pistol.

"Case," Colt said, and stepping forward, eased the gun from her fingers. "If you're going to shoot someone, you should probably use real bullets. These mounted shooting blanks aren't very effective."

"I'll keep that in mind," she said, and turning toward Emily, took a deep breath. "What's going on?"

"What do you mean?"

Outside, an engine roared to life. Tires squealed on the gravel drive.

"Max Barrenger is an—" She paused. "He's not good enough to peel your carrots, Em. Why were you interested in him?"

Emily swallowed. "He's wealthy."

"Uh huh."

"And handsome."

Casie shrugged.

"And you know I've always been attracted to . . ." She paused, mind spinning, nerves cranked up tight. "It's Alexander."

They stared at her as if she'd lost her mind. And maybe she had. Maybe she finally and truly had.

"Lincoln Alexander? Our guest?" Casie guessed.

She jerked a nod.

"What about him?"

"I lied."

They waited in silence.

"I knew him from . . . from before."

"And?" Colt shifted his weight. His scowl had returned.

"We just called him Linc. When I was . . ." She closed her eyes for a second. "I used to . . . I lived on the streets for a while."

"Okay."

"Linc took me in. I thought he was an okay guy. But he . . ." She exhaled. "He's really smart. Could orchestrate . . ." She shook her head. "There was a bunch of us. Half dozen at least. We were panhandlers." She felt a muscle twitch in her cheek. "Thieves. I wanted to get out for months, but he . . . he's very persuasive."

"I'll call the sheriff," Colt said and stepped toward the phone, but she grabbed his arm.

"No. Please. I . . ." Fear had turned to bitter terror. "I couldn't stand to lose . . . I know I don't deserve her." She tightened her fingers in his sleeve. "I know I don't deserve any of this."

"What are you talking about?"

"I was a criminal," she said. "I'd go to jail, too."

Colt let his shoulders drop and glanced toward Casie. "You got something with a little more firepower than that thing?" he asked, indicating the pistol.

Casie shifted her attention to Emily. Her focus felt dark and heavy.

"Case?" Colt said.

She turned her gaze reluctantly back to him. "Let's not do anything rash," she said.

He raised his brows as he motioned toward the pistol. "Are you kidding me?"

"I never meant to put anyone in danger." Emily inhaled, lifted her chin, faced the firing squad. "I should leave," she said and stepped toward the stairway.

"What?" Casie asked.

"What!" Colt snapped.

"He's just here because of me." Her throat felt tight, her legs rubbery. "Me and the baby."

"I'll get the rifle," Casie said and Colt nodded.

CHAPTER 28

Christmas Eve day dawned cold and silent. Every bush was frosted white, every branch rimed with crystal.

Sophie had returned to her room after morning chores and remained there still, though it was well past noon. Ty hadn't shown his face since the previous day. Colt, however, had stayed the night. To make sure Lincoln Alexander, or whatever his name was, didn't return, he'd said. He had stepped outside hours earlier. Either he was cleaning the cattle pens or he was patrolling the perimeter like an overzealous cattle dog.

Even Emily, usually so hopelessly optimistic, looked grim as she stirred the contents of a battered steel pot.

"Why don't you take a nap while Bliss is still content," Casie said. From the living room, the baby cooed quietly. "Don't worry about meals today."

"It's just soup," Emily said, and crushing a bit of dried something in her hands, added it to the steaming contents. "But it's done."

The stairs creaked under Casie's footsteps.

Sophie was still locked away in her bedroom. "Dinner's ready." Silence met the announcement. "I can bring something up, if you—" she began, but the door opened in a moment. Sophie's eyes looked tired, but dry. Her mouth was pursed in her signature sign of anger.

"How are you doing?" Casie asked.

"Fine," she said and moved toward the stairs.

The girl's attack on Ty ate at Casie, but it seemed like a less-than-perfect time to bring it up.

Back in the kitchen, Emily was dishing soup into oversized mugs.

Sophie glanced at the table. Her lips twitched. Her complexion was pale. "Where is everyone?"

"Lincoln had to . . ." Casie paused. No good could come of spilling Em's secrets of the night before. "Lincoln left last night," she said simply.

"How about . . ." Sophie paused. Her eyes looked bruised. "Everyone else?"

"Colt should be in soon," Casie said, and knew she was avoiding the subject. "He's—"

"If you want Ty around, you should quit publicly humiliating him," Emily said.

Casie held her breath. Looking from one combatant to the other, she waited for Sophie to explode, but the girl's voice was low when she finally spoke.

"He might as well know the truth now."

Emily faced her square on. "What truth's that?"

The girl shrugged as she slipped into the nearest chair. "I'm a . . ." She paused and pursed her lips again as if to control her ire. "He's got to learn not to trust people."

"Sophie—" Casie began, but Emily interrupted.

"No, she's right." Her expression was tired, resigned. "Relationships never work out."

"That's not true."

"Yeah?" Emily said. Both girls were staring at her with varying degrees of disdain and hope. "Name one that has."

Casie flinched. Emily's traitorous thoughts weren't far from her own, but it was her responsibility to give them hope. Yet, suddenly, she couldn't think of a single working relationship.

"See?" Emily said. "It's not even worth trying to work things out when—"

"My parents," Casie said.

There was a moment's hesitation and then both girls snorted.

"Okay, they weren't perfect, but I think . . ." A dozen memories of angry confrontations roared through Casie's mind. But the distress caused by those conflicts had faded somewhere along the way, making the arguments seem dim and her own re-action to them rather infantile. Life wasn't idyllic, after all. People yelled and whined and pouted and moved on. It was human nature. She didn't have to like it. "I know they cared about each other. Dad—"

"Oh please . . ." Emily's tone was disgusted as she took fresh rolls from the oven. "You're so weirded out by your parents' relationship, you throw away love with both hands."

"That's not true."

"Are you messing with me?" she asked, facing Casie like an angry pugilist. "Colt works like a field slave around here and you don't give him the time of—"

"I know you care about Mr. Dickenson," Casie said, cutting in before the girl felt the need to revisit every menial task Colt had undertaken in the past six months. "And I'm glad you do. But he's not the kind to settle down on—"

Emily snorted.

Casie tightened her fists. "I realize you think you understand him. But I've known him a lot longer than you have, and he's not the sort of guy to spend day after day milking goats and changing diapers."

"What do you think he's *been* doing?"

"I . . ." Casie began, but just then the doorbell rang. They held their collective breath as someone stepped inside.

"Anybody home?" Cindy Dickenson's voice was clear and cheery.

Casie flipped her gaze from one girl to the next, silently de-bating whether Colt's mother could have heard their conversation.

"Yeah," Emily said and hurried toward the entryway. "Come in."

In a second, Cindy Dickenson entered the kitchen carrying a covered casserole dish.

She glanced at the faces around her. Unless she had all the in-tuition of a brick, she could probably sense the angst. "I know

Emily's the best cook in the world," she said without preamble, "but I had to get this out of the house and I thought maybe you could use it."

Emily rushed forward to relieve the older woman of her burden. "That's really nice of you," she said, and setting the dish on the table, removed the foil cover. Inside, baked lasagna still bubbled with melding layers of cheese and noodles. "But why couldn't *you* use it?"

"Because she likes to torture me," Monty said and trundled in, carrying a covered tray. "Afternoon, ladies."

"Hello, Mr. Dickenson." Casie felt her face heat. What were the chances that their conversation had gone unheard?

"Maybe your wife's just trying to keep you around for a while," Emily suggested, addressing Monty. "Lasagna isn't exactly fat free."

He shook his head. "She's mean-spirited, is what she is."

Cindy turned toward him with a scowl. "If I'm mean-spirited, you're weak-willed."

Casie winced.

"Listen, woman, I've busted my hump for you and the kids for—" he began, then stopped abruptly. "What's wrong?"

"Nothing. I'm fine," his wife said, but she was gripping the edge of the table with plump fingers gone pale at the tips.

"Here, sit down," Monty insisted, and taking her arm in a firm grip, turned her toward the nearest chair.

She put a hand on his arm, steadying herself. Their eyes met, his worried, hers soft. "I'm okay now," she said.

"Are you sure?" His voice was no more than a low rumble of worry. His eyes were intense, absolutely focused, as if nothing else in the world mattered a whit.

"Of course, I'm sure. It's nothing," she said.

"Do you want me to carry you to the truck?" he asked and curved a protective arm around her shoulders.

She tsked, color returning to her cheeks like a flood. "Don't be silly."

"I still can, you know," he said. A spark of devilishness shone in his deep-water eyes.

"You think I don't know that?" Blushing, she slipped her arm through his as they turned to go.

They walked out side by side. His eyes were for her alone. He murmured something too quiet for the girls to hear, but his wife chuckled softly and swatted his arm with her free hand.

The threesome in the kitchen stood immobilized for the count of five, then turned like automatons to fiddle with nothing in particular. Bliss made quiet baby noises from the living room, but otherwise the house was absolutely silent until Colt Dickenson stepped inside. The collar of his canvas coat was popped up against the dark skin of his throat. "What did my folks want?" he asked.

The women turned as one to stare at him.

"What?" he asked.

Emily blinked and turned away, hiding her face as she tossed rolls into a basket.

Sophie pursed her lips and spooned up a bit of soup.

"What's going on?" Colt asked, tone dubious.

"Nothing," Casie said but her voice sounded strained even to herself. She cleared her throat and cut into the lasagna. "Your mom just dropped this off."

He nodded. "She feeling okay?"

"I think she was a little dizzy."

His worried expression was reminiscent of his father's. "She's going in for another battery of tests after the first of the year."

"I'm sorry," Casie said, and despite the passing of years, remembered her own mother's medical battles with a pang of guilt-riddled sorrow. "That's got to be hard for her."

"It's worse for Dad." Hanging up his coat, he stepped fully into the kitchen. "Sometimes I catch him staring at her like she's made of glass."

He slipped into a chair. Dinner was a quiet affair. Afterward, Sophie cleared the dishes as Emily ran water into the sink.

"Oh sh—" She gritted her teeth, dreadlocks bouncing. "Shoot!" she said.

Casie glanced up from storing the remaining lasagna. "What's wrong?"

"Drain's clogged again."

"I'll take care of it," she said and hurried to fetch the plunger, but when she returned Colt tried to take it from her hands. "I can do it."

"So can I," he countered.

"Go . . ." She shook her head, feeling oddly manic. "Watch television or something."

"That's a good idea," he said. "I think I'll catch up on my soaps while you do all the manual labor."

"I don't do all the—"

"Oh, for Pete's sake!" Emily snapped. "Let him take care of the drain."

They turned to her in tandem surprise, then zipped their gazes toward each other and away.

"Okay," Casie said, and clearing her throat, relinquished the plunger.

"I'm sorry," Emily said and turned to rest her hands on the edge of the counter.

"You all right?" Colt asked.

"Sure. I'm fine," she said and formed another stack of dirty dishes.

Colt raised his brows. Casie shrugged, uncertain.

Bliss squawked from her bassinet.

"I'll get her," Sophie said and hurried from the room.

"I'm sorry about Barrenger," Colt said and pushed the plunger into the sink drain.

Emily shrugged.

"Looks like it's really stuck this time," he said and pushed his sleeves up dark-skinned forearms.

Casie forced herself to turn away. So what if he was still here, still hanging around, still helping out? It didn't mean anything. He had to be *somewhere* between rodeo queens.

"Maybe we should think about replacing the trap underneath," he suggested.

"Don't worry about it," Casie said and turned to watch as he relinquished the plunger and unbuttoned his shirt.

"What are you doing?" she asked. Beside her, Emily was absolutely silent.

He hung the garment over the back of a nearby chair. Dark biceps bunched beneath the sleeves of his white T-shirt. He glanced at her. "I'm getting kinda hot."

She felt a little flushed herself. "You don't . . . you don't have to do this," she reminded him, but her voice sounded faint.

"Don't think this is altruistic. Em promised to make rosettes. I'm afraid she'll back out if the sink doesn't work," he said and returned to his task with renewed vigor. His forearms knotted like vibrant roots. His biceps bunched as he leaned into the job, and the muscles in his back bulged, straining against the wear-softened fabric of his shirt.

"Holy crap," Sophie rasped, returning to the kitchen. Casie managed to pull her gaze from Colt long enough to glance in her direction. The girl's lips were parted slightly as she watched Colt work. Em's expression was just as enraptured.

"Right now I think you're the dumbest woman I've ever met," she breathed.

Casie shifted her attention to Bliss. But she found no support there; the baby's eyes were wide, and a tiny dollop of drool was just slipping from her cupid's-bow lips.

CHAPTER 29

Casie sat bolt upright. It was as black as pitch outside her bedroom window, but something had awakened her, footsteps on gravel, maybe, or . . .

A noise groaned from below stairs. Breath held, she stepped out of bed. The floor creaked beneath her feet. The yard was dark and empty but for Puke and . . .

Her breath froze in her throat. Was that a footprint in the new snow? A scratch of noise sounded from below again. Swallowing, she slipped her .45 from the gun belt that hung in the closet and crept downstairs. She flipped the living room switch. Light bathed the room, bringing normalcy with it. There was nothing out of the ordinary. Stepping into the kitchen, she lit that as well. Security seeped in. A dozen brown eggs sat in a wooden bowl on the counter. Black walnuts occupied a basket on the table.

Casie exhaled heavily and ran a glass of water from the tap. Christmas had come and gone. As had Colt. After spending a few additional nights on the couch, he had finally begun returning to his parents' ranch in the evenings. Not that it mattered. She was an independent woman, but perhaps she *was* a little jumpier without him there. After all, she was currently standing in the middle of her kitchen holding a cold pistol and a tepid glass of water.

Silently laughing at herself, she set the .45 beside the walnuts and glanced out the window. Jack was trotting across the yard, black body barely visible in the darkness. He must have made the noise that woke her. Perhaps he'd spotted a skunk. Sometimes the semi-dormant wildlife left their dens to forage for food this time of year. It was nice to have a watchdog to convince them to move along.

Grateful and oddly lonely, Casie pulled a bag of whole wheat bread from the cupboard. A few table scraps never hurt anyone, she decided, and venturing to the entry, slipped into a pair of over-boots before leaning outside.

"Jack," she called quietly, but he was nowhere to be seen. "Come on, boy," she said, and folding her arms across her chest, stepped onto the porch. The moon was a shiny trinket in the western sky, the world below just as silvery. She drew a deep breath and walked to the railing. She'd seen this view a thousand times. But she never tired of the long sweep of hills, the endless horizon. Near the hip shed, Jack reappeared. "There you are. Don't you want—" she began, but just then a noise scraped the floor behind her. She spun toward it.

"Who's there?" Her voice was raspy.

A black shadow separated itself from the murky dimness.

It was a man. She knew that much, but no more. She darted her eyes toward the door, wondering if she could beat him inside.

"Who are you?"

The silence dragged on, but finally he spoke.

"Lincoln."

Lincoln Alexander? Frozen air rasped against her throat. "What are you doing here?"

"I need to see Ellie."

"What?" If she bolted into the house, could she slam the door before he got inside?

"When I knew her, she called herself Ellie." His voice was very low, very quiet. "Ellie Casper."

She shook her head. "You need to leave. Now! You need to—"

"I need to see my baby."

Her lungs felt constricted. "Emily told us all about you, but I won't call the sheriff if—"

"I was an art student at USD when we met."

She jerked her gaze toward the door again, desperately longing to be inside.

"She was a barista at the Jumping Bean."

Casie scowled as mismatched pieces of Emily's story settled in around her like flotsam from a shipwreck.

"She was always laughing. Always upbeat. That's what drew me at first. Things were tough at home. My folks wanted me to be an engineer. Dad was sick and . . ." He paused. "She didn't tell me she had a boyfriend." He took another step forward. Casie shuffled away.

"Please leave," she whispered.

"Then I saw the bruises and—"

"Linc!" Emily's voice shot through the night like a bullet.

Casie jerked toward her. "Get back in the house!" she rasped, but the girl just stepped onto the porch.

"What are you doing here?" she asked.

"Bliss is mine, isn't she?"

Emily glanced toward Casie, eyes wide and bright in the darkness.

"Isn't she?" he asked again.

"I called Mr. Dickenson. He'll be here any minute."

"I shouldn't have left," he said. "I know that now."

"I'm going to call the sheriff," Emily warned and backed toward the house.

"Just let me hold her first."

"Get inside! Lock the door!" Casie ordered, but Emily remained where she was, gaze caught fast on the young man who shivered on the porch.

"She's not yours," Emily said.

"Whose then?"

She lifted her chin a little. "She's Flynn's."

He stood very still for a second, then exhaled softly. "You were always the best liar I've ever met."

"I'm not lying."

"You're unpredictable, El. And sometimes you're a little crazy. But you're not stupid."

"I'm not lying!"

He shook his head. "You wouldn't have gone back to that bastard. Not even with me gone. You knew you deserved better than that."

"You don't know me."

"I want to. I—"

"What's going on?" Casie asked.

Emily remained perfectly still for a moment, then turned robotically toward her. Even in the dim light the agony in her eyes was clear. "He's . . ." She paused, silently fighting demons. "He's *not* a thief. That was someone else." She cleared her throat. "Linc wouldn't steal any . . . well, not . . . he took some potpies from the school cafeteria once. And a cheesecake." Her face looked eerily pale in the dim light. "When I didn't have enough money to pay for . . ." She paused. ". . . Anything."

"What is he to you?" Casie asked.

She exhaled heavily, breath white in the near darkness. "He's . . . he was a friend. At least I thought he was. I thought—"

"I *am* your friend, El. But I couldn't find you. I looked. Then someone said . . ." He shook his head. "I was sure you wouldn't really be here. When I saw Sophie all bundled up, riding a horse, I thought maybe they'd mistaken her for you. But then I . . ." His words stopped. "I tried to leave . . . to stay out of your life, but . . ." He shrugged.

Casie shivered. The boy looked smaller somehow and painfully thin. "This isn't a good time for this."

He nodded, as if agreeing, but didn't move away. "I have to talk to her."

"Maybe tomorrow when—"

"I would have waited if I could. I would have . . ." He tightened his fists and turned back toward Emily. "I should have called you."

The girl snorted a laugh. "Ya think?"

"It's just . . ." He glanced away, eyes bright in the ambient light. "I panicked."

"Yeah. Me too. But then *I* was the one who was pregnant."

"I didn't know!" he said and jerked forward, but just then

Colt's truck careened into the yard. In a moment he was stalking across the gravel toward the porch.

"What's going on?" His voice was no more than a growl. He carried a rifle in his right hand.

"I have no idea," Casie said.

"Em?" he asked, turning toward her.

She met his gaze, but turned away in a moment. "I didn't . . ." She paused. "His name's David Lincoln."

"I don't care what his name is. I just want to know if I should shoot him or not."

Her lips moved. There were tears in her eyes. "Not," she said finally.

"Okay." He nodded once. "Then let's get him inside before we have to explain why he died of hypothermia on the porch."

In a second they were ensconced in the kitchen. Colt's hair stood up at odd angles. His eyes still looked sleepy and the flannel shirt he wore in lieu of a coat was buttoned wrong.

"We got any coffee?" he asked.

Casie shook her head.

Lincoln tightened his fists. "Can I talk to Ellie alone?"

Colt scowled. "Who the hell is Ellie?"

Casie shrugged once.

Emily cleared her throat. "They used to call me El."

Lincoln shuffled his feet. "I just want a few minutes to talk to—"

"No," Colt said, and settling his hips against the counter, propped the butt of the rifle against his thigh. "Whatever you got to say, say it now."

The boy fidgeted, then turned his attention back to Emily. "I know I don't have any rights to the baby. But—"

"Wait a minute," Colt said. Settling the Ruger more comfortably against his leg, he turned toward the boy. "Are you a thief or what?"

Lincoln's lips moved for a second. He shifted his gaze to Emily. She remained atypically silent. "When I was five I stole a pack of gum."

Colt lowered his brows and glanced at Emily. She turned her eyes aside.

"But later on . . ." Linc tightened his fists rhythmically. "I snuck quarters onto the counter to pay for it."

"Because you felt guilty?" Colt kept his glower focused on Emily. She didn't return his stare.

"Because my brother said thieves go to hell."

"What did he say about people who lie to folks who love you?" Colt asked.

Em jerked her eyes toward Colt. They were bright with tears, but he didn't shift his gaze away. She swallowed and glanced aside.

"It's not her fault," Linc said and stepped toward her, but Colt raised his rifle.

"How 'bout you just stay over on that side of the room?"

"Okay," he agreed, and backing away, took a deep breath.

"So . . ." Colt shuffled his dark gaze from one to the other, then gritted his teeth and forced a lighter tone. It sounded odd in the strained quiet. "How'd you two kids meet?"

Emily pursed her lips.

"I used to go into the coffee shop where she worked."

"Coffee," Colt said. His voice sounded a little dreamy. "You sure we don't have any of that?"

"I'll make some!" Emily sounded relieved to be busy and hurried toward the counter.

"She was . . ." Linc shrugged jerkily. There was something in his eyes. Anger or hope or disappointment or terror. It was impossible to tell. "I knew she was special."

"She makes pretty good coffee," Colt said. His tone was grudging. "If you like it strong."

"I don't like it at all."

"That's just one of the reasons I don't trust you," Colt said and shifted the Ruger a little.

"Colt," Casie chastised quietly, then turned to the boy. "Go on."

Lincoln swallowed. "I'd go in there and study, maybe buy a scone if I could afford it. Watch her."

Emily's movements looked stiff and ungainly as she dumped grounds into the coffeepot.

"I didn't know she was spoken for."

"You had a boyfriend?" Colt asked.

She didn't answer.

"His name was Flynn. There was some talk about him having a police record, but I thought he was an okay guy." His brows dipped a little. "Till I realized he and his buddies were stealing stuff." A muscle jumped in his jaw. "Till I noticed the bruises on El's neck."

Water splashed across the counter.

"Sorry," Emily said and immediately began mopping it up.

Silence filled the room for a second.

"Go on," Colt said. His voice was gritty.

Lincoln shrugged. The movement was awkward, but maybe the presence of Colt's rifle made it a little difficult to relax. "I didn't know why a girl like her would put up with . . ." He shrugged. "We got to talking." He cleared his throat. "One thing led to another thing."

"Another thing like sex?" Colt asked.

Emily swung around to face him, eyes wide.

"It wasn't like that," Lincoln said, words rushed. "I was in l—" He swallowed. "She moved in with me. I lived off campus. It was a dump. But having her there . . ." He paused, exhaled, shifted his gaze to her, then dragged it away. "Everything was going great. . . ." His voice trailed away. He shrugged.

"Seems to me we're missing a part of this little yarn," Colt said.

The boy exhaled. "Maybe it was *too* great."

"I don't think I've ever experienced that."

"I got scared. I mean, I wasn't ready to get married. Shi—"

"Don't swear," Colt said. "Casie doesn't like it."

Lincoln looked nervously from one to the other. "Sorry." He cleared his throat. "I wasn't even nineteen and I thought—"

"You could do better?" Colt asked.

"No! No. It's not that, I just . . . She told me she was late the same day I was heading back to Detroit to see my folks." He shook his head. "I planned to go back. Hell—"

"Quit—"

"Sorry. I mean . . ." He exhaled, skinny and devastatingly young. "I'd been offered a free ride at Oakland, so I thought maybe I should take advantage of that, and my buddies were throwing a party and . . ." He glanced at Casie, winced, and continued on a different tack. "Dad was sick. He wasn't doing well so—" He shrugged.

"So you stayed home to help with him?" Casie asked.

"No. I—" he began and straightened his spine with what looked like painful resolve. "I went to Cancun with my buddies so I could be a chickenshit bastard a little while longer."

They stared at him, but he had turned his gaze back to Emily.

"I convinced myself that you would have called if were pregnant. I mean . . ." He shook his head. "Why didn't you call?"

She stared at him. "I did call," she said. "I believe I asked your mother to have you get back to me."

He held her eyes for a fraction of a second before moving his guiltily away. "Why didn't you call *again?*" The words were almost inaudible.

Colt shifted the rifle. Linc winced.

"We've all made mistakes." Casie kept her voice soft, but Colt heard her. He tilted the Ruger's muzzle back toward the ceiling.

"So the baby's his?" Colt asked.

Emily snapped her panicked gaze to his. "I don't know who the father is. I mean . . ." She laughed. The sound was harsh. "How should I know—"

"Emily!" Colt barked. Even Casie jumped.

A tear slipped from the corner of the girl's eye. "She's *mine,*" she whispered. "Nobody else's."

Lincoln winced. "I'm not trying to take her from you, El. But I messed up with my dad." He swallowed. His eyes were bright with tears. "And sometimes you don't get second—"

"I don't care!" she rasped. "I don't care that your father was a genius and your mother's a saint. I don't care that you all lit sparklers on the Fourth of July and stocked food shelves on

New Year's Eve. You can't have Bliss. She's *mine!*" she repeated. The words were whispered. "She's all I've got. All I've ever wanted."

The world was silent for one long moment, waiting.

"Is he the father?" Colt asked finally.

Emily closed her eyes and swallowed. "Yeah," she said. "He is."

CHAPTER 30

The sun peeked with cheeky optimism through winter's gossamer veil.

The six weeks since Christmas had been productive ones. The haybine had been fixed, as had the roof on the corncrib. Lumpkin had moved into the barn with the new lambs, which had begun to arrive in earnest.

Ty watched as Casie slipped a halter over Chesapeake's nose. He didn't like to have her working with stallions; they were too unpredictable, too aggressive. But he wasn't the boss of her. Then again, neither was Colt, but Ty was pretty sure that rodeo cowboy would show up before long. He'd putter around the fences, tightening up loose wires and pounding in stray nails, staying close while Casie threw a saddle on the bay's back. Colt Dickenson might not be the savviest horse in the herd, but so far Casie's refusals hadn't chased him off. He had to get points for persistence. Which was more than could be said for Ty himself. He glanced surreptitiously toward the arena where Sophie put Freedom over a homemade double oxer. Her hair, bright as a harvest moon, flared out behind as the mare cleared the two vertical jumps. The sight of her face so alive made his breath catch in his throat.

"Careful," Linc said and tossed a pair of unidentified cables over his back as he made his way toward the ancient pickup truck parked beside the baling equipment.

Ty wasn't sure what to think about Lincoln Alexander, aka David Lincoln. A month ago he'd taken an apartment in Hope Springs. He paid the rent by working part time at the garage and made pocket change by selling his sculptures somewhere east of the Mississippi, but he seemed to spend most of his time at the Lazy. Ty didn't really think the ranch needed another man hanging around, but Emily sang a lot these days and laughed even more, so he was willing to reserve judgment. "Careful of what?"

Linc jerked his chin toward the arena where Sophie had just dismounted and was talking to her mare. "If you don't exhale every once in a while, you're gonna pass flat out."

Ty scowled. He and Soph hadn't exchanged more than a dozen words since before Christmas. For days, he had been absolutely certain she was out of line; he wasn't smug. And he sure as hell didn't think he was better than her. But in retrospect, he realized that knowing Casie had changed him. He felt different now, bigger somehow, whole, and maybe that swagger showed through.

"You're doing it again," Linc said.

Ty turned away from the sight of her. She was not magical. She was just a girl, he told himself, but somehow that didn't ring true in his soul. He blushed at the thought.

Linc chuckled as he pushed up the hood of the ancient Dodge.

"You ain't exactly top dog around here, you know," Ty said. His tone sounded a little pouty.

"Top dog?" Linc grinned and shook his head as he stared into the unfathomable depths of the old pickup's engine. "I'm still in the dog's *house*."

Ty straightened his back. He'd heard a truncated story of the other's relationship to Emily. He didn't know how much he had missed, but it hardly mattered. "Em deserves better than you," he said.

Linc caught his gaze, all trace of humor gone. "That's why I'm trying to *be* better than me."

"Yeah?"

"Yeah."

"Yeah what?" Emily asked and walked in. She was wearing a chunky knit sweater that exactly matched her tiny daughter's. Both were nubby. Bliss's looked like hers had been made for a three-armed hunchback.

Ty waited for the other boy to mention that fact. Colt certainly would have teased her about her lack of knitting skills, but David Lincoln seemed to be struck momentarily dumb. "Hey, Em," he managed finally, but his tone was funny. He'd given up calling her Ellie a couple weeks ago.

"Hey." Her cheeks were a little pink as she avoided Lincoln's gaze and latched onto Ty's. "I'm having trouble with the drain again."

Ty set aside the halter he was carrying, ready to help out. But a thought struck him suddenly. Chances were this David Lincoln guy was never going to be good enough for Emily, but maybe she didn't know that and maybe she needed a chance to figure it out on her own.

"There's a strawberry strudel in it for you if you'll try to fix it," she said, never shifting her gaze to the older boy's.

Ty glanced toward Lincoln. His brows were pulled low. He shuffled his feet and looked a little like he'd swallowed a land mine. Turned out there wasn't hardly nobody that did this love thing very well, he thought. But it could be that everyone should have the opportunity to fail.

"I'm kind of busy right now," Ty said.

Emily scowled before finally glancing toward her baby's daddy. Behind him, the truck's driver's door stood open. The new leather seat gleamed a bright, cool red in the overhead lights. She took in the half dozen parts that littered the tarp on the floor, then bit her lip for a second. "How about you?" she asked. Her voice was very soft. "Could you—"

"Yes!" Lincoln said, and wiping his hands on a towel, stepped toward her. Their gazes met in one sharp clash and then they turned in tandem toward the house, walking side by side, arms almost touching, tiny Bliss little more than a comma between their bodies as they strode uphill. Lincoln spoke. Emily glanced up to catch his eyes.

And there was something in her expression, some glimmer of hope so bright it made Ty's gut cramp up.

"He's not as bad as you think."

Ty jerked around at the sound of Sophie's voice and hoped rather wildly there weren't tears in his eyes. He busied his hands, doing God knows what. "I didn't say he was bad," he said.

"I know you don't think anybody can be good enough for her."

He shrugged.

She glanced sideways. Perfection in profile. "She . . ." She paused, then exhaled and let her shoulders drop a little as if forcing out the tension. She'd left her mare outside, but carried her English saddle, barely enough leather to fry up for supper, as the old codgers would say.

Ty focused all his attention on that saddle. Looking at her straight on just made him loopy.

"I'm sorry." Her words brought his attention back to her face with a snap. Her lips were pursed, her expression haughty, and for a moment he was absolutely certain he had heard her wrong.

"What?"

She raised one regal brow. "I said . . ." She gritted her teeth. "I apologized."

"Oh." As far as he could recall he had never been privy to such a thing. "Thank you?" He was pretty sure that was the proper thing to say, though her presence made it nearly impossible to be certain of anything.

She scowled at him. "For saying you thought you were better than I am."

He nodded. "I . . ." Would it look bad if he bolted out the door and hid in the sheep barn? "I don't think—"

"Well, you are."

He stopped, blinked, and scowled.

"You're kind," she said. Her voice had lowered. She cleared

her throat. "You're loyal. You're hardworking, and your *stupid* hands . . ." She stopped and shifted her gaze abruptly away as if the hills beyond the wide-flung doors called her name.

He stared at her. Could be he wasn't the only one who was crazy around here.

"I'd just . . ." She glanced at him again. A flicker of despair shone in her lost-girl eyes. "I'd like to be friends."

Something warm and hopeful unfurled softly in the middle of his being. "I thought we *was* friends, Soph."

She swallowed, pretty neck drawing his gaze. "Well, I . . . I was . . ." She raised her chin and tightened her jaw, but damned if she didn't look like she was about to cry. "I was an idiot."

He couldn't look away, but he managed to force a shrug. "Couple a words," he said. "That don't make no difference between real friends."

The world went silent. He was holding his breath again. But maybe she was, too. And then she smiled, the tiniest curve of a grin, and he couldn't resist slipping his stupid fingers around hers. Warmth slipped up his arm, enveloping his being, like sunlight against bare skin.

From the pen on the far side of the barn, Casie buckled Chesapeake's throatlatch and felt her heart swell as she watched the young couple trail hand in hand back to the riding arena. There would be fights again. There would be insecurities and wounded pride and bruised feelings, but that's what life was about. For right now, her favorite people in the world were happy.

And that was enough. More than one could ask for, as Emily would say. Far more than one should expect. She wouldn't overburden fate by asking for more. Wouldn't tip the world into despair by insisting on perfection.

Her mind wandered dreamily. Maybe Lincoln and Emily would marry. Little Bliss could be the flower girl, decked out in a poorly knit white dress that dragged down to her feet on one side and hiked up to her chubby knees on the other. She would toddle down the aisle holding Aunt Casie's hand. Ty would smile. Really smile to see Emily so happy, and all would be right with the world.

From his pickup truck, Colt watched Casie lead Chesapeake out of his corral. Sunlight glimmered on her hair, and her lips, so sweet and seductive, curled up the slightest bit as if she was just about to smile.

Well, he didn't care if she was just this side of euphoria. He was about to ruin her day. Again. He was about to break his word and his own rules and a thousand self-warnings and ask her again to . . .

It all happened so fast that even though he replayed the moment a thousand times in his mind, he would never truly know what happened. He would never understand what went wrong or what he could have done to change the course of the universe.

One moment she was walking, shoulders back, lips canted into that fairy-princess smile of hers. And the next the stallion was rearing, hooves thrashing. It was just like that. One second all was well. There was hope. There was reason and sunshine and tomorrows.

And the next she was on the ground.

"Casie!"

He was out of his truck and running before another thought registered in his brain. The world stood still around him. No sound, no thought. His footsteps were as silent as death as he raced toward her.

There was nothing but Casie. On the ground. Unmoving. Silent. He collapsed beside her.

"Case!" He reached for her. Her body was as limp as a sodden rag. He rolled her over, breath burning in his throat. Her head flopped back. Golden hair was sprayed across her brow. He pushed it aside with trembling hands. Her eyes had fallen closed. "Casie!"

She didn't blink, didn't speak, didn't move in his arms.

He'd been ungrateful. Asked too much. The thought exploded in his mind.

"Help me!" He yelled the words, desperately cradling her lifeless body against his own. "Somebody! Help me!"

He saw Ty spin toward them. Saw him sprint across the yard, snow flying in his wake.

Emily stepped onto the porch and shaded her eyes. Her mouth moved. The door slammed, but there was no sound. Only emptiness. Only never-ending nothingness.

"Don't do this! Don't! We're supposed to spend our lives together." His words were guttural as he clenched her to his chest.

Behind him, Ty panted up and stood unmoving.

Colt curled over her, rocking her in his arms.

And then her hand moved on his sleeve.

He opened his eyes slowly. Her fingers were pale. He stared at them for a breathless second, then shot his gaze to her face.

"Say yes," she said.

"Casie!" His heart burst into motion. "What the devil are you thinking? You scared the living hell out of me."

The shadow of an angel's smile played around her lips. "Say yes," she repeated.

He scowled, new worries crowding in. "Are you . . ." His cheeks felt wet. He wiped the back of his glove across his face. "Where does it hurt? Don't move. We'll get an ambulance."

"Marry me."

He loosened his grip a little, failing to breathe again. "You must have hit your head harder than I thought."

Her lips cranked up another quarter of an inch. "Could be Chester knocked some sense into it. Marry me."

"What about . . ." His world felt upside down, topsy-turvy and crazy hopeful. "What about your hungry horse syndrome?"

"Screw it," she said.

His heart was bursting in his chest, sending sparks of lightning spearing through his body. "What about the fights?"

"Fights?"

"The ones we're going to have about the kids, and the stray men, and that *damned* stallion."

Her grin lifted another notch. "We're keeping the stallion."

"We're not—" he began, but in that second she kissed him.

And, suddenly, all was right with the world.

FINALLY HOME

Lois Greiman

About This Guide

The suggested questions are included
to enhance your group's
reading of this book.

DISCUSSION QUESTIONS

1. Sophie's parents have a checkered past. Despite that, do you think it would have been best for them to stay together for their daughter's sake?

2. Good marriages, such as the one Colt's parents enjoy, are rare. Do you believe that having such an example will make it easier for Colt to make a solid family of his own?

3. Emily Kane has endured a great deal, including the abandonment of her baby's father. Should she take him back for the sake of her baby?

4. Casie Carmichael believes she is better suited for a stable, even boring, relationship than an exciting one. Is she a fool to believe she can build a life with a rodeo cowboy like Colt Dickenson?

5. What about you? Would you prefer to have an exciting relationship, or a solid but somewhat less exhilarating one?

6. South Dakota's climate can be intimidating, as ranch life can be. Do you think the challenges would be worth the effort?

7. Sophie Jaegar is an intelligent, talented young woman who will have many opportunities in the future. Would it be a mistake for her to pursue a path in an equestrian field despite the fact that money and advancement are probably limited?

8. Sophie Jaegar and Ty Roberts come from very different backgrounds. Do you think opposites truly do attract? And if so, are those relationships likely to fail?

9. Even though Colt Dickenson was attracted to Casie Carmichael in high school, he didn't pursue her. Why is he so determined to win her love now?

10. Is there a message you will take away from this book? If so, what is it?